VIKING
Sworn Brother

TIM SEVERIN, explorer, film-maker and lecturer, has made many expeditions, from his crossing of the Atlantic in a medieval leather boat in *The Brendan Voyage* to, most recently, *In Search of Moby Dick* and *Seeking Robinson Crusoe*. He has won the Thomas Cook Travel Book Award, the Book of the Sea Award, a Christopher Prize, and the literary medal of the Académie de la Marine. *Viking — Odinn's Child*, was his first novel and the final book in this trilogy will be *Viking — King's Man*.

TIM SEVERIN

VIKING
Sworn Brother

PAN BOOKS

First published 2005 by Macmillan

This edition published 2005 by Pan Books
an imprint of Pan Macmillan Ltd
Pan Macmillan, 20 New Wharf Road, London N1 9RR
Basingstoke and Oxford
Associated companies throughout the world
www.panmacmillan.com

ISBN 0 330 43821 2

1 3 5 7 9 8 6 4 2

A CIP catalogue record for this book is available from
the British Library.

Typeset by SetSystems Ltd, Saffron Walden, Essex
Printed and bound in Great Britain by
Mackays of Chatham plc, Chatham, Kent

All Pan Macmillan titles are available from www.panmacmillan.com
or from Bookpost by telephoning +44 (0)1624 677237

VIKING:
SWORN BROTHER

✳

To my holy and blessed master, Abbot Geraldus,

As requested of your unworthy servant, I send this, the second of the writings of the false monk Thangbrand. Alas, I must warn you that many times the work is even more disturbing than its antecedent. So deeply did the author's life descend into iniquity that many times I have been obliged, when reading his blasphemies, to set aside the pages that I might pray to Our Lord to cleanse my mind of such abominations and beseech Him to forgive the sinner who penned them. For here is a tale of continuing deceit and idolatry, of wantonness and wicked sin as well as violent death. Truly, the coils of deception, fraud and murder drag almost all men down to perdition.

The edges of many pages are scorched and burned by fire. From this I deduce that this Pharisee began to write his tale of depravity before the great conflagration so sadly destroyed our holy cathedral church of St Peter at York on 19 September in the year of our Lord 1069. By diligent enquiry I have learned that the holocaust revealed a secret cavity in the wall of the cathedral library, in which these writings had been concealed. A God-fearing member of our flock, making this discovery, brought the documents to my predecessor as librarian with joy, believing them to contain pious scripture. Lest further pages be discovered to dismay the unwary, I took it upon myself to visit the scene of that devastation and search the ruins. By God's mercy I found no further

3

examples of the reprobate's writings, but with a heavy heart I observed that nothing now remains of our once-great cathedral church, neither the portico of St Gregory, nor the glass windows nor the panelled ceilings. Gone are the thirty altars. Gone too is the great altar to St Paul. So fierce was the heat of the fire that I found spatterings of once-molten tin from the bellcote roof. Even the great bell, fallen from the tower, lay misshapen and dumb. Mysterious indeed are the ways of the Lord that these profane words of the ungodly should survive such destruction.

So great is my abhorrence of what has emerged from that hidden pustule of impiety that I have been unable to complete my reading of all that was found. There remains one more bundle of documents which I have not dared to examine.

On behalf of our community, I pray for your inspired guidance and that the Almighty Lord may keep you securely in bliss. Amen.

Aethelred
Sacristan and Librarian
Written in the month of October in the Year of our Lord One thousand and seventy-one.

ONE

I LOST MY virginity – to a king's wife.

Few people can make such a claim, least of all when hunched over a desk in a monastery scriptorium while pretending to make a fair copy of St Luke's gospel, though in fact writing a life's chronicle. But that is how it was and I remember the scene clearly.

The two of us lay in the elegant royal bed, Aelfgifu snuggled luxuriously against me, her head resting on my shoulder, one arm flung contentedly across my ribs as if to own me. I could smell a faint perfume from the glossy sweep of dark chestnut hair which spread across my chest and cascaded down onto the pillow we shared. If Aelfgifu felt any qualms, as the woman who had just introduced a nineteen-year-old to the delights of lovemaking but who was already the wife of Knut, the most powerful ruler of the northern lands, she did not show them. She lay completely at ease, motionless. All I could feel was the faint pulse of her heart and the regular waft of her breath across my skin. I lay just as still. I neither dared to move nor wanted to. The enormity and the wonder of what had happened had yet to ebb. For the first time in my life I had experienced utter joy in the embrace of a beautiful woman. Here was a marvel which once tasted could never be forgotten.

The distant clang of a church bell broke into my reverie. The sound slid through the window embrasure high in the queen's chambers and disturbed our quiet tranquillity. It was repeated, then joined by another bell and then another. Their metallic clamour reminded me where I was: London. No other city that I had visited boasted so many churches of the White Christ. They were springing up everywhere and the king was doing nothing to obstruct their construction, the king whose wife was now lying beside me, skin to skin.

The sound of the church bells made Aelfgifu stir. 'So, my little courtier,' she murmured, her voice muffled against my chest, 'you had better tell me something about yourself. My servants inform me that your name is Thorgils, but no one seems to know much about you. It's said you have come recently from Iceland. Is that correct?'

'Yes, in a way,' I replied tentatively. I paused, for I did not know how to address her. Should I call her 'my lady'? Or would that seem servile after the recent delight of our mingling, which she had encouraged with her caresses, and which had wrung from me the most intimate words? I hugged her closer and tried to combine both affection and deference in my reply, though I suspect my voice was trembling slightly.

'I arrived in London only two weeks ago. I came in the company of an Icelandic skald. He's taken me on as his pupil to learn how compose court poetry. He's hoping to find employment with . . .' Here my voice trailed away in embarrassment, for I was about to say 'the king'. Of course Aelfgifu guessed my words. She gave my ribs a little squeeze of encouragement and said, 'So that's why you were standing among my husband's skalds at the palace assembly. Go on.' She did not raise her head from my shoulder. Indeed, she pressed her body even more closely against me.

'I met the skald – his name's Herfid – last autumn on the island of Orkney off the Scottish coast, where I had been dropped off by a ship that rescued me from the sea of Ireland. It's a complicated story, but the sailors found me in a small boat that

was sinking. They were very kind to me, and so was Herfid.'
Tactfully I omitted to mention that I had been found drifting in
what was hardly more than a leaky wickerwork bowl covered
with cowskin, after I had been deliberately set afloat. I doubted
whether Aelfgifu knew that this is a traditional punishment levied
on convicted criminals by the Irish. My accusers had been monks
too squeamish to spill blood. And while it was true that I had
stolen their property — five decorative stones prised from a bible
cover — I had only taken the baubles in an act of desperation and
I felt not a shred of remorse. Certainly I did not see myself as a
jewel thief. But I thought this would be a foolish revelation to
make to the warm, soft woman curled up against me, particularly
when the only item she was wearing was a valuable-looking
necklace of silver coins.

'What about your family?' asked Aelfgifu, as if to satisfy
herself on an important point.

'I don't have one,' I replied. 'I never really knew my mother.
She died while I was a small child. She was part Irish, I'm told,
and a few years ago I travelled to Ireland to find out more about
her, but I never succeeded in learning anything. Anyhow, she
didn't live with my father and she had already sent me off to stay
with him by the time she died. My father, Leif, owns one of the
largest farms in a country called Greenland. I spent most of my
childhood there and in an even more remote land called Vinland.
When I was old enough to try to make my own living I had the
idea of becoming a professional skald as I've always enjoyed
story-telling. All the best skalds come from Iceland, so I thought
I would try my luck there.'

Again, I was being sparing with the truth. I did not tell
Aelfgifu that my father Leif, known to his colleagues as 'the
Lucky', had never been married to my mother, either in the
Christian or pagan rite. Nor that Leif's official wife had repudiated
her husband's illegitimate son and refused to have me in her
household. That was why I had spent most of my life being
shuttled from one country to the next, searching for some stability

and purpose. But it occurred to me at that moment, as I lay next to Aelfgifu, that perhaps my father's luck spirit, his hamingja as the Norse say, had transferred to me. How else could I explain the fact that I had lost my virginity to the consort of Knut, ruler of England, and royal claimant to the thrones of Denmark and Norway?

It all happened so suddenly. I had arrived in London with my master Herfid only ten days earlier. He and the other skalds had been invited to a royal assembly held by King Knut to announce the start of his new campaign in Denmark, and I had gone along as Herfid's attendant. During the king's speech from the throne, I had been aware that someone in Knut's entourage was staring at me as I stood among the royal skalds. I had no idea who Aelfgifu was, only that, when our eyes met, there was no mistaking the appetite in her gaze. The day after Knut sailed for Denmark, taking his army with him, I had received a summons to attend Aelfgifu's private apartments at the palace.

'Greenland, Iceland, Ireland, Scotland . . . you are a wanderer, aren't you, my little courtier,' Aelfgifu said, 'and I've never even heard of Vinland.' She rolled onto one side and propped her head on a hand, so that she could trace the profile of my face, from forehead to chin, with her finger. It was to become a habit of hers. 'You're like my husband,' she said without embarrassment. 'It's all that Norse blood, never at home, always rushing about, constantly on the move, with a wanderlust that wants to look beyond the horizon or incite some action. I don't even try to understand it. I grew up in the heart of the English countryside, about as far from the sea as you can get. It's a calmer life, and though it can be a little dull at times, it's what I like. Anyhow, dullness can always be brightened up if you know what you are doing.'

I should have guessed her meaning, but I was too naive; besides, I was smitten by her sophistication and beauty. I was so intoxicated with what had happened that I was incapable of asking myself why a queen should take up with a young man so rapidly.

I was yet to learn how a woman can be attracted instantly and overwhelmingly by a man, and that women who live close to the seat of power can indulge their craving with speed and certainty if they wish. That is their prerogative. Years later I saw an empress go so far as to share her realm with a young man – half her age – who took her fancy, though of course I never stood in that relationship to my wondrous Aelfgifu. She cared for me, of that I am sure, but she was worldly enough to measure out her affection to me warily, according to opportunity. For my part, I should have taken heed of the risk that came from an affair with the king's wife, but I was so swept away by my feelings that nothing on earth would have deterred me from adoring her.

'Come,' she said abruptly, 'it's time to get up. My husband may be away on another of those ambitious military expeditions of his, but if I'm not seen about the palace for several hours people might get curious as to where I am and what I'm doing. The palace is full of spies and gossips, and my prim and prudish rival would be only too delighted to have a stick to beat me with.'

Here I should note that Aelfgifu was not Knut's only wife. He had married her to gain political advantage when he and his father, Svein Forkbeard, were plotting to extend their control beyond the half of England which the Danes already held after more than a century of Viking raids across what they called the 'English Sea'. Aelfgifu's people were Saxon aristocracy. Her father had been an ealdorman, their highest rank of nobility, who owned extensive lands in the border country where the Danish possessions rubbed up against the kingdom of the English ruler, Ethelred. Forkbeard calculated that if his son and heir had a high-born Saxon as wife, the neighbouring ealdormen would be more willing to defect to the Danish cause than to serve their own native monarch, whom they had caustically nicknamed 'the Ill-Advised' for his uncanny ability to wait until the last moment before taking any action and then do the wrong thing at exactly the wrong time. Knut was twenty-four years old when he took Aelfgifu to be his wife, she was two years younger. By the time Aelfgifu invited me to her

bedchamber four years later, she was a mature and ripe woman
despite her youthful appearance and beauty, and her ambitious
husband had risen to become the undisputed king of all England,
for Ethelred was in his grave, and – as a step to reassure the
English nobility – Knut had married Ethelred's widow, Emma.

Emma was fourteen years older than Knut, and Knut had not
bothered to divorce Aelfgifu. The only people who might have
objected to his bigamy, namely the Christian priests who infested
Emma's household, had found a typically weasel excuse. Knut,
they said, had never properly married Aelfgifu because there had
been no Christian wedding. In their phrase it was a marriage 'in
the Danish custom', *ad mores danaos* – how they loved their
church Latin – and did not need to be set aside. Now, behind
their hands, they were calling Aelfgifu 'the concubine'. By contrast
Knut's earls, his personal retinue of noblemen from Denmark and
the Norse lands, approved the dual marriage. In their opinion this
was how great kings should behave in matters of state and they
liked Aelfgifu. With her slender figure and grace, she was a far
more attractive sight at royal assemblies than the dried-up widow
Emma with her entourage of whispering prelates. They found that
Aelfgifu behaved more in the way that a well-regarded woman in
the Norse world should: she was down to earth, independent
minded and at times – as I was shortly to discover – she was an
accomplished schemer.

Aelfgifu rose from our love bed with typical decisiveness. She
slid abruptly to the side, stepped onto the floor – giving me a
heart-melting glimpse of her curved back and hips – and, picking
up the pale grey and silver shift that she had discarded an hour
earlier, slid the garment over her nakedness. Then she turned to
me, as I lay there, almost paralysed with fresh longing. 'I'll
arrange for my maid to show you discreetly out of the palace. She
can be trusted. Wait until I contact you again. You've got another
journey to make, though not nearly as far as your previous ones.'
Then she turned and vanished behind a screen.

Still in a daze, I reached the lodging house where the royal skalds were accommodated. I found that my master, Herfid, had scarcely noticed my absence. A small and diffident man, he wore clothes cut in a style that had gone out of fashion at least a generation ago, and it was easy to guess he was a skald because the moment he opened his mouth you heard the Icelandic accent and the old-fashioned phrases and obscure words of his profession. As usual, when I entered, he was in another world, seated at the bare table in the main room talking to himself. His lips moved as he tried out various possibilities. 'Battle wolf, battle gleam, beam of war,' he muttered. After a moment's incomprehension I realised he was in the middle of composing a poem and having difficulty in finding the right words. As part of my skald's apprenticeship, he had explained to me that when composing poetry it was vital to avoid plain words for common objects. Instead you referred to them obliquely, using a substitute term or phrase − a kenning − taken if possible from our Norse traditions of our Elder Way. Poor Herfid was making heavy weather of it. 'Whetstone's hollow, hard ring, shield's grief, battle icicle,' he tried to himself. 'No, no, that won't do. Too banal. Ottar the Black used it in a poem only last year.'

By then I had worked out that he was trying to find a different way of saying 'a sword'.

'Herfid!' I said firmly, interrupting his thoughts. He looked up, irritated for a moment by the intrusion. Then he saw who it was and his habitual good humour returned.

'Ah, Thorgils! It's good to see you, though this is a rather lacklustre and empty house since the other skalds sallied forth to accompany the king on his campaign in Denmark. I fear that I've brought you to a dead end. There will be no chance of royal patronage until Knut gets back, and in the meantime I doubt if we'll find anyone else who is willing to pay for good-quality praise poems. I thought that perhaps one of his great earls whom he has left behind here in England, might be sufficiently cultured to want something elegantly phrased in the old style. But I'm told they are a boorish lot. Picked for their fighting ability rather than their appreciation of the finer points of versifying.'

'How about the queen?' I asked, deliberately disingenuous. 'Wouldn't she want some poetry?'

Herfid misunderstood. 'The queen!' he snorted. 'She only wants new prayers or perhaps one of those dreary hymns, all repetitions and chanting, remarkably tedious stuff. And she's got plenty of priests to supply that. The very mention of any of the Aesir would probably make her swoon. She positively hates the Old Gods.'

'I didn't mean Queen Emma,' I said. 'I meant the other one, Aelfgifu.'

'Oh her. I don't know much about her. She's keeping pretty much in the background. Anyhow queens don't employ skalds. They're more interested in romantic harp songs and that sort of frippery.'

'What about Thorkel, the vice-regent, then? I'm told that Knut has placed Thorkel in charge of the country while he is away. Wouldn't he appreciate a praise poem or two? Everyone says he's one of the old school, a true Viking. Fought as a mercenary, absolute believer in the Elder Faith, wears Thor's hammer as an amulet.'

'Yes, indeed, and you should hear him swear when he's angry,' said Herfid cheering up slightly. 'He spits out more names for the Old Gods than even I've heard. He also blasphemes mightily against those White Christ priests. I've been told that when he's drunk he refers to Queen Emma as Bakrauf. I just hope that not too many of the Saxons hear or understand.'

I knew what he meant. In Norse lore a bakrauf was a wizened old hag, a troll wife, and her name translates as 'arse hole'.

'So why don't you attach yourself to Thorkel's household as a skald?' I insisted.

'That's a thought,' Herfid said. 'But I'll have to be cautious. If word gets back to Knut that the vice-regent is surrounding himself with royal trappings, like a personal skald, the king may think that he is putting on airs and wants to be England's ruler. Knut delegated Thorkel to look after the military side of things, put down any local troubles with a firm hand and so forth, but Archbishop Wulfstan is in charge of the civil administration and the legal side. It's a neat balance: the heathen kept in check by the Christian.' Herfid, who was a kindly man, sighed. 'Whatever happens, even if I get an appointment with Thorkel, I'm afraid that there won't be much of an opportunity for you to shine as my pupil. A vice-regent is not as wealthy as a king, and his largesse is less. You're welcome to stay on with me as an apprentice, but I can't possibly pay you anything. We'll be lucky if we have enough to eat.'

A page boy solved my predicament three days later when the lad knocked at the door of our lodgings with a message for me. I was to report to the queen's chamberlain ready to join her entourage, which was leaving for her home country of Northampton. It took me only a moment to pack. All the clothing I owned, apart from the drab tunic, shoes and hose that I wore every day, was a plum-coloured costume Herfid had given me so that I could appear reasonably well dressed at court. This garment I stuffed into the worn satchel of heavy leather I had stitched for myself in Ireland when I had lived among the monks there. Then I said goodbye to Herfid, promising him that I would try to keep in touch. He was still struggling to find a suitable substitute phrase to fit the metre of his rhyme. 'How about "death's flame"? That's a good kenning for a sword,' I suggested as I turned to leave with the satchel over my shoulder.

He looked at me with a smile of pure delight. 'Perfect!' he said, 'It fits exactly. You've not entirely ignored my teaching. I hope that one day you'll find some use for your gift with words.'

In the palace courtyard Aelfgifu's entourage was already waiting, four horse-drawn carts with massive wooden wheels to haul the baggage and transport the womenfolk, a dozen or so riding animals, and an escort of a couple of Knut's mounted huscarls. The last were no more than token protection, as the countryside had been remarkably peaceful since Knut came to the throne. The English, after years of fighting off Viking raiders or being squeezed for the taxes to buy them off with Danegeld, were so exhausted that they would have welcomed any overlord just as long he brought peace. Knut had done better. He had promised to rule the Saxons with the same laws they had under a Saxon king, and he showed his trust in his subjects – and reduced their tax burden – by sending away his army of mercenaries, a rough lot drawn from half the countries across the Channel and the English Sea. But Knut was too canny to leave himself entirely vulnerable to armed rebellion. He surrounded himself with his huscarls, three hundred of them all armed to the teeth. Any man who joined his elite guard was required to own, as a personal possession, a long two-edged sword with gold inlay in the grip. Knut knew well that only a genuine fighter would own such an expensive weapon and only a man of substance could afford one. His palace regiment was composed of professional full-time fighting men whose trade was warfare. Never before had the English seen such a compact and lethal fighting force, or one with weaponry so stylish.

So I was surprised to observe that the two huscarls detailed to escort Queen Aelfgifu were both severely maimed. One had a stump where his right hand should be, and the other had lost a leg below the knee and walked on a wooden limb. Then I remembered that Knut had taken the huscarl regiment on his campaign in Denmark; only the invalids had been left behind. Even as I watched the huscarls prepare to mount their stallions, I was already revising my opinion of their disabilities. The one-legged man limped to his horse, and though he was encumbered with a round wooden shield slung across his back, he bent down and removed his wooden leg and, with it still in his hand, balanced for a moment on a single foot before he gave a brisk, one-legged hop and swung himself into the saddle. There he tucked the false limb into a leather loop for safe keeping, and began to tie a leather strap around his waist to fix himself more firmly in place.

'Come on, stop fiddling about. It's time to ride!' he bellowed cheerfully at his companion, who was using one hand and his teeth to untangle his horse's knotted reins, and getting ready to wrap them around the stump of his arm, 'Even Tyr didn't take so long to get Gleipnir ready for Fenrir.'

'Shut up, Treeleg, or I'll come across and knock that stupid grin off your face,' came the reply, but I could see that the one-handed man was flattered. And rightly so. Every Old Believer knows that Tyr is the bravest of the Old Gods, the Aesirs. It was Tyr who volunteered to put his hand into the mouth of the Fenrir, the hell wolf, to lull the beast's suspicions while the other Gods placed Gleipnir, the magic fetter, on the hell wolf to restrain him. The dwarves had made the fetter from six magical ingredients – 'the sound of a cat's footfall, a woman's beard, a mountain's roots, a bear's sinews, a fish's breath and a bird's spit' – and Gleipnir did not burst even when the hell hound felt his bonds tightening and struggled with a fiend's strength. Meanwhile brave Tyr lost his hand to the hell wolf's bite.

Aelfgifu's chamberlain was glaring at me. 'Are you Thorgils?' he asked curtly. 'You're late. Ever ridden a horse before?'

I nodded cautiously. In Iceland I had occasionally ridden the sturdy little Icelandic horses. But they stood close enough to the ground for the rider not to get hurt when he fell off, and there were no roads, only tracks across the moors, so the landing was usually soft enough if you were not so unlucky as to fall on a rock. But I did not fancy trying to get on the back of anything resembling the bad-tempered stallions the two huscarls were now astride. To my relief the chamberlain nodded towards a shaggy and dispirited-looking mare tied up to the tail of one of the carts. Her aged head was drooping. 'Take that animal. Or walk.' Soon our motley cavalcade was creaking and clopping its way out of the city, and I was wondering whether there had not been a change of plan. Nowhere could I see my adored Aelfgifu.

She joined us in a thunder of cantering hooves when we had already crawled along for some five miles. 'Here she comes, riding like a Valkyrie as usual,' I heard the one-handed huscarl remark approvingly to his colleague, as they turned in their saddles to watch the young queen approach. On my plodding creature I twisted round as well, trying not to make my interest obvious, but my heart was pounding. There she was, riding like a man, her loose hair streaming out behind her. With a pang of jealousy I noted that she was accompanied by two or three young noblemen, Saxons by the look of them. A moment later the little group were swirling past us, chattering and whooping with delight as they took up their places as the head of the little group, then reined in their horses to match our trudging progress. Clumping along on my ugly nag, I felt hot and ashamed. I had not really expected that Aelfgifu would even glance at me, but I was so lovelorn that I still hoped she would catch my eye. She had ignored me entirely.

For four unhappy days I stayed at the back of the little column, and the most I ever saw of Aelfgifu was an occasional glimpse of her shapely back among the leading horsemen with her companions. It was torture for me whenever one of the young men leaned across towards her to exchange some confidence, or I saw her throw back her head and laugh at a witty remark. Sour with jealousy, I tried to learn who her companions were, but my fellow travellers were a taciturn lot. They could only tell me that they were high-born Saxons, ealdormen's spawn.

The journey was torture for another reason. My lacklustre mount proved to be the most leaden-footed, iron-mouthed creature that ever escaped the butcher's knife. The brute plodded along, slamming down her feet so that the impact of each hoof fall rattled up my spine. My saddle, the cheapest variety and made of wood, was an agony. Each time I dismounted I hobbled like a crone, so stiff that I could not walk properly. Life on the road was no better. I had to work for every yard of progress, kicking and slapping at the flanks of the sluggish creature to make her go forward. And when the mare decided to leave the main track and head for a mouthful of spring grass, there was nothing I could do to prevent her. I hit her between the ears with a hazel rod I cut for the purpose, and heaved on the reins. But the creature merely turned her ugly head to one side and kept walking in a straight line towards her target. On one embarrassing occasion she tripped and the two of us went sprawling in the dirt. As soon as the mare had her head down and started eating, I was helpless. I pulled on the reins till my arms ached and kicked her in the ribs, but there was no response. Only when the obstinate brute had eaten her fill would she raise her head and lumber back to the main track while I swore in rage.

'Try to keep up with the group,' One Hand warned me gruffly as he rode back down the column to see that all was in order. 'I don't want any stragglers.'

'I'm sorry,' I replied. 'I'm having difficulty controlling my horse.'

'If it *is* a horse' commented the huscarl, regarding the ill-shapen monster. 'I don't think I've ever seen such an ugly nag. Has it got a name?'

'I don't know,' I said, and then added without thinking, 'I'm calling her Jarnvidja.'

The huscarl gave me a funny look, before wheeling about and riding off. Jarnvidja means 'iron hag' and I realised, like Bakrauf, it is the name of a troll wife.

My dawdling horse allowed me plenty of opportunity to observe the countryside of England. The land was astonishingly prosperous despite the recent wars. Village followed village in quick succession. Most were neat and well tended – a dozen or so thatched houses constructed with walls of wattle and daub or wooden planks and set on either side of the muddy street or at a crossroads. Many had gardens front and back and, beyond their barns, pigsties and sheep sheds, were well-tended fields stretching away to the edge of forests or moorland. If the place was important enough there might be a larger house for the local magnate with its little chapel, or even a small church built of wood. Sometimes I noticed a stonemason at work, laying the foundations for a more substantial church tower. It seemed that the worship of the White Christ was spreading at remarkable speed, even in the countryside. I never saw a shrine to Old Ways, only tattered little strips of votive rags hanging from every great oak tree we passed, indicating that the Elder Faith had not entirely vanished.

Our party was travelling across country in an almost straight line and I thought this strange. The roads and tracks I had known in Iceland and Ireland meandered here and there, keeping to the high ground to avoid boglands and turning aside to shun the thickest forests. But the English road cut straight across country, or nearly so. When I looked more closely, I realised that our heavy carts were rolling and creaking along a prepared track, rutted and battered but still discernible, with occasional paving slabs and a raised embankment.

When I enquired, I was told that this was a legacy of the Roman days, a road called Watling Street and that, although the original bridges and causeways had long since collapsed or been washed away, it was the duty of the local villages to maintain and repair the track. They often failed in their task, and we found ourselves splashing across fords or paying ferrymen to take us across rivers in small barges and row boats.

It was at a water splash that the appalling Jarnvidja finally disgraced me. As usual, she was plodding along at the rear of the column when she smelled water up ahead. Being thirsty, she simply barged her way forward past the wagons and other horses. Aelfgifu and her companions had already reached the ford, and their horses were standing in the shallows, cooling their feet while their riders chatted. By then I had lost all control over Jarnvidja, and my hideous mount came sliding and slithering down the bank, rudely shouldering aside a couple of horses. As I tugged futilely on the reins, Jarnvidja splashed monstrously through the shallows, her great hooves sending up a muddy spray which drenched the finery of the Saxon nobles, and spattered across the queen herself.

Then the brute stopped, plunged her ugly snout into the water and began to suck up her drink noisily, while I was forced to sit on her broad back, crimson with embarrassment, and Aelfgifu's companions glared at me as they brushed off the muck.

On the fifth day we turned aside from Watling Street and rode down a broad track through a dense forest of beech and oak until we came to our destination. Aelfgifu's home was more heavily protected that earlier settlements I had seen. It was what the Saxons call a burh and was surrounded by a massive earth bank and a heavy wooden palisade. All around for a space of about a hundred paces the forest had been cleared back to allow a field of fire for archers in case of attack. Inside the rampart the ground was laid out to accommodate a lord and his retinue. There were dormitories for servants, a small barracks for the soldiery, storehouses and a large banqueting hall next to the lord's own dwelling, a substantial manor house. As our travel-stained group entered the main gate, the inhabitants lined up to greet us. Amid the reunions, gossip and exchanges of news, I saw the two huscarls head straight for the manor house, and — to my disappointment — Aelgifu and her attendant women disappear into a separate building, the women's quarters. I dismounted and stretched my back, glad at last to be rid of my torment on the Iron Hag. A servant came forward to take the mare from me, and I was heartily glad to see her gone. Her final act of treachery was to step heavily on my foot as she was led away, and I hope never to see her again.

I was wondering what I should do and where I should go, when a man whom I guessed was the local steward appeared. He had a list in his hand. 'Who are you?' he asked.

'Thorgils,' I replied.

He looked down his list, then said, 'Can't see your name here. Must have been a last-minute addition. Until I get this sorted out, you can go and help out Edgar.'

'Edgar?' I queried.

But the steward was already waving me away, too busy to

explain details. He had pointed vaguely towards a side gate. Whoever Edgar was, it seemed that I would find him outside the palisade.

My satchel slung over my shoulder, I walked out through the gate. In the distance I could see a low wooden building, and a small cottage. I walked towards them and as I drew closer my heart sank. I heard the barking and hubbub of dogs and realised that I was approaching a kennel. Earlier, in Ireland, I had been dog boy to the Norse king, Sigtryggr of Dublin, and it had not been a success. I had been put in charge of two Irish wolfhounds and they had run away from me. Now I could hear at least a dozen dogs, maybe more, and smell their unmistakably pungent odour. It was beginning to rain, one of those sudden heavy showers so frequent in an English spring time, and I looked for somewhere to shelter. I did not want to risk being bitten, so I swerved aside and ran towards a small shed set close to the edge of the forest.

The door was not locked and I pulled it open. It was gloomy inside, the only light coming through cracks in walls made from loosely woven wattle. When my eyes had adjusted to the darkness, I saw that the shed was completely empty except for several stout posts driven into the earth floor, over which had been strewn a thin layer of sand. From each post extended a number of short wooden poles, covered with sacking or bound with leather, and sitting on the poles were birds. They ranged in size from scarcely bigger than my hand to a creature as large as a barnyard cockerel. The shed was eerily quiet. I heard only the distant howling of the dogs and the patter of rain on the thatched roof. The birds were silent, except for the occasional rustle of a wing and a scratching sound as they shifted their claws on the perches. I stepped forward to examine them more closely, gingerly treading past them as they turned their heads to follow my progress. I realised that they were following me by sound not by sight, for they were blind. Or rather, they could not see me because they were wearing leather hoods on their heads. Then I stopped dead in my tracks and a great wave of homesickness suddenly swept over me.

In front of me, sitting on a perch well away from the others, was a bird I recognised at once. Its feathers were pale grey, almost white, and speckled with blackish brown spots, like a sheet of parchment on which a scribe had sprinkled spots of ink. Even in the half-light I could see that, though hunched up and miserable, it was a spear falcon.

The spear falcons are princes among the birds of prey. As a child in Greenland I had seen these magnificent birds hunting ptarmigan on the moors, and our trappers occasionally tangled them in nets or climbed the cliffs to take them as fledglings, for they are the most precious of our Greenlandic exports. We sent away five or six falcons in a year to the traders in Iceland, and I heard that they were then sold on for a great price to wealthy magnates in Norway or the southern lands. To see one of these birds, in the centre of damp, green England, cooped up and far from its natural home, made me feel it was a kindred soul, an exile, and the scene squeezed at my heart.

The spear falcon was in moult. That was why it was looking so dejected, its feathers dishevelled and awry. The bird sensed my presence and turned its head towards me. I crept forward and then I saw: its eyes were sewn shut. A thin thread had been stitched through each of the lower eyelids, and then led up over the bird's head, pulling the eyelid up. The two threads were tied together in a knot over the head, holding up the lids. Tentatively I stretched out my hand, fearing to frighten the bird, yet wanting to unpick the knot and release the eyes. I felt the creature's unhappy fate was a symbol of my predicament. My hand was hovering over the bird's head, no more than six inches away, when suddenly my left wrist was seized from behind and my arm twisted up violently between my shoulder blades. Wiry fingers clamped on the back of my neck, and a voice hissed ferociously in my ear, 'Touch that bird and I'll break first your arm and then your neck!' Then I was pushed forward so that I was forced to bend double at the waist. Next my attacker turned and marched me, still bent over, out through the shed door and into the open. There he deftly kicked my feet from under me so that I fell headlong in the mud. Winded, I lay gasping for a moment, shocked by the lightning attack. My assailant had dropped on top of me and was holding me face down, one knee in my back. I could not turn my head to see who he was, so I blurted out, 'I was looking for Edgar.' Above me, a voice seething with anger said, 'You've found him.'

TWO

MY ATTACKER RELEASED his grip and allowed me to roll over and look up. A small, thick-set man was standing over me, dressed in a patched and worn tunic, heavy hose and scuffed leather leggings. His grey hair was cropped close to his skull, and I guessed he must be in his mid-fifties. What struck me most was how battered and weatherbeaten he looked. Deep lines were etched across his face and his cheeks were mottled with dark red blotches as if someone had scoured them with sand. An angry scowl pulled his eyebrows so far down that his eyes almost disappeared into his skull. He looked thoroughly dangerous, and I noted a well-used dagger with a stag-horn handle tucked into his leather belt and wondered why he had not drawn it. Then I remembered how easily he had bundled me out of the shed, as if I was no more than a child.

'What were you doing in the hawk shed?' he demanded furiously. He spoke the language of the Saxons, close enough to my native Norse for me to understand, but with a country accent, deep and deliberate, so that I had to listen closely. 'Who gave you permission to go in there?'

'I told you,' I replied placatingly, 'I was looking for Edgar. I had no idea that I was doing any harm.'

'And the gyrfalcon? What were you doing near it? What were you trying? To steal it?'

'No,' I said. 'I wanted to remove the thread so that it could open its eyes.'

'And who said you could do that?' He was growing even more angry, and I was worried that he would lose control and give me a beating. There was no answer to his question, so I kept silent.

'Imbecile! Do you know what would have happened? The bird would have panicked, left its perch, thrashed around. Escaped or damaged itself. It's in no condition to fly. And that bird, for your information, is worth ten times as much as you are, probably more, you miserable lout.'

'I'm sorry,' I said. 'I recognised the bird and I've never seen them with their eyes sewn shut before.'

My reply set him off again. 'What do you mean "recognised?"' he snarled. 'There are no more than five or six birds like that in the whole of England. That's a royal bird.'

'Where I come from, there are quite a few.'

'So you're a liar as well as a thief.'

'No, believe me. I come from a place where those birds build their nests and raise their young. I only entered the shed to look for you, if you are Edgar, because I was told to find him and report to him for work.'

'I asked for a kennelhand, not a thieving Dane with sticky fingers like all the rest of them. I can recognise your ugly accent,' he growled. 'Get on your feet,' and he let loose a kick to help me up. 'We'll soon learn whether you're telling the truth.'

He marched me back to the burh and checked my story with Aelfgifu's harassed steward. When the steward confirmed who I was, Edgar spat deliberately – the gob of spittle just missed me – and announced, 'We'll see about that then.'

This time we returned to the kennels and Edgar lifted the latch on the low gate which led into the dog-run. Instantly a hysterical brown, white and tan cascade of tail-wagging confusion swirled forward and engulfed us. The dogs barked and howled, though whether with enthusiasm or hunger I could not tell. Some leaped up at Edgar in affection, others pushed and shoved to get closer, a few cringed back, or ran off into the corner and defecated in their excitement. The kennel smelled abominable, and I felt a sharp pain in my calf where one mistrustful dog had run round behind me to give me an experimental bite. Edgar was completely at ease. He plunged his hands into the heaving mass of dog flesh, petting them, rubbing ears fondly, calling their names, casually knocking aside the more exuberant animals which tried to leap up and lick his face. He was in his element, but for me it was a vision of the abyss.

'This is where you will work,' he said bluntly.

I must have looked aghast, for he allowed himself the glimmer of a smile. 'I'll show your duties.' He crossed to the far side of the dog-run, where a long, low shed was built against the fence. He dragged open the ill-fitting door and we went inside. The interior was almost as bare as the hawk shed, only this time there was no sand on the earth floor and instead of bird perches, a wide wooden platform had been constructed down one side of the building. The platform was made of rough wooden planks, raised about a foot above the ground on short posts. Its surface was covered with a thick layer of straw, which Edgar pointed at. 'I want that turned over daily, so that it's well aired. Pick up any droppings and put them outside. When you've a sackful of turds, you'll be carrying it to the tannery for the leather-makers. Nothing like a strong solution of dog shit to soften the surface of hides. Then every three days, when the straw is too soiled, you change all the bedding. I'll show you later where to find fresh straw.'

Next he pointed out three low troughs. 'Keep these topped up with drinking water for the dogs. If they get fouled, you're to take them outside and empty them – I don't want the floor in here any more damp than it already is – then refill them.' As he made his remark about the damp floor, he glanced towards a wooden post hammered into the ground about halfway along the shed. The post was wrapped with straw and there was an obvious damp patch around it. I realised it was a urinating post. 'Every

three days you change that straw as well. Let the dogs out into
the run first thing every morning. That's when you will change
their straw bedding. They're to be fed once a day – mostly stale
bread, but also meat scraps from the main kitchen, whatever is
left over. You are to check through the scraps to make sure that
there's nothing harmful in the swill. If any dog is sick or off-
colour, and there's usually one or two, you're to let me know at
once.'

'Where will I find you?' I asked.

'I live in the cottage opposite the hawk shed. Behind my house
you'll find the lean-to where the straw is kept. If I'm not at home,
probably because I'm out in the forest, check with my wife before
you touch any of the stores. She'll keep an eye on you to make
sure that you're doing your job thoroughly. Any questions?'

By now we had re-emerged from the dog shed and were back
at the entrance to the dog-run. 'No,' I said, 'you've made everything very clear. Where do I sleep?'

He gave me a look of pure malice. 'Where do you expect?
With the dogs, of course. That's the right place for a kennelman.'

My next question was on the tip of my tongue, when the
expression on his face decided me not to give him the satisfaction
of asking it. I was going to enquire, 'What about my food?
Where do I take my meals?' But I already knew the answer –
'With the dogs. You eat what they do.'

I was right. The next days were among the most vile that I
ever spent and I have lived under some unspeakable conditions.
I ate and I slept with the dogs. I picked out the better scraps from
their food for my own meals, I caught their fleas and I spent a
good deal of my time avoiding their teeth. I loathed them, and
took to carrying a cudgel – which I hid under the dog platform
whenever Edgar appeared – and used it to clout any dog that
came too close to me, though some of the nastier ones still tried
to circle round behind me and attack. The experience gave me
ample time to wonder how on earth people could become fond of
their dogs, least of all such unlovely hounds as these. In Ireland

the clan chiefs had been proud of their wolfhounds, and I had understood why. Their dogs were resplendent, elegant animals, aristocratic with their long legs and haughty pace. But Edgar's pack was, to all appearances, a bunch of curs. Half the height of a wolfhound, they had short faces, sharp snouts and untidy fur. The predominant colour was a drab brown, though a few had patches of black or of tan, and one dog would have been all white if it had not kept rolling in the filthiness. It was incredible to me that anyone would take the trouble to keep a pack of them. Several months later I learned that they were known as 'Briton hounds' and their forebears had been greatly valued as hunting dogs by those same Romans who had built the Watling Street. My informant was a monk whose abbot was a sporting priest and ran a pack of them, and he told me that these Briton hounds were valued for their courage, their tenacity and their ability to follow the scent whether in the air or on the ground. How the dogs managed to follow a scent amazed me, for they themselves stank exceedingly. In an attempt to keep my purple tunic from being tainted, I took the precaution of hanging my faithful leather satchel from a peg in one of the upright posts, as high up as I could manage, for I knew for certain that, within hours, I reeked as much as my canine companions.

Edgar came to visit the kennel both morning and afternoon to check on me as well as his noxious hounds. He would enter the dog-run and wade nonchalantly through the riot of animals. He had an uncanny ability to spot any of them that were cut, scratched or damaged in any way. Then he would reach out and grab the dog and haul it close. With complete assurance he folded back ears, prised apart toes looking for thorns, and casually pulled aside private parts, which he called their yard and stones, to check that they were not sore or bleeding. If he found a gash, he produced a needle and thread, and with one knee pinned down the dog while he stitched up the wound. Occasionally, if the dog was troublesome, he would call on me to assist by holding it, and of course I got badly bitten. Seeing the blood dripping from my hand, Edgar gave a satisfied laugh. 'Teach you to stick your hand in his mouth,' he jeered, making me think instantly of the one-handed huscarl. 'Better than a cat bite. That'd go bad on you. A dog bite is clean and healthy. Or at least it is if the dog isn't mad.' The dog which had bitten me certainly didn't look mad, so I sucked at the puncture wounds left by its teeth and said nothing. But Edgar wasn't going to miss his opportunity. 'Do you know what you do if you get bitten by a mad dog?' he asked with relish. 'You can't suck hard enough to get out the rottenness. So you get a good strong barnyard cock, and strip off his feathers, all of them, until he is arse naked. Then you clap his fundament on the wound and give him a bad fright. That way he clenches up his gut and sucks out the wound.' He guffawed.

My ordeal would have lasted much longer but for the fact that I mislaid a dog on the fourth day. Edgar had told me to take the pack to a grassy area a few hundred paces from the kennel. There the animals were encouraged to chew the blades of grass for their health. During that short excursion I managed to lose track of the number of hounds I took with me, and when I brought them back into the dog-run I failed to notice that one was missing. Only when I was shutting the dogs up for the night and took a head count, did I realise my error. I closed the kennel door behind me, and walked back to the grassy area to see if I could find the missing hound. I did not call the dog because I did not know its name and, just as importantly, I did not want to alert Edgar to my blunder. He had been so hostile about the possible loss of a hawk that I was sure he would be furious over a missing dog. I walked quietly, hoping to spot the runaway lurking somewhere. There was no dog by the grass patch, and, thinking that the animal might have found its way to the back door of Edgar's cottage to scavenge, I went to check. Just as I rounded the corner of the little house, I heard a slight clatter, and there was Edgar.

He was kneeling on the ground with his back to me. In front of him was a square of white cloth spread on the earth. Lying on the cloth where he had just dropped them lay a scatter of half a dozen flat lathes. Edgar, who had been looking down at them intently, swung round in surprise.

'What do they say?' I asked, hoping to forestall the outburst of anger.

He regarded me with suspicion. 'None of your business,' he retorted. I began to walk away when, unexpectedly from behind me, I heard him say, 'Can you read the wands?'

I turned back and replied cautiously, 'In my country we prefer to throw dice or a tafl. And we bind our wands together like a book.'

'What's a tafl?'

'A board which has markers. With practice one can read the signs.'

'But you do use wands?'

'Some of the older people still do, or knuckle bones of animals.'

'Then tell me what you think these wands say.'

I walked over to where the white cloth lay on the ground, and counted six of the wooden lathes scattered on it. Edgar was holding a seventh in his hand. One of the lathes on the ground was painted with a red band. I knew it must be the master. Three of the wands on the ground were slightly shorter than the others.

'What do you read?' Edgar asked. There was a pleading note in his voice.

I looked down. 'The answer is confused,' I said. I bent down and picked up one of the lathes. It was slightly askew, lying across another wand. I turned it over, and read the sign marked on it. 'Tyr,' I said, 'the God of death and war.'

Edgar looked puzzled for an instant and then the blood drained from his face, leaving the ruddy spots on his cheekbones even brighter. 'Tiw? You know how to read the marks? Are you sure?'

'Yes, of course,' I replied, showing him the marked face of the wand. The symbol on it was the shape of an arrow. 'I'm a devotee of Odinn and it was Odinn who learned the secret of the runes and taught them to mankind. Also he invented fortune dice. It's very plain. That rune is Tyr's own sign. Nothing else.'

Edgar's voice was unsteady as he said, 'That must mean that she is dead.'

'Who?'

'My daughter. Four years ago a gang of your Danish bandits took her away during the troubles. They couldn't attack the burh – the palisade was too strong for them – so they made a quick sweep around the perimeter, beat my youngest son so badly that he lost an eye and dragged off the girl. She was just twelve. We've not heard a word from her since.'

'Is that what you wanted to know when you cast the wands? What had become of her.'

'Yes,' he replied.

'Then don't give up hope,' I said. 'The wand of Tyr was lying across another wand, and that signifies the meaning is unclear or reversed. So your daughter may be alive. Would you like me to cast the sticks again for you?'

The huntsman shook his head. 'No,' he said. 'Three casts at a time is enough. Any more would be an affront to the Gods and, besides, the sun has set and now the hour is no longer propitious.'

Then his suspicions came back with a rush. 'How do I know you're not lying to me about the runes, like you lied about the gyrfalcon.'

'There's no reason for me to lie,' I answered, and began picking up the wands, the master rod first and then the three shorter, calling out their names, 'rainbow, warrior queen, firm belief.' Then, collecting the longer ones, I announced, 'The key-holder, joy,' and taking the last one from Edgar's fingers I said, 'festivity.'

To establish my credentials even more clearly, I asked inno-cenctly, 'You don't use the wand of darkness, the snake wand?'

Edgar looked dumbfounded. He was, as I later found out, a countryman at heart, and he believed implicitly in the Saxon wands, as they are called in England where they are much used in divination and prophecy. But only the most skilled employ the eighth wand, the snake wand. It has a baleful influence which affects all the other wands and most people, being only human, prefer a happy outcome to the shoot, as the Saxons call the casting of the rods. Frankly I thought the Saxon wands were elementary. In Iceland my rune master Thrand had taught me to read much more sophisticated versions. There the wands are fastened to a leather cord, fanned out and used like an almanac, the meanings read from runes cut on both sides. These runes – like most seidr or magic – reverse the normal forms. The runes are written backwards, as if seen in a mirror.

'Tell my wife what you just said about our daughter,' Edgar announced. 'It may comfort her. She has been grieving for the girl these four years past.' He ushered me into the cottage – it was no more than a large single room, divided across the middle into a living area and a bedroom. There was an open fire at the gable wall, a plain table and two benches. At Edgar's prompting I repeated my reading of the wands to Edgar's wife, Judith. The poor woman looked pitifully trustful of my interpretation and timidly asked if I would like some proper food. I suspected that she thought that her husband had been treating me very unfairly. But Edgar's loathing was understandable if he thought I was a Dane, like the raiders who had kidnapped his daughter and maimed his son.

Edgar was obviously weighing me up. 'Where did you say you come from?' he asked suddenly.

'From Iceland and before that from Greenland.'

'But you speak like a Dane.'

'Same words, yes,' I said, 'but I say them differently, and I use some words that are only used in Iceland. A bit like your Saxon. I'm sure you've noticed how foreigners from other parts of England speak it differently and have words that you don't understand.'

'Prove to me that you come from this other place, this Greenland or whatever you call it.'

'I'm afraid I don't know how to.'

Edgar thought for a moment, and then said suddenly, 'Gyrfal-con. You said you come from a place where the bird builds its nests and raises its young. And I know that it does not do so in the Danes' country, but somewhere further away. So if you are really from that place, then you know all about the bird and its habits.'

'What can I tell you?' I asked.

He looked cunning, then said, 'Answer me this: is the gyrfal-con a hawk of the tower, or a hawk of the hand?'

I had no idea what he was talking about and when I looked baffled he was triumphant. 'Just as I thought. You don't know any-thing about them.'

'No,' I said 'It's just that I don't understand your question. But I could recognise a gyrfalcon if I saw it hunting.'

'So tell me how.'

'When I watched the wild spear falcons in Greenland, they would fly down from the cliffs and perch on some vantage point on the moors, like a high rock or hill crest. There the bird sat, watching out for its prey. It was looking for its food, another bird we call rjupa, like your partridge. When the spear falcon sees a rjupa, it launches from its perch and flies low at tremendous speed, faster and faster, and then strikes the rjupa, knocking it to the ground, dead.'

'And what does it do at the last moment before it strikes?' Edgar asked.

'The spear falcon suddenly rises, to gain height, and then come smashing down on its prey.'

'Right,' announced Edgar, finally persuaded. 'That's what the gyr does and that's why it can be a hawk of the tower and also a hawk of the fist, and very few hunting birds can be both.'

'I still don't know what you mean,' I said. 'What's a bird of the tower?'

'A bird that towers or waits on, as we say. Hovers in the sky

above the master, waiting for the right moment, then drops down
on its prey. Peregrine falcons do that naturally and, with patience,
gyrfalcons can be taught to hunt that way. A hawk of the fist is
one that is carried on the hand or wrist while hunting, and thrown
off the hand to chase down the quarry.'

Thus my knowledge of the habits of the wild gyrfalcon and
the art of divination rescued me from the ordeal of those noxious
dog kennels, though Edgar confessed some weeks later that he
would not have kept me living in the kennels indefinitely because
he had recognised that I did not have the makings of a kennelman.
'Mind you, I can't understand anyone who doesn't get along with
dogs,' he added. 'Seems unnatural.'

'They stink exceedingly,' I pointed out. 'It took me days to
wash off their stench. Quite why the English love their dogs so
much baffles me. They never stop talking about them. Sometimes
they seem to prefer them to their own children.'

'Not just the English,' Edgar said, 'That pack belongs to Knut,
and when he shows up here half his Danish friends bring along
their own dogs, which they add to the pack. It's a cursed nuisance
as the dogs start fighting amongst themselves.'

'Precisely,' I commented. 'When it comes to dogs, neither
Saxon nor Dane seems to have any common sense. In Greenland,
in times of famine, we ate them.'

By the time of that conversation I was being treated as a
member of Edgar's family. I had been allocated a corner of their
cottage where I could hang my satchel and find a sleeping place,
and Judith, who was as trusting as her husband had been initially
wary, was spoiling me as if I was her favourite nephew. She
would fish out for me the best bits of meat from the stewpot that
simmered constantly over her cooking fire. I have rarely been fed
so well. Officially Edgar was the royal huntsman, an important
post which made him responsible for arranging the hunts when
Knut came to visit. But Edgar also had a neat sideline in poaching.
He quietly set nets for small game – hares were a favourite prey

– and would come back to the cottage in the first light of dawn, his leggings wet with dew, and a couple of plump hares dangling from his hand.

As spring turned to summer, I realised that I was very privileged. July is the hungry month before the crops have been harvested, and normal folk must live on the sweepings of their storehouses and grain bins. They eat hard, gritty bread made from bran, old husks and ground-up peas. But in Edgar's house our stockpot was always well supplied, and with the hunting season approaching Edgar began to take me into the forest to scout for the biggest game of all – red-deer stags. This was Edgar at his best – quiet, confident and willing to teach me. He was like Herfid explaining the skald's techniques, or the monks in Ireland when they taught me French, Latin and a little Greek, and how to read and write the foreign scripts, or my seidr master Thrand in Iceland as he tutored me in the mysteries of the Elder Faith.

Edgar took me with him as he quietly followed the deer paths through the forest of oak and beech, and smaller thickets of alder and ash. He showed me how to judge the size of a deer from the size of the hoof prints, and how to tell whether the stag was walking, running or moving at a trot. After he had located a stag large enough to be hunted by the king's pack, we would return again and again to note the stag's regular haunts and observe its daily routine. 'Look closely,' he would say to me, pulling aside a bush. 'This is where he slept last night. See how the grass and weeds are flattened down. And here are the marks where his knees pressed the earth as he got to his feet at dawn. He's a big stag all right, probably twelve points on his antlers, a royal beast . . . and in good condition too,' he added, poking open one of the stag's turds. 'He's tall, that one, and holds his head well. Here's where his antlers scraped the tree when passing.'

Nor was Edgar confused when, as happened, the tracks of two stags crossed in the forest. 'The one we want is the stag who veered off to the right. He's the better one,' he told me quietly. 'The other one is too thin.'

'How do you know?' I whispered, for the size of the tracks looked the same to me.

Edgar made me kneel on the ground and sight along the second line of tracks. 'See anything different?' he asked.

I shook my head.

'Observe the pattern of the slots' – this was his name for the hoof marks – 'you can see the difference between the fore and back feet, and how this stag was running. His hind feet strike the ground in front of the marks made by his fore feet, and that means he is thin. A well-fed, fat stag is too big in the body for his legs to over-reach in this way.'

It was on one of these scouting trips into the forest that Edgar came close to treating me with deference, a far cry from his earlier harassment. He was, as I had noted, someone who believed deeply in signs and portents and the hidden world which underlies our own. I did not find this strange, for I had been trained in these beliefs through my education in the Elder Faith. In some sacred matters Edgar and I had much in common. He respected many of my Gods, though under slightly different names. Odinn, my special God, he knew as Wotan; Tiw was his name for Tyr the War God, as I had noted; and red-bearded Thor he referred to as Thunor. But Edgar had other gods too, and many of them were entirely new to me. There were elves and sprites, Sickness Gods and Name Gods, House Gods and Weather Gods, Water Gods and Tree Gods, and he was forever making little signs or gestures to placate them, sprinkling a few drops of soup on the flames of the fire, or breaking off a supple twig to twist into a wreath and lay on a mossy stone.

On the day in question we were moving quietly through beech forest on the trail of a promising stag, when his slots led us to a quiet glade among the trees. In the centre of the glade stood a single, great oak tree, very ancient, its trunk half rotten and moss-speckled. At the base of the oak someone had built a low wall of loose stones. Coming closer I saw that the wall protected the mouth of a small well. Edgar had already picked up a small stone and now he took it across to the trunk of the tree and pushed it into a crevice in the bark. I saw other stones tucked away here and there, and guessed that this was a wishing tree.

'Newly married couples come to ask for babies,' Edgar said. 'Each stone represents their desire. I thought a stone put there might help to bring my daughter back.' He gestured to the well itself. 'Before girls marry they come here too, and drop a straw down into the well, to count the bubbles that rise. Each bubble represents one year before they find their husband.'

His remark touched a raw spot in my feelings. I broke off a twig and leaned over to drop it into the well. Not far below, I could see the dark reflection of the black water. My wish, of course, was not to know my marriage date, but when I would next see Aelfgifu, for I had been pining for her and did not know why I had not heard from her. On every possible occasion I had taken the chance to go from Edgar's cottage up to the burh in the hopes of glimpsing her. But always I had been disappointed.

Now, as I leaned forward over the well, and before I dropped the twig, something happened which was totally unforeseen.

Since I was six or seven, I have known I am one of those few people who are gifted with what others call the second sight. My Irish mother had been famous for it and I must have inherited it from her. From time to time I had experienced strange presentiments, intuitions and out-of-body sensations. I had even seen the spirits of those who were dead or the shadows of those about to die. These experiences were random, unexpected. Sometimes months and even years would pass between one occurrence and the next. A wise woman in Orkney – herself the possessor of the sight – had diagnosed that I only responded to the spirit world when in the company of someone else who already had the power. She said that I was some sort of spirit mirror.

What happened next proved her wrong.

As I leaned over to drop the twig, I looked down at the glint of black water and suddenly felt ill. At first I thought it was that sensation which comes when a person looks down from a great height, and feels as if he or she is falling and is overtaken by sudden faintness. But the surface of the inky pool was hardly more than an arm's length away. My giddiness then changed to a numb paralysis. I felt an icy cold; a terrible pain shot through me, spreading to every part of my body, and I feared I was going to faint. My vision went cloudy and I wanted to retch. But almost as quickly my vision cleared. I saw again the silhouette of my head in the water below, framed by the rim of the well and the sky above it. But this time, as I watched, I saw — quite distinctly — the reflection of someone moving up behind me, holding something up in the air about to strike me, them a metallic flash, and I felt a terrible presentiment of fear.

At that moment I must have fainted away, because I came back to my senses with Edgar shaking me. I was lying on the ground beside the well. He was looking frightened.

'What happened to you?' he asked.

'I don't know,' I replied. 'I had a seizure. I went somewhere else.'

'Woden spoke to you?' he asked, awe in his voice.

'No. I heard nothing, only saw an attack. It was some sort of warning.'

Edgar helped me to my feet and guided me to a fallen log where I could sit down.

'Here, rest for a while. Is that the first attack you have had?'

'Like that one, yes.' I replied. 'I've had visions before, but never in a calm, quiet place like this. Only at times of stress or when I was in the company of a volva or seidrman.'

'What are those?' he asked.

'It's the Norse way of describing the women and men who communicate with the spirit world.'

Edgar understood immediately. 'There's a person like that over to the west, a good two days' walk. An old woman. She too lives by a well. Takes a sip or two of the water, and when the mood is on her, goes into a trance. Some people call her a witch

and the priests have cursed her. But often her prophecies come
true, though no one else would drink the water from this well. It
gives you a bad gut if you do, and there's something mysterious
about the well itself. The waters suddenly gush up and overflow
as a warning that a dreadful catastrophe will occur. The last time
that happened was before Ashington Battle, when the Danes
defeated our men.'

'Were you there?' I asked, still feeling faint.

'Yes,' Edgar replied, 'with the Saxon levies and armed with
my hunting bow. It was useless. We were betrayed by one of our
own leaders and I was lucky to get away with my life. If the
waters of the well had been able to warn us about traitors, I
would have slit his throat for him, for all that he was an ealdorman.'

I hardly heard what Edgar was saying because, as my head
cleared, I was trying to puzzle out what could have caused my
vision.

Then, in a sudden flash of comprehension, I understood: I was
sensitive to the spirit world not only when in the company of
someone who also possessed the second sight, but *by place*. If I
found myself where the veil between the real world and the spirit
world is thin, then I would respond to the presence of mysterious
forces. Like a wisp of grass which bends to the unseen wind, long
before a human feels it on his skin, I would pick up the emanations
of the otherworld. The realisation made me uneasy because I
feared that I had no way of knowing whether I was in such a
sacred place before another vision overcame me.

IT WAS A WEEK after my vision in the forest and Edgar was in
high good humour. 'South wind and a cloudy sky proclaim a
hunting morning,' he announced, prodding me with the toe of
his shoe as I lay half-asleep among my blanket in the corner of
his cottage. He was very fond of his proverbs.

'Time for your first hunt, Thorgils. I've got a feeling that you'll bring us luck.'

It was barely light enough to see by, yet he was already dressed in clothes I had never seen before. He was wearing green from head to toe. I struggled out from under my blanket.

'Here, put these on,' he said, throwing at me in succession a tunic, leggings and a cloak with a soft hood. They were all of green. Mystified, I dressed and followed him out into the cold morning air. Edgar was testing a hunting bow, drawing it back and then releasing it. The bow was painted green too.

'Should I get the dogs?' I asked.

'No, not today. We take only one.'

I said nothing, though I wondered what use it was to have a pack, feed them, clean them, exercise them, and then not use them when you went hunting.

Edgar guessed my thoughts. 'Hunting with a pack is playtime for kings, an entertainment. Today we hunt for meat, not fun. Besides, what we are doing is much more delicate and skilled. So mark my words and follow my instructions carefully. Ah! Here they are,' and he looked towards the burh.

Three green-clad horsemen were riding towards us. One man I did not recognise, though he seemed to be a servant. To my surprise, the other two riders were the huscarls who had accompanied us from London. I still thought of them as One-Hand Tyr and Treeleg. Edgar told me that their true names were Gisli and Kjartan. Both looked in a thoroughly good humour.

'Perfect day for the hunt!' called out Kjartan cheerfully. He was the one missing a hand. 'Got everything ready, Edgar?' They both seemed to be on familiar terms with the royal huntsman.

'Just off to fetch Cabal,' answered Edgar and hurried to the kennel. He returned, leading a dog I had noticed during my unhappy days as a kennelman because it was different from the rest of the pack. This particular dog did not bite or yap, or run around like a maniac. Larger than the others, it was dark brown with a drooping muzzle and a mournful look. It kept to itself and was a steady, quiet, sensible creature. I had almost liked it.

'Mount up!' Edgar said to me. I looked puzzled. I could see no spare horse. There were only three, and each already had a rider. 'Here, lad,' called out Kjartan, leaning down from his saddle and holding out his one remaining hand for me to grasp. It seemed that we were to ride two-up on the animals. Edgar had already sprung up on the saddle behind the servant. One thing about hunting, I thought to myself as I scrambled up behind the huscarl and grabbed him round the waist to steady myself, it's a great leveller – it makes huntsman, huscarl, servant and former kennelman all equal.

'Never been hunting like this before?' Kjartan asked me over his shoulder. He spoke kindly and was obviously looking forward to the day's events. I wondered how he could go hunting when he lacked a hand. He could not pull a bow, and he was not even carrying a spear. His only weapon was a scramsaxe, the long-bladed knife of all trades.

'No, sir,' I replied. 'I've done a bit of hunting on foot, small animals mostly, in the forest. But not from horseback.'

'Well, wait and see,' Kjartan said. 'This will be part on horse and part on foot. Edgar knows what he is doing, so it should be successful. We only have to do what he says, though luck plays a certain part, as well as skill. The red deer are just getting into their fat time. Good eating.' He began humming gently to himself.

We rode into the forest to an area where Edgar and I had recently noted the slots of a red-deer stag and his group of four or five hinds. As we approached the place, the dog, which had been running beside the horses, began to cast back and forth, sniffing the ground and searching. 'Great dog, Cabal, good fellow,' said Kjartan. 'Getting old and a bit stiff in the limbs, but if any dog can find deer, he can. And he never gives up. Great heart.' Another besotted dog lover, I thought to myself, but I had to admire the serious attention that old Cabal was giving to every bush and thicket, running here and there, sniffing. From time to time he halted and put his great muzzle up into the air, trying to catch the faintest whiff of scent.

'There!' said Kjartan quietly. He had been watching Cabal and the dog had dropped his muzzle very close to the ground and was moving forward through the forest, clearly tracking a quarry. 'Silent as he should be,' grunted Kjartan approvingly. When I failed to appreciate the compliment for the dog, he went on, 'Most dogs start to bark or whine when they catch the scent of deer, but not old Cabal. Specially trained to stay silent so as not alarm the quarry.'

We had slowed our horses to the gentlest of walks and I noticed that the riders were taking care to make as little noise as possible. Kjartan glanced across at Edgar, and when Edgar signalled with a nod, our little group stopped immediately. The servant dismounted, took Cabal's leash and led the dog quietly to where he could fasten the leash to a sapling. Cabal, still silent, lay contentedly down on the grass and lowered his head on his paws. It seemed his job was done.

The servant returned and we all closed up in a small circle to listen to Edgar. He spoke in a soft whisper.

'I think we'll find the deer just ahead and we've come to them upwind, so that's good. You, Aelfric,' here he indicated the servant, 'mount up with Gisli, Thorgils stays with Kjartan and I'll walk. We'll leave the extra horse here.'

At his signal, the five of us and the two horses moved forward cautiously. We emerged into an area of the forest where the trees thinned out. To our right, between the trees, I glimpsed a movement, and then another. It was a red-deer hind and her companion. Then I saw the little group – the stag and his four hinds.

'Now we go across the face of the deer,' Kjartan whispered to me. He clearly wanted me to appreciate the subtlety of the chase. I heard the brief creak of leather and to my astonishment one-legged Gisli unfastened his special leather belt, slid out of the saddle, and dropped to the ground. I noticed that he landed on the side of the horse away from the deer, shielded from their sight. He stood grasping the stirrup leather in one hand to keep himself upright as he strapped on his wooden leg. He did not carry a crutch, instead he had a heavy bow in his hand. Edgar moved up to stand beside him. He too was behind the horse and hidden from the deer. When Edgar gave his next signal, the two horses moved out in the open, three men riding and two men walking alongside and hidden from the deer. The stag and his hinds immediately raised their heads and watched our distant procession. Now I understood. The deer were not alarmed by men on horseback, provided they rode gently and quietly and kept their distance. They were accepted as another form of forest animal. I noticed how Edgar and Gisli timed their paces on foot so that they moved with the horses' legs.

'Not quite another Sleipnir,' I whispered to Kjartan. He nodded. Sleipnir, Odinn's horse, has eight legs so that it can travel at tremendous speed. To the deer, our horses must have looked as if they each had six legs.

Fifty paces further on I realised that one-legged Gisli was no longer with us. Glancing back, I saw he was standing in front of a young oak tree, motionless. Dressed in green, he was almost impossible to see. He had let go of the stirrup leather just as the horse passed the tree, used his bow as a crutch, and was now in position. A few paces further on, Edgar did the same. He too was almost invisible. We were setting an ambush.

Kjartan, Aelfric and I rode on, then began to circle to the right. We reached the far side of the clearing and at the edge of the trees Kjartan said quietly, 'Thorgils, this is where you drop off. Stand in front of that tree there. Stay absolutely still. Only move if you see the deer heading your way and not towards Edgar and Gisli.' I slipped off the horse and did as I had been ordered, waiting quietly as Kjartan and the servant rode on.

For what seemed a long time I stood, not moving a muscle, and wondering what would happen next. Then I heard it, a single faint sound – chkkk! Very, very slowly I turned my head towards the noise. I heard it repeated, softly, almost languidly from far away. A moment later I heard the gentle crack of a twig, and into my line of vision walked one of the red-deer hinds. She was perhaps twenty paces away, moving gently through the forest, stopping now and again to snatch a mouthful of food, then moving on. Then I saw another hind and caught a glimpse of the stag itself. All the animals were on the move, unhurried yet heading in the same direction. Chkk! Again I heard the strange sound, and behind the deer I saw Kjartan on his horse. He was riding on a loose rein, barely moving, drifting through the forest behind the deer, not hurrying, but turning his horse this way and that as if the animal was feeding. The sound was Kjartan softly clicking his tongue. A moment later I glimpsed the second rider, Aelfric, and heard a gentle, deliberate tap as he struck his saddle lightly with a willow switch. The soft sounds made the deer move forward, unalarmed. Directly ahead Edgar and Gisli waited.

With excruciating slowness the quarry moved forward. As they drew level with my position, I hardly dared to breath. Slowly I turned my head to look for Edgar. He was so motionless that it took me a moment to detect his position. He was standing with his bow pulled back and an arrow on the string as the leading deer approached him. An elderly hind, she was almost upon Edgar when she realised that she was staring straight into the eyes of her hunter. Her head came up suddenly, she flared her nostrils and tensed her muscles to leap away. At that instant Edgar loosed. From that short range I clearly heard the thunk of the arrow hitting her chest.

Now all chaos broke loose. The stag and other hinds awoke to their danger and began to run. I heard another thump and guessed that Gisli had shot an arrow. A young hind and the stag turned back and broke away towards me. They came bounding through the trees, the stag taking great leaps, his antlers crashing against the branches. I stepped forward so the deer could see me and raised my arms. The hind swerved in panic, slipped on the greasy ground, scrambled to her feet and darted away to safety.

But the great stag, fearing that his flight was blocked, doubled back and headed to where Edgar stood. By then Edgar had a second arrow nocked to his bow string and was waiting. The stag saw Edgar, accelerated and veered past him. Smoothly Edgar swivelled at the hips, his bow pulled so far back that the arrow's feathers were at his right ear, and he loosed just as the prey sped past. It was a perfect passing shot, which brought a shout of approval from Kjartan. The arrow struck the great stag between the ribs. I saw the beast falter in its stride, recover, and then go bounding away through the bushes with a great thrashing of branches which dwindled in the distance until the only sound was the patter of twigs and leaves falling to the ground.

Gisli's shot had also hit its mark. Two hinds, his and Edgar's, lay dead on the forest floor.

'Good shooting,' called out Kjartan as he rode up to the ambush.

'Lucky the stag broke to my left,' said Edgar. He was trying to sound matter of fact, though I knew he was delighted. 'Had he gone the other side of me, it would have been a more awkward shot, swinging away from my leading foot.'

Aelfric had already run off to retrieve Cabal and the dog swiftly picked up the scent of the wounded stag. The trail of blood was hard to miss, and after a couple of hundred paces we came across Edgar's arrow, lying where it had fallen from the wounded animal. 'Gut shot,' said Edgar, showing me the metal barbs. 'You can see traces of his stomach contents. This won't be a long pursuit. Bright clear blood would mean a superficial wound and a long chase.'

He was right. We tracked the stag for less than a mile, and found it dead in a thicket. Losing no time, the servant began to skin the carcass and butcher the meat, and Edgar rewarded Cabal with a choice titbit.

'Located the big stag without trouble, Gisli,' Kjartan called out as we arrived back to where Gisli was standing at the ambush site. The one-legged huscarl had been unable to join the pursuit.

'Five deer found and three killed. That was a nice shot of yours. Fifty paces at least.'

'One advantage to losing a leg, my friend,' Gisli replied. 'When you use a crutch to help you hobble around, it strengthens the arms and shoulders.'

THREE

WE DELIVERED THE venison to the burh, where the earldorman's cooks were preparing the great feast which, by Saxon custom, celebrates the binding of the harvest sheaves.

'The royal huntsman is always invited and gets an honoured place,' Edgar said to me. 'And so he should – he provides the best of the festival food. As my assistant, Thorgils, you're expected to be there as well. Make sure you're suitably dressed.'

So it was that I found myself at the door of the burh's great hall five days later, wearing my purple tunic, which had been freshly cleaned by Edgar's wife, Judith. I was having difficulty in controlling my excitement. Aelfgifu must surely be at the banquet, I thought to myself.

'Who's going to be at the high table?' I asked a fellow guest as we waited for the horn blast to signal that we could enter the hall.

'Ealdorman Aelfhelm is the official host,' he replied.

'Is he Aelfgifu's father?' 'No. Her father was executed by that fool Ethelred on suspicion of disloyalty long before Knut came to power. Aelfhelm is her uncle. He has an old-fashioned view of how to conduct a banquet so I expect Aelfgifu will be a cup-bearer.'

When the blaedhorn sounded, we filed into the great hall to

find our places. I had been allocated to sit at a long table facing towards the centre of the hall, which had been left clear for the servitors who brought our food and for the entertainment to follow. A similar long table had been placed on the far side, and to my right, raised up on a platform, was the table at which ealdorman Aelfhelm and his important guests would dine. Our humbler board was set with wooden plates, mugs and cowhorn spoons, but the ealdorman's guests had an embroidered linen tablecloth and their drinking vessels were expensive imports, goblets of green glass. We lesser folk had just taken our places when another horn blast announced the entry of the ealdorman. He came in with his wife and a cluster of nobles. Most were Saxons, but among them I noticed Gisli and Kjartan, wearing their gold-hilted huscarl swords and looking much more dignified than the green-clad hunters I had accompanied five days earlier. Still there was no sign of Aelfgifu.

The ealdorman and his party took their seats along one side of the high table, looking down at us. Then came a third horn blast, and from the left-hand side of the hall appeared a small procession of women. Leading them was Aelfgifu. I recognised her at once and felt a surge of pride. She had chosen to wear the same close-fitting sky-blue dress in which I had first seen her at Knut's Easter assembly in London. Then her long hair had hung loose, held with a single gold fillet. Now her hair was coiled up on her head, to reveal the slender white neck I remembered so well. I could not keep my eyes from her. She walked forward at the head of the procession, looking demurely down at the ground and holding a silver jug. Stepping up to her uncle's table, she filled the glass goblet of the chief guest, then her uncle's glass and then the noble next in rank. Judging by the colour of the liquid she poured, their drink was also a luxurious import – red wine. Her formal duty done, Aelfgifu handed the jug to a servant and walked to take her own seat. To my chagrin she was placed at the far end of the high table, and from where I sat my neighbour blocked my line of sight.

The cooks had excelled themselves. Even I, who was used to eating Edgar's game stews, was impressed by the variety and quality of the dishes. There were joints of pork and mutton, rounds of blood sausage and pies and pastes of freshwater fish – pike, perch, eel – with sweet pastries too. We were offered white bread, unlike the everyday rough bread, and of course there was the venison which Edgar had contributed, now brought in ceremonially on iron spits. I tried leaning forward and then back on my bench, attempting to get another glimpse of Aelfgifu. But my immediate neighbour on my right was a big, hulking man – the burh's ironworker as it turned out – and he was soon irritated by my fidgeting.

'Here,' he said, 'settle down and get on with the meal. Not often that you have a chance to eat such fine food –' he belched happily – 'or as much to drink.'

Of course, we were not offered wine, but on the table were heavy bowls made from local clay, which gave a deep grey sheen to the pottery. They contained a drink which I had not tasted before.

'Cider,' commented my burly neighbour as he enthusiastically used a wooden scoop to refill his wooden cup and mine. He had an enormous thirst and throughout the meal gulped cup after cup. I tried to avoid his friendly insistence to keep pace, but it proved difficult, even when I switched to drinking mead flavoured with myrtlewort in the hope that he would leave me alone. The leather mead bottle was in the hands of an overly efficient servant, and every time I put down my cup he topped it up again. Gradually, and for almost the first time in my life, I was getting drunk.

As the banquet progressed, the entertainers came on. A pair of jugglers skipped into the open space between the tables and began throwing batons and balls in the air and doing somersaults. It was uninspiring stuff, so there were catcalls and rude comments, and the jugglers left, looking cross. The audience perked up when the next act came on – a troop of performing dogs. They were dressed in coloured jackets and fancy collars and had been trained to scamper about in patterns, to duck and roll over, to walk on two feet and jump through hoops or over a bar. The audience shouted with approval as the bar rose higher and higher, and threw scraps of meat and chicken into the arena as rewards. Next it was the turn of the ealdorman's scop to come forward. He was the Saxon version of our Norse skald, and his duty was to declaim verses in praise of his lord and compose poems in honour of the chief guest. Remembering my time as an apprentice skald, I listened carefully. But I was not overly impressed. The ealdorman's scop had a mumbling delivery and I thought that his verses were mundane. I suspected they were stock lines which he changed to suit the particular individual at his lord's table, filling in the names of whoever was present that day. When the scop had finished and the final lines of poetry died away, there was an awkward silence.

'Where's the gleeman?' called down the ealdorman, and I saw the steward hurry up to the high table and say something to his master. The steward was looking unhappy.

'The gleeman's probably failed to show,' slurred my neighbour. The cider was making him alternately cantankerous and genial. 'He's become very unreliable. Meant to travel from one festival to another, but often has too much of a hangover to remember his next engagement.'

The steward was heading towards a small crowd of onlookers standing at the back of the hall. They were mostly women, kitchen workers. I saw him approach one young woman at the front of the crowd, take her by the wrist and try to bring her forward. For a moment she resisted and then I saw a harp being passed to her from somewhere at the back of the room. She beckoned to a youth sitting at the far table and he got to his feet. By now an attendant had placed two stools in the middle of the cleared space and the young man and woman – I could see that they were brother and sister – came forward and, after paying their respects to the ealdorman, sat down. The young man produced a bone whistle from his tunic and fingered a few experimental notes.

The crowd fell silent as his sister began to tune her harp. It was different from the harps I had known in Ireland. The Irish instrument is strung with twenty or more wires of bronze, while the harp the girl was holding was lighter, smaller, and had only a dozen strings. When she plucked it I realised it was corded with gut. But the simpler instrument suited her voice, which was pure, untrained and clear. She sang a number of songs, while her brother accompanied her on his whistle. The songs were about love and war and travel, and were plain enough, and no worse for that. The ealdorman and his guests listened for most of the time, only occasionally talking among themselves, and I judged that the stand-in musicians had done well.

When they finished, the dancing began. The young man on the whistle was joined by other local musicians, playing pan pipes, shaking rattles and beating tambourines. People left their benches and started to dance in the centre of the hall. Determined to enjoy themselves, men coaxed women out of the crowd of onlookers, and the music became more cheerful and spirited and everyone began to clap and sing. None of the august guests danced, of course, they merely looked on. I could see that the dancing was uncomplicated, a few steps forward, a few steps back, a sideways shuffle. To escape from my drunken neighbour, whose head was beginning to loll heavily against my shoulder, I decided to try. A little fuddled, I rose from my bench and joined the dancers. Among the line of women and girls coming towards me, I realised, was the girl harpist. She was wearing a bodice of russet red and a skirt of contrasting brown, which showed off her figure, and with her brown hair cut short and lightly freckled skin, she was the picture of fresh womanhood. Each time we passed she gave my hand a little squeeze. Gradually the music grew faster and faster, and the circles whirled with increasing speed, until we were short of breath. The music rose to a crescendo and then stopped abruptly. Laughing and smiling, the dancers staggered to a halt and there in front of me was the harpist girl. She stood before me, triumphant with her evening's success. Still intoxicated, I reached forward, took her in my arms and gave her a kiss. A heartbeat later, I heard a short, loud crash. It was a sound that few people in that gathering could have ever heard in their lives – the sound of expensive glass shattering. I looked up and there was Aelfgifu, standing up. She had flung her goblet on the table. As her uncle and his guests looked up in amazement, Aelfgifu stalked out of the hall, her back rigid with anger.

Swaying tipsily, I suddenly felt wretched. I knew that I had offended the woman I adored.

'WAR, HUNTING AND love are as full of trouble as they are of pleasure.' Edgar launched another of his proverbs at me next morning, as we were getting ready to visit the hawk shed, which he called the hack house, and feed the hawks.

'What do you mean?' I asked, though I had a shrewd idea why he had mentioned love.

'Our lady's got a quick temper.'

'What makes you say that?'

'Come on, lad. I've known Aelfgifu since she was a skinny girl growing up. As a youngster she was always trying to get away from the stuffiness of the burh. Used to spend half her days with my wife and me down at the cottage. Playing around like any ordinary child, though she tended to get into more mischief than most. A real little vixen she could be when she was caught out. But she's got a good heart and we love her still. And we were very proud when she was wed to Knut, though by then she had become a grand lady.'

'What's that got to do with her bad temper?'

Edgar paused with his hand on the door into the hack house, and there was a glint of amusement in his eyes as he looked straight at me. 'Don't think you're the first young man she's taken a fancy to,' he said. 'Soon after you arrived, it was clear that you were not cut out to be kennelman. I began wondering why you were brought all the way from London and I asked the steward, who told me that you had been included in my lady's travelling party on her particular instructions. So I had my guess, but I wasn't sure until I saw her tantrum last night. No harm in that,' he went on, 'Aelfgifu's not been so well treated these past months, what with that other queen, Emma, and Knut being away all the time. I'd say she has a right to her own life. And she's been more than good to me and my wife. When our daughter was taken by the Danes, it was Aelfgifu who offered to pay her ransom if she was ever located. And she would still do so.'

THE HAWKING SEASON was now upon us, and for the previous two months we had been preparing Edgar's hunting birds as they emerged from their moult. The hack house contained three peregrine falcons, a merlin, and a pair of small sparrowhawks, as well as the costly gyrfalcon which had first got me into trouble. The gyrfalcon, Edgar pointed out, was worth its weight in pure silver or 'the price of three male slaves or perhaps four useless kennelmen'. He and I would go into the hack house every day, to 'man' the birds as he put it. This meant picking them up and getting them used to being handled by humans while feeding them special titbits to increase their strength and condition as their new feathers grew. Edgar proved to be just as expert with birds as he was with hounds. He favoured a diet of goslings, eels and adders for the long-winged falcons and mice for the short-winged hawks. Now I learned why there was sandy floor beneath their perches: it allowed us to find and collect the droppings from each bird, which Edgar examined with close attention. He explained that hunting birds could suffer from almost-human ailments, including itch, rheum, worms, mouth ulcers and cough. When Edgar detected a suspicion of gout in one of the peregrines, an older bird, he sent me to find a hedgehog for it to eat, which he pronounced to be the only cure.

Most of the birds, with the exception of the gyrfalcon and one of the sparrowhawks, were already trained. When they had their new feathers, it was only necessary to reintroduce them to their hunting duties. But the gyrfalcon had recently arrived in the hack house when I first saw it. That was why its eyelids had been sewn shut. 'It keeps the bird calm and quiet when it's being transported,' Edgar explained. 'Once it arrives in its new home, I ease the thread little by little so that the bird looks out on its surroundings gradually and settles in without stress. It may seem cruel, but the only other method is to enclose its head in a leather hood, and I don't like to do that to a bird captured after it has learned to hunt in the wild. Putting on the hood too soon can cause chafing and distress.'

Edgar also had a warning. 'A dog comes to depend upon its master, but a hunting bird keeps its independence,' he said. 'You may tame and train a bird to work with you, and there is no greater pleasure in any sport than to fly your bird and see it take its prey and then return to your hand. But always remember that the moment the bird takes to the air it has the choice of liberty. It may fly away and never return. Then you will suffer falconer's heartbreak.'

Their free spirit attracted me to the hunting birds and I quickly found that I had a natural talent for handling them. Edgar started me off with one of the little sparrowhawks, the least valuable of his charges. He chose the one which had never yet been trained and showed me how to tie six-inch strips of leather to the bird's ankles with a special knot, then slip a longer leash through the metal rings at their ends. He equipped me with a falconer's protective glove, and each day I fed the hawk its diet of fresh mouse, encouraging it to leap from the perch to the warm carcass in my hand. The sparrowhawk was shrill and bad tempered when it first arrived – a sure sign, according to Edgar, that it had been taken from the nest as a fledgling and not caught after it had left the nest – yet within two weeks I had it hopping back and forth like a garden pet. Edgar confessed he had never seen a sparrowhawk tamed so fast. 'You seem to have a way with women,' he commented, slily because only the female sparrowhawk is any use for hunting.

Not long afterwards he decided that I was the right person to train the gyrfalcon. It was a bold decision and may have been superstitious on Edgar's part, thinking that I would have some special understanding of the spear falcon because I came from its homeland. But Edgar knew that I had been brought to Northampton at the express wish of Aelfgifu, and he may have been playing a deeper game. He made me the gyrfalcon's keeper. I handled her – she was also a female – two or three times each day, fed her, bathed her once a week in a bath of yellow powder to get rid of lice, gave her chicken wings to tug and twist as she stood on her perch so her neck and body muscles grew strong, and held out my glove, a much stouter one this time, so she could hop from perch to hand. Within a month the gyrfalcon was quiet enough to wear a leather hood without alarm, and she and I were allowed outside the hack house, where the splendid white and speckled bird flew on a long leash to reach lumps of meat I placed on a stump of wood. A week after that and Edgar was tossing into the air a leather sock dressed with pigeon's wings, and the gyrfalcon, still tethered, was flying off from my glove to strike the lure and pin it to the ground and earn a reward of gosling. 'You have the makings of a first-class falconer,' Edgar commented and I glowed with satisfaction.

Two days after Aelgifu's outburst at the banquet, we allowed the gyrfalcon to fly free for the first time. It was a critical and delicate moment in her training. Soon after dawn Edgar and I carried the falcon to a quiet spot, well away from the burh. Edgar whirled the lure on its cord. Standing fifty paces away with the gyrfalcon on my glove, I lifted off the leather hood, loosed the leather straps, and raised my arm on high. The falcon caught sight at once of the whirling lure, thrust off from the glove with a powerful leap that I felt right to my shoulder, and flashed straight at the target in a single, deadly swoop. She hit the leather lure with a solid thump that tore the tethering cord from Edgar's grasp, then carried the lure and its trailing cord up into a tree. For a moment Edgar and I stood aghast, wondering if the falcon would now take her chance to fly free. There was nothing we could do. But when I slowly held up my arm again, the gyrfalcon dropped quietly from her branch, glided back to my glove and settled there. I rewarded her with a morsel of raw pigeon's breast.

'So she finally comes to claim her royal prerogative,' Edgar said quietly to me as he saw who was waiting beside the hack house as we walked back. Aclfgifu was standing there, accompanied by two attendants. For a moment I resented the mischievous implication in Edgar's comment, but then a familiar feeling washed over me. I felt light-headed at being in the presence of the most beautiful and desirable woman in existence.

'Good morning, my lady,' said Edgar. 'Come to see your falcon?'

'Yes, Edgar,' she replied. 'Is the bird ready yet?'

'Not quite, my lady. Another week or ten days of training and we should have her fit for the hunt.'

'And have you thought of a name for her?' asked Aelfgifu.

'Well, Thorgils here has,' said Edgar.

Aelfgifu turned towards me as if seeing me for the first time in her life. 'So what name have you chosen to call my falcon?' she asked. 'I trust it is one I will approve.'

'I call the falcon Habrok,' I answered. 'It means high breeches, after the fluffy feathers on its legs.'

She gave a slight smile which made my heart lurch. 'I know it does; Habrok was also the "finest of all hawks" according to the tales of the ancient Gods, was it not? A good name.'

I felt as if I was walking on air.

'Edgar,' she went on, 'I'll keep you to your promise. In ten days from now I begin hawking. I need to get out into the countryside and relax. Two hunts a week if the hawks stay fit.'

So began the most idyllic autumn I ever spent in England. On hawking days Aelfgifu would arrive at the hack house on horseback, usually with a single woman attendant. Occasionally she came alone. Edgar and I, also mounted, would be waiting for her. The hawks we carried depended on our prey. Edgar usually brought one of the peregrines, myself the gyrfalcon, and Aelfgifu accepted from us the merlin or one of the sparrowhawks, which were lighter birds and more suitable for a woman to carry. We always rode to the same spot, a broad area of open land, a mix of heath and marsh, where the hunting birds had room to fly.

There we tethered the horses, leaving them in the care of Aelfgifu's servant, and the three of us would walk across the open ground with its tussock grass and small bushes, its ponds and ditches, ideal country for the game we sought. Here Edgar would loose his favourite peregrine, and the experienced bird would mount higher and higher in the sky over his head and wait, circling, until it could see its target. With the peregrine in position, we advanced on foot, perhaps startling a duck from a ditch or a woodcock from the brushwood. As the panicked creature rose into the air, the peregrine far above would note the direction of its flight and begin its dive. Plummeting through the air, making minute adjustments for the speed of its prey, it hurtled down towards its target like a feathered thunderbolt from Thor. Sometimes it killed with the first strike. At other times it might miss its stoop as the quarry jinked or dived, and then the peregrine would mount again to launch another attack or pursue the quarry at ground level. Occasionally, but not often, the peregrine would fail, and then Edgar and I would whirl our lures and coax the disappointed and angry bird to return to human hand.

'Would you like to fly Habrok next?' Edgar asked Aelfgifu halfway through our first afternoon of hunting and he set my heart racing. The gyrfalcon was a royal bird, fit for a king to fly, and a queen, of course. But Habrok was too heavy for Aelfgifu to carry, so it was I who stood beside her ready to cast the falcon off. As luck would have it, the next game we saw was a hare. It sprang out of a clump of grass, a fine animal, sleek and strong, and went bounding away arrogantly, ears up, a sure sign that it was confident of escape. I glanced at Aelfgifu and she nodded. With one hand I slipped Habrok's leash – the hood was already off – and tossed the splendid bird clear. For a moment she faltered, then caught a distant glimpse of her prey leaping through the rough grass and reeds. A few wing beats to gain height and have a clear sight of the hare, then Habrok sped towards the fleeing animal. The hare realised its danger and increased its pace, swerved and sought protection in a thicket of grass at the very instant the falcon shot by. Habrok curved up into the air, turned and swooped again, this time attacking from the other side. The hare, alarmed, broke cover and began to run towards the woods, ears back, full pace now, straining every sinew. Again it was lucky. As she was about to strike, the gyrfalcon was foiled by an intervening bush and forced to check her dive. Now the hare was nearing refuge and almost safe. Suddenly, Habrok shot ahead of her prey, turned and came straight at the hare from ahead. There was a tremendous flurry, a swirl of fur and feather, and predator and prey vanished into the thick grass. I ran forward, guided by the faint jingle of the bells on Habrok's legs. As I parted the grass, I came upon the hawk, standing on the dead carcass. She had bitten through the hare's neck, using the sharp point on her beak which Edgar called the 'falcon's tooth' and was beginning to feed, tearing open the fur to get at the warm flesh. I let Habrok feed for a moment, then gently picked her up and hooded her.

'Don't allow a hunting bird to eat too much from its prey, or it will not want to hunt again that day,' Edgar had instructed. Now he too came running up, delighted with the performance in front of Aelfgifu. 'Could not have done better,' he exulted. 'No peregrine could have matched that. Only a gyrfalcon will pursue and pursue its prey, and never give up,' and then he could not resist adding, 'rather like its owner.'

But the hunt was not the main reason why I remember those glorious afternoons. Our hunting took us deep into the marshy heath, and after an hour or so, when we were a safe distance from the attendant watching our horses, Edgar would hang back or take a different path, tactfully leaving Aelfgifu and me alone together. Then we would find a quiet spot, screened by tall reeds and grasses, and I would set Habrok down on a temporary perch, a branch curved over and the two ends pushed into the earth to make a hoop. And there, while the falcon sat quietly under her hood, Aelfgifu and I would make love. Under the vault of England's summer sky we were in a blissful world of our own. And when Edgar judged that it was time to return to the burh, we would hear him approaching in the distance, softly jingling a hawk bell to give us warning so that we were dressed and ready when he arrived.

On one such hawking excursion – it must have been the third or fourth time that Aelfgifu and I were walking the marshland together – we came across a small abandoned shelter at the tip of a tongue of land which projected into a mere. Who had made the secluded hut of interlaced reeds and heather it was impossible to know, probably a wild fowler come to take birds from the mere by stealth. At any rate Aelfgifu and I claimed it for our own as our love bower, and it became our habit to direct our steps towards it, and spent the afternoon there curled up in one another's arms while Edgar stood guard at the neck of land.

These were times of glorious pleasure and intimacy: and at last I could tell Aelfgifu how much I longed for her and how inadequate I felt, she being so much more experienced and high born.

'Love needs no teaching,' she replied softly and with that characteristic habit of hers she ran the tip of her finger along the profile of my face. We were lying naked, side by side, so her finger continued across my chest and belly. 'And haven't you ever heard the saying that love makes all men equal? That means women too.'

I bent over to brush my lips across her cheek and she smiled with contentment.

'And speaking of teaching, Edgar tells me that you trained Habrok in less than five weeks. That you have a natural way with hunting birds. Why do you think that is?'

'I don't know,' I replied, 'but maybe it has something to do with my veneration for Odinn. Since I was a child in Greenland I have been attracted to Odinn's ways. He is the God whose accomplishments I most admire. He gave mankind so much of what we possess – whether poetry or self-knowledge or the master spells – and he is always seeking to learn more. So much so that he sacrificed the sight of one eye to gain extra wisdom. He comes in many forms, but to any person who wanders as far from home as I have done, Odinn can be an inspiration. He is ever the traveller himself and a seeker after truths. That is why I venerate him as Odinn the wanderer, the empowerer of journeys.'

'So what, my little courtier, has your devotion to Odinn to do with birds and teaching them?' she enquired. 'I thought that Odinn is the God of War, bringing victory on the battlefield. That, at least, is how my husband and his war captains regard him. They invoke Odinn before their campaigns. While their priests do the same to the White Christ.'

'Odinn is the God of victories, yes, and the God of the dead too,' I answered. 'But do you know how he learned the secret of poetry and gave it to men?'

'Tell me,' Aelfgifu said, nestling closer.

'Poetry is the mead of the Gods, created from their spittle, which ran in the veins of the creature Kvasir. But Kvasir was killed by evil dwarves, who preserved his blood in three great cauldrons. When these cauldrons passed into the possession of the giant Suttung and his daughter Gunnlod, Odinn took it upon himself to steal the mead. He changed himself into a snake –

Odinn is a shape-changer, as is often said – and crept through a hole in the mountain which guarded Suttung's lair, and seduced Gunnlod into allowing him three sips, one at each cauldron. Such was Odinn's power that he drained each cauldron dry. Then he changed himself into an eagle to fly back to Asgard, the home of the Gods, with the precious liquid in his throat. But the giant Suttung also changed himself into a great eagle and pursued Odinn, chasing him as fast as Edgar's peregrine chases a fleeing hawk. Suttung would have overtaken Odinn, if Odinn had not spewed out a few drops of the mead and thus lightened of his precious load managed to reach the safety of Asgard just ahead of his pursuer. He escaped by the narrowest of margins. Suttung had come so close that when he swung his sword at the fleeing Odinn-eagle, Odinn was forced to dodge and dive and the sword cut away the tips of his tail feathers.'

'A charming story,' said Aelfgifu as I finished. 'But is it true?'

'Look over there,' I answered, rolling onto my side, and pointing to where Habrok sat quietly on her perch. 'Ever since Odinn lost his tail feathers to Suttung's sword, all hawks and falcons have been born with short tail feathers.'

Just then the gentle tinkle of Edgar's hawk bells warned us it was time to return to the burh.

Our idyll could not last for ever and there was to be just one more tryst at our hidden refuge before its sanctuary was destroyed. The day was sultry with the threat of a thunderstorm and, for some reason, when Aelfgifu arrived to meet Edgar and myself she had no attendant with her but had chosen to bring her lapdog. To most people it was an appealing little creature, brown and white, constantly alert, with bright intelligent eyes. But I knew Edgar's view of lapdogs – he thought they were spoiled pests – and I had a sense of foreboding which, mistakenly, I put down to my usual dislike of dogs.

Aelfgifu detected our disapproval and was adamant. 'I insist Maccus comes with us today. He too needs his fun in the country. He will not disturb Habrok or the other hawks.'

So we rode out, Maccus riding on the pommel of Aelfgifu's saddle, until we tethered our mounts at the usual place and walked into the marshland. Maccus bounced happily ahead through the undergrowth and long grass, his ears flapping. He even put up a partridge, which Habrok struck down in a dazzling attacking flight. 'Look!' said Aelfgifu to me, 'I don't know why you and Edgar made such long faces about the little dog. He's proving himself useful.'

It was when she and I were once again in our bower and had made love that Maccus barked excitedly. A moment later I heard Edgar's warning bell ring urgently. Aelfgifu and I dressed quickly. Hurriedly I picked up Habrok and tried to pretend that we had been waiting in ambush by the mere. It was too late. A servant, Aelfgifu's old nursemaid, had been sent to find her mistress as she was wanted at the burh, and Maccus's enthusiastic barking had led her to where Edgar was standing guard. Edgar tried to distract the servant from advancing along the little causeway leading to the bower, but the dog went dashing out from our little hut and eagerly led her servant to our trysting place. Not till much later did I know what harm had been done.

We were returning to our horses when Edgar glanced behind us and saw, high in the sky, a lone heron flying towards his roost. The bird was moving through the air with broad, measured wing beats, his winding course following the line of the stream that would lead him to his home. The arrival of the servant had ruined our sport so Edgar thought perhaps he could retrieve our day's enjoyment. A heron is the peregrine's greatest prey. So Edgar loosed his peregrine and the faithful bird began to mount. The peregrine spiralled upwards, not underneath the heron but adjacent to the great bird's flight so as not to alarm her quarry. When she had reached her height, she turned and came slicing down, hurtling through the air at such a pace that it was difficult to follow the stoop. But the heron was courageous. At the last moment the great bird swerved, and tilted up, showing its fearsome beak and claws. Edgar's peregrine swerved aside, overshot, and a moment later was climbing back into the sky to gain height for a second onslaught. This was the rare opportunity that Edgar and I had discussed a dozen times: the chance to launch Habrok against a heron.

'Quick, Thorgils. Let Habrok fly!' Edgar called urgently.

Both of us knew that a gyrfalcon will only attack a heron if there is an experienced bird to imitate. I fumbled for the leash and reached out to remove the leather hood, but a strange presentiment came over me. I felt as if my hands were shackled.

'Hurry, Thorgils, hurry! There's not much time. The peregrine's got one more chance, and then the heron will be among the trees.'

But I could not go on. I looked across at Edgar. 'I'm sorry,' I said. 'There's something wrong. I must not fly Habrok. I don't know why.'

Edgar was getting angry. I could see the scowl developing, the eyes sinking back into his head, his jaw set. Then he looked into my face and it was like the day at the well in the forest. The words died in his throat, and he said, 'Thorgils, are you feeling all right? You look odd.'

'It's fine,' I replied. 'The feeling is over. I don't know what it was.'

Edgar took Habruk from me, removed hood and leash, and with a single gesture let loose the falcon. Habrok rose and rose in the air, and for a moment we were sure that the gyrfalcon would join the waiting peregrine and learn its trade. But then, the white and speckled bird seemed to sense some ancient call, and instead of flying up to join the waiting peregrine, Habrok changed direction and with steady sure wingbeats began to fly towards the north. From the ground we watched the falcon disappearing, flying strongly until we could see it no more.

Edgar could not forgive himself for allowing Habrok to fly. For the next two weeks he kept on saying to me, 'I should have realised when I saw your face. There was something there that neither of us could know.' The shocking loss brought all our hawking to a halt. The spirit had gone out of us, we grieved and, of course, I had lost my link with Aelfgifu.

THE RHYTHM OF the hunting year had to go on. We fed and doctored the remaining birds, even if we did not fly them, and walked the dogs. There was a new kennelman, who was excellent at his job, taking the pack each day to an area of stony ground where the exercise toughened their paws. In the evenings he bathed any cuts and bruises in a mixture of vinegar and soot until they were fit to run on any surface. Edgar wanted the pack ready for the first boar hunt of the year, which takes place at the festival the White Christ devotees call Michael's Mass. He and I returned to our scouting trips in the forest, looking this time for the tracks of a suitable boar, old and massive enough to be a worthy opponent.

'The boar hunt is very different from the hunting of the stag and much more dangerous,' Edgar told me. 'Boar hunting is like training for a battle. You must plan your campaign, deploy your forces, launch your attack and then there is the ultimate test – close combat with a foe who can kill you.'

'Do many lose their lives?'

'The boar, of course,' he answered. 'And dogs too. It can be a messy business. A dog gets too close and the boar will slash him. Occasionally a horse slips, or a man loses his footing when the boar charges, and if he falls the wrong way then the files can disembowel him.'

'The files?'

'The tusks. Look closely when the boar is cornered, though not too closely for your own safety, and you will see him gnash his teeth. He is using the upper ones to sharpen his lower tusks, as a reaper employs his whetstone to put a keen edge on his scythe. The boar's weapons can be deadly.'

'It sounds as if you are less enthusiastic about the boar hunt than pursuing the stag.'

Edgar shrugged. 'It's my duty as huntsman to see that my

master and his guests enjoy their sport to the full, that the boar is killed so its fearsome head is brought on a platter into the banquet and paraded before the applauding guests. If the boar escapes, then everyone goes home feeling that their battle honour has been diminished, and the banquet is a dismal affair. But for the hunt itself, I personally don't find there is much skill to it. The hunted boar travels most often in a straight line. His scent is easy for the dogs to follow, unlike the canny stag who leaps beside his own track to confuse the trail, or doubles back, or runs through water to perplex the scenting pursuit.'

It still took us three days of searching the forest, and the help of Cabal's questing nose to find the quarry we were seeking. Edgar calculated from the mighty size of its droppings that the boar was enormous. His opinion was confirmed when we came across the boar's marking tree. The rub marks extended an arm's length above the ground and there were white gashes in the bark. 'See there, Thorgils, that is where he has marked his territory by scratching his back and sides. He's getting ready for the rutting season when he will fight the other boars. Those white slashes are file marks.' Then we found the wallow where the creature had rested and Edgar laid his hand on the mud to check how long the creature had been away. He drew his hand back thoughtfully. 'Still warm,' he said, 'the animal is not far off. We'd best leave quietly because I have a feeling that he is close by.'

'Will we scare him off?' I asked.

'No. This boar is a strange one. Not just big, but arrogant. He must have heard us approaching. A boar sees very poorly, but he hears better than any other creature in the forest. Yet only at the last moment did this one leave his bed. He fears nothing. He may still be lurking nearby, in some thicket, even preparing to rush on us – it has happened in the past, a sudden unprovoked attack – and we have not thought to bring our boar spears.'

Cautiously we withdrew and the moment we got back to Edgar's cottage he took down his boar spears from where they hung suspended on cords from the rafters. Their stout shafts were of ash and the metal heads were the shape of slender chestnut leaves, with a wickedly narrow tip. I noticed the heavy crosspiece a little way below the metal head.

'That's to stop the spear head piercing so deep into the boar that he can reach you with his tusks,' Edgar said. 'A charging boar knows no pain. In his fury he will spit himself even to his death, just to get at his enemy, especially if he is already wounded. Here, Thorgils, take this spear and make sure that you put a keen edge on it just in case you have to meet his charge, though that is not our job. Tomorrow, on the day of the hunt, our task is only to find the boar and run him until he is exhausted and turns to fight. Then we stand aside and let our masters make the kill and gain the honour.'

I hefted the heavy spear in my hand and wondered if I would be brave enough or capable of withstanding the assault.

'Oh, one more thing,' Edgar said, tossing me a roll of leather. 'Tomorrow wear these. Even if you are faced with a young boar, he can do some damage with his tusks as he slips by you.'

I unrolled the leather, and found they were a pair of heavy leggings. At knee level they were cut clean through in several places as though by the sharpest knife.

By coincidence, Michael's Mass of the Christians falls near the equinox when, for Old Believers, the barrier which separates the spirit world from our own grows thin. So I was not surprised when Judith, Edgar's wife, shyly approached me and asked if I would cast the Saxon wands at sunset. As before, she wanted to know if she would ever see her missing daughter again and what the future held for her sundered family. I took the white cloth that Edgar had used and with a nub of charcoal drew the pattern of nine squares as my mentors in Iceland had taught me before I laid the sheet upon the ground. Also, to please Judith, I carved and marked the eighth wand, the sinuous snake wand, and included it when I made my throw. Three times I threw the wands into the cloth's central square, and three times the answer came back the same. But I could not fathom it, and feared to explain it to Judith, not only because I was perplexed but because the snake wand was so dominant on each cast. That signalled some sort of death, and certain death because the snake wand lay across the master wand. Yet there was a contradiction too because all three times the wands gave me back, clearly and unambiguously, the signs and symbols for Frey, he who governs rain and the crops and rules prosperity and wealth. Frey is a God of birth, not death. I was baffled, and told Judith something bland, mumbling about Frey and the future. She went away happy, thinking, I suspect, that Frey's dominance – he is the God shown with the huge phallus – meant that perhaps her daughter would one day present her with grandchildren.

The morning of the hunt dawned with the dogs barking and baying in excitement, the kennelman yelling to keep them in order, and the boisterous shouts of our masters, who arrived to begin the chase. The hunt marshal was Aelfgifu's uncle, the earldorman, and it was his glory that was to be burnished that day. Aelfhelm had brought along a dozen friends, almost all of whom had attended the sheave-day feast, and once again I noticed the two huscarls. Even with their disabilities, they were prepared to pursue the boar. There were no women in the group. This was men's work.

We sorted out the chaos at the kennels and moved off, the lords mounted on their best horses, Edgar and myself on ponies, and a dozen or so churls and slaves running along beside us. They were to act as horse holders once we found our boar. From that moment forward the hunt would be on foot.

Edgar had already calculated the line the boar would run once he was moved so, as we rode, we dropped off small groups of dogs with their handlers at strategic spots, where they could be released to intercept and turn the fleeing boar.

Within an hour the first deep voices of the older dogs announced they had found their quarry. Then a crash of sound from the pack told us that they were onto the boar. Almost at once there was a piercing yelp of agony and I saw Edgar and the ealdorman exchange glances.

'Beware, my lord,' Edgar said. 'That's not a beast that runs. It stands and fights.'

We slipped from our horses and walked through the forest. But that day's hunting was a calamity. There was no chase, no hallooing or blasts on the horn, no occasion to use the dogs we had so carefully positioned. Instead we came upon the boar, standing at the foot of a great tree, champing its teeth, flecks of foam in its jaws. But this was not a boar at bay. It was a boar defiant. It was challenging its attackers, and the circling pack of dogs howled and barked in frustration. Not one dog dared to close with it and I could see why. Two dogs lay on the ground, disembowelled and dead. Another was trying to drag itself away, using only its forepaws, because its back was broken. The kennelman ran forward to restrain his other dogs. The boar stood, black and menacing, the ridge of bristle on his back erect, his head held low, looking with murderous short-sighted eyes.

'Watch the ears, my lord, watch the ears,' Edgar cautioned.

The ealdorman had courage, there was no doubt about that. He gripped the handle of his spear and walked forward towards the boar, defying it. I saw the beast's ears go flat against his skull, a sure sign that he was about to charge. The boar's black body quivered and suddenly exploded into action. The legs and hooves moved so fast that they seemed a single blur.

The ealdorman knew what he was doing. He stood his ground, the boar spear held at an angle sloping slightly downwards so as to take the charge on its tip. His aim was true. The boar impaled itself on the leaf-shaped tip and gave a mighty squeal of anger. It seemed to be a death strike, but the ealdorman was perhaps too slow. The sheer weight of the boar's charge knocked him off his feet and he was tossed aside. He fell and those near him heard his arm crack.

The boar rushed on, the spear projecting from its side. It darted through the circle of dogs and men unopposed. It ran in a frenzy of pain, a dark red stripe of blood oozing from its flank. We followed at the double, led by Edgar, boar spear in his hand, the dogs howling with fear and excitement. The beast did not go far, it was too badly hurt. We could easily follow the crashing sound of its reckless run. Then suddenly the noise stopped. Edgar halted immediately, and gasping for breath, held up his hand. 'All hold! All hold!' He walked forward very slowly and cautiously. I followed, but he waved at me to keep a safe distance. We moved between the trees and saw and heard nothing. The boar's blood trail led to a tangled thicket of briars and brushwood, a woven mass of thorn and branches, impossible to penetrate even for the dogs. We could see the battered and torn leaves and broken twigs which marked the tunnel of its blind, impetuous entry.

I heard the sudden intake of breath of a man in pain. Looking round, I saw the ealdorman clutching his broken arm, He had stumbled through the wood to find us. With him were three of his high-born guests. They looked drawn and shaken.

'Give me a moment to prepare myself, my lord,' said Edgar. 'Then I'll go in after him.'

The ealdorman said nothing. He was dizzy with pain and shock. Seeing what Edgar proposed, I made a move to join him, but a single firm hand fell on my shoulder. 'Stand still, lad,' said a voice and I glanced round. I was being held back by Kjartan the one-handed huscarl. 'You'd only get in his way.'

I looked at Edgar. He was removing his leather leggings so he would be less hampered. He turned towards his lord and saluted him, a short movement of the boar spear held up to the sky, then he faced the thicket, shifted his boar spear to his left hand holding it close to the metal head, dropped to his knees and began to crawl into the tunnel. Straight towards the waiting beast.

We held our breath, expecting any moment the boar's suicidal charge, but nothing came.

'Maybe the boar's already dead in there,' I whispered to Kjartan.

'I hope so. If not, Edgar's only chance will be to kneel and take the charge head on, the spear point in the boar's chest, butt planted in the ground.'

Still there was no sound except our breathing and the whimper of a nervous dog. We strained to hear any noise from the thicket. None came.

Then, incredibly, we heard Edgar's voice in a low, guttural chant, almost a growl. 'Out! Out! Out!'

'By the belt of Thor!' muttered Kjartan. 'I heard that sound when we fought King Ethelred at Ashington, The place I lost my hand. It's the war call of the Saxons. That is how they taunt their foe. He's challenging the boar.'

Suddenly there came a tearing, crashing, rushing sound, an upheaval in the thicket, and the boar came blundering out, unsteady on its feet, weaving and slipping on the ground, its legs losing purchase. It stumbled past us and ran another hundred paces, then slipped one more time and fell on its side. The yelping pack closed upon it now it was helpless. The kennelman ran up with a knife to cut the boar's throat. I did not see the end, for already I was on my hands and knees crawling through the tunnel to find Edgar. I came across him doubled up in agony, his boar spear tangled in the underbrush, his hands clasped across his belly. 'Easy now,' I told him, 'I have to get you clear.' Slowly I dragged him, crawling backwards until I felt helping hands reach over me to grab Edgar by his shoulders and pull him free.

They laid him on the ground and Kjartan reached down to draw Edgar's hands aside so he could inspect the wound. As Edgar hands came away, I saw that the tusks had gutted him. His entrails lay exposed. He knew he was dying, his eyes shut tight with pain.

He died without saying another word, at the feet of his master, the ealdorman whose honour he had protected.

Only then did I know the real message in the wands was not about Edgar's missing daughter. The wands had pointed to the truth, yet I had been too dull to see it. The snake wand had meant death; that much I had understood. But the appearance of Frey stood not for prosperity and fertility, but because the God's familiar is Gullinborsti, the immortal boar who pulls his chariot.

FOUR

LONDON WAS SOGGY and miserable under a rain-shrouded sky when I arrived back there a week after Michael's Mass. I was still trying to come to terms with Edgar's death. The festivities in the burh had been dismal, with the ealdorman injured, Edgar dead, and the premature onset of gales and heavy rain showers to remind us that the English countryside is no place to spend a winter. Edgar's death had hit me hard. The wiry huntsman had been so competent, so sure of himself, that he had seemed indestructible. I told myself that he would have accepted his death as a risk of his profession and that he had died honourably and would have found a place in Valholl, or wherever it was that his own Gods rewarded those who died a worthy death. His wife Judith, however, was left numbed by her loss. First her daughter and now her husband had been taken away from her, and she was distraught. Aelfhelm, the ealdorman, behaved nobly. When we brought Edgar's body back to the huntsman's cottage, he had promised Judith that he would remember her husband's sacrifice. She could continue to live in her home, and Edgar's son would be employed as assistant to whoever was appointed the new royal huntsman. If the young man proved as capable as his father had been, then there was every reason why he would eventually succeed his father. Yet when I went to say goodbye to Judith on the day Aelfgifu and her entourage set out for London, she could only press my hand in hers and murmur, 'Thorgils, take care of yourself. Remember your days with us. Remember how Edgar . . .' but she did not finish what she had to say because she choked and began to weep.

It had rained for most of our journey south-east as our glum little procession travelled the same road that had taken us to Northampton in the spring. And I had another worry. 'Far from court, far from care,' had been one of Edgar's many proverbs and, as the capital drew nearer, I began for the first time to appreciate the danger of my affair with Aelfgifu. I was still very much in love with her and I longed to see her and hold her. Yet I knew that the risks of discovery in London would be far greater than in our secluded rural world. There was a rumour that Knut was shortly to return from Denmark to England now that the summer campaigning season was over. Naturally Aelfgifu as his queen, or rather as one of his queens, should be on hand to greet him. She had chosen to come to London because Emma, the other wife, was installed in Winchester, which Knut regarded as his English capital. Naturally there was gossipy speculation as to which city, and which wife, he would return to if he did come. As events turned out, he did not return to England that winter, but continued to leave the affairs of the kingdom under the joint control of Earl Thorkel the Tall and Archbishop Wulfstan.

While the staff were unloading the carts at the palace, I approached Aelfgifu's chamberlain and asked if he had any orders for me, only to be told that he had no instructions. I was not on the official list of the queen's retinue. He suggested I should return to my original lodgings at the skalds' house, where he would send for me if I was wanted.

Feeling rejected, I walked through the sodden streets, skirting around the murky puddles in the unpaved roadway and ducking to avoid the dripping run-off from the thatched roofs. When I reached the lodging house, the place was shuttered and locked. I hammered on the door until a neighbour called out to say that

the housekeeper was away visiting her family, and expected back
that evening. I was soaked by the time she finally returned and let
me in. She told me that all the skalds who had regular employment
with Knut were still in Denmark. Those, like my absent-minded
mentor Herfid who had no official appointment at court, had
packed up and drifted away. I asked if I could stay in the lodgings
for a few days until my future was clear.

It was a week before Aelfgifu sent a messenger to fetch me
and I went with high hopes, remembering my last visit to her
rooms in the palace. This time I was shown to an audience room,
not to her private chamber. Aelfgifu was seated at a table, sorting
through a box of jewellery.

'Thorgils,' she began, and the tone of her voice warned me at
once that she was going to be businesslike. This was not a lover's
tryst. I noticed, however, that she waited until the messenger who
fetched me had left the room before she spoke. 'I have to talk to
you about life in London.' She paused, and I could see that she
was trying to find a way between her private feelings and her
caution. 'London is not like Northampton. This palace has many
ears and eyes, and there are those who, from jealousy or ambition,
would do anything to damage me.'

'My lady, I would never do anything to put you at risk,' I
blurted out.

'I know,' she said, 'but you cannot hide your feelings. Your
love is written in your face. That is one thing that I found so
appealing when we were in the country. Don't you remember
how Edgar would joke about it – he used to say, "Love and a
cough cannot be hid". He had so many of those proverbs.' Here
she paused wistfully for a moment. 'So, however much you may
try to conceal your love, I don't think you would be successful.
And if that love was constantly on display before me, I cannot
guarantee that I might not respond and reveal all.'

Anguished, I wondered for a moment if she would forbid me
to see her ever again, but I had misjudged her.

She went on. 'I have been thinking about how it might be

possible for us to meet from time to time – not often, but at least when it is safe to do so.'

My spirits soared. I would do anything to see her. I would trust to her guidance, however much it might hurt me.

Aelfgifu was playing with the contents of the jewellery box, lifting up a necklace or a pendant, letting it slide back through her fingers, then picking up a ring or a brooch and turning it so that the workmanship or the stones caught the light. For a moment she seemed distracted.

'There is a way, but you will have to be most discreet,' she said.

'Please tell me. I'll do whatever you wish,' I replied.

'I've arranged for you to stay with Brithmaer. You don't know him yet, but he is the man who supplies me with most of my jewels. He came to visit me this morning to show me his latest stock, and I told him that in future I preferred to have my own agent staying at his premises, someone who knows my tastes' – she said this without a trace of irony – 'so that when anything interesting comes in from abroad, I will see it without delay.'

'I don't know anything about jewellery, but, of course, I'll do whatever is necessary,' I promised her.

'I've asked Brithmaer to give you some training. You'll have plenty of time to learn. Of course he won't instruct you himself, but one of his craftsmen will. Now go. I will send for you when I judge it to be safe.'

One of Aelfgifu's servants showed me the way to Brithmaer's premises, which was just as well because it was a long walk from the palace to the heart of the city, near the new stone church of St Paul, where the land slopes towards the Thames waterfront. Riverside London reminded me of Dublin, only it was very much bigger. Here was the same stench of fetid foreshore, the same jostle and tangle of muddy lanes leading inland from the wharves, the same dank spread of drab houses. However, London's houses were more substantial, stout timbers replacing Dublin's daub and wattle. The servant took me down a lane leading to the river, and

if he had not stopped at the door of the building, I would have
mistaken Brithmaer's home for a warehouse, and a very solid one
at that.

A small spy hatch opened in answer to our knock. When the
servant identified himself, the massive door was opened and, as
soon as I was inside, closed firmly behind me. The palace servant
was not allowed to enter.

I found myself blinking to adjust to the dimness. I was in an
antechamber. The place was dark because the barred windows
were small and high up in the walls. The man who had let me in
looked more like a rough blacksmith than a fine jeweller and I
quickly concluded that he was more of a guard than a doorkeeper.
He grunted when I gave him my name and gestured for me to
follow him. As I crossed the darkened room, I became aware of
a muffled sound. It was an uninterrupted chinking and clinking, a
metallic sound, irregular but insistent which seemed to come
through rear wall of the room. I could not imagine what was
causing it.

There was a small door to one side, which led on to a narrow
stairway, and that in turn brought us up to the upper floor of the
building. From the outside the house had seemed workmanlike,
even grim, but on the upper floor I found accommodation more
comfortable than in the palace I had just left. I was shown into
what was the first of a series of large, airy rooms. It was clearly a
reception room and expensively furnished. The wall hangings
were artfully woven in muted golds and greens and I imagined
they must have been imported from the Frankish lands. The
chairs were plain but valuable and the table was spread with a
patterned carpet, a fashion I had never seen before. Sculpted
bronze candle holders, even some glass panes in the windows
instead of the usual window panes of horn, spoke of wealth and
discreet good taste. The sole occupant of the room was seated at
the table, an old man quietly eating an apple.

'So you are to be the queen's viewer,' he said. By his dress
and manner he was clearly the owner of the establishment. He

was wearing a dark grey tunic of old-fashioned cut with comfort-able loose pantaloons. On his feet were well-worn but beautiful stitched slippers. Had he been standing, I doubted that he would have come only halfway up my chest, and I observed that he had developed the forward stoop of the very old. He held his head hunched down carefully into his shoulders and the hand that held the apple, was mottled with age. Yet his small, narrow face with its slightly hooked nose and close-set eyes, was a youthful pink, as if he had never been exposed to the wind and rain. His hair, which he had kept despite his age, was pure white. He looked very carefully preserved. It was impossible to read any expression in the watery, bright blue eyes which regarded me shrewdly.

'Do you know anything about jewellery and fine metals?' he asked.

I was about to tell this delicate gnome of a man that I had lived for two years in an Irish monastery where master craftsmen produced exquisite objects for the glory of God – reliquaries, platens, bishops' crosses and so forth – made in gold and silver and inlaid with enamel and precious stones. But when I saw those neutral, watchful eyes, I decided only to answer, 'I would be pleased to learn.'

'Very well. Naturally I am happy to accede to the queen's request. She is one of my best customers. We'll provide you with board and lodging – rent free of course, though nothing was said about paying any wages.' Then, speaking to the doorkeeper who had stood behind me, he said, 'Call Thurulf. Tell him that I want a word.'

The servant left by a different door from the one we had entered through and, as he opened it, that same puzzling sound came bursting in, at much greater volume. It seemed to be coming from below. Now I remembered a similar sound. As a boy, I had been befriended by Tyrkir the metalworker and had helped him at his forge. When Tyrkir was beating out a heavy lump of iron, he would relax between the blows by letting his hammer bounce lightly on the anvil. This is what I was hearing. It sounded as if a dozen Tyrkirs were letting their hammers tap idly in a continuous, irregular ringing chorus.

Another burst of the sound accompanied the young man who now stepped into the reception room. Thurulf was about my age, about eighteen or nineteen, though taller. A well-set-up young man, his cheerful countenance was fringed by a straggly reddish-orange beard which made up for the fact that he was going prematurely bald. His face was ruddy and he was sweating.

'Thurulf, be so kind as to show our young friend Thorgils to a guest room – the end room, I think. He will be staying with us for some time. Then you might bring him down to the exchange later in the afternoon.' With studied courtesy the old man waited until I was walking out of the door before he turned back to take the next bite of his apple.

I followed Thurulf's broad back as he stepped out onto an internal balcony, which ran the entire length of the building, and found myself looking down on a curious sight.

Laid out below me was a long workshop. It must have been at least forty paces in length and perhaps ten paces broad. It had the same small high windows protected with heavy bars which I had seen in the ground-floor antechamber. Now I noticed that the outer wall was at least three feet thick. A heavy, narrow work-bench, set high and securely fixed, ran for the full length of the wall. At the bench a dozen men sat on stools. They were facing the wall, away from me, so I could only see the backs of their heads and they were bowed over their work, so I could not make out what they were doing. All I could see was that each man held a small hammer in one hand and what looked like a heavy, blunt peg in the other. Each worker was making the same action, again and again and again. From a box beside him he lifted an item so small that he was obliged to pick it up carefully between forefinger and thumb, then he placed it in front of him. Next he set the peg in position and struck the butt end with his hammer. It was the metallic sound of this blow repeated regularly by a dozen men, which I had been hearing from the moment I had entered Brithmaer's premises.

Looking down on the line of stooped, hammer-wielding workmen as they beat out their rhythm, I wished Herfid the skald had been standing beside me. I knew exactly what he would have said: he would have taken one glance and burst out, 'Ivaldi's Sons!' for they would have reminded him of the dwarves who created the equipment of the Gods: Odinn's spear, Thor's hammer and the golden wig for Sif, Thor's wife, after she had been shorn by the wicked Loki.

Thurulf led me along the balcony to the last door on the right and showed me into a small sleeping room. It had a pair of wooden beds, set into the walls like mangers, and I put my leather satchel on one of them to claim it. The battered satchel was my only baggage.

'What are all those men with the hammers doing?' I asked Thurulf.

He looked puzzled by my ignorance. 'You meant with striking irons?'

'The men in the workshop down there.'

'They're making money.' I must have looked mystified, for Thurulf went on, 'Didn't you know that my uncle Brithmaer is the king's chief moneyer?'

'I thought he was the royal jeweller.'

Thurulf laughed. 'He's that also in a small way. He makes far more money by making money, so to speak, than by supplying the palace with gems. Here, I'll show you.' And he led me back to the balcony and down a wooden ladder, which led directly to the floor of the workshop.

We walked over to the heavy bench and stood beside one of the workmen. He did not lift his head to acknowledge our presence or break the steady rhythm of his hammer. In his left hand was the metal peg which Thurulf called the 'striking iron'. I could see that it was a blunt metal chisel about five inches long and square in section, with a flat tip. With the hand that held the striking iron, the man stretched out to a wooden box on the bench beside him, and used finger and thumb to pick up a small, thin, metal disc. He then placed the disc carefully on the flat top of a similar metal peg fixed into the heavy wooden bench in front of him. Then, as the little disc balanced there, the workman brought the striking iron into position on top of it, and gave the butt of the iron a smart blow with his hammer. Lifting the iron, he used his right hand to pick up the metal disc and drop it into a wooden tray on his right-hand side.

Thurulf reached out, took one of the metal discs from the first box and handed it to me. It was about the size of my fingernail and I saw that it was plain unmarked silver. Thurulf took back the disc, returned it to the box, then picked up a disc from the tray on the workman's right. This too he handed to me, and I saw that on one side the disc bore a stylised picture of the king's head. Around the margin were stamped the letters KNUT, a small cross, and a leaf pattern. Turning the disc over, I saw the leaf pattern repeated and over it was stamped a larger cross. This time the lettering read BRTHMR. I was holding one of Knut's pennies.

Thurulf took back the penny, carefully replaced it in the box of finished coins and, holding me by the arm, led me away from the workmen so we could speak more easily over the constant ringing of the hammers.

'My uncle holds the king's licence to make his money,' he said. He still had to raise his voice to make himself heard clearly. 'In fact, he's just been named a mint master, so he's the most important moneyer in London.'

'You mean, there are other workshops like this?'

'Oh yes, at least another dozen in London. I'm not sure of the exact number. And there are several score more moneyers in towns scattered all around England, all doing the same work, though each moneyer has his own mark on the coins he stamps. That's in case of error or forgery so the king's officials can trace a coin back to its maker. My own family are moneyers up in

Anglia, from Norwich, and I've been sent here to gain experience under my uncle.'

'It must cost the king a great deal to keep so many moneyers employed,' I said wonderingly.

Thurulf laughed at my naivety. 'Not at all. Quite the reverse. He does not pay them. They pay him.'

When he saw that I was baffled again, Thurulf went on, 'The moneyers pay the king's officials for the right to stamp money, and they take a commission on all the coins they produce.'

'Then who's paying the commission, and who supplies the silver which is turned into coins?'

'That's the beauty of it,' said Thurulf. 'Every so often, the king announces a change to the design of his coins and withdraws the old style from circulation. IIis subjects have to bring the moneyers all their old coins. These are then melted down for the new issue, and the new coins are given out, but not to the same value as those that were given in. There is a deduction of five to fifteen per cent. It's a simple and effective royal tax, and of course the moneyers get their share.'

'So why don't the people just keep their old pennies and use them amongst themselves as currency?'

'Some do and they value their old coins by their weight of silver when they come to trading. But the king's advisers are a clever lot and they've found a way round that too. When you pay royal taxes, whether as fines or trade licences or whatever, the tax collectors only accept the current issue of coins. So you have to use new coins and, of course, if you fail to pay the tax collectors, they impose more fines and that means you have to obtain more coins of the new issue. It's a system of pure genius.'

'Don't people complain, or at least try to melt down their own old coins and stamp out a copy of the new design?'

Thurulf looked mildly shocked. 'That's forgery! Anyone caught making false coins has their right hand cut off. The same penalty, incidentally, applies to any moneyer caught producing coins which are fake or under weight. And the merchants don't complain about the system because the royal stamp on coins is a guarantee of quality. All over Europe the coins of England are regarded as the most trustworthy.'

I looked at the number of men working at the benches, and the porters and assistants who were moving around, carrying bags of silver blanks and finished coins. There must have been at least thirty of them.

'Isn't there a risk that some of the workers will steal? After all, a single penny must represent at least a day's wage for them, and a coin or two would be very easy to carry away.'

'That's why my uncle has designed the premises with that balcony so he can appear from his rooms at any time and look down into the workshop to see what's going on, but the counting is far more effective. A moneyer's job might seem to be nothing but organising a lot of men to hammer out coins while he himself endures the din. But the real chore is the endless counting. Everything is counted in and out. The number of blanks issued to each worker, the number of finished coins he returns, the number of damaged coins, the number of coins received in for melting down, their precise weight, and so on. It's endless, this counting and recounting, checking and rechecking, and everything of value is stored in the strongrooms behind you.' He pointed to a row of small rooms located directly under his uncle's rooms. Brithmaer, I thought to myself, ate and slept on top of his money like a Norse troll guarding his most valuable possessions.

I saw what I thought might be a flaw in the moneyer's defences. 'What about the striking irons?' I asked. 'Couldn't someone copy one of them, or steal one, and start making coins that are indistinguishable from the genuine article?'

Thurulf shook his head. 'It takes great skill to craft a striking iron. The metal is particularly hard. The shank is of iron, but the flat head is steel. To engrave the right image takes a master craftsman. New striking irons are issued by the king's officers when the design of the coin changes. Each moneyer has to buy them from the iron-maker, and return all the striking irons of the older design. More counting out and counting in.' He sighed. 'But recently my uncle was authorised to have a master craftsman engrave irons here on the premises and that's a great relief. After all he's been a moneyer for nearly forty years.'

'You mean your uncle is a moneyer for the Saxon kings, as well as for Knut?'

'Oh yes,' said Thurulf cheerfully. 'He was a moneyer for Ethelred the Ill-Advised long before Knut came along. That's why my uncle has amassed such a fortune. Kings may change, but the moneyers stay the same and go on making their commissions.'

LATER THAT AFTERNOON Thurulf took me to see his uncle at what he called 'the exchange'. It was another sturdy building, closer to the waterfront, where the little stream called the Walbrook empties into the Thames near the wharves. There I found Brithmaer sitting at a table in a back room, writing figures in a ledger. He glanced up as I came in, again with that bland and careful look. 'Did Thurulf show you the jewellery stock?'

'Not yet,' I answered. 'He showed me the coin makers, and then we went to eat at a tavern near the docks.'

Brithmaer did not react. 'No matter. Now that you're here, I'll explain how the jewellery side of my business operates, so you can do whatever it is that the queen wants.'

He nodded towards three or four locked chests on the floor beside him. 'This is where the preliminary assessment is made. When foreign merchants arrive in London port, they usually visit this office first of all. They need to pay the port dues to the harbour reeve and, as this is a royal tax, they have to pay in English coin. If they don't have any English coin they come to my office. I give them good English silver stamped with the king's head in exchange for their own foreign coins or whatever they have to offer. Most of the exchange work is straightforward, and done in the front office. My clerks know the comparative value of Frisian coins, Frankish coins, coins from Dublin and so forth. If they don't recognise a coin, they weigh it and place a value on the metal content. But occasionally we get items brought to us like this.'

He pulled out a heavy iron key and unlocked the largest of the chests. Opening the lid, he reached in and produced an ornate buckle, which glinted gold in the weak afternoon light.

'As you can see, this is valuable, but how valuable? What is it worth in English coin, do you think? Maybe you would care to give me an opinion.'

He passed the buckle over to me. I knew he was testing me so I looked at it cautiously. Compared to the metalwork I had seen in my Irish monastery, it was crude stuff. Also it had been damaged. I weighed it in my hand. For something that looked like gold, it was remarkably light. 'I have no idea of the value,' I said, 'but I don't think it would be worth very much.'

'It's not,' the old man said. 'It's not genuine gold, but gilt over a bronze base. I would say it was once part of a horse harness belonging to some showy chief, perhaps among the Wendish people. It's amazing what shows up in the hands of the merchants, particularly if they come from the northern lands. Everyone knows the reputation of the Norse as raiders. A merchant may come in from Sweden looking to exchange a pile of broken silver bits and some foreign coins, then find he has not enough value for what he needs, reach into his purse and produce this—'

The old man rummaged in the chest, and pulled out something I recognised at once. It was a small reliquary, no bigger than the palm of my hand and made in the shape of a tiny casket. It was crafted in silver and bronze, and decorated with gold inlay. Doubtless it had been looted from an Irish monastery. It was an accomplished piece of metalwork.

'So what do you think that one is worth?'

Again I exercised caution. Something about Brithmaer's attitude sent me a warning signal.

'I'm sorry,' I said, 'I have no idea. I don't know what it is used for or how much precious metal is in it.'

'Neither did the illiterate barbarian who brought it in to me,' said the old man. 'For him it was just a pretty bauble, and because his wife or mistress could not wear it as a brooch or hang it round her neck as a pendant, he couldn't find a use for it.'

'So why did you buy it?'

'Because I could get a bargain.'

Brithmaer dropped back the lid of the chest. 'Enough. I presume that your job is to be here at the exchange so that, when a merchant or a sailor comes in with something similar, you are on hand to assess whether the queen would like to add it to her jewellery collection. If you go to the front office, my clerks will find a space for you.'

So began a long, tedious spell for me. I was not born to be a shopkeeper. I lack the patience to sit for hours gazing vacantly out of the door or, when the weather allows, to stand in the street, hovering to greet a potential customer with an attentive smile. And because it was the start of winter and the sailing season was at an end, very few ships were working upriver with cargoes from the Continent. So there were very few clients. Indeed there were almost no visitors to Brithmaer's exchange, except for two or three merchants who seemed to be regular customers. When they arrived, they did not deal with the clerks in the front room but were shown directly to see Brithmaer in his office in the back. Then the door was firmly closed.

Whenever the boredom got too great to endure, I would slip out of the building, stroll down to the wharves and find a spot out of the wind. There I would stand and gaze at the waters of the Thames sliding past me with their endless patterns and ripples, and I would mark the slow passage of time by the inexorable rise and fall of the tideline on the river's muddy foreshore, and ache for Aelfgifu. She never sent me word.

FIVE

BY MID-DECEMBER I was so racked by longing to see Aelgifu that I asked Brithmaer for permission to look through his existing stock of jewellery for items which might catch the queen's eye. He sent me to Thurulf with a note telling him to show me the inventory in the strongroom. Thurulf was glad to see me. We had adjacent rooms at Brithmaer's home, but each morning went our separate ways – I to the exchange, Thurulf to the workshop floor. Once or twice a week we met up after working hours and, if we could avoid Brithmaer's attention, slipped out of the house to visit the taverns by the docks. We always timed our return to be outside the heavily guarded door to the mint when Brithmaer's two night workers reported for duty, and we entered – unnoticed, we hoped – with them. The night workers were both veterans of the moneyer's bench, too old and worn-out for full-time labour. One had an eye disease and was nearly blind, so he sat at the bench and worked by touch. The other was stone deaf after years among the din of hammers. The men spent a few hours each night at their well-remembered places at the workbench, in lamplight, and I would often fall asleep to the patient clink, clink of their hammers. The general opinion was that it was an act of charity for Brithmaer to give them part-time employment.

'What are you doing here at this time of day?' said Thurulf, obviously pleased when I showed up mid-morning with Brith-maer's note. He was glumly counting up the contents of the bags of the old-issue coins stored in the strongroom before they were melted down for new coinage. It was a job he particularly loathed. 'The bags never seem to grow any less,' he said. 'Goes to prove that people are hoarders. Just when you think you've cleared the backlog, another batch of old coins comes in.'

Thurulf put aside the wooden tally stick on which he was cutting the number of bags of coin, a notch for each bag. Locking the door behind him, he took me to where the jewellery was kept. At the far end of the minting floor was the workroom for the craftsman who cut the faces of the striking irons. He was a suspicious, surly figure and unpopular with the other workers, who resented that he was paid far more than them. I never learned his name because he only came to the mint one day a week, went straight to his workroom and locked himself inside to get on with his job.

'There's not enough work in preparing striking irons to keep a craftsman employed, even one day a week,' explained Thurulf, relishing his chance to display his moneyer's expertise. 'When all the striking irons for a new coin issue have been made, another full set of irons won't be needed until the king decides a new design for his coin, and that might not be for several years. In the meantime the work is mainly repairing and refacing damaged and worn-out striking irons. So my uncle decided that his craftsman might as well make and repair jewellery during his extra hours.'

Thurulf pushed open the door to the workroom. It was a cubbyhole equipped with the same sort of heavy workbench that was used in the main workshop, a small crucible for melting metal and an array of punches and engraving tools for cutting the faces of the striking irons. The only difference was the large iron-bound chest tucked under the bench. I helped Thurulf tug this out and heave it up on the bench. He unlocked it, rummaged inside and produced some jewellery, which he spread out. 'It's mostly repairs,' he said, 'replacing a missing stone in a necklace, tightening up the mounts, mending a clasp, straightening, cleaning and polishing an item so that it will catch the customer's eye. A lot of what is here is rubbish – imitation gold, low-grade silver, broken odds and ends.'

He picked through the better pieces on the bench, and selected a handsome pendant, silver with a blue stone set in its centre and an attractive pattern of curved lines radiating from the mount. 'Here,' he said, 'you can see how this pendant is hung on a chain through that loop. When my uncle acquired the piece, the loop was cracked and flattened and our man had to reshape and solder it. Then he went over the decoration lines again with his engraving tool – they were a bit faded – and made them more distinct.'

I took the pendant from Thurulf. It was easy to detect where the mend had been done and the scratches of the new engraving. 'Your man's not very skilled, is he?' I commented.

'Frankly, no. But then most of our clients aren't too discerning,' said Thrulf blithely. 'He's a working engraver,, not an artist. Now look at this. Here's something he could repair if only he had the right stones to fill the holes.' He handed me a necklace made of red amber beads strung on a silver chain. After every third bead a crystal, the size of half a walnut, was held in a fine silver claw. Like nuggets of smooth, fresh ice, the crystals threw back the light from flat surfaces cut and polished on them. Originally there had been seven crystals, but now three of them were missing, though the silver mounts remained. Had the necklace been entire, it would have been spectacular. As it was, it looked like a gap-toothed grin.

'I thought you said your uncle's workshop made jewellery,' I commented.

'Nothing complicated,' Thurulf replied, lifting a leather pouch from the chest and unfastening the drawstring. 'This is what we specialise in,' and he pulled out a necklace.

My heart gave a little lurch. It was a necklace, made very

simply by joining a chain of silver coins together with links of gold. I had seen one around Aelfgifu's neck. It was the only item she had worn on the day we first made love.

'Your uncle said that I could look through the chest to pick out anything which I thought the queen might like.'

'Go ahead,' said Thurulf amiably, 'though I doubt that you'll find much that has been overlooked. My uncle knows his clients and his stock down to the tiniest item.'

He was right. I picked through the box of broken jewellery and managed to find no more than a couple of bead necklaces, some heavy brooches, and a finger ring which I thought might please Aelfgifu. They added up to a feeble excuse to visit her.

'Would it be possible to make up a coin necklace for her?' I enquired. 'I know that she would like that.'

'You'd have to ask my uncle,' Thurulf said. 'He's the coin expert. Even hoards them. But that's what you'd expect from a moneyer, I suppose. Here, I'll show you.'

He tipped the contents of a second pouch over the workbench and a cascade of coins tumbled out in a little pile. I picked through them, turning them over in my fingers. They were of all different sizes, some broad and thin, others as thick and chunky as nuggets. Most were silver, but some were gold or copper or bronze, and a few were even struck from lead. Some had holes in the centre, others were hexagons or little squares, though the majority were round, or nearly so. Many were smooth with handling, but occasionally you could still see the writing clearly and the images. On one coin I read the Greek script that the Irish monks had taught me; on another I saw runes that I had learned in Iceland. On several was a script with curves and loops like the surface of the sea riffled by a breeze. Nearly all were stamped with symbols – pyramids, squares, a sword, a tree, a leaf, several crosses, the head of a king, a God shown with two faces, and one with two triangles which overlapped to make a six-pointed star.

I slid the coins about on the bench like counters in a board game, trying to align a sequence that would make a handsome

necklace for my love. Instead I found my thoughts flying out like
Hugin and Munin, Odinn's birds, his scouts who fly out across
the world to observe and report to their master all that happens.
By what routes, I wondered, had these strange coins reached a
little box in a strongroom belonging to a moneyer for King Knut?
How far had they come? Who had made them and why were
these symbols chosen? My fingertips sensed a vast, unknown
world that I had never imagined, a world across which these little
rounds and squares of precious metal had travelled by paths I
would like to explore.

I assembled a row of coins, alternately gold and silver, that
looked well. But when I turned them over to check their reverse
sides, I was disappointed. Three of the coins were blemished.
Someone had dug fierce little nicks in the surface with something
sharp. 'A pity about those nicks and pits,' I said. 'They ruin the
surface and destroy the images.'

'You find those marks all the time,' Thurulf said casually.
'Nearly half the old-issue silver coins that we get from the
northern lands carry those cuts and scratches. It's something
foreigners do to them, especially in Sweden and the land of the
Rus. They don't trust coins. They think they might be fakes: a
lead base coated with silver, or a bronze core which has a gold
wash applied to make it look like solid gold. It's possible to
achieve that effect, even in this small workshop. So when they are
offered a coin in payment, they jab the point of a knife into it or
scratch the surface to check that the metal is genuine all the way
through.'

I abandoned the idea of making up a coin necklace for
Aelfgifu, and instead prepared a package of the necklaces and
brooches which I thought might please her. Thurulf wrote down
a careful list of what I was taking. Then we left and locked the
strongroom, and one of Brithmaer's burly watchmen escorted me
and the jewellery to the palace.

I asked to see the queen's chamberlain and told him that I had
samples of jewellery for the queen to view. He kept me waiting

for an hour before he returned to say that the queen was too busy. I was to return the same day the following week to seek another appointment.

As I was emerging from the palace gate, a leather stump tapped me on the shoulder and a voice said, 'If it isn't my young friend, the huntsman.' I turned to see Kjartan the one-handed huscarl. 'Someone said you had found a job with Brithmaer the moneyer,' he said, 'but by the glum look on your face, it would seem that you had found Fafnir's golden hoard and then lost it again.'

I mumbled something about having to return to Brithmaer's workshop. My escort, the watchman, was already looking impatient. 'Not so fast,' the huscarl said. 'At year's end we hold our gemot, the dedication feast. Most of the brigade is still in Denmark with Knut, but there are enough of us semi-pensioners and a few back on home leave for us to make a gathering. Each huscarl is expected to bring one orderly. To honour the memory of our good friend Edgar I would like you to be my attendant. Do you accept?'

'With pleasure, sir,' I replied.

'I've just one condition to make,' said Kjartan. 'For Aesir's sake, get yourself a new set of clothes. That plum-coloured tunic you wore last time at Northampton was beginning to look very shabby. I want my attendant to be turned out smartly.'

The huscarl had a point, I thought, as I pulled my much-worn tunic out of the satchel when I got back to my room. The garment was spotted and stained and a seam had split. The tunic was getting a little too small for me. I had filled out since coming to England, partly due to exercise and good meals when living with Edgar but more from all the ale I was drinking. For a moment I thought of borrowing something to wear from Thurulf, but I decided I would be adrift in his larger garments. Besides, I was already in his debt for our visits to the taverns. I received board and lodging from Brithmaer but no wage, so my friend was always buying the drinks.

If I was to have a new tunic, I had to pay a tailor, and I believed I knew how to raise the money. Better still, I would be able to show my love for Aelfgifu.

When Thurulf had shown me the amber necklace with its missing crystals, I had immediately thought of my satchel. Closed deep in a slit in the thick leather where I had stitched them three years earlier were the five stones I had prised from an ornate bible cover in a fit of rage against the Irish monks who I felt had betrayed me, before I fled their monastery. I had no idea what the stolen stones were worth, but that was not the point. Four of the stones were crystals and they matched the stones missing from the necklace.

I suppose only someone so much in love as I was would have dreamed what I now proposed: I would sell the stones to Brithmaer. With the money from the sale I could repay my debt to Thurulf and still have more than sufficient to purchase new clothes for the banquet. Best of all, I was sure that once Brithmaer had the stones he would tell his craftsman to set them in the necklace. Then, at last, I would have some jewellery worthy to offer the queen.

With a silent prayer of thanks to Odinn I took down the satchel from its peg, slit open the hiding place and, like squeezing roe from a fish, pressed out the stones into the palm of my hand.

'HOW MANY OF these do you have,' asked Brithmaer. We were sitting in his private room at the rear of the exchange when I handed him one of the gleaming flat stones to inspect.

'Four in all,' I said. 'They match.'

The mint master turned the stone over in his hand, and looked at me thoughtfully. Again I noted the guarded expression in his eyes. 'May I see the others?'

I handed over three more stones, and he held them up to the light one by one. He was still expressionless.

'Rock crystal,' he announced dismissively. 'Eye-catching, but of little value on their own.'

'There's a damaged necklace in the jewellery coffer which lacks similar stones. I thought that—'

'I'm perfectly aware of what jewellery is in my inventory,' he interrupted. 'These may not fit the settings. So before I make you an offer I'll have to check if they suit.'

'I think you'll find they are the right size,' I volunteered.

I thought I detected a slight chill, a deliberate closeness in the glance that met this remark. It was difficult to judge because Brithmaer masked his feelings so well.

His next question was certainly one he asked every customer who brought in precious stones to try to sell.

'Have you got anything else you would like me to take a look at?'

I produced the fifth of my stolen stones. It was smaller than the others and dull by comparison. It was a very deep red, nearly as dark as the colour of drying blood. In size and shape it resembled nothing so much as a large bean.

Brithmaer took the stone from me, and once again held it up to the daylight. By chance – or maybe by Odinn's intervention – the winter sun broke through the cloud cover at that moment and briefly flooded the world outside with a luminous light, which reflected off the surface of the Thames and came pouring in through the window. As I looked at the little red stone held up between Brithmaer's forefinger and thumb, I saw something unexpected. Inside it appeared a sudden vivid flicker of colour. It reminded me of an ember deep inside the ashes of a fire which feels a draught and briefly gives off a radiant glow that animates the entire hearth. But the glow the stone gave off was more alive. It travelled back and forth as if a shard from Mjollnir's lightning flash when Thor throws his hammer lay imprisoned within the stone.

For the first and only time in my meetings with Brithmaer, I saw him drop his guard. He froze, hand in the air, for a moment. I heard a quick, slight intake of breath, and then he rotated the stone and again the interior lit up, a living red gleam flickering back and forth. Somewhere inside the jewel was a quality which rested until summoned into life by motion and light.

Very slowly Brithmaer turned to face me – I heard him exhale as he regained his composure.

'And where did you get this?' he asked softly.

'I would rather not say.'

'Probably with good reason.'

I knew that something untoward had entered our conversation. 'Can you tell me anything about the stone?' I asked.

Again there was a long pause as Brithmaer looked at me with those washed-out blue, rheumy eyes, carefully considering before he spoke.

'If I thought you were stupid or gullible, I would tell you that this stone is nothing more than red glass, cleverly made but of little value. However, I have already observed that you are neither simple nor credulous. You saw the fire flickering within the stone, as well as I did.'

'Yes,' I replied. 'I've had the stone in my possession for a while, but this is the first time I've looked at it carefully. Until now I kept it hidden.'

'A wise precaution,' said Brithmaer drily. 'Have you any idea what you have here?'

I stayed silent. With Brithmaer silence was the wiser course.

He rolled the stone gently between his fingers. 'All my life I have been a moneyer who also dealt in jewels. As did my father before me. In that time I've seen many stones, brought to me from many different sources. Some were precious, others not, some badly cut, others raw and unworked. Often they were nothing more than pretty lumps of coloured rock. Until now I have never seen a stone like this, but only heard of its existence. It is a type of ruby known vulgarly and for obvious reasons as a fire ruby. No one knows for sure where such gems originate, though I would make a guess. In my father's time we used to receive many coins, mostly silver but a few of gold, which bore the curling script of the Arabs. So many were reaching us that the moneyers found it convenient to base their system of weights and measures on these foreign coins. Our coins were little more than substitutes, reminted from their metal.'

Brithmaer was looking pensively at the little stone as it lay in his palm. Now that the sunlight no longer struck it directly, the stone lay lifeless, nothing more than a pleasant dark-red bead.

'At the time of the Arab coins I heard reports about the fire rubies, how they glow when the light strikes them in a certain way. The men who described these stones were usually the same men who dealt in the Arab coins, and I conjectured that fire rubies came along the same routes as the Arab coins. But it was impossible to learn more. I was told only that these gems originated even further away, where the desert lands rose again to mountains. Here the fire gems were mined.'

The mint master leaned forward to hand me back the little stone. 'I'll let you know whether I want to buy the rock crystals, but I suggest you keep this gem somewhere very safe.'

I took his hint. For the next few days I kept the fire ruby concealed in a crack behind the headboard of my manger bed, and when Brithmaer decided he would buy the rock crystals and have his workman repair the faulty necklace, I went to the pedlars' market. There, using a fraction of his purchase price, I bought a cheap and ugly amulet. It was meant to be one of Odinn's birds, but was so badly cast in lead that you could not tell whether it was eagle, raven, or an owl. Yet its body was fat enough for my purposes. I scraped out a cavity, inserted the ruby and sealed the hole. Thereafter I wore it on a leather thong around my neck and learned to smile sheepishly when people asked me why I wore a barnyard fowl as a pendant.

My other purchases took a little longer: a tunic of fine English wool, yellow with an embroidered border; a new set of hose in brown; gaiters of the same hue; and garters to match the tunic. I also ordered new footwear – a pair of soft shoes in the latest style, also in yellow with a brown pattern embossed across the toe. 'Don't you want to take away the leather scraps with you, young master, so you can make an offering for your Gods?' asked the cobbler with a grin. The cross displayed in his workshop denoted he was a follower of the White Christ. He had recognised me as a northerner by my accent, and was teasing me about our belief that on the terrible day of Ragnarok, when the hell wolf Fenrir swallows Odinn, it will be his son Vidar who will avenge him. Vidar will step onto the wolf's fanged lower jaw with one foot and tear away the upper jaw with his bare hands. So his shoe must be thick, made from all the clippings and scraps that shoe-makers have thrown away since the beginning of time. The cobbler had made his jibe good-humouredly, so I answered in the same spirit, 'No thanks. But I'll remember to come back to you when I need a pair of sandals that will walk on water.'

Kjartan raised an appreciative eyebrow when he saw my finery as I presented myself at the huscarl barracks on the morning of the gemot. 'Well, well, a handsome show. No one will think me poorly attended.' He was looking resplendent in the formal armour of a king's bodyguard. Over his court tunic he wore a corselet of burnished metal plates, and the helmet on his head had curlicues of gold inlay. In addition to his huscarl's sword at his hip, with its gold inlay handle, a Danish fighting axe hung from his left shoulder on a silver chain. In his left hand he gripped a battle spear with a polished head, which for a moment reminded me of Edgar's death facing the charging boar. But the item which caught my eye was the torc of twisted gold wire wrapped around his arm, the same one that lacked a hand. He noticed my glance and said, 'That was royal recompense for my injury at Ashington.'

Kjartan cautioned me as we walked towards the barrack's mess hall, and his words reminded me of Aelfgifu's mistrust of palace intrigue. 'I rely on you to keep silent about what you witness today,' he said, 'There are many who would like to see all the veteran huscarls purged. The tide of affairs is moving against us, at least in England. We have fewer and fewer opportunities to celebrate our traditions, and our enemies would use our ceremonies to denounce us as evil pagans. The Elder Ways offend the bishops and archbishops as well as the king's church advisers. So your task today will be to serve as my cup-bearer at the feast and to be discreet.'

Kjartan and I were among the last to enter the hall. There were no trumpet blasts or grand arrivals and no women. About forty huscarls were already standing in the room, dressed in their finery. There was no sense of rank or social standing. Instead an air of fellowship prevailed. One man I recognised instantly, for he stood a head taller than anyone else in the room, which was remarkable in itself because the huscarls were mostly big men. The giant was Thorkel the Tall, the king's vice-regent. When the group around him parted, I saw that his legs were freakishly long, almost as if he were wearing the stilts some jugglers use in their performances. It made him look ungainly, as his body was of normal proportions, though the arms were long and dangled oddly by his sides. When he listened to his companions Thorkel was obliged to bend over to bring his head closer. He reminded me of a bird I had occasionally seen when hawking in the marshes with Edgar – the wandering stork.

'Where do you want me to stand?' I said quietly to Kjartan. I did not want to disgrace him in etiquette. There was no division of the tables as at Ealdorman Aelfhelm's feast, where the seating arrangement distinguished between commoner and nobly born. Now a single large table stood in the middle of the room, one place of honour at its head, benches down each side. Service trestles had been set up in one corner for the tubs of mead and ale, and somewhere I could smell roasting flesh, so a kitchen was nearby.

'Stand behind me when the company moves to table. Huscarls are seated by eminence of military prowess and length of service, not because they are high born or well connected,' he replied. 'After that, just watch what the other cup-bearers do and follow their example.'

At that moment I saw Thorkel move towards the place of honour at the head of the table. When all the huscarls had taken their places on the benches, we cup-bearers placed before them their drinking horns already filled with mead. I could not see a single glass goblet or a drop of wine. Still seated, Thorkel called a toast to Odinn, then a toast to Thor, then a toast to Tyr, and a toast to Frey. Hurrying back and forth from the service trestles to refill the drinking horns for each toast, I could see that the cup-bearers were going to be kept busy.

Finally Thorkel called the minni, the remembrance toast to the dead comrades of the fellowship. 'They who died honorably, may we meet them in Valholl,' he announced.

'In Valholl,' his listeners chorused.

Thorkel unfolded his great length from his chair and rose to speak. 'I stand here as the representative of the king. On his behalf I will accept renewal of the fellowship. I begin with Earl Eirikr. Do you renew your pledge of allegiance to the king and the brotherhood?' A richly dressed veteran seated closest on the bench to Thorkel stood up and announced in a loud voice that he would serve and protect the king, and obey the rules of the brotherhood. I knew him as one of Knut's most successful war captains, who had also served his father Forkbeard before him. For this service Eirikr had received great estates far in the north of England, making him one of the wealthiest of Knut's nobles. Both his arms sported heavy gold torcs, which were marks of royal favour. Now I knew why Herfid the skald loved to refer to Knut as the 'generous ring giver'.

So it went on. One after another the names of the huscarls were called out, and each man stood up to renew his oath for the coming year. Then, after the pledges were all received, Thorkel called out the name of three of the huscarls who were in England but had failed to attend the gemot.

'What is your verdict?' he asked the assembled company.

'A fine of three mancus of gold, payable to the fellowship,' a voice said promptly. I guessed that this was customary forfeit.

'Agreed?' asked Thorkel.

'Agreed,' came back the response.

I was beginning to understand that the huscarls ruled themselves by general vote.

Thorkel moved on to a more serious violation of their code. 'I have received a complaint from Hrani, now serving with the king in Denmark. He states that Hakon was asked to look after his horse, specifically his best battle charger, for him. The horse was too sickly to be shipped with the army for Denmark. Hrani goes on to state that the horse was neglected and has since died. I have established these facts as true. What is your verdict?'

'Ten mancus fine!' shouted someone.

'No, fifteen!' called another voice, a little drunkenly I thought.

'And demotion by four places,' called another voice.

Thorkel then put the matter to a vote. When it was passed, a shame-faced huscarl stood up and moved four places further away from the head of the table before sitting down among his comrades.

'All that talk of horses reminds me that I'm getting hungry,' a wag shouted out. It was definitely a tipsy voice. It was beginning to be difficult to hear Thorkel above the general background hubbub.

'Who's the glum-looking fellow at the end of the table?' I asked Gisli's cup-bearer, a quiet young man with an unfortunate strawberry birthmark on his neck. He glanced across to the huscarl sitting silently by himself. 'I don't know his name. But he's in disgrace. He committed three transgressions of the rules and has been banished to the lowest end of the table. No one is allowed to talk to him. He'll be lucky if his messmates don't start throwing meat bones and scraps of food at him after the meal. That's their privilege.'

Suddenly a great cheer went up. From the side room where

the cooks had been at work four men appeared. They were carrying between them the body of a small ox, spit roasted, which they lifted over the heads of the revellers and placed on the centre of the table. The head of the ox was brought in separately and displayed on a long iron spike driven into the floor. An even louder cheer greeted the four men when they appeared a second time with another burden. This time the carcass they carried was the body of a horse. This too had been roasted and its ribs stood up like the fingers of a splayed hand. The roast horse was also placed on the table and its head on a second spike beside the ox's. Then the cooks withdrew, and the huscarls fell upon the food, hacking it up with their daggers, and passing chunks up the table. 'Thank the Gods we can still eat real meat on feast days whatever those lily-white priests say,' a whiskery veteran announced to no one in particular, chewing heartily, his beard already daubed with morsels of horse flesh. 'Makes no sense that the White Christ priests forbid their followers to eat horse flesh. Can't think why they don't ban mutton when they spend so much time talking about the Lamb of God.'

As the pace of eating slowed, I noticed the cooks and other servitors leave the mess hall. Only the huscarls and their cup-bearers remained. Then I saw Thorkel nod to the disgraced huscarl seated at the end of the table. It must have been some sort of pre-arranged signal for the man got up from his place and walked across to the double entrance doors. Closing them, he picked up a wooden bar and dropped the timber into two frame slots. The door was now effectively barred from the inside. Whatever was now going to take place inside the mess hall was definitely a private matter.

Someone hammered on the table with his sword hilt, calling for silence. A hush fell over the assembled company, and into that silence came a sound I had last heard in Ireland three years before, at the feast of a minor Irish king. It was an eerie wailing. At first it seemed to be unearthly, without rhythm or tune until you listened closely. It was a sound that could make the hairs stand up on the back of your neck — a single bagpipe, hauntingly played. I listened carefully, trying to locate the sound. It seemed to be coming from the side room where the cooks had worked. As I looked in that direction, through the doorway stepped a figure that made the blood rush to my head. It was a man and his head was completely invisible inside a terrifying mask made from gilded basketwork. It covered the wearer down to his shoulders, leaving only eye holes for him to see his way from as he advanced into the room. He man was wearing the head of a giant bird.

And there was no doubt that he was a man because, except for the mask, he was stark naked.

I knew at once who was represented. The man held in each hand a long spear, the symbol of Odinn, his ash spear Gungnir, the 'swaying one'.

As the bagpipe continued to play, the naked man began to dance. Deliberately at first, lifting each spear in turn and bringing its butt end down with a thump on the ground in time with the music. As the music quickened, so too did the dancing figure, turning and cavorting, leaping in sidelong jumps down one side of the table, then up the other. As the cadence of his dance became familiar, the huscarls took up the rhythm, beating gently at the start and then with increasing fervour on the table with their hands, their dagger handles, and chanting, Odinn! Odinn! Odinn!' The figure whirled, holding out the two spears so they whistled through the air, and he leaped and leaped again. I saw several of the older huscarls reach out and dip their hands in the bloody juices of the horse carcass and mark their own foreheads with a bloody stripe, dedicating themselves to the All-Father.

Then, as unexpectedly as he had arrived, the masked figure darted out of sight back into the room he had come from.

Again the bagpipe began to play, and this time the musician emerged from his hiding place. He was a young man and he was playing a smaller pipe than those I knew from Ireland. He took up his station behind Earl Eirikr and I guessed that the Northumbrian earl had brought the piper with him for our entertainment.

He had also hired a professional mimer, for the next person to appear from the side room with a dramatic leap was dressed in the costume of a hero, with helmet, armour and a light sword. It took only moments for the audience to recognise he was playing the role of Sigurd in the lay of Fafnir. They roared their approval as he mimed the ambush from the trench in which the hidden Sigurd stabs upwards into Fafnir's slithering belly and the gold-guarding dragon dies. Then, in a sinuous movement the actor changed character and became Regin, Sigurd's evil foster-father, who arrives upon the scene and asks Sigurd to cook the dragon's heart so he may eat it. Another leap sideways and the mimer became Sigurd, licking his burned thumb as he cooks the meat, and from that taste learns the language of birds, who tell him that the treacherous Regin intends to murder him. A sham sword fight, and Sigurd killed the evil foster-father, ending his display by dragging away two imaginary chests of dragon's gold. And not entirely imaginary gold either, for several of the huscarls threw gold and silver coins on the floor as a mark of their appreciation.

At this point Thorkel and several of the more senior huscarls left the hall. They must have known that the gemot could last far into the night, and into the next day as well, and that the celebrations would soon grow even more ribald and disorderly. But Kjartan made no move to go, so I kept to my cup-bearer's duties as the evening grew more and more raucous. Prodigious quantities of mead and ale were consumed, and the liquor loosened tongues. I had not anticipated the strength of dislike that the traditional huscarls showed towards the White Christ faction at court. They talked of the Christians as devious, smug and crafty. The special targets for their odium were the queen, Emma of Normandy, and the king's chief lawmaker, Archbishop Wulfstan. A very drunk huscarl pulled out a long white shirt – he must have brought it with him for that purpose – and waved it in the air to attract the attention of his drinking companions. Unsteadily he got to his feet, pulled it on over his own head and mimicked the act of Christian prayer, shouting, 'I've been prepared for baptism three times, and each time the priests paid me a month's wages and gave me a fine white shirt.'

'Easy money,' yelled a companion drunkenly. 'I collected four payments; it's a new version of the Danegeld'.

This drew a roar of drunken laughter. Then the assembly began to chant a name. 'Thyrmr! Thyrmr! Remember Thyrmr!' and the huscarl took off his white shirt and threw it into the corner of the room. 'Thyrmr! Thyrmr!' chanted the men, now completely intoxicated, and they began picking up the remnants of the meal, and throwing the chewed bones and discarded gristle in the direction of the crumpled cloth.

'I thought they were going to throw the bones at the disgraced huscarl,' I muttered to Gisli's cup-bearer.

'He's in luck tonight,' he answered. 'Instead they're celebrating the day that one of the Saxon high priests, an archbishop, I think his name was Alfheah, got himself killed. A man named Thyrmr did it, smacked the archbishop on the back of his head with the flat of his battleaxe at the end of a particularly boisterous feast after everyone had pelted the priest with ox bones.'

This drunken boasting was infantile and pointless, I thought to myself as I watched the stumbling drunkards. It was the response of men who felt outmanouevred by their rivals. This hollow mummery was not the way to protect the future veneration of the Old Gods.

I grew more and more depressed as the evening degenerated into brutishness. The only moment I raised a smile was when the company began to chant a lewd little ditty about Queen Emma and her priestly entourage. The words were clever and I found myself joining in the refrain, 'Bakrauf! Bakrauf!' I realised I was thick tongued and slurring my words, even though I had been trying to stay sober. So when Kjartan slumped from his seat, completely drunk, I beckoned to Gisli's cup-bearer to help me, and together we carried the one-armed huscarl back to his barracks bed. Then I started out on the long walk back through London to reach my own room, hoping that the chilly winter air and the exercise would clear my head.

I scratched quietly at the heavy door of the mint. It was long past the time that Thurulf and I normally returned from tavern, but I had bribed the door keeper, who was by now quite accustomed to my drinking excursions. He must have been waiting by the door, for he opened it almost at once, and I went in, walking as quietly and as straight as my drunkenness would allow. I was just sober enough to realise that it would be foolish to use the stairs to the upper floor that went past Brithmaer's chambers. A creaking floorboard or falling up the stairs would attract attention. I decided to go to my room by the far stair, which led directly from the workshop floor to the balcony. I removed my smart yellow shoes, and holding them in my hand, walked quietly along the length of the workshop, trying to keep in a straight line. In a pool of lantern light at the far end of the workshop, the two elderly men were still at the coining bench. I could see them bent over, tapping out the little coins. Neither of them was aware of my approach – one because eye disease had damaged his sight, the other because he was concentrating hard on his work and, being deaf, would not have heard me even if I had not been barefoot. I was more drunk than I thought and I swayed and swerved in my walk enough to brush against the deaf man. It gave him such a shock that he started upright and fumbled his work. The striking iron dropped to the floor, as he turned to see what was behind him. In tipsy embarrassment I put my finger to my lips, entreating silence. Then, concentrating ferociously as only a drunkard can, I managed to bend over without tumbling headlong, picked up his striking iron from the ground, and returned it to him. A glint of silver caught my eye. It was the coin he had just struck. It too had fallen to the floor. Risking another attack of sot's vertigo, I picked up the coin and put it in his hands. Then with an exaggerated salute, I turned and wove my way to the staircase, then climbed it hand over hand like a novice sailor, and eventually toppled into my manger bed.

I awoke next morning with a vile headache and the taste of stale mead in my mouth. As I was bent over a bucket of well water, trying to wash my bleary eyes, my position bent over the bucket reminded me of something that had puzzled me. I recalled something strange when I leaned down and picked up the old man's striking iron and the dropped coin. I could not remember exactly what it was. Then I remembered: as I placed the coin into the workman's palm, a gleam of lantern light had fallen across it. The freshly minted coin was a silver penny. But the face I saw stamped on the coin was not Knut's familiar image, but someone else's.

Or was I too drunk to know the difference? The mystery nagged at me all morning until I realised that I could check. The striking irons used at night were kept for safe keeping in the jewellery workshop, and so mid-morning I reminded Brithmaer that the crystal necklace should be repaired by now and asked if I might visit the workshop to examine it.

Thurulf opened the door to the strongroom and wandered off, leaving me on my own. A few moments was all the time I needed to locate the striking irons that the two night workers used. They were tucked away out of sight under the workbench, wrapped in a leather cloth. There was also a lump of old wax, tossed aside when the engraver had made moulds for repairing jewellery. I nipped off two little pellets of wax and pressed them between the faces of the striking irons and their counterparts, then replaced the nightworkers' tools. When Thurulf returned, I was admiring the rock crystals in their new settings.

I was so eager to examine the wax impressions that I had scarcely gone a hundred paces on my way back to the exchange when I shook them out from my sleeve. Even the simplest pedlar would have recognised the patterns pressed on them. There was no mystery: they could be found in half the markets in the land,

and they lay in the mint's storerooms by the thousand – the king's head on the striking irons was that of King Ethelred the Ill-Advised, dead these four years past. On their reverse, one wax impression bore the mark of a moneyer in Derby and the other a moneyer in Winchester. I was intrigued. Why would Brithmaer secretly be making coins that were out of date? Why would he want coins that were already valueless and should be melted down, and that at a discount?

There seemed no logic to it, and in the tavern that evening I casually asked Thurulf if he had heard of a moneyer in Derby by the name of Guner. He told that the name was vaguely familiar, but he thought that the man was long since dead.

I drank little, telling Thurulf that I was still queasy from the huscarls' gemot. In fact I wanted to look my best the following morning for that was when I had arranged with Aelfgifu's chamberlain that I would return with a selection of jewellery for her inspection.

Aelfgifu was in a mischievous mood. Her eyes sparkled when – at last – she managed to dismiss her attendants, telling them that she would try on the jewels in private. It seemed a feeble excuse to me, but she carried it off, and moments later we were in the private bedchamber where she had first taught me how to love.

'Let me look at you!' she gloated, making me stand back so she could admire the effect of my new tunic. 'Yellow and brown and black. The colours really suit you – you look good enough to eat. Come, let me taste you.' And she walked across and threw her arms around me.

Feeling the softness of her breasts, I was flooded by my own craving. Our mouths met, and I realised that if my longing had been acute, hers was also. Previously in that room our love had been tender and forbearing, with Aelfgifu leading my novice hesitancy. Now we both plunged into the certainty of our passion, greedy for one another, tumbling together on the bed. Within moments we were naked and making love with desperate urgency until the first wave of passion had spent itself. Only then did Aelfgifu disengage herself and, as always, run her finger down my profile. 'What was it you wanted to show me?' she asked teasingly.

I rolled over to the side of the bed and reached down to pick up the bag of jewellery, and tipped it out on the sheet. As I had hoped, she pounced immediately on the crystal and amber necklace.

'It's beautiful' she exclaimed. 'Here help me put it on,' and she turned so that I could fasten the clasp at the nape of her neck. When she turned back again to face me, her eyes shining to match the crystals, I could have imagined no better place for the gems that I had stolen. Now they lay supported on the sweet curves of her breasts. What would the Irish monks have thought? I wondered.

Somehow Aelfgifu had arranged that we could be alone together for several hours, and in that time we were unrestrained. We made love light-heartedly and often. We delighted in one another's bodies. Aelfgifu was provocative in her response when I covered her with jewellery — the necklace, of course, but also bracelets on her ankles and wrists, a pendant as a belt, and two magnificently gaudy brooches to cup her breasts, all at once.

When we had laughed and loved one another to exhaustion and were lying side by side, I told her about the fire ruby hidden in the amulet of lead — she had lifted it from my neck after the first encounter, saying the lump would give her bruises. She listened to my story and before I had finished, had guessed my intention. 'Thorgils,' she said gently, 'I don't want to have that stone. You are not to give it to me. I have a feeling that stone should remain with you. It has your spirit. Somewhere inside you flickers that same light, which needs someone to make it glow,' and gently she leaned over and began to lick my chest.

SIX

GREAT HAPPINESS; GREAT danger – another of Edgar's proverbs. Only two days after my impassioned visit to Aelfgifu, I was shaken awake by Brithmaer's door keeper. A palace messenger was waiting for me in the street, he grunted, on an urgent matter. Groggy with sleep since it was not yet dawn, I dressed in my tunic, elated that this summons to the queen's apartments had come so soon after our last tryst.

But when I opened the door to the street, I did not recognise the messenger standing there in the half-dark. He was sombrely dressed and looked more like a minor clerk than a royal servant.

'Your name is Thorgils?' he enquired.

'Yes,' I replied, puzzled. 'What can I do for you?'

'Come with me, please,' the man said. 'You have a meeting with Archbishop Wulfstan.'

A chill came over me. Archbishop Wulfstan, co-regent of England, was no friend to followers of the Old Ways, and by reputation was the cleverest man in the kingdom. For an instant I wondered what business he had with someone as insignificant as myself. Then a hard knot formed in my stomach. The only person who connected me with matters of state was Aelfgifu.

The messenger led me to the royal chancery, a melancholy building at the rear of the palace where I was shown to an empty waiting room. It was still only an hour after daybreak when I was ushered into the archbishop's council chamber, yet the king's chief minister was already deep in his work. Flanked by two priests as his secretaries, Wulfstan was seated at a table listening to some notes being read to him in Latin. He looked up as I entered, and I saw that he must have been well past his sixtieth year. He had a seamless face, scrubbed and pink, a few wisps of white hair remained on his scalp and his hands, which were folded on the table, were soft and white. His serene demeanour and the benign smile he directed towards me as I entered gave him the appearance of a kindly grandfather. But that agreeable impression withered the moment he spoke. His voice was so quiet that I had to strain to hear him, yet it carried a menace far more frightening than if he had shouted aloud. Worse was his choice of words: 'The fly that plays too long in the candle singes his wings at last.'

I felt as if I was about to faint.

One of the notaries passed a sheet of parchment to the archbishop. 'Your name, Thorgils, is a pagan one, is it not? You are an un-believer?' Wulfstan asked.

I nodded.

'Would that be why you attended the banquet at the huscarls' mess hall the other evening? I understand that certain gross ceremonies were conducted during the course of the meal.'

'I attended only as a cup-bearer, my lord,' I said, wondering who was the informer who had told the archbishop about the evening's events. 'I was a bystander.'

'Not entirely, I think,' said the archbishop consulting his notes. 'It is reported that at times you participated in the debauchery. Apparently you also enthusiastically joined in the chorus of a blasphemous and scurrilous song, which might be said to be treasonable and is certainly seditious.'

'I don't know what you mean, my lord,' I answered.

'Let me give you an example. The song noted here apparently referred to our noble Queen Emma, and repeatedly, as a Bakrauf.'

I stayed silent.

'You know what Bakrauf means?'

Still I said nothing,

'You ought to be aware,' the archbishop went on unrelentingly, 'that for a number of years I served as Archbishop of York. In that city the majority of the citizens are Norse and speak their donsk tunga, as they call it. I made it my business to learn the langage fluently, so I do not need my staff to tell me that the word Bakrauf means the human fundament, or in a more civilised speech, an anus. Hardly a fitting description of the wife of the king of England, do you think? Sufficient cause for the culprit to suffer some sort of punishment – like having his tongue cut out, perhaps?' The archbishop spoke in little more than a gentle whisper. Yet there was no mistaking that he meant his threat. I recalled that he was famous for the virulent sermons he delivered under the name of 'the Wolf'. I wondered where this line of questioning was leading.

'Do you deny the charge? There are at least three witnesses to the fact that you participated in the chorus and with apparent relish.'

'My lord,' I answered, 'I was fuddled at the time, having taken too much drink.'

'Hardly an excuse.'

'I mean I misunderstood the meaning of the word Bakrauf,' I pleaded. 'I know that Bakrauf means anus in the donsk tunga, but I was thinking in Latin, and those who taught me Latin told me that anus means "an old woman". They never said that it might also mean part of the human body. Of course I humbly apologise for referring to the queen as an old woman.'

Wulfstan, who had begun to look bored, suddenly became more attentive. 'So Thorgils knows his Latin, does he?' he mumured. 'And how is that?'

'Monks in Ireland taught me, my lord,' I said. I did not add that, judging from his conversation in Latin with the notaries when I came in, my command of the language was probably better than his own.

Wulfstan grimaced. 'Those benighted Irish monks,' he observed sourly. 'A cluster of thorns in the flesh of the true Church.' He noticed the lead amulet hanging round my neck. 'If you studied with the Irish monks, how is it that you were not baptised? You should be wearing a Christian cross around your neck. Not a pagan sign.'

'I never completed the necessary instruction, my lord.'

Wulfstan must have accepted that I was not easily intimidated, for he tried another approach, still in the same soft, menacing voice. 'Whether Christian or not, you are subject to the king's laws while you are in his realm. Did those Irish monks teach you also about the law?'

His enquiry was so barbed that I could not resist replying, 'They taught me – "the more laws, the more offenders".'

It was a stupid and provocative reply. I had no idea that Wulfstan and his staff had laboured for the past two years at drawing up a legal code for Knut and prided themselves on their diligence. Even if the archbishop had known that it was a quotation from Tacitus expounded to me in the classroom by the monks, he would have been annoyed.

'Let me tell you the fifty-third clause in King Knut's legal code,' Wulfstan went on grimly. 'It concerns the penalty for adultery. It states that any married woman who commits adultery will forfeit all the property she owns. Moreover she will lose her ears and nose.'

I knew that he had come to the point of our interview.

'I understand, my lord. A married woman, you said. Do you mean a woman married according to the laws of the Church? Openly recognised as such?'

The 'Wolf' regarded me malevolently. He knew that I was referring to Aelfgifu's status as 'the concubine' in the eyes of the Church, which refused to consider her as a legal wife.

'Enough of this sophistry. You know exactly what I am talking about. I summoned you here to give you a choice. We are well informed of your behaviour with regard to a certain person close to the king. Either you agree to act as an agent for this office, informing this chancery of what goes on within the palace, or it will be arranged that you are brought before a court on a charge of adultery.'

'I see that I have no choice in the matter, my lord,' I answered.

'He that steals honey should beware of the sting,' said the archbishop with an air of smug finality. He rivalled Edgar in his love of proverbs. 'Now you must live with the consequences. Return to your lodgings and think over how you may best serve this office. And you may rest assured that you are being watched, as you have been for the past month and more. It would be futile to try to flee the king's justice.'

I returned to Brithmaer's mint just long enough to change out of my court clothes, pack them into my satchel and put on my travelling garments. I had come to a decision even as the archbishop set out his ultimatum. I knew that I could not betray Aelfgifu by becoming a spy for Wulfstan, nor could I stay in London. My position would be intolerable if I did. When Knut returned to England, Wulfstan would not need to bring an accusation of adultery against me, only to hint to the king that Aelfgifu had been unfaithful. Then I would be the cause of the disgrace of the woman I adored. Better I fled the kingdom than ruin her life.

My first step was to take the two little wax moulds pressed from the striking irons of Brithmaer's elderly workmen, and bring them to the huscarls' barracks. There I asked to see Kjartan. 'I've come to say goodbye,' I told him, 'and to ask a favour. If you hear that some accident has befallen me, or if I fail to contact you with a message before the spring, I want you to take these two pieces of wax and give them to Thorkel the Tall. Tell him that they came from the workshop of Brithmaer the moneyer while Knut was the king of England. Thorkel will know what to do.'

Kjartan took the two small discs of wax in his single hand, and looked at me steadily. There was neither surprise nor question in his eyes. 'You have my word on it,' he said. 'I have the feeling that it would be tactless of me to ask why your departure from London is so sudden. Doubtless you have your reasons, and anyhow I have a strong feeling that one day I will be hearing more about you. In the meantime, may Odinn Farmognudr, the jourey empowerer', protect you.'

Within the hour I was back at Brithmaer's exchange office on the waterfront and I asked if I could speak to him in private. He was standing at the window of the room where he met his private clients, looking out on the wintry grey river, when I made my request.

'I need to leave England without the knowledge of the authorities and you can help me,' I said.

'Really. What makes you think that?' he answered blandly.

'Because new-minted coins bear a dead king's mark.'

Slowly and deliberately Brithmaer turned his head and looked straight at me. For the second time that day an old man regarded me with strong dislike.

'I always thought you were a spy,' he said coldly.

'No,' I replied, 'I did not come to you as a spy. I was sent in good faith by the queen. What I learned has nothing to do with Aelfgifu.'

'So what is it that you have learned?'

'I know that you are forging the king's coinage. And that you are not alone in this felony, though I would not be wrong in believing you are the prime agent.'

Brithmaer was calm. 'And how do you think that this felony, as you call it, is enacted? Everyone knows that the coinage of England is the most strictly controlled in all Europe and the penalties for forgery are severe. Counterfeit coins would be noticed immediately by the king's officers and traced back to the forger. He would be lucky only to lose a hand, more likely it would be his life. Only a fool or a knave would seek to forge the coins of the king of England.'

'Of the present king of England, yes,' I replied, 'but not the coins of a previous king.'

'Go on,' said Brithmaer. There was an edge to his voice now.

'I discovered quite by accident that the two elderly workers who strike coins at night in your workshop are not producing coins with the head of Knut. They make coins which carry the head and markings of King Ethelred. At first it made no sense, but then I saw coins which had arrived from the northern lands, from Sweden and Norway. Many of them had the test marks, the nicks and scratches. Most of them were old, from Ethelred's times, when the English paid vast amounts of Danegeld to buy off the raiders. It seems that huge numbers of Ethelred's coins are in circulation in the north lands, and now they are coming back in trade. Thurulf spends a great deal of time counting them in the storerooms.'

'There's nothing wrong with that,' Brithmaer murmured.

'No, but Thurulf remarked to me how the numbers of the old coins never seemed to diminish, but kept piling up. That made me think about something else which was not quite right. I had noticed that here in the exchange you accept large amounts of inferior jewellery made with base metals and cheap alloys. You say it is for the jewellery business, yet your so-called jeweller is nothing more than a workaday craftsman. He is an engraver, familiar with the cutting and maintenance of striking irons and he knows nothing about jewellery. Yet I found very little of the broken jewellery. It had disappeared. Then I realised that the engraver had the skill and equipment in his workshop to melt down the low-grade metals, and turn out blanks for stamping into coins.'

'You seem to have done a great deal of imagining,' said Brithmaer. 'Your story is a fantasy. Who would want low-grade coins from a dead king?'

'That is the clever part,' I replied. 'It would be reckless to issue forged coins in England. They would be quickly identified. But forge coins which you then issue in the north lands, where the coins of England are regarded as honest, and few people would detect that the coins were counterfeit. Cutting or nicking the coins would not reveal the purity of the metal. And if it did, and the coins are revealed as fakes, then the coins carry the markings of long-dead moneyers, and could never be traced back to their maker. However, there has to be one more link in the chain.'

'And that is?'

'The link that interests me now. You can obtain the base metals from the cheap jewellery, make low-grade coins, forge the marks of other moneyers, but you still need to distribute the coins in the north lands. And for that you need the cooperation of dishonest merchants and ship owners who make regular trading voyages there and put the coins into general circulation. These, I suspect, are the people who visit your private office, even in winter. So my request to you now is that you will arrange with one of these men for me to be smuggled aboard ship, no questions asked. It is in your interests. Once I am out of England, I would no longer be in a position to report you to the authorities.'

'Would it not be more sensible for me to arrange for you to vanish permanently?' Brithmaer said. He was no more emotional than if he was suggesting a money-changing commission.

'Two wax impressions taken from the striking irons used in the forgery will be delivered to the king's regent if I vanish mysteriously or fail to report by springtime.'

Brithmaer regarded me thoughtfully. There was a long pause while he considered his alternatives. 'Very well. I'll make the arrangements you request. There's a merchant ship due to visit King's Lynn in two week's time. The captain trades from Norway and is one of the very few who makes the winter crossing of the English Sea. I will send you to King's Lynn with Thurulf. It's about time he returned to Norwich, which is nearby. If he meets up with any of the king's officials he will say that you are travelling as his assistant. I will also write a note to inform the ship captain that you are to be taken on as supercargo. It would be hypocritical to wish you a safe journey. Indeed, I hope I never see you again. Should you ever return to England, I think you will find no trace of the conspiracy which you say you have uncovered.'

And with that I left the service of Brithmaer the king's moneyer, and master forger. I never saw him again, but I did not forget him. For years to come, every time I was offered an English coin in payment or as change in a market place, I turned it over to see the name of the maker and rejected it if it had been minted in Derby or in Winchester.

SEVEN

'YOU ICELANDERS REALLY get around, don't you?' commented Brithmaer's accomplice as he watched the low coastline of England disappear in our wake. The Norwegian shipmaster had not informed the port reeve of our impending departure before he ordered his crew to weigh anchor on the early tide. I suspected the harbour official was accustomed to seeing our ship slip out of port at strange hours and had been bribed to look the other way.

I barely heard the captain's comment, for I was still brooding on the thought that every mile was taking me further away from Aelfgifu. Unhappiness had haunted me throughout the three-day journey to King's Lynn with Thurulf. We had travelled on ponies, with two servants leading a brace of packhorses and I did not know how much Brithmaer had told his nephew about why I had to travel posing as his assistant or the need for discretion. Our servants blew loudly on trumpets and rang bells whenever we approached settlements or passed through woodland, and I had suggested to Thurulf that it might be wiser to proceed with less ostentation, as I did not wish to attract the attention of the authorities.

Thurulf grinned back at me and said, 'Quite the reverse. If we used the king's highway in a manner that might be considered surreptitious, people would take us to be skulking criminals or robbers. Then they would be entitled to attack, even kill us. Honest travellers are required to announce their presence with as much fanfare as possible.'

Thurulf had brought me to the quay where the Norwegian vessel was berthed. There he handed me over to her captain with a note from Brithmaer to say that I was to be taken abroad, on a one-way trip, and that it would be wise to keep me out of sight until we left England. Then he had turned back to rejoin his family in Norwich. The gloom of parting from a friend was added to my heartache for Aelfgifu.

'Know someone by the name of Grettir Asmundarson, by any chance? He's one of your countrymen.' The captain's voice again broke into my thoughts. The name was vaguely familiar, but for a moment I couldn't place it. 'Got quite a reputation. They call him Grettir the Strong. Killed his first man when he was only sixteen and was condemned to three year's exile. Decided to spend part of it in Norway. He asked me to make some purchases for him while I was in England, but they cost rather more than I had anticipated. I'm hoping you could tell me the best way of dealing with him so he'll pay up without any trouble. He's a dangerous character, quick to anger.' The captain was trying to strike up a conversation so he could find out just who I was.

'I don't think I know him,' I answered, but the word outlaw had jogged my memory. The last time I had seen Grettir Asmundarson had been six years earlier in Iceland. I remembered a young man sitting on a bench in a farmyard, whittling on a piece of wood. He had been much the same age as myself, with middling brown hair, freckles and fair skin. But where I am quite slender and lightly built, he had been broad and thickset, though only of average height, and while I am normally self-possessed and calm by nature, Grettir had given the impression of being hot-headed and highly strung. I remembered how the little shavings had jumped up into the air with each slice of the sharp blade as if he was suppressing some sort of explosive anger. Even at that age Grettir exuded an air of violent, unpredictable menace.

'Troublemaker from the day he was born, and got worse as he grew up,' said the captain. 'Deliberately provoked his father at every turn, though his parent was a decent enough man by all accounts, a steady farmer. The son refused to help out with the farmyard chores. Broke the wings and legs of the geese when he was sent to put them in their house in the evening, killed the goslings, mutilated his father's favourite horse when he was asked to look after it. Cut the skin all along the animal's spine so the poor creature reared up when you laid a hand on its back. A thoroughly bad lot. His father would have thrown him out of the house, but for the fact that his mother was always asking that he should be given a second chance. Typical of a mother's spoiled pet, if you ask me.'

'What made him kill a man?' I asked.

'Quarrelled over a bag of dried food, would you believe. Hardly a reason to attack someone so viciously.'

I remembered the jumping wood shavings, and wondered if Grettir Asmundarson was touched in the head.

'Anyway, you'll soon have your chance to make your own judgement. If this wind holds steady on the quarter, our first landfall will be the place where he's staying with his half-brother Thorstein. Quite a different type, Thorstein, as even-tempered and steady as Grettir is touchy and wild. Got the nickname "the Galleon" because he has a rolling stride to his walk, just like a ship in a beam sea.'

I saw what the captain meant when we dropped anchor in the bay in front of Thorstein's farm in the Tonsberg district of Norway three days later. The two brothers met us on the beach. Thorstein, tall and calm, was waiting for us, feet planted stolidly on the shingle; Grettir, a head shorter, tramped back and forth nervously. He was a squat volcano, ready to erupt. But when our eyes met, I felt that shock of recognition I had experienced half a dozen times in my life: I had seen the same look in the eyes of a native shaman in Vinland, in the expression of the mother of the Earl of Orkney who was a noted sibyl, in the glance of the wife of King Sigtryggr of Dublin, whom many considered a witch, and in the faraway stare of the veteran warrior Thrand, my tutor in Iceland, who had taught me the rune spells. It was the look of someone who possessed the second sight, and I knew that Grettir Asmundarson saw things hidden from more normal people, as I do. Yet I had no premonition that Grettir was to become my closest friend.

We began by treating one another warily, almost with distrust. No one would ever call Grettir easygoing or amiable. He had a natural reticence which people mistook for surliness, and he met every friendly remark with a curt response which often caused offence and gave the impression that he discouraged human contact. I doubt if the two of us exchanged more than half a dozen sentences in as many days as we sailed on along the coast towards the Norwegian capital at Nidaros. Grettir had asked if he might join our ship as he intended to present himself at the Norwegian court and petition for a post in the royal household, his family being distant relatives of the Norwegian king, Olaf.

Our passage was by the usual route, along the sheltered channel between the outer islands and the rocky coast, with its succession of tall headlands and fiord entrances. The sailing was easy and we were in no hurry. By mid-afternoon our skipper would pick a convenient anchorage and we would moor for the night, dropping anchor and laying out a stern line to a convenient rock. Often we would go ashore to cook our meal and set up tents on the beach rather than sleep aboard. It was at one of these anchorages as the sun was setting that I noticed a strange light suddenly blaze out from the summit of the nearest headland. It flared up for a moment as if someone had lit a raging fire in the mouth of a cave, then quickly extinguished it. When I drew the skipper's attention to the phenomenon, I was met with a blank look. He had seen nothing. 'There's no one living up on that headland. Only an old barrow grave,' he said. 'Burial place for the local family who own all the land in the area. The only time they go there is when they have another corpse. It has proved to

be a lucky place for them. The current head of the family is called
Thorfinn, and when he buried his father Kar the Old, the ghost
of the dead man came back and haunted the area so persistently
that the other local farmers decided to leave. After that, Thorfinn
was able to buy up all the best land.' Then he added tactfully,
'You must have seen a trick of the light. Maybe a shiny piece of
rock reflecting the last rays of the setting run.'

The rest of the crew looked at me sideways, as if I had been
hallucinating, so I let the matter drop. But after we had finished
our evening meal and the men had wrapped themselves in their
heavy sea cloaks and settled down for the night, Grettir sidled
across to me and said quietly, 'That blaze was nothing to do with
the sun's rays. I saw it too. You and I know what a fire shining
out from the earth means: gold underground.'

He paused for a moment then murmured, 'I'm going up there
to take a closer look. Care to come with me?'

I glanced round at the others. Most of the crew were half
asleep. For a moment I hesitated. I was not at all sure that I
wanted to go clambering around the dark countryside with a man
who had been convicted of murder. But then my curiosity got the
better of me. 'All right' I whispered. 'Let me get my boots on.'

Moments later Grettir and I had left the camp and were
picking our way between the black shapes of the boulders on the
beach. It was a dry, clear night, warm for that time of year, with
a few clouds moving across the face of the moon but leaving us
enough moonlight to see our way to the base of the headland and
begin our climb. As we moved higher, I could make out the
distinct humpbacked profile of the grave barrow up ahead of us,
curving against the starry sky. I also noticed something else: each
time clouds covered the moon and darkness suddenly cloaked us,
Grettir would hesitate, and I heard his breath come more quickly.
I felt his sudden onset of panic, and I realised that Grettir the
Strong, notorious murderer and outlaw, was desperately afraid of
the dark.

We followed a narrow path used by the funeral parties until

it brought us out onto a small, grassy area around the grave
barrow itself. Grettir looked away to our left out over the black
sheen of the sea, its surface pricked with the reflection of the
stars. 'Fine place for a burial,' he said. 'When I die, I hope I'll
finish up in a spot like this, where the helmsmen of passing ships
can point out my last resting place.' Given Grettir's reputation as
a youthful homicide, I wondered what his epitaph might be.

'Come on, Thorgils,' he said and began to clamber up the
grassy side of the barrow mound. I followed him until we were
both standing on the top of the whale-backed hillock. Grettir
produced a heavy metal bar from under his cloak.

'What are you doing?' I asked, though the answer was
obvious.

'I'm going to break in and take the grave goods,' he answered
jauntily. 'Here, give me a hand.' And he began digging a hole
down through the turf which covered the tomb. Grave-robbing
was a new experience for me, yet when I saw the furious energy
with which Grettir hacked and stabbed at the soil with his iron
bar, I decided it would be wiser to humour him. I was frightened
of what he might do if I tried to restrain him. Taking it in turns
to excavate, we burrowed down to the outer roof of the tomb.
When the point of the iron bar struck the roof timbers of the
vault, Gettir gave a grunt of satisfaction, and with a few powerful
blows punched a hole large enough for him to climb down into
the tomb.

'Stand guard here for me, will you?' he asked. 'In case I get
stuck down there and need help to climb out.' He was unwinding
a rope from around his waist, and I realised that plundering the
tomb had been his intention from the moment he had suggested
that he and I climb to the headland.

A moment later Grettir was lowering himself down into the
black hole and I could hear his voice as he vanished into the
gloom. For a moment I thought he was speaking to me, and tried
to make out what he was saying. But then I realised that he was
talking to himself. He was making a noise to keep up his courage,

to compensate for his terror of the dark. His words, echoing up from the entrance hole into the tomb, made no sense. Then came a sudden loud crash, followed immediately by a loud yell of bravado. There was another crash, and another, and I guessed he was flailing about in the dark, floundering and tripping over one obstacle after another, falling over the grave goods in the dark, driven by his determination to carry out the robbery, yet gripped by a sense of panic.

The racket finally ended and then I heard Grettir's voice call up to me, 'Hang onto the rope! I'm ready to climb up.'

I braced on the rope and soon Grettir's head and shoulders appeared through the hole in the roof of the tomb, and he hauled himself out onto the grass. Then he turned round and began to pull on the rope, until its end appeared attached to a bundle. He had used his tunic as a sack to hold the various items he had collected. He laid them out on the grass to inspect. There were several bronze dishes, some buckles and strap ends from horse harness, a silver cup, and two silver arm rings. The finest item was a short sword which the dead man would have carried if the Valkyries selected him for a warrior's afterlife in Valholl. Grettir slid the weapon out of its sheath and in a glimmer of moonlight I could see the intricate patterns a master swordsmith had worked into the metal of the blade.

'That's a noble weapon,' I commented.

'Yes, I had to fight the haugbui for it,' Grettir replied. 'He was reluctant to give it up.'

'The mound dweller?' I asked.

'He was waiting for me, seated in the dead man's chair,' Grettir said. 'I was groping around in the darkness, gathering the grave goods, when I put my hand on his leg and he jumped to his feet and attacked me. I had to fight him in the dark, as he tried to embrace me in his death grip. But finally I managed to cut off his head and kill him. I laid him out face down, with his head between his buttocks. That way he will never live again.'

I wondered if Grettir was telling the truth. Had there really

been a haugbui? Everyone knows stories about the spirits of the
dead who live in the darkness of tombs, ready to protect the
treasures there. Sometimes they take substantial form as draugr,
the walking dead who emerge and walk the earth, and frighten
men, just as the ghost of Kar the Old had scared away the local
farmers. Cutting off a haugbui's head and placing it on the
buttocks is the only way to lay the creature finally to rest. Or was
Grettir spinning me a tale to account for the noise and clatter of
his robbery, his senseless loud talk and the shouts of bravado?
Was he ashamed to admit that Grettir the Strong was terrified of
the dark, and that all that had happened was that he had blundered
into the skeleton of Kar the Old seated on his funeral chair? For
the sake of Grettir's self-esteem I did not question his tale of the
barrow wight, but I knew for sure that he was more fearful of the
dark than a six-year-old child.

Grettir's self-confidence and bravado were still evident the next
morning when the camp awoke and he made no attempt to hide
his new acquisitions. I was surprised that he even took his loot
with us when we went to visit Thorfinn's farm to buy ship's stores.
When Grettir brazenly laid out the grave goods on the farmhouse
table, Thorfinn recognised them at once.

'Where did you find these?' he asked.

'In the tomb on the hill,' Grettir replied. 'The ghost of Kar
the Old is not that fearsome after all. You'd better keep hold of
them.'

Thorfinn must have known Grettir's reputation because he
avoided any confrontation. 'Well, it's true that buried treasure
is no use to anyone,' he said amiably. 'You have my thanks for
restoring these heirlooms to us. Can I offer you some reward for
your courage?'

Grettir shrugged dismissively. 'No. I have no need for such
things, only for an increase to my honour, though I will keep the
sword as a reminder of this day,' he said. He then rudely turned
on his heel and walked out of the farmhouse, taking the fine short
sword and leaving the rest of the grave goods on the table.

I mulled over that answer as I walked back to the ship, trying to understand what drove Grettir. If he had plundered the barrow in order to gain the admiration of the others for his courage, why did he behave so churlishly afterwards? Why was he always so rude and quarrelsome?

I fell into step with him. Typically, he was walking by himself, well away from the rest of our group.

'That man whose death got you outlawed from Iceland, why did you kill him?' I asked. 'Killing someone over something as trifling as a bag of food doesn't seem to be a way of gaining honour or renown.'

'It was a mistake,' Grettir replied. 'At the age of sixteen I didn't realise my own strength. I was travelling across the moors with some of my father's neighbours when I discovered that the satchel of dried food I had tied to my saddle was missing. I turned back to the place where we had stopped to rest our horses, and found someone else already searching in the grass. He said that he too had left his food bag behind. A moment later he gave a cry and held up a bag, saying that he had found what he was looking for. I went over to check and it seemed to me that the bag was mine. When I tried to take it from him, he snatched out his axe without warning and aimed a blow at me. I grabbed the axe handle, turned the blade around and struck back at him. But he lost his grip and the axe suddenly came free, so I struck him square on the skull. He died instantly.'

'Didn't you try to explain this to the others when they found out what had happened?' I asked.

'It would have done no good – there were no witnesses. Anyhow the man was dead and I was the killer,' said Grettir. 'It goes against my nature to heed the opinions of others. I don't seek either their approval or their disdain. What matters will be the reputation I leave behind me for later generations.'

He spoke so openly and with such conviction that I felt he was acknowledging a bond between us, a comradeship which had started when we pillaged the barrow together. My intuition was to prove correct, but I failed to discern that Grettir was also casting the shadow of his own downfall.

The sailors thought Grettir had been a rash fool to interfere with the spirits of the dead. All day they kept muttering among themselves that his stupidity would bring down misfortune on us. One or two Christians among them made the sign of the cross to keep off the evil eye. Their disquiet was confirmed when we got back to where we had moored the ship. In our absence a gust of wind had shifted the vessel on her anchorage and brought her broadside to the rocky beach. The anchor had lost its grip and she had been driven ashore. By the time we got back, the boat was lying canted over, stoved in, sea water swilling in her bilge. The damage to her planking was so severe that her captain decided we had no choice but to abandon the vessel and march overland to Nidaros, carrying the most valuable of our trade goods. There was nothing to do but wade out in the shallows and salvage what we could. I noticed that the sailors took care to keep as far away from Grettir as possible. They blamed him for the calamity and expected that further disaster would follow. I was the only person to walk beside him.

Our progress was dishearteningly slow. By sea it would have taken two days to reach the Norwegian capital, but the land path twisted and turned as it followed the coast, skirting the bays and fiords. The extra distance added two weeks to our journey. Whenever we came to the mouth of a fiord, we tried to reduce the detour by bargaining with a local farmer to ferry us across, paying him with trade goods or, I supposed, some of Brithmaer's false coin. Even so, we had to wait for the farmer to fetch his small boat, then wait again as he rowed us across the water two or three passengers at a time.

Finally came an evening when we found ourselves on the beach at the entrance to a fiord, facing across open water to a farmhouse we could see on the opposite bank. We were chilled to the bone, tired and miserable. We tried to attract the farmer's attention so he would come across to fetch us, but it was late in the day and there was no reaction from the far shore, though we could see smoke rising from the smoke hole in the farmhouse roof. The spot where we were standing was utterly bleak, a bare beach of pebbles backed by a steep cliff. There were a few sticks of damp driftwood, enough to make a small fire if we could get one started, but our tinder was soaked. We slid our packs off our backs and slumped down on the shingle, resigned to spending a cold and hungry night.

It was at that moment that Grettir suddenly announced he would swim across the fiord to reach the farm on the other side. Everyone looked at him as if he was insane. The distance was too great for any but the strongest swimmer, and it was nearly dark already. But, typically, Grettir paid no attention. The farm would have a stock of dry firewood, he said. He would bring back some of it and a lighted brand so we could warm ourselves and cook a meal. As we watched in disbelief, he began to strip off his clothes until he was wearing nothing but his undershirt and a pair of loose woollen trousers, and a moment later he was wading into the water. I watched his head dwindle in the distance as he struck out for the far shore, and I recalled his words that he lived for honour and fame. I wondered if he might not drown in this new act of bravado.

It was well past midnight and a thick fog had settled over the fiord, when we heard the sound of splashes and Grettir reappeared out of the darkness. He was reeling with exhaustion but, to our astonishment, held in his arms a small wooden tub. 'Enough sticks to make a fire and there are some burning embers in the bottom,' he said, then sat down abruptly, unable to stand any longer. I noticed a fresh bruise on his forehead and that one hand was bleeding from a deep cut. Also he was shaking and I got the impression that it was not just from cold.

As the sailors busied themselves with making a campfire, I led Grettir to one side. 'What's the matter?' I asked, wrapping my warm sea cloak around him. 'What happened?'

He gave me an anguished look. 'It was like that business with the food bag all over again.'

'What do you mean?'

'When I reached the other side of the fiord there was just enough light for me to see my way to what we thought was a farmhouse. It turned out that it wasn't a farm, but one of those shelters built along the coast as refuges for sailors trapped by bad weather. I could hear sounds of singing and laughter inside, so I went up and pushed at the door. The lock was flimsy and broke easily. I stumbled in on about a dozen men, sailors by the look of them. Everyone was roaring drunk, lolling about and scarcely able to stand. There was a blazing fire in the middle of the room. I thought it was useless to ask the drunkards for help. They were too far gone to have understood what I wanted. Instead I went straight up to the fire and took the wooden tub of dry kindling that was next to it. Then I pulled a burning brand out of the hearth. That was when one of the drunks attacked me. He yelled out that I was some sort of troll or water demon appearing out of the night. He lumbered across the room and took a swipe at me. I knocked him down easily enough and the next moment all his companions were bellowing and lurching to their feet and trying to get at me. They picked up logs from the fire and tried to rush me. They must have been heaping straw on the fire, for there were a lot of sparks and embers flying about. I pulled a burning log out of the fire and kept swinging it at them as I backed away to the door. Then I made a dash for it, ran for the water, threw myself in and began swimming to get back here.' He shivered again and pulled the sea cloak tighter around him.

I sat with him through the rest of that black night. Grettir stayed hunched on a rock, brooding and nursing his injured hand. My presence seemed to calm him, and he took comfort from my stories as I passed the hours in telling him about my time as a youngster growing up in Greenland and the days that I had spent in the little Norse settlement in Vinland until the natives had driven us away. At first light the sailors began to stir, grumbling and shivering. One of the sailors was blowing on the embers to rekindle the fire when someone said in appalled tones, 'Look over there!' Everyone turned to stare across the water. The sun had risen above the cliff behind us, and the blanket of fog was breaking up. An early shaft of bright sunlight struck the far side of the fiord at the spot where the wooden building had stood. Only now it was gone. Instead there was a pile of blackened timber, from which rose a thin plume of grey smoke. The place had been incinerated.

There was a dismayed silence. The sailors turned to look at Grettir. He too was gazing at the smouldering wreckage. His face betrayed utter consternation. No one said a word: the sailors were scared of Grettir's strength and temper and Grettir was too shocked to speak. I held my tongue because no one would believe any other explanation: in everyone's mind Grettir the hooligan and brawler had struck again.

Within the hour a small boat was seen. A farmer from further along the fiord had noticed the smoke and was rowing down to investigate. When he ferried us across, we went to inspect the burned-out refuge. The devastation was total. The place had burned to the ground and there was no sign of the drunken sailors who had been inside. We presumed that they had perished in the blaze.

A sombre group huddled around the charred beams. 'It is not for us to judge this matter,' announced our skipper. 'Only the king's court can do that. And that must wait until a proper complaint has been made. But I speak for all the crew when I say that we will no longer accept Grettir among us. He is luck-cursed. Whatever the rights and wrongs of last night's events, he brings catastrophe with him wherever he goes and whatever he does. We renounce his company and will no longer travel with him. He must go his own way.'

Grettir made no attempt to protest his innocence or even to say farewell. He picked up his pack, slung it over his shoulder, turned and began to walk away. It was exactly what I had expected he would do.

A moment later I realised that it was what I would have done too. Grettir and I were very alike. We were two outsiders. To protect ourselves we had developed our own sense of stubborn independence. But whereas I understood that my sense of exclusion came from my rootless childhood and from scarcely knowing my parents, I feared that Grettir would grow only more bewildered and angry at misadventures which were unforeseen and apparently random. He did not realise how often he brought calamity upon himself by his waywardness or by acting without first considering the consequences. Grettir had qualities which I admired – audacity, single-mindedness, bravery. If someone was on hand to rein him in, stand by his side in times of crisis, Grettir would be a remarkable and true companion.

Another of Edgar's proverbs echoed in my memory. 'Have patience with a friend,' Edgar used to say, 'rather than lose him for ever.' Before Grettir had gone more than a few steps I shouldered my satchel and hurried to join him.

GRETTIR'S EVIL REPUTATION travelled before us. By the time the two of us reached Nidaros, the whole town was talking about the holocaust. The men who had perished in the blaze were a boat crew from Iceland, all members of a single family. Their father, Thorir, who was in Nidaros at the time, had already brought a complaint against Grettir for homicide. Nor had our former shipmates helped Grettir's case. They had arrived in Nidaros before us, and had spread a damning account of how he had returned battered and bruised from his swim across the fiord. Of course they barely mentioned that Grettir had risked his life to bring them fire and relieve their distress and, wittingly or not, they smeared his name further by adding lurid details of his grave robbery.

The Norwegian king, Olaf, summoned Grettir to the palace to stand judgement, and I went with him, intending to act as a favourable witness. The hearing was held in the great hall of the royal residence and King Olaf himself conducted the enquiry with proper formality. He listened to the dead men's father state his case, then asked our former companions to recount their version of that fateful evening. Finally he turned to Grettir to ask him what he had to say. Stubbornly Grettir remained silent, glowering at the king, and I felt it was left to me to speak up. So I repeated what Grettir had told me about the drunkards using burning firebrands as weapons. When I had finished, the king asked Grettir, 'Do you have anything to add?'

'The sots in the house were all alive when I left them,' was his only comment.

King Olaf was fair-minded as well as patient. 'All the evidence I have heard today is conjectural, as none of the participants survived except Grettir,' he said, 'and Grettir's statement must be treated with caution as he is the defendant in this case. So it will be difficult to arrive at the truth. My own opinion is that Grettir is probably innocent of the charge of deliberate murder because he had no motive to set fire to the building.'

I was about to congratulate Grettir on the royal verdict, when King Olaf continued. 'I have therefore decided that the best way to settle the matter is that Grettir Asmundarson submits himself to ordeal in my new church and in the presence of the faithful. The ordeal to be that of hot iron.'

I had completely forgotten that King Olaf never missed a chance to demonstrate the advantages of Christianity. A fervent believer in the White Christ, he wanted all his subjects to adopt the faith and follow Christian customs. Trial by ordeal was one of them. Of course, trials to test for guilt or innocence were also a part of the Old Ways, usually by armed combat, man to man, arranged between plaintiff and accused. But the Christians had come up with much more ingenious tests. They dropped the accused into narrow wells to see if the guilty sank or the innocent swam. They obliged others to pluck stones out of boiling water to observe whether the scald wounds then festered; or – as was proposed for Grettir – they made them hold a red-hot lump of iron and watched to see how far they could walk before their hands blistered mortally. And, for some curious reason, they thought it more authentic and righteous if the ordeals by steam and fire were conducted in a church.

A packed congregation assembled to witness Grettir's test. Their expectant faces revealed how notorious my friend had already become. Apparently the stories of his exploits were common knowledge: how he had tackled a rogue bear and killed the animal single-handed, and – in an uncomfortable echo of his present situation – how he had locked a marauding gang of dangerous berserks into a wooden shed and burned the place down, killing them all. Now the audience turned up to see whether Grettir could endure the pain of holding a lump of scorching iron in the palms of his hands while he walked ten paces. I slipped quietly into the church ahead of Grettir, though I had no idea how I could help him. The best I could do, while the congregation chanted a prayer to their God, was to repeat over and over again a galdr verse I had learned long ago, the seventh of Odinn's spells, which will quench a blazing fire.

Odinn heard my appeal, for when Grettir entered the church and began to walk up the aisle to where the priest and his assistant stood waiting by the brazier, a young man darted out from the congregation, and began to caper and dance beside Grettir. He was a fanatical Christian devotee. He was grimacing and shouting, waving his arms and cursing. Grettir was a vile heathen, the youth shouted, he should never be allowed inside a church or permitted to tread on sacred ground. Rolling his eyes and dribbling, he began to taunt Grettir, hurling a torrent of abuse until finally Grettir swung his arm and fetched his tormentor such a crack on the side of the head that the youth went spinning away, pitching face down in the aisle. The congregation gasped. They waited for the youth to get back to his feet, but he lay there motionless. Grettir said not a word, but stood patiently. Someone knelt down beside the lad and turned him over.

'He's dead' he said, looking up. 'His neck's broken.'

There was an awful silence, then the priest raised his voice.

'Violent death in God's House! Murder in the face of our Lord!' he screamed.

Grettir began to retreat slowly down the aisle towards the door. The people's fear of him was so great that no one dared to move. Before Grettir reached the door King Olaf, who had been in the front of the church to witness the ordeal, intervened. He must have realised that his show of Christian justice was turning sour. 'Grettir!' he called, 'no man is unlucky or as ill-fated as you. Your quick temper has destroyed your chance to prove your innocence or guilt. I hereby pronounce that you must leave this kingdom and return to your own country. In view of the provocation you have suffered, you will be permitted a grace period of six months. But you are never to return to Norway.'

FOR DAYS GRETTIR and I searched for a ship that would take us back to Tonsberg, where his brother Thorstein lived. But it was hard to find a captain who would accept us aboard. Seamen are more superstitious than most and Grettir was said to be the most luckless man alive. If he did not cause mischief himself, his misfortune would drag down those around him. Nor were his enemies satisfied with King Olaf's verdict. Grettir and I were in a shoreside tavern, seated in a back room and whiling away one of those dark and dreary Norwegian winter afternoons when Thorir's family decided to take their revenge. Five of them burst into the room, armed with spears and axes. Four of the attackers made straight for Grettir, while the fifth turned his attention on me. I was taken completely unawares – before I could get to my feet my attacker had struck me hard on the side of the head with the butt of his spear. I crashed backward from my seat, my head so filled with pain that I could hardly see. When my vision cleared, I saw that Grettir had picked up a bench and was using it as his weapon. His strength was prodigious. He handled the heavy bench as if it was a fighting staff, first sweeping the legs from under two of his assailants, and then bringing the heavy furniture down on the shoulder of a third with a massive thump. The man howled and clutched at his now useless arm. The fourth man, seeing his opening, rushed at Grettir from one side with an axe. Grettir dodged and, as the man overreached, my friend effortlessly plucked the weapon from his grasp. The balance of the contest changed in an instant. Seeing that Grettir was now armed and dangerous, the attackers jostled one another as they headed for the door. The man who had knocked me down raised his spear to skewer me. Compared with Grettir, I was a helpless target. In a flash Grettir turned and used his free hand to wrench the spear from my attacker, and he too ran out of the door and slammed it hard behind him.

'Are you all right?' Grettir asked as I struggled groggily to my feet. My head felt as if it was split.

'Yes, I'll be fine. Just give me a moment.'

I could hear our opponents just outside the door, shouting insults and calling out that they had not finished with us. Grettir cocked his head on one side to listen. I saw him heft the captured spear in one hand to find its balance point and draw back his arm in the throwing position. Then he hurled the spear straight at the door. His strength was so great that the weapon splintered right through the wood panel. I heard a yelp of pain. Moments later the attackers had gone.

'I'm sorry. I didn't mean for our friendship to bring you into danger,' Grettir said to me quietly. 'That was not your quarrel.'

'What is friendship for if not to hold things in common, including another's battles?' I said. Despite my aching head, I felt a new self-confidence welling up within me. I knew that since Edgar's death and my parting from Aelfgifu, I had been adrift, and that my day-to-day existence had been aimless. But now my life had taken a new shape: Grettir had acknowledged me as his friend.

EIGHT

'IT'S THE STRENGTH in his arms that does it,' said Thorstein Galleon to me two weeks later. Grettir and I had finally found a ship, an Icelandic vessel and at a bandit's price, to take us to Tonsberg, where the three of us – Thorstein, Grettir and I – were now seated in the kitchen at Thorstein's farm. 'Look here, see my arm.' And Thorstein rolled back his sleeve. 'People would say that I'm well muscled. But take a look at Grettir's arms. They're more like oxen's hocks. And he's got the strength in his chest and shoulders to back them up. We used to have contests when we were children, seeing who could pick up the heaviest stones or throw them the furthest. Grettir always won and by the time he was in his early teens people started taking bets on whether he could lift a particularly heavy boulder they selected. Yet to look at him you would never know how strong he is. Not until he takes off his tunic, that is. That is why people misjudge him so often. They get into a fight with him or an argument, and finish up the worse off. If Grettir was a big man, massive and fearsome to look at, he would not have half the trouble he seems to attract. People would steer clear.'

Grettir, as usual, was adding little to the conversation. He sat there, listening to his half-brother ramble on. I could see that there was considerable affection between them, though for the most part it was unspoken. We were lazing away the day, waiting for the captain who had brought us to decide whether he would risk sailing onward to Iceland. My friend had announced that he had decided to go home, even if it meant breaking the terms of his three-year exile. He had confided to me that although his sentence of lesser outlawry still had six months to run, as far as he was concerned the matter was over and done with. He felt he had spent enough time abroad to cancel the blood debt to the Icelandic family of the man he had killed. Now that I knew him better, I realised that his unfinished sentence had become an attraction rather than a deterrent. He was thinking he would gain fame – or notoriety – as the man brave enough to adjust his time of exile out of a sense of self-justice.

When Grettir told Thorstein of his decision to return home, his half-brother pondered the matter for several moments, then said in his deep rumbling voice, 'I doubt that your father will be too pleased to see you, or even speak to you. But remember me to our mother and tell her that I am well and prospering here in Norway. Whatever happens, I want you to know that you can always count on my support. And if worst comes to worst, and you get yourself unjustly killed, I swear that I will hunt down the killer and avenge you. This I pledge.'

Though Grettir had promised our avaricious captain that he would double his usual fee for the passage to Iceland, the skipper had already delayed his departure three times, not because he was fearful of Grettir's bad luck, but because he was uneasy about running into a late winter gale. He was mercenary but he was also a good seaman. Even now he was aboard his ship in the little creek close below Thorstein's farm, gazing up anxiously at the sky, watching which way the clouds were going, and offering up prayers to Njord, God of the winds and waves. He knew that an open-sea crossing to Iceland was not something to undertake lightly at that time of year.

Sailors give nicknames to their ships. I have sailed on 'Plunger', which pitched badly in the waves; 'Griper' was almost impossible to sail close to the wind, and 'The Sieve' obviously needed constant bailing. The ship we now expected to carry us to Iceland was known to her crew as 'The Clog'. The man who had built her many years earlier had intended a vessel nearly twice the size and he had constructed the fore part of the ship before realising that he was running out of funds. Iceland has no ship-building timber, and the wood for her vessels has to be imported from Norway. The price of timber soared that year, and 'The Clog's' builder was already deep in debt. So he had truncated his ship, making her stern with whatever material he had left over. The result was that the bow of 'The Clog' was a fine, sea-kindly prow. But the stern was a sorry affair, stunted, clumsy and awkward. And it turned out to be nearly the death of us.

Her captain knew that he needed six days of settled weather to make his passage in 'The Clog', as she was such a slow and heavy sailer. 'We could be lucky and have a week of favourable east winds at this season,' he said, 'but then again it can turn nasty in a few hours and we'd be in real trouble.'

Eventually his weather sense, or perhaps his enthusiasm for our passage money, persuaded him that the right moment had come and we set sail. At first everything went well. The east wind held and we plodded west, passing through an area where we saw many whales and knew we had cleared the rocks and cliffs of Farroes. Though I was a paying passenger, I took my turn to prepare meals on the flat hearth stone at the base of the mast, and I helped to handle sails, bail out the bilges, and generally showed willing. Grettir, by contrast, sank into one of his surly moods. He lay about the deck, wrapped in his cloak and picking the most sheltered spots, where he was in the way of the working crew. Even when it was obvious that he was a hindrance, he refused to shift, and the vessel's regular eight-man crew were too frightened of his brawler's reputation to kick him out of the way. Instead they glared at him, made loud remarks about lazy louts and generally worked themselves into a state of rightful indignation about his idleness. Grettir only sneered back at them and called

them lubberly clowns, no better than seagoing serfs. Being
Grettir's friend and companion I was thoroughly embarrassed by
his churlish behaviour, though I knew better than to interfere.
Anything I said when he was in that sullen mood was likely to
make him even more obstinate. So I put up with the scornful
remarks of my shipmates when they enquired how I managed to
maintain a friendship with such a boor. I held my tongue and
remembered how, without Grettir's intervention, I would probably
have ended my life in a Nidaros tavern brawl.

'The Clog' trudged along. Despite her age, she was doing all
that was asked of her thanks to the hard-working crew and the
good weather. Unfortunately, though, the weather proved a cruel
fraud. The same east wind which was pushing us along our route
so satisfactorily, gradually grew in strength. At first no one
complained. The increase in the wind was by small degrees and
easily handled. The crew reduced sail and looked pleased. 'The
Clog' was now moving through the water as fast as any of them
could remember and in the right direction. In the evening the
wind strength rose a little more. The sailors doubled the ropes
which supported the single mast, lowered the mainyard a fraction,
and checked that there was nothing loose on deck that might roll
free and do damage. The younger mariners began to look slightly
apprehensive. During the third night at sea we began to hear the
telltale sound of the wind moaning in the rigging, a sign that 'The
Clog' was coming under increasing stress. When dawn broke, the
sea all around us was heaving in rank upon rank of great waves,
their tops streaked with foam. Now the older members of the
crew began to be concerned. They checked the bilges to see how
much water was seeping through the hull's seams. The ship was
labouring, and if you listened closely you could hear the deep
groans of the heavier timbers in contrast to the shrieking clamour
of the wind. By noon the captain had ordered the crew to take
down the mainsail entirely and rig a makeshift storm sail on a
short spar just above deck level. This storm sail was no bigger
than a man's cloak, but by then the wind had risen to such

strength that the tiny sail was enough to allow the helmsman to steer the ship. Only the captain himself and his most experienced crewman were at the rudder because each breaking wave was threatening to yaw the ship and send her out of control. In those vile conditions there was no question of trying to steer our intended course, nor of heaving to and waiting for the gale to blow itself out. 'The Clog' was too clumsy to ride the waves ahull. They would roll her. Our best tactic was to steer directly downwind, allowing the great waves to roll harmlessly under her.

This was when the original failure of her construction began to tell. A deep-sea merchant ship, properly built to our favoured Norse design, would have had a neat stern, so she rose effortlessly to the following waves, as a sea-kindly gull sits on the water. But 'The Clog's broad, ugly stern was too ungainly. She did not lift with the waves, but instead squatted down awkwardly and presented a bluff barrier to the force of the sea. And the sea responded in anger. Wave after wave broke violently against that clumsy stern. We felt each impact shake the length of the little vessel. And the crest of every wave came rearing up and toppled onto the deck, washing forward and then cascading into the open hold. Even the least experienced seafarer would have seen the danger: if our vessel took on too much water, she would either founder from the added weight or the swirl of the water in the hold would make her dangerously unstable. Then she would simply roll over and die, taking all of us with her.

Without being told, our crew – myself included – bailed frantically, trying to return the sea water to where it belonged. It was back-breaking, endless labour. We were using wooden buckets, and they had to be hoisted up from the bilge by one man to a helper on deck, who then crossed to the lee rail, emptied the bucket over the side, lurched his way back across the heaving and slippery deck, and lowered back the bucket down to the man working in the bilge. It became a never-ending, desperate cycle as more and more water came gushing in over 'The Clog's' ill-begotten stern. Our skipper did what he could to help. He steered the ship to each wave, trying to avoid the direct impact on the stern, and he ordered the now-useless mainsail to be rigged as a breakwater to divert the crests that leaped aboard. But the respite was only temporary. After a day of unremitting bailing, we could feel 'The Clog' beginning to lose the battle. Hour by hour she became more sluggish, and the man who stood in the bilge to bail was now up to his thighs in water. The previous day he had been able to see his knees. Our ship was slowly settling into her grave.

All the time, as we struggled to save the ship, Grettir lay on deck like a dead man, his face turned to the bulwark, soaked to the skin and ignoring us. It was difficult to credit his behaviour. At first I thought he was one of those unfortunates who are so seasick that all feeling leaves them and they become like the living dead, unable to stir whatever the emergency. But not Grettir. From time to time I saw him turn over to ease his bones on the hard deck. I found his attitude inexplicable and wondered if he was so fatalistic that he had decided to meet calmly whatever death the Norns had decreed him.

But I had mistaken my friend. On the fourth morning of our voyage, after we had passed an awful night, bailing constantly until we were so exhausted that we could scarcely stand, Grettir suddenly sat up and stretched his arms. He glanced over to where we were standing, our eyes red-rimmed with tiredness, muscles aching. There was no mistaking our expressions of dislike as we saw him finally take an interest in our plight. He did not say a word, but got up and walked over to the edge of the open hatch leading to the hold and jumped down. Silently Grettir held out his hand to the man who was standing there, crotch deep in the water. He took the bailing bucket from him, waved him away, then scooped up a bucket full of water and passed it up to the sailor who had been emptying the bucket over the rail. Grettir made the lift look effortless even though he had to reach above his head. When the bucket was empty, it was handed back and Grettir repeated his action so smoothly and quickly that the full

bucket was back on deck level before the startled sailor was ready
to receive it. He staggered across the pitching deck and emptied
its contents over the side, while my friend stood in the bilge and
waited his return. Now Grettir caught my eye and gestured towards
a second bucket lashed with its lanyard to the mast step. I saw
immediately what he meant, so fetched the bucket and passed it
down to him. He filled that bucket, too, and handed it back up to
me so I could dump the water over the rail. Back and forth we
went, the sailor and I, emptying our buckets as fast as the two of
us could cross the deck while Grettir stayed below and went on
scooping and filling our loads. When I was too tired to continue,
I handed my bucket to a second sailor, as did my workmate. Grettir
did not break his rhythm. Nor did he falter when the second pair
of helpers had to rest, but kept on filling bucket after bucket with
water from the bilge.

He kept up his amazing feat for eight hours, with only a short
break after every five hundredth bucket. None of us would have
believed such stamina was possible. He was tireless and kept pace
with the crew as they worked in relays. The men who had glared
and complained about his indolence, now looked at him in awe.
Inspired, they found an endurance of their own and worked, turn
and turn about, to win the race against the water level in the
bilge. Without Grettir, they and their ship would be lost and they
knew it. For my part, I knew that Grettir was saving my life for
a second time and that I owed him my unswerving friendship.

'The Clog' nearly overshot Iceland altogether as she ran
before that tyrannical east wind. When the gale finally eased, our
shaken skipper managed to edge his ship into the lee of the land
off the Hvit River and we found that, by 'The Clog's' lumbering
standards, we had made a record passage. Our sailors went ashore
boasting about their prowess, though their greatest applause was
reserved for Grettir. He was the hero of the hour. The skipper
went so far as to hand him back half our passage money and
announced that Grettir was welcome to stay on board as long as

he wished. After such a shockingly desperate voyage the skipper vowed that he would keep 'The Clog' safely at anchor until the proper sailing season.

'Why don't you take up his offer, at least for a day or two?' I suggested to Grettir. 'You stay on board. It will give me a chance to go ashore and find out what sort of a reception you may get when people learn that you have returned before completing your three-year exile.'

'Thorgils, you know very well that I don't care what people will do and say. I'm planning to go to see my mother, Gerdis, to bring her news about Thorstein, and find out how the rest of my family is getting on. I left two brothers here in Iceland when I went away, and I fear that I abandoned them just when they needed me most. We were in the middle of a feud with neighbours and there was talk of bloodshed and reprisals. I want to know how that quarrel turned out. If it is unresolved, then perhaps there's something I can do. So I'll find a good, swift horse to carry me across country to our family home.'

'Look, Grettir,' I told him. 'I spent some time in this district when I was a lad and I know the leading chieftain – Snorri Godi. Let me get his opinion about whether there is any way you can get the final part of your sentence waived.'

'It will be a wonder if Snorri Godi is still alive. He must be an old man now,' said Grettir. 'I know his reputation as a shrewd lawgiver. So he's not likely to approve of someone flouting the rules of outlawry.'

'Snorri always treated me fairly,' I answered. 'Maybe he'll agree to act as an intermediary if you offer to pay compensation to the family of the man killed in the quarrel over the bag of food. It wouldn't cost very much because you've already served most of the sentence.'

But when I put that suggestion to Snorri Godi two days later, his response came as a body blow. He said quietly, 'So you haven't heard the Althing's decision?'

'What do you mean?' I asked.

I had travelled a day's journey to Snorri's substantial farm-house, and the farm looked even more prosperous than I remembered it. Snorri himself now had a head of snow-white hair, but his eyes were as I remembered them – grey and watchful.

'At the last meeting of the Althing, Thorir of Gard, the father of those lads who died in the fire in Norway, brought forward a new complaint against Grettir. He accused him of murdering his sons in a deliberate act. He was very persuasive and provided complete details of the outrage. He contended that the deed was so foul that Grettir should be declared skogarmadur.'

The word skogarmadur dismayed me. In Iceland it is never used in jest. It means 'a forest man', and describes someone found guilty of a crime so repugnant that the offender is condemned to live outside civilised society for ever. It means full outlawry and banishment for life. If the annual lawgiving assembly of the Icelanders, the Althing, passes such a sentence, there can be neither an appeal nor a pardon.

'No one at the Althing wanted to convict Grettir of such a heinous crime without hearing his side of the affair,' Snorri went on, 'but there was no one to speak up for him, and Thorir was so vehement that in the end Grettir was made a full outlaw. Now there is nothing that can be done to reverse the verdict. You'd better go back and warn your friend Grettir that every man's hand is against him. He will be hunted down like vermin. Anyone who meets him is entitled to kill him, casually or deliberately. In addition, Thorir is offering a handsome reward to anyone who executes him.'

'But what about Grettir's family?' I asked 'Weren't they represented at the Althing? Why didn't they speak up for him?'

'Grettir's father died while his son was abroad. And the most competent of his brothers, Atli, whom everyone liked and would have listened to, was killed in that deadly feud which the Asmundarsons are pursuing with the faction led by Thorbjorn Oxenmight. And, Thorgils, you'd better be careful too. Don't let yourself get drawn into that feud because of your relationship with Grettir.

Remember that the law states that anyone who helps or harbours
a forest man is an accessory to his crime and therefore forfeits his
own goods. My advice to you is to have as little as possible to do
with Grettir in the future. Once you have delivered your message
to him, put as much space as possible between yourself and your
murderous friend. Go and build yourself a normal life. Why don't
you settle down, get married, raise a family, find your place in
a community?'

I was aghast. Grettir had come home believing that he was
entitled to live a normal life. Instead he stood condemned in his
absence of a crime which I was convinced he did not commit.
The effect of such injustice on his already brooding character
would be calamitous. He would find himself even further isolated
from normal society.

I knew that his chances of survival were negligible. No forest
man had ever lived to old age unless he fled abroad and never
returned to Iceland. In effect I had lost my friend. It was as if he
was already dead.

To my surprise Grettir was not in the least perturbed to hear
that he been declared a skogarmadur. 'Cheer up, Thorgils,' he
said. 'Don't look so glum. If they are going to hunt down and kill
their outlaw, they'll have to catch me first. I have no intention of
running away and I've friends and allies in Iceland who'll ignore
the Althing's decision and give me food and a roof over my head
when I need it. I'll just have to be careful when I call on my
mother. I'll have to do that in secret. Then I'll see how matters
turn out once people hear that Grettir the Strong is back.'

'I'll go with you,' I said.

'No you won't, my friend,' he replied. 'Snorri was wise in
that regard. You really ought to try settling down. You are at
the right age for marriage, and you should look around for a
wife and perhaps start a family. If I need your help, then I'll call
on you for it. In the meantime I can look after myself very
adequately.'

The two of us were standing on the brow of a low hill

overlooking the anchorage where 'The Clog' was riding at anchor. In contrast to the foul weather of our voyage from Norway, it was a warm and sunny day, almost spring-like. I had suggested to Grettir that we walk up there as I had important news to tell him in private. Grettir reached down to pluck a wisp of grass, and tossed it nonchalantly into the air as if he didn't have a care in the world. The breeze caught the blades of grass and carried them away. 'I like this country,' he said. 'It's my home, and no man will chase me away from it. I believe I can live off this land and it will take care of me.'

'You'll need more than just the ability to live off the land,' I said.

'There's a saying that goes "Bare is the back of the brotherless,"' Grettir answered. He was carrying the sword we had plundered from the barrow grave, and now he pulled it from its scabbard and used the point to carve out a long strip of turf. He did not cut the ends but left them attached to the ground. Then he picked up his spear – since the attack at the tavern he never went anywhere unless fully armed – and used it to prop up the strip of turf so that it formed an arch. 'Here, hold out your right hand,' he said to me. When I did so, he delicately drew the blade of his sword across the palm of my hand. It felt like the touch of a feather, yet the blood began to flow. He shifted the sword to his left hand, to make a similar cut on his right palm. He held out his hand, and our palms met and the blood mingled. Then we ducked under the arch of turf, straightening up as we emerged on the other side. 'Now we are fostbraedralag,' said Grettir. 'We are sworn brothers. It is a loyalty that cannot be sundered as long as either of us is alive.'

Looking back on that ceremony under the arch of turf, I realise that it was another of the defining moments of my adult life. I, who had never really known my mother and whose father had been aloof and distant, had found true kindred at last. Had my life been otherwise, perhaps I would have natural brothers and sisters or, in the manner of many Norse families, I would have been fostered out and gained an alternative family of foster-brothers and -sisters with whom I could have been close and intimate. But that never happened. Instead I had gained a sworn brother by a decision made between two adults and that made our bond even stronger.

'Well, sworn brother,' said Grettir with a mischievous glint in his eye, 'I've got my first request of you.'

'What's that?' I asked.

'I want you to help me steal a horse.'

So before the next daybreak Grettir and I dressed in dark clothes and crept to a meadow where he had seen a handsome black mare. Under cover of darkness, we managed to coax the mare away from the herd, far enough for Grettir to put a bridle on her, jump on her back and begin his journey home. Thus a friendship which began with grave robbery celebrated its formal recognition with a horse theft.

NINE

WRITING THIS MEMOIR of my life I now come to one of its less happy episodes, namely my first marriage. Brief and cheerless, that marriage now seems so distant that I have to strain to recall the details. Yet it was to have important consequences and that is why I must include it in my tale.

Her name was Gunnhildr. She was four years older than myself, taller by half a head and tending to overweight, with milky pale skin, blonde hair of remarkable fineness and pale blue eyes which bulged when she was angry. Her father was a moderately well-to-do farmer up in the north-west district, and while he was far from pleased with the match, he knew it was the best that could be managed. His daughter, the third of five, had recently been divorced for reasons which I never fully discovered. Perhaps I should have taken this as a warning and been more cautious, for – as I was to find out – it is far easier for a woman to divorce a man in Norse society than the other way around and divorce can be a costly affair – for the man.

Before a marriage is agreed in Iceland, two financial settlements are made. One comes from the bride's family and is a contribution to the couple to help them get started. That investment remains the bride's property. If the marriage fails, she keeps it. By contrast the price put into the marriage by her husband's side, the mundur, is held as common property, and in the event of divorce may be claimed by the bride if she can show that her husband was in any way at fault. Understandably, the haggling between the families of groom and bride over the size of the mundur can take up a considerable time before a marriage, but should the marriage collapse, the rancour over which partner was at fault takes even longer.

Why did I get married? I suppose it was because Grettir had recommended it and Snorri Godi, who was regarded as a very astute man, had done the same. That, at least, would have been my superficial reason, but deeper down I suppose that Grettir's departure to seek his own family had left me feeling insecure. Also Snorri, after making the initial suggestion, then proceeded actively to find me a wife, which left me little option. Like many men who are approaching the loss of their prestige and power, he could not resist meddling in the affairs of others, however insignificant they might be.

And I was certainly insignificant. Born illegitimate and sent away by my mother at the age of two to a father who had remarried and largely ignored me, I could offer neither support nor prospects to a wife. Nor would it have been wise to tell her that I was sworn brother to the most notorious outlaw in the land. So, instead, I kept quiet and let Snorri do the negotiating for me. I suppose his reputation as the foremost chieftain of the district was in my favour, or perhaps he had some hidden understanding with Gunnhildr's father, Audun. Whatever the background, Snorri invited me to stay at his home while he arranged the details, and all went smoothly until the matter of mundur came up. Old Audun, a grasping and pompous man if there ever was one, asked what bride price I was prepared to pay for what he called his 'exquisite daughter'. If Odinn had been kinder to me at that moment, I would have said that I was penniless and the negotiations would have collapsed. As it was, I foolishly offered to contribute a single jewel, but one so rare that nothing like it had been seen in Iceland. Audun was sceptical at first, then curious, and when I melted down the clumsy lead bird of my amulet and produced the fire ruby he looked amazed.

The greater impact was made on his daughter. The moment Gunnhildr saw that gem she had to have it. She was determined to flaunt it before her sisters. It was her way of paying them back for years of spiteful remarks about her frumpiness. And once Gunnhildr decided that she wanted something nothing would stop her, as her father well knew. So the last of old Audun's objections to our marriage disappeared and he agreed to the match. My future in-laws agreed to provide Gunnhildr and myself with a small outlying farmstead as her dowry, while the gem was my mundur. At the last moment, either because the thought of parting with my talisman and its association with my life in England was so painful, or because of a premonition, I made Gunnhildr and Audun agree that if the marriage failed I would be allowed to redeem the jewel on payment of a sum which was the equivalent value of the farmstead. The price of the gem was set at thirty marks of silver, a sum that was to cloud my next few years.

Our wedding was such a subdued affair that it was barely noticed in the neighbourhood. Even Snorri was absent, having taken to his bed with an attack of fever and Gunnhildr dressed up only in order to display the fire ruby. I was taken aback to discover that the ceremony was to be conducted by an itinerant priest. He was one of those Christian holy men who had begun to appear in increasing numbers in the countryside, travelling from farm to farm to persuade the women to accept their faith and baptise their children, and railing all the while against what they described as the barbaric and heathen Old Ways. During the wedding ceremony I realised that my bride was a rabid Christian. She stood beside me, sweating slightly in her wedding finery, and calling out the responses in her unmelodious voice so devoutly and harshly that I knew she believed the priest's every incantation. Now and again, I noticed, she fondled the fire ruby possessively as it dangled between her ample breasts.

The wedding feast was as skimpy as my father-in-law could

get away with, and then my wife and I were conducted to our farmstead by a small group of her relatives, then left alone. Later that evening Gunnhildr made it clear that physical relations between us were out of the question. She had given herself to the White Christ, she informed me loftily, and close contact with a non-believer like myself was repugnant to her. It was a reaction which I did not care to challenge. On the walk to our new home I had been pondering on the fact that my marriage was probably the worst mistake I had yet made in my life.

Matters did not improve. I quickly learned that my in-laws' wedding gift of the farmstead was self-serving in the extreme. The farm lay just too distant from their own home for them to work it themselves. My father-in-law had been too parsimonious to hire a steward to live there and run it, and too jealous of his neighbours to rent them the lands and pasture. By installing a compliant son-in-law he thought he had found his ideal solution. I was expected to bring the farm into good order, then hand on to him a significant portion of the hay, meat or cheese it produced. In short, I was his lackey.

Nor did Gunnhildr intend to spend much time there with me. Once she had acquired a husband or, rather, once she had got her hands on the fire ruby, she reverted to her previous way of life. To her credit she was a competent housekeeper, and she was quick to clean up the farmhouse, which had been left unoccupied for several years and make the place habitable in a basic way. But then she began to spend more and more time back at her parent's house, staying the nights there on the excuse that it was too far to return to her marital home. Or she went off on visits to her gang of women friends. They were an intimidating group. All were recent and ardent converts to Christianity, so they spent a good deal of their time congratulating one another on the superior merits of their new faith and complaining of the coarseness of the one they now spurned.

I must admit that Gunnhildr would have found me a thoroughly unsatisfactory helpmeet had she stayed at home. I was completely unsuited to farm work. I found it depressing to get up every morning and pick up the same tools, walk the same paths, round up the same cattle, cut hay from the same patch, repair the same rickety outhouse and return to the same lumpy mattress, which, thankfully, I had to myself. To put it bluntly, I preferred Gunnhildr in her absence because I found her company to be shallow, tedious and ignorant. When I compared her to Aelfgifu I almost wept with frustration. Gunnhildr had an uncanny ability to interrupt my thoughts with observations of breathtaking banality, and her sole interest in her fellow humans appeared to be based on their financial worth, an attitude she doubtless learned from her money-grubbing father. To spite him, I did as little work on the farm as possible.

Naturally the other farmers in the area, who were hard-working men, thought me a good-for-nothing and shunned my company. So rather than stay and mind the cattle and cut hay for the winter, I went on excursions to visit my mentor Thrand, who had instructed me in the Old Ways when I was in my teens. Thrand lived only half a day's travel away and, compared with white-haired Snorri, I found him remarkably little changed. He was still the gaunt, soldierly figure whom I remembered, plainly dressed and living simply in his small cabin with its array of foreign trophies hung on the wall. He greeted me with genuine affection, telling me that he had heard that I was back in the district. He had not attended my wedding, he added, because he found it difficult to support the prating of so many Christians.

We slipped back easily into the old routine of tutor and pupil. When I told Thrand that I had become a devotee of Odinn in his role as traveller and enquirer, he suggested I memorise the Havamal, the song of Odinn, 'Let the Havamal be your guide for the future,' he suggested. 'In cleaving to Odinn's words you will find wisdom and solace. Your friend Grettir, for example: he wants to be remembered for what he was, for his good repute, and Odinn has something to say on that very subject,' and here Thrand quoted:

'Cattle die, kinsmen die,
you yourself die,
But words of glory never die
for the man who achieves good name.

'Cattle die, kinsmen die,
you yourself die.
I know one thing that never dies,
the fame of each man dead.'

On another day, when I made some wry comment about
Gunnhildr and her disappointing behaviour, Thrand promptly
recited another of Odinn's verses:

'The love of women whose hearts are false
is like driving an unshod steed over slippery ice,
a two-year-old, frolicsome, badly broken,
or like being in a rudderless boat in a storm.'

This led me to ask, 'Have you ever been married yourself?'
Thrand shook his head. 'No. The idea of marriage never
appealed to me, and at an age when I might have married, it was
not allowed.'
'What do you mean "not allowed"?'
'The felag, the fellowship, forbade it and I took my vows
seriously.'
'What fellowship was that?' I asked, hoping to learn something
of Thrand's enigmatic past, which the old soldier had never talked
about.
But Thrand said only, 'It was the greatest of all the felags, at
that time at least. It was at the height of its glory. Now, though,
it is much reduced. Few would believe how much it was once
admired throughout the northern lands.'
On occasions like this I had the feeling that Thrand sensed
that the beliefs he held, and had taught me, were in final retreat,
that an era was drawing to a close.

'Do you think that Ragnarok, the great day of reckoning, is soon?' I asked him.

'We haven't yet heard Heimdall the watchman of the Gods blow the Gjallahorn to announce the approach of the massed forces of havoc,' he answered, 'but I fear that even with his wariness Heimdall may overlook the closer danger. His hearing may be so acute that he can hear the grass growing, and his sight so keen that he can see a hundred leagues in every direction by day or night, but he does not realise that true destruction often creeps in disguise. The agents of the White Christ could prove to be the harbingers of a blight just as damaging as all the giants and trolls and forces of destruction that have been foretold for so long.'

'Can nothing be done about it?' I asked.

'It is not possible to bend fate, nor can one stand against nature,' he replied. 'At first I thought that the Christians and the Old Believers had enough in common to be able to coexist. We all believe that mankind is descended from just one man and one woman. For the Christians it is Adam and Eve, for us it is Ask and Embla, whom Odinn brought to life. So we agree on our origins, but when it comes to the afterlife we are too far apart. The Christians call us pagans and dirty heathens because we eat horse-flesh and make animal sacrifice. But, for me, a greater filthiness is to dig a pit for the corpse of a warrior and put him in the ground to be eaten by worms and turned to slime. How can they do that? A warrior deserves his funeral pyre, which will send his spirit to Valholl to feast there until he joins the defenders on the day of Ragnarok. I fear that if more and more warriors take the White Christ faith, there will be a sadly depleted army to follow Odin, Frey and Thor at the great conflict.'

THROUGHOUT THAT SUMMER and autumn I heard reports of my sworn brother Grettir. His exploits were the main topic of conversation among the farmers of the region. Whenever I called

on my father-in-law, Audun, to discuss my progress with the out-
farm, I was regaled with the latest episode in Grettir's deeds.
Audun's gossip made my visits bearable because I was missing
my sworn brother, though I was very careful not to reveal that I
knew that 'cursed outlaw', as Audun called him. I learned that
Grettir had succeeded in visiting his mother without alerting
anyone else in the household. He had called at her house after
dark, approaching the farmhouse along a narrow ravine that led
to the side door, from where he found his way along the unlit
passage to the room where his mother slept. With a mother's
intuition she had identified the intruder in the darkness, and after
greeting him had told him the dismal details of how Atli his older
brother had been murdered by Thorbjorn Oxenmight and his
faction. Grettir had then hidden in his mother's house until he
was able to confirm that Thorbjorn Oxenmight was on his own
farm and accompanied by only his farm workers.

'And do you know what that scoundrel Grettir did then?' said
Audun, snorting with indignation. 'He rode right over to the
Oxenmight's place, in broad daylight, a helmet on his head, a
long spear in one hand and that fancy sword of his at his belt.
He came on Oxenmight and his son working in the hayfields,
gathering up the early hay and stacking it. They recognised
Grettir at once and knew why he had come. Fortunately they had
brought their weapons with them to the meadow, and so Thorbjorn and his lad devised what they thought was an effective
defence. Oxenmight would confront Grettir to distract him, while
his son armed with an axe worked his way round behind the
outlaw and struck him in the back.'

'And did the plan work?'

My father-in-law let out the self-satisfied grunt of a storyteller
who knows he has his audience on tenterhooks. 'It nearly did,' he
said. 'A servant woman saw the whole affair. She saw Grettir
stop, then sit down on the ground and start fiddling with the head
of the spear. Apparently he was removing the pin which holds the
spear head to the shaft. If he missed his throw, he didn't want

Oxenmight pulling the spear out of the ground and using it against him. But when Grettir threw the spear at Oxenmight the head came off too early and the spear went harmlessly astray. That left Grettir armed with his sword and a small shield against the grown man and the youth. Oxenmight did not get his name for nothing, so it seemed that the odds were now against Grettir.'

'I've heard that Grettir is not the sort of man to back off from a fight,' I said.

'He didn't. Grettir went up to Oxenmight and the two men started to circle one another, holding their swords. Oxenmight's lad saw his chance to slip around behind Grettir and bury the axe in his spine. He was just about to make his stroke when Grettir lifted up his sword to hack at Oxenmight and saw the lad out of the corner of his eye. Instead of bringing the sword forwards, he kept swinging it up and over and brought it down back-handed on the boy's head. The blow split the lad's skull like a turnip. Meanwhile his father had seen his opening and rushed forward, but Grettir deflected his sword blow with his shield, and then took a cut at his opponent. That Grettir is so strong that his sword smashed right through Oxenmight's shield as if it was made of straw, and struck his opponent in the neck. Killed him on the spot. Grettir returned immediately to his mother's house and announced to her that he had avenged the death of her oldest son Atli. She was delighted and told Grettir that he was a worthy member of her family, but that he had better be careful as Oxenmight's people would be sure to seek retribution.'

'Where's Grettir now?' I asked, trying not to seem too interested.

'Can't be sure,' Audun answered. 'He went over to see Snorri Godi and asked if he could stay there, but Snorri turned him down. There's a rumour that Grettir is hiding out with one of the farmers over in Westfiords.'

Later my obnoxious father-in-law informed me that Grettir had surfaced on the moors, living rough and keeping himself fed by making raids on the local farmsteads or sheepstealing. He was moving from place to place, usually alone but sometimes in the company of one or two other outlaws.

It was not until the spring that I met Grettir again and then completely unexpectedly. I was on my way to visit Thrand when I encountered a large group of farmers, about twenty of them. From their manner I saw at once that they were very excited, and to my surprise I saw Grettir among them. He was in the middle of the group, being led along on a rope with his hands tied behind his back.

'Can you tell me what's going on?' I asked the farmer at the head of the group.

'It's Grettir the Strong. We finally caught him,' said one of the farmers, a big, red-faced man dressed in homespun clothes. He was looking very pleased with himself. 'One of our shepherds reported seeing him on the moors, and we got together and stalked him. We had been suffering from his raids and he had got over-confident. He was asleep when we found him, and we managed to get close enough to overpower him, though a couple of us got badly bruised in the scuffle.'

'So where are you taking him?' I asked.

'We can't decide,' said the farmer. 'No one wants to take charge of him until we can bring him before our local chieftain for judgement. He's too strong and violent, and he would be a menace if kept captive.'

I glanced over at Grettir. He was standing, with his hands still bound behind his back and looking stone-faced. He did not acknowledge that he knew me. The rest of the farmers had halted and were continuing with what was obviously a long-running argument, whether to hand Grettir over to Thorir of Gard for the reward or to the local chieftain for a trial.

'Let's hang him here and now,' said one of the captors. Judging by the bruise on his face, he was one of the men whom Grettir had hit during the capture. 'That way, we can take the corpse to Thorir of Gard and claim the reward.' There was a murmur of agreement from some of his companions, though the rest were looking doubtful. In a few moments they would reach a decision and there would be no chance to influence them.

'I want to speak up for Grettir,' I called out. 'I sailed with him last year, and if he hadn't been on board our ship would have foundered. He saved my life and the lives of the rest of the crew. He's not a common criminal and he was convicted at the Althing without a chance to defend himself. If any of you have suffered from his robberies, I promise I will make good the loss.' Then I had an inspiration. 'It will be to your credit if you are generous enough to spare his life. People will talk about how magnanimous you were and remember the deed. I suggest that you make Grettir swear that he will move away from this district, and not prey on you any more. And that he'll not take his revenge on any one of you. He's a man of honour and will keep his word.'

It was the mention of honour and fame that swayed them. In every farmer, however humble, there lurked a shred of that same sense of honour and thirst for fame that Grettir had expressed to me. There was a general muttering as they discussed my proposal. It became clear that they were relieved that they would not have the dirty work of taking the outlaw's life. Finally – after a long and awkward pause – their spokesman accepted my suggestion.

'All right, then,' he said. 'If Grettir clears off and agrees never to trouble us again, we'll let him go.' Looking at Grettir, he asked, 'Do you give us your word?'

Grettir nodded.

Someone untied Grettir's bonds, loosening the knots cautiously and then stood back.

Grettir rubbed his wrists and then walked across to embrace me. 'Thank you, sworn brother,' he said. Then he stepped aside from the path and struck out across the moor.

Grettir kept his word to the farmers. He never came back into the district, but stayed away and made his home in a cave on the far side of the moor. For my part, the revelation that I was Grettir's sworn brother put an end to my quiet life. Some of my neighbours now looked at me with curiosity, others gave me a

wide berth, and Gunnhildr flew into a rage. When she heard what
had happened, she confronted me. Not only was I an unbeliever,
she shrilled, I was consorting with the worst sort of criminals.
Grettir was the spawn of the devil, a creature of Satan. He was
twisted and evil. She had heard that he was a warlock, in touch
with demons and ghouls.

Accustomed to my wife's ready grievances, I said nothing,
and was vaguely relieved when she announced that she would in
future live with her parents, and that if I continued my friendship
with Grettir she would seriously consider a divorce.

My promise to pay compensation to the farmers Grettir had
robbed contributed significantly to Gunnhildr's anger. The truth
was that I could not afford the reparations. I was penniless and
little more than a tenant for my father-in-law. Gunnhildr was
very much her father's daughter, so prising money out of her
grasp in order to pay the farmers was nigh impossible. It was
useless to ask if she would let me use any of our joint property
to settle the farmers' claims, and the only item of value which I
had ever owned — the fire ruby — was now Gunnhildr's mundur,
and no longer mine, even as surety for a loan. For a few days
after my encounter with Grettir I was hopeful that his victims
would not hold me to my promise, and I would see nothing more
of them. But though the farmers had an appetite for honour and
renown, they were still peasants at heart and they valued hard
cash. A succession of men showed up at my door, claiming that
they had been robbed by my sworn brother and asking for recompense. One said he had been held up on the roadway and his
horse stolen from him; another that valuable clothing had been
stripped from him at knife point; several claimed that Grettir had
rustled their sheep and cattle. Of course there was no way of
knowing whether their claims were genuine. The sheep and cattle
might have wandered off on their own, and I was fairly sure that
the values the owners put on their losses were often exaggerated.
But I had appealed to their sense of honour when obtaining Grettir's freedom and, after taking such a high-minded stance, I was

hardly in a position to quibble over the precise cost of their claims. I found myself faced with a sum that I had no hope of paying off.

Thrand, of course, had heard what had happened. On my next visit to his house, he noticed that I looked distracted and asked the reason. When I told him that I was worried about my debts, he merely asked, 'How much is it that you owe?'

'A little less than seven marks in all,' I said.

He walked across to his bed where it stood against the wall, reached underneath and pulled out a small, locked chest. Placing it on the table between us, he produced a key. When he threw back the lid, I found myself looking at a sight I had last seen when I had worked for Brithmaer the moneyer. The strong box was two-thirds full of silver. Very little was in coin. I saw bits and fragments of jewellery, segments of silver torcs, broken pieces of silver plate, half a silver brooch, several flattened finger rings. They were jumbled together where Thrand had tossed them casually into his hoard chest. From my days as a novice monk I recognised part of a silver altar cross, and – with a little lurch of my heart – I saw a piece of jewellery inscribed with the same sinuous writing that had been on the silver coins of Aelfgifu's favourite necklace.

'You know how to use this, I imagine,' Thrand asked, picking something out from the clutter. At first sight I thought it was one of the metal styluses that I had used in my writing lessons in the monastery. But Thrand was searching for two more items. When he put them together I recognised a weighing scale, similar to the ones that Brithmaer had used, but smaller and constructed so that it could be dismantled, suitable for a traveller.

'Here,' Thrand said. 'Hold these.'

He sifted through his hoard, picking out the pieces for me to weigh as I told him how much I owed to each farmer. Once or twice, when he could not find a piece of silver that matched the sum, he took out his sword, laid a larger piece of silver on the table, and chopped off the correct weight. 'That's how we did it

in the old days,' he commented, 'when we divided up the spoils.
No bothering with coins; a mark of silver is just as good by
weight as when it is stamped with a king's head.' Sometimes more
so, I thought, remembering Brithmaer's forgeries.

I was tactful enough not to ask Thrand where he had acquired
his treasure and said only, 'I give you my word that I will repay
your generosity when I have the chance.'

In reply he said, 'This is a gift, Thorgils. It does me no good
locked away here in a box,' and he quoted the Havamal again:

> 'If wealth a man has won for himself
> Let him never suffer in need
> Oft he saves for a foe what he plans for a friend
> For much goes worse than we wish.'

When I had paid off the last of Grettir's victims, I decided it
was time to pay a visit to my sworn brother. I had no idea where
to find him, so I set off across the moors in the direction that he
had taken when I had saved him from the angry farmers. As it
turned out, Grettir saw me coming from a distance away. He had
made his lair in a cave on high ground, from where he could keep
a watch for the approach of strangers, and he came down the
hillside to greet me. He led me back to his cave, the two of us
scrambling up a near-vertical rock face to reach his home. He
had hung a grey blanket across the entrance, the colour matching the rock so that you did not realise that the cave was there
until you were a few paces away. Inside were a fireplace, a place
to sleep, where he had laid out his leather sleeping sack, and a
store of dried food. He took his drinking water from a small rill
that drained at the foot of the cliff. When I commented on a pile
of fist-sized rocks that he had stacked near the entrance of the
cave, he explained that he had collected them to use as missiles.
'If anyone tries to storm the cave,' he said, 'there's only one
approach, and that is straight up the cliff. I can keep them at bay
for hours.'

I noticed a second leather sleeping sack, thrown in a heap on the far side of the cave. 'Who does that belong to?' I asked.

'A man called Stuv Redbeard. He's an outlaw like myself. He's gone off to raid for food. He should be back soon.'

Redbeard returned that evening, carrying a shoulder of dried lamb and a bag of whey he had stolen from an unguarded shepherd's hut. From the moment that I laid eyes on Stuv Redbeard I was worried. There was a shiftiness about him which put me on my guard. When he left the cave for a moment, I took the chance to ask Grettir about him.

'How long have you known Stuv? Do you trust him?' I asked

'Not entirely,' Grettir replied. 'I know there are men who would kill me for the price on my head. Last autumn a man came to the moor and joined me, claiming to be an outlaw like myself and needing shelter. One night he crept up on me, thinking I was asleep. He had a dagger in his hand, and intended to stab me, but I awoke in time, and managed to grab the weapon from him. I made him confess that he was a professional killer, hoping to win my blood money from Thorir of Gard.'

'Thorir is offering twenty-four marks of silver for your head and Oxenmight's family have promised to match that sum for anyone who kills you,' I said. 'It's twice as much as the highest reward ever offered for the death of a skogarmadur.'

'Well, that night creeper didn't get to collect it,' Grettir said. 'I killed him with his own dagger, carried his body over to the nearest lake, weighed the corpse down with stones and dumped him in.'

'So why are you now taking the risk of sharing your lair with that Redbeard? He could also be after the reward money.'

'It's a risk I'm prepared to take,' Grettir replied. 'I make sure that I keep an eye on him, but I would rather have company, however suspect it might be, than live here out on the moors by myself. At least after sunset.'

I remembered that, for all his ferocity and reputation, Grettir was still mortally afraid of the dark. I knew it was useless to try to persuade him that his childish dread was putting his life in danger.

My fears were well-founded. Over the next few weeks I was rarely at my father-in-law's farm as I was spending most of my time on the moor. I brought Grettir regular deliveries of food and clothing, and the two of us would sit for hours at the entrance to the cave, looking out across the moor as I relayed to him news of what was happening in the outside world. Grettir's family and friends had been negotiating with Oxenmight's people in an attempt to settle their feud, and the two sides had agreed that the deaths of Oxenmight and Grettir's brother Atli should cancel each other out. Grettir's supporters even collected enough money to offer a heavy compensation to Thorir of Gard for the death of his sons. But Thorir refused to be placated. Nothing less than Grettir's death would satisfy him.

It was on one of these visits to carry supplies to Grettir that I found the cave unoccupied. It was a warm day and I guessed that he had gone to the nearby lake to bathe and wash his clothes. Leaving my parcel of food, I started off across the moor to find him. The lake lay on the far side of a low rise in the ground. As I came to the top of the slope, I found myself looking down on a shallow expanse of water fringed with reeds and with one or two small islands in the centre. From my vantage point I could see Grettir in the water, far out from the shoreline. Much closer to the bank was his fellow outlaw, Stuv Redbeard. Clearly they had both decided to go for a swim, stripped off their clothes and left them on the bank. I watched Redbeard wade out of the water, return to his pile of clothes and get dressed quickly. There was something about his hasty movements which was suspicious. I saw him pick up his sword, unsheathe it and then slink back to where he could crouch down among the reeds in ambush. The distance was too great for me to shout a warning to Grettir, who was now approaching the landing place. I saw him reach the shallows, stand up and begin to wade towards the bank, pulling at the reeds for support as his feet moved through the slippery lake bottom. He was naked and I realised that this was the moment that Redbeard had been waiting for, perhaps for months. He had Grettir at his mercy.

Even as I watched, I saw Redbeard suddenly rise up from his ambush and the flash of his blade as he slashed at Grettir. Grettir's reaction was astonishingly swift. He must have sensed the blow coming, for he flung himself backwards into the water with a tremendous splash, and the sword stroke missed. Redbeard immediately raised his sword for a second strike. But Grettir had disappeared. The ripples still spread out from where he had flung himself back into the water, and Redbeard stood poised, head thrust forward, watching for his prey to surface, his sword at the ready. He watched and watched, and both of us became increasingly puzzled as Grettir did not reappear. For a moment I wondered whether Grettir had been caught by the tip of the sword and drowned. It was too far for me to see whether there was any blood floating to the surface. The water of the lake was a dark peaty brown, and the only sign of the struggle was the broad patch of dirty yellow where Grettir's feet had disturbed the mud as he fell backwards. This opaque patch was my sworn brother's salvation. As time passed, Redbeard concentrated his gaze in that area.

Then I noticed the reeds quiver a short distance to Redbeard's left. From my vantage point I saw them bend and stir gently: their movement was tracing a line from the water's edge to where Redbeard was standing. I realised that Grettir must have swum underwater to the bank, hauled himself out and was stalking his prey. In his eagerness Redbeard stepped forward, wading up to his knees in the water, still holding his sword with the point downward, ready to stab. But now it was Redbeard who was edging into danger. He was facing the lake, ready to pounce, when Grettir burst from the reeds behind him. I was reminded of the way that the boar had charged from the thicket when I was hunting with Edgar in England. Once again the charging animal was lethal. Grettir, stark naked, flung himself out of the reeds and

onto Redbeard's back. The force of the impact knocked Redbeard
into the lake. I saw Grettir reach forward right-handed, and pluck
the sword from his attacker's hand. Then with his left arm, Grettir
spun Redbeard over in the water, and plunged the sword in the
man's belly. By then I was running down the slope, heart pounding, until I slithered to a stop beside Grettir and clasped him to
me. Redbeard's body lay face down where he had intended my
sworn brother to die.

Again, I was more badly shaken by the attack than Grettir.
He was so accustomed to violence and assault that he recovered
quickly from the ambush. Nevertheless, seeing him so narrowly
escape death made me distraught. I was shaking with relief as we
walked back together to the cave, leaving his would-be killer's
body drifting on the surface of the lake for all to see. 'It will be a
warning to others,' Grettir said. 'My whereabouts is not a secret
any longer.'

'You'll have to find another refuge,' I told him. 'Staying on
the moor is getting too dangerous. Sooner or later, you'll be trapped here and find yourself outnumbered.'

'I know, Thorgils,' he answered. 'I need to find somewhere so
remote that no one will plague me, a place where the landowner
is discreet and willing to ignore my presence.'

'Why don't we consult your mother? She may know someone
who will offer you the hideaway you need. Until we get her
answer, come and stay with me. Gunnhildr, my wife, is hardly
ever at home. I can smuggle you into the house and you can hide
there until we can pick the moment to travel to your mother's
place.'

As matters turned out, Grettir stayed with me for more than
two weeks. Redbeard's body was found and Oxenmight's friends
assembled to make a sweep of the moor nearby, looking for
Grettir. They eventually discovered his cave, and I had a feeling
that they suspected that I was harbouring the fugitive, for more
than once I thought I saw a watcher on the hillside above my
house. Only when the hunt had been abandoned did I think it

safe for Grettir to make the journey to his mother's home, and even then I insisted that I accompany him in case we encountered trouble on the road.

My caution was justified. We had gone only half a day's travel when we came face to face on the path with a man I recognised. He was one of Snorri Godi's sons, a tall, well-set-up man in his thirties by the name of Thorodd. I remembered him as a rather quiet, decent fellow. Yet as he drew level with us, he suddenly stepped right into Grettir's path, drew his sword and announced, 'Guard yourself, skogarmadur.' I must have gaped with surprise, for I did not remember Thorodd as being the least belligerent.

'What are you doing, Thorodd?' I blurted. 'Don't you recognise me? I'm Thorgils. We used to know one another when I lived at your father's farm.'

'Stay out of this,' he snapped back at me. 'Everyone knows of your association with Grettir. I'll attend to you later. Right now I intend to deal with the outlaw.'

'Don't be mad,' I insisted. 'You've got no quarrel with Grettir. Let us pass on peacefully. Just forget you've seen us.'

For his response, Thorodd struck me hard in the stomach with the pommel of his sword, knocking the wind out of me. I sat down abruptly on the roadside, clutching my guts.

Grettir had not moved until he saw me hit. Then he drew his own sword and waited for Thorodd to strike the first blow. I could see from the way Thorodd advanced on Grettir that he was a competent fighter. The speed and accuracy of the hilt blow that had knocked me down was impressive and I guessed that Thorodd had received enough weapon-training to deal with the average farmer. But Thorodd was not fighting an ordinary opponent. He was attacking the man reputed to be the strongest in Iceland.

Thorodd launched his first blow, a high cut that, if it had landed, would have separated Grettir's head from his shoulders. Almost nonchalantly Grettir raised his small wooden shield and deflected the blow as if he was swatting aside an insect. Thorodd recovered his balance and launched a second stroke, this time aimed at Grettir's legs in the hopes of laming him. Again Grettir warded off the blow, using his sword to block the attack. The two sword blades met with a ringing clash. For his third stroke Thorodd tried using all his strength to swing back-handed at Grettir's right side. Without even moving his feet, Grettir moved his wooden shield across to stop the blow. Thorodd, now panting with exertion, tried a direct stab. He lunged, with the point of his sword aimed at Grettir's belly. Again, the shield blocked the attack.

Thorodd stepped back, calculating how he could get past Grettir's guard. At that moment Grettir decided he had had enough of the onslaught and that his opponent was serious about killing him. In absolute silence, which was more terrifying than if he had given a berserker's battle roar, my sworn brother advanced on Thorodd and rained down on him a series of heavy sword blows that resembled a blacksmith beating on a forge. There was nothing subtle about Grettir's assault. He did not bother to feint or conceal the direction of the next blow, but relied entirely on brute strength. He moved forward, striking downward repeatedly on his hapless victim's defence. Thorodd raised his shield to block the blows, but each time Grettir's sword struck the shield I saw the arm shake beneath it and Thorodd stagger slightly. Grettir could have swung below the shield to cut at Thorodd's body, or struck at Thorodd's head. But he did not bother. He simply hammered on the shield, his blows so fast and so hard that Thorodd was forced to give ground. Step by step Thorodd was driven back, and I saw that Grettir was not even trying to kill his enemy, only to pound him into submission. After twenty or thirty heavy blows, Thorodd could withstand the onslaught no longer. First his shield arm began to droop, then his backward steps became more and more shaky, until he sank to his knees, still desperately trying to keep up his defence. Finally his shield, which had begun to splinter and crack, broke in half, and Thorodd was left kneeling defenceless on the soggy ground.

'Stop!' I shouted at Grettir, for I had got my breath back. But my warning was unnecessary. Now that Grettir had belaboured his opponent into submission, he stood back. He was not even out of breath.

I went across to where Thorodd was still kneeling, his body bowed forward in exhaustion. Putting an arm around his waist, I helped him to his feet.

'What on earth possessed you?' I asked. 'Did you really think that you could defeat Grettir the Strong?'

Thorodd was gasping for air. His shield arm was so numb that it hung uselessly. 'I hoped to win back my father's favour,' he groaned. 'I quarrelled with him so badly that he ordered me out of his house, saying that I had to prove my worth before he would accept me back again. He shouted at me that I had to do something spectacular – like dealing with an outlaw. I had no idea that I would run into Grettir. That was something the Gods put in my way.'

'Go back to your father,' I advised him, 'and tell him what happened. The wreckage of your shield should prove that you are telling the truth, and surely he'll accept that anyone courageous enough to tackle Grettir single-handed has proved his worth. Tell him also that Grettir's quarrel is only with those who have harmed his family. If he has robbed others or caused them injury, the sole motive has been his own survival.'

When Thorodd had limped away, Grettir insisted that I turn back to my house. 'It's less than half a day's walk from here to my mother's place,' he said, 'and that is just where my enemies will be on the lookout for me. It will be easier for one man to approach unobserved than for two of us. And after I have spoken to her and decided where I will go next, I will send you word where to find me.'

'I think we should have some way of checking that any message that passes between us is genuine,' I said. 'Now I have been seen in your company, people may use our friendship to lure you out of hiding and trap you.'

'You're always the clever and cautious one, Thorgils,' said

Grettir with a slight smile. 'Any time a message passes between us, the bearer can begin by quoting one of Odinn's sayings. That should keep you happy.'

I walked back home, worrying that Grettir would fall into an ambush as he approached his mother's house. But it was I who found calamity waiting at my door.

I almost walked right past them without noticing. Only when I was level, within touching distance, did I realise they were there. They were waiting for me and, though they were motionless, they were as dangerous as any killer waiting to pounce with a dagger.

Scorn poles – two of them were planted upright in the ground just beside my front door. I could guess who had erected them there because one was a likeness of myself carved with physical details that only someone intimate could have known. The second wooden pole was less elaborate, but there was no mistaking the broad shoulders of the man it portrayed. To make sure, the carver had scratched in runes the name 'Grettir'. The two poles were adult height, very obviously male, and both faced in the same direction, towards the door. One scorn pole was placed close behind the other, almost touching. The message was explicit, obvious to every passer-by: Grettir and Thorgils were lovers.

My initial shock of comprehension was quickly replaced by cold fury. I was outraged. I felt cheated and damaged, my closest friendship defiled. I knew, of course, that Gunnhildr must have arranged for the scorn poles to be carved and then planted for all to see. It was a public accusation, and – worse – in the same way that the sentence of full outlawry can never be appealed against, so the public accusation of man-love can never be effectively denied if it is made from within a marriage. In that regard I now shared Grettir's fate: he had been found guilty of a crime he did not commit and which he had no opportunity to deny; I had been accused unjustly of acts against which there was no way to defend myself.

Disgusted, I pushed open the door of the house and gathered up a few clothes, thrusting them angrily into a travelling satchel.

I vowed that I would never again enter that odious house, or work one more hour on the farm for old Audun's benefit, or speak to my treacherous wife. Slinging the satchel over my shoulder, I stormed out of the building feeling utterly betrayed.

OF COURSE I went to Thrand. Of all the people who had ever guided and advised me, Thrand had always been the most staunch. When I told him about the scorn poles and asked how I could fight back against the slur, he brought me to my senses.

'The more you stamp on a turd,' he said bluntly, 'the further it spreads. Let the matter alone, there's nothing you can do about it.'

It was good advice, but I was too angry and resentful to accept it outright.

'What about Grettir?' I said. 'Should I tell him? And how will he react?'

'Grettir's got far more serious threats to think about,' said Thrand. 'Of course, he will get to know about the scorn poles like everyone else. All you can do is make sure that he hears the news before it is common gossip. Then it is for him to decide if he wants to do anything about it. But, as I said, a public denial is useless. Let the matter drop, ignore it, wait for the uproar to die down and for the next new scandal to erupt and smother it. If you tell me where to find him, I'll go to see Grettir and talk with him.'

'He'll still be hiding out at his mother's house,' I replied. 'Should I do anything about Gunnhildr?'

'Well, for a start you can expect that she will bring divorce proceedings against you. She's probably lined up some hostile witnesses already, rehearsing them to appear at the next district gathering to support her claim.'

'I'll go there myself and deny the accusation,' I said defiantly, still stung by the injustice of my predicament.

'I doubt that will do much good,' said Thrand calmly. 'For

any chance of success you'll need to be represented by skilful advocates at the court, and there's no one you know who can act in that capacity.'

'Maybe I could ask Snorri Godi,' I suggested.

'Snorri Godi is unlikely to act on your behalf. He helped to arrange the match in the first place and he will look foolish trying to act for an aggrieved spouse. The best you can expect from him is that he might help to recover your mundur, the fire ruby. And when it comes to keeping the jewel from falling permanently into Gunnhildr's hands, I think I can be of use.'

'How can you help?' I asked, but Thrand did not answer. He only advised me to get a good night's sleep so as to have a clear head in the morning. That was impossible. It was long after nightfall before I fell into a restless slumber, plagued by black dreams in which I was pursued by a death hag. When I woke, it was to find Thrand gone.

He came back four days later, and in his absence I alternately seethed with anger at Gunnhildr and concocted wild plots to avenge myself for her perfidy, or I felt sorry for myself and wondered how to escape from this crisis.

Thrand was as calm as always when he returned. 'Gunnhildr has announced publicly that she is seeking a divorce,' he confirmed. 'She and her father are claiming back the farm. It was her dowry, so that is just a formality. But they also want to keep your mundur, the fire ruby, as you are the one at fault.' My face must have showed my vexation and despair.

'The divorce is all but guaranteed,' Thrand went on, 'but for the moment you need not worry about the fire ruby. It is in safe hands.'

'What do you mean?' I asked.

'Snorri Godi has it. I went to see Snorri Godi and reminded him about the initial agreement at the time of your marriage: that the mundur was to be valued at thirty marks and could be redeemed in the event of a divorce. He said that his inclination was not to get involved in such a messy business, but because Grettir had spared his son Thorodd's life he would use his influence to get Audun and Gunnhildr to hand the jewel over to him, and he would hold it in safe keeping until you could provide thirty marks to redeem it.'

'I'm surprised that Gunnhildr or that miserly father of hers agreed to such a proposal,' I said. 'They are so grasping that they wouldn't accept a verbal assurance. They know that I could never raise thirty marks.'

'Snorri Godi told them that the sum is guaranteed. He is holding a surety for that amount.'

'What do you mean? Snorri won't lie about something like that.'

'He didn't,' said Thrand. 'I've left thirty marks of hack silver with him.'

I was stunned.

But Thrand had not finished. 'I also went to see Grettir and had a talk with him, told him about the scorn poles and asked him what he wanted to do about it. As I expected, he took the matter in his stride. Commented that far worse things were being said about him and one more false accusation would make no difference. When I suggested that he could solve all his problems by leaving the country and that you would probably go with him, he answered that he had no intention of running away from his enemies, which you knew already. Also to tell you that his younger brother, Illugi, has now grown to manhood, and that he felt he should stay to protect him. Grettir still feels guilty that he deserted his older brother Atli, who was killed during his first outlawry. He asked me to wish you well on your travels.'

'My travels?' I asked.

'Yes,' Thrand replied 'I told Grettir that you and I were leaving Iceland for a while, long enough for the scandal to die down and for you to have a chance to win the thirty marks to redeem your mundur.'

'Thrand,' I said, 'I'm deeply grateful to you for the money you have left with Snorri Godi, but there's no reason for you to desert your farm.'

Thrand shrugged. 'I have been sitting too long in this quiet corner. I feel the wanderlust coming back, and I want to return to the places I knew as a young man, the places where I won my silver. Who knows – you may do the same.'

'You never told me where or how you got your hoard,' I said.

'Until now there was no need. Besides, I had my reasons for remaining silent,' he answered. 'But you should know that I fought with the felag, with the Jomsvikings.'

Every boy in Iceland who dreamed of plunder and martial glory had heard about the Jomsvikings, but I had not known whether they were mythical or whether they really existed. If Thrand said they were real, then I was prepared to take his word on it.

'What did Grettir say when you told him that you and I would be going abroad?'

'He quoted some lines from the Havamal:

> "A better burden may no man bear
> For wanderings wide than wisdom
> It is better than wealth on unknown ways
> And in grief a refuge it gives." '

Thrand looked at me and with a note of compassion in his voice said, 'Appropriate, don't you think?'

TEN

JOMSBURG WAS AN indistinct smudge on the horizon for half
a day. Since first light our ship, a weather-beaten merchantman
owned by a syndicate of Wendish traders, had been edging slowly
towards the home of the Jomsvikings, yet by noon we did not
seem to have come any closer. After the dramatic cliffs and rocky
shores of Iceland and Norway, I was disappointed by the apparently featureless Baltic coast ahead. Its monotony was accentuated
by the grey overcast sky reflected in murky water under our keel.
Thrand and I had already spent two weeks on the voyage and I
was impatient to reach our destination. I stood gripping the
weather shrouds as if I could drag the vessel bodily forward.

'We'll arrive at the time the Gods have decided, and that will
be soon enough,' said Thrand, noting my mood.

'Is that where you won your hoard?' I asked, staring towards
the dark line on the horizon where the sky met the sea.

'Not here, but in the company of comrades who lived here,'
he replied.

'When was the last time you saw them?'

'Not since the great battle in Jorunga Bay against Earl Haakon
of Norway more than thirty years ago.'

'Do you have any idea what might have happened to them
since then? Have you heard anything?'

'No, not after our defeat,' he answered and walked away to the far side of the deck and stood staring down into the water, his face expressionless.

I would have left the matter there if one of the Wendish sailors had not sidled up to me. Ever since Thrand and I had joined the ship as passengers, the man had been glancing at my taciturn companion, trying not to let his curiosity show. Now as our ship crept closer to Jomsburg, the sailor took his chance to ask the question that had been on his mind for days.

'Old Jomsviking, eh?' he enquired in his heavily accented Norse, jerking his head at Thrand.

'I don't know,' I replied.

'Looks Jomsviking, sure,' said the sailor. 'Going to Jomi. Maybe for his friends. But not many to find now. They liked to die.'

I waited for a few moments and then crossed to where Thrand stood watching the water rippling gently past our scuffed hull and asked him what the sailor had meant. There was a long silence before the tall Icelander finally replied and he spoke so quietly that I had to strain to hear him. For the first time in all the years I had known him, Thrand's voice had a tremor of emotion. Whether it was sorrow, pride or shame, I could not tell.

'Only eighty came out of the sea battle alive; eighty of all those who did not turn their backs on the enemy. They took refuge on an island and ten of them died of exposure before the enemy hunted them down and brought the survivors before their executioner. Thorkel Leira was his name. Earl Haakon had ordered that no Jomsviking was to be left alive. Their hands and legs were bound so tightly that a stick had to be thrust through their hair – they took great pride in braiding their hair before battle – and each man was half-carried to his fate, as if he was a dead animal brought home on a pole after the hunt. The headsman asked the same question of each man, "Are you afraid of dying?"'

'What did they reply?'

'Some answered, "I am content to die," or words to that

effect. Others insisted that they be allowed to face the headsman's
sword so they could see the blow coming. One man's last request
was that his hands should be untied so he could hold a dagger in
the air while his head was lopped from his shoulders.'

'Why such a strange request?' I commented. 'What could he
have been thinking of?'

'He said that in the Jomsviking barracks he and his companions had often discussed if the mind resides in the head or in
the body, and now he had the chance to settle the matter. He had
decided to hold up the dagger after death, so if he let it drop
when his head left his body, then his head was the seat of his
decision. However, if the dagger stayed clutched in his hand, then
his body had made the decision and was sticking to it.'

'And what was the outcome of the experiment?'

'The dagger hit the ground before his body.'

'If I understood the Wend properly, he said that a few of the
Jomsvikings survived. So why did Earl Haakon spare their lives
when he had sworn to kill them all?'

Thrand smiled grimly. 'It was Sven the son of Bui's doing.
He had exceptional yellow hair, long and glossy, and he was very
proud of it. He grew it almost to his waist and spent a great deal
of time combing and arranging it. When his turn came to go
before the executioner he asked for someone to be assigned to
hold up his hair so it did not get bloodstained when his head came
off. Thorkel Leira agreed, and told his chief assistant to hold the
hair to one side. Then just as Thorkel made his sword stroke,
Sven jerked his head forward, pulling the assistant off balance so
the sword struck the man's wrists, cutting off a hand. Of course
Thorkel Leira was furious and was about to take a second cut at
Sven and behead him properly when Earl Haakon, who had seen
what happened, intervened. He said that the Jomsvikings were
proving so awkward even in the manner of their death, that it
would be easier to set the remainder free if they promised never
to take up arms against him again. He knew that a Jomsviking
honours his word.'

'How many were left alive to make that promise?'

'Just twenty-five of the eighty who were captured,' Thrand answered, and before I could put the obvious question he added, 'and, yes, I was one of them.'

It was dusk by the time our ship entered the channel leading to Jomsburg itself, and by then I realised I had been mistaken about the apparent monotony of the coastline. The final stages of our approach revealed a long line of cliffs, not ragged and raw as in Iceland, but a regular wall of brown and grey rock. At its foot a beach of rocks and boulders gradually changed to a long strip of white sand backed by dunes. Here we turned into a river mouth to find a town built on an island where a steep hill rose close to the bank. Its summit provided the site for the stronghold of the Jomsvikings. Watchtowers dominated a palisaded citadel and two long breastworks extended down the slope of the hill to enclose a military harbour within the protective perimeter. Heading for the commercial wharves, our ship continued upstream, and I noticed Thrand look into the mouth of the Jomsviking harbour as we passed. He must not have liked what he saw. The pilings which fronted the river were in poor condition, their timbers soggy and rotten. Two massive wooden gates faced with iron plates had formerly protected the entrance – in times of siege they could be swung closed, sealing off the harbour inside. Now they were sagging and askew, and the ramparts which had allowed the defenders to hurl missiles at their attackers were crumbling. The stronghold of the Jomsvikings looked rundown.

As soon as we docked, Thrand and I left the ship and set off for the citadel. The town looked prosperous enough and was far larger than I had expected, with a regular grid pattern of streets and numerous stalls, warehouses and shops, now shuttered up for the night. It was when we began to climb the hill towards the Jomsviking citadel that signs of neglect reappeared. The roadway was potholed and weeds grew along each side. Nor was the main gateway leading into the citadel properly guarded. A trio of bored soldiers made no attempt to stop us as we walked through the gate into the main enclosure. The space inside was a large oval and in its centre was a parade ground. On each side stood four large barn-like structures, which were clearly barracks. Each building was at least eighty paces in length, and solidly built from heavy tree trunks in blockhouse construction, with a roof of wooden shingles. I noted that three of the barracks were derelict. Their roofs had holes and in several places the roof ridges sagged. Only the fourth barrack block, the one nearest the entrance gate, was still in use. Its roof was neatly patched, smoke arose from several chimney holes, and at least a score of men were seated on benches at the main doorway, talking or playing a board game set on a trestle table between them.

As Thrand and I walked towards them, they looked up. Thrand was still twenty paces away when I saw one of the men rise to his feet. He was a leathery-looking character, dressed in sombre civilian clothes but with the unmistakable bearing of a professional warrior. Judging by his grey hair, he was about the same age as my companion. Suddenly he slammed his hand down on the table, making the game pieces jump into the air. 'Thrand!' he called. 'By the head of Hymir's ox! it must be Thrand. I would know those long shanks anywhere!' He hurried across to my companion and seized him in a bear hug. 'I never thought to see you again!' he cried. 'Where have you been all these years? I heard rumours that you were with a raiding party in the Irish Sea, but that was at least ten years back and since then there was no further news.'

'I've been living quietly in Iceland,' answered Thrand, 'until I felt it was time to see what had happened to the old felag.'

'Things aren't at all what they used to be, as you can see,' said the old soldier, waving at the empty barrack buildings. 'But never mind, that will change. We're gaining recruits, though not as many as I would wish and we are not as strict as before about their qualifications. Here, let me introduce you.'

Proudly he steered Thrand towards the group of loungers and began to make introductions. Thrand, he boasted to them, had

been a member of the brotherhood in the glory days, had fought
Earl Haakon's men at Jorunga Bay and survived. He was a
warrior of experience and knew what it was like to be a true
Jomsviking. His description of my companion was so extravagant
that I began to wonder if there was a purpose behind it, and
looked more closely at his audience. They were a mixed lot. Some
were scarred warriors, while others were considerably younger
without a martial bearing. Nor, judging by their appearance, were
they all Norsemen. Several had square Wendish faces; others were
narrow jawed with foxy eyes and probably came from the Permian
regions further north. Their only common feature was that they
all wore good daggers, and many were dressed in the padded
jerkins which are worn beneath the chain-mail shirt the northerners call a byrnie.

'Who's your companion?' asked Thrand's acquaintance, whose
name I later found out was Arne.

'He is called Thorgils. He came with me from Iceland.'

'Is he a fighting man?'

'More of a traveller and observer,' said Thrand, 'He is a
devotee of Odinn the Far-farer.'

'Well, Odinn is the God of battles, too, so he may find himself
at home among us—'

Thrand interrupted him. 'To whom should I report?'

Arne checked his enthusiasm and looked a little awkward. He
drew Thrand away from the group, out of earshot, and I followed.

'It's not like the old days, at least not yet,' Arne told us. 'The
felag all but disintegrated after the disaster against Earl Haakon.
There were so few left to continue the fellowship – only a couple
of dozen who were on sick leave or had stayed behind to garrison
Jomsburg, plus the handful of battle survivors. And many of
them, like yourself, we never thought to see again. Of course, the
others were too ashamed to return.'

'You had better explain to Thorgils,' said Thrand. He had
noticed that I was listening. 'If you want to recruit him to the
fellowship, he should know the truth.'

Arne spat in the dust. 'Sigvaldi, Thorkel and the others – they and their crews withdrew from the battle line when they saw that our ships were heavily outnumbered by the Norwegians. They broke their solemn vow as Jomsvikings and retreated, leaving the likes of Thrand to face the enemy unsupported. Their bad faith did more damage to the felag than losing the battle. Defeat and death we were prepared for, but against cowardice and dishonour we had no defence.'

Thrand later told me his comrades were so ashamed when several Jomsviking ships deserted the battle line that they debated whether to challenge their colleagues and fight them in order to obliterate the dishonour. As it was, they hurled spears and stones at their retreating boats and shouted curses in their wake, before turning to face the Norwegian onslaught.

Arne continued. 'Sigvaldi was among the first to run away, and the worst thing about it was that he was our leader. In those days we all swore to follow just one man as our absolute commander. He decided everything for the felag, whether it was the division of our booty or the settlement of quarrels between us. And when a leader fails so abjectly, it is difficult afterwards to regain respect for leadership. That is why now we rule ourselves by council – a gathering of the senior men decides what we should do. I've little doubt, Thrand, that you will be elected to that council.'

Thrand was looking across at the barracks where a couple of women were loitering. 'I see there are other changes too,' he remarked.

Arne followed his gaze. 'Yes,' he said, 'but you know as well as I do that the regulation forbidding women into the fortress was frequently ignored. Women were smuggled into the barracks and Sigvaldi turned a blind eye to the practice. He said that it was better to have the women here than for the men to slip away into the town and stay there without permission.'

Thrand said nothing, but every line of his face showed his disapproval.

'There's one rule which you will be glad we have set aside,' Arne added slyly. 'We no longer insist that every member of the felag must be between the ages of eighteen and fifty. You and I are getting long in the tooth, and the council has agreed to admit every man who has battle experience, whatever his age, provided he is still fit enough to hold spear and shield in the first or second line. To back them up, we've put in place a training programme for all our new recruits.'

Over the next four weeks I learned what he meant. I was assigned to the training platoon, while Thrand was received back into the ranks of the Jomsvikings and, as Arne had predicted, voted onto their council within days. My fellow recruits were a ragbag assortment of volunteers – Saxons, Wagrians, Polabians, Pomeranians and others. Their reasons for joining the fellowship were as varied as their origins. I found myself learning the rudiments of warfare alongside malcontents and misfits, fugitives escaping justice and opportunists who had come to Jomsburg in the hope of winning plunder. There was also a handful of adventurers and romantics who genuinely hoped to restore the past glory of what had once been the most famous and respected military brotherhood of the northern lands.

We came under the authority of a crop-headed, irascible instructor who reminded me of one of Edgar's hunting dogs, the short-legged variety we put down a badger hole to flush out the occupant, which has a habit of suddenly twisting round and giving its handler a nasty bite. Like the little yapping dogs, our instructor had a loud and incessant bark. He was an Abodrite, a member of the tribe on whose territory Jomsburg had been built, and he never lost an opportunity to show up our ignorance. On the very first day of training he took us into the Jomsviking armoury. We looked around in awe. The Jomsviking weapons store had once equipped a battle group of a thousand men and it still held an impressive array of arms. Many were now rusty and blunt, but the best of them were still greased and arranged on their wooden racks by a crippled armourer, who remembered the days when a dozen smiths and their assistants had wrought and repaired hundreds of swords, axes and spearheads to equip the felag.

'Pick out the weapon you would take into battle if you could carry only one weapon and nothing else,' snapped our instructor, pointing to the largest man in our group, a big shambling Dane, who stood bemused by the choice. After a moment's hesitation, the Dane reached out and selected a heavy sword. Its blade was as long as my arm, and it had a workmanlike brass handle. It seemed a sensible selection.

Without a word our instructor took up a shield with a metal rim and told the Dane. 'Now take a swing at me.'

The Dane, irritated by the instructor's cocksure manner, did as he was told. He lashed out at the instructor, who deftly interposed his shield, edge on. The heavy sword blade met the metal rim and promptly snapped, the blade spinning away from the handle. The instructor stepped up close to the Dane, rammed his shield boss into the Dane's stomach, and the big man fell on the ground in a heap.

'Swords may look good,' announced the instructor, 'but unless you know their true quality don't trust them. They're treacherous in your hand, and you won't find the very best blades in an armoury.'

He caught my eye. 'Here you, the Icelander, what should he have chosen as his weapon?'

The answer was obvious. 'He should have chosen a good spear,' I said.

'And what would you do with it? Throw it at your enemy?'

I remembered how Grettir had lost the head of his spear when he threw it at Oxenmight. 'No, I would use it like a lance, thrusting at my opponent, keeping him at a distance, until I found an opening.'

'Right. So that's what I'm going to teach you lot. Swords are first-class weapons when they are in skilled hands and under the right circumstances. But for well-trained troops the real killing tool is the humble spear, straight and true, and with a shaft of hardened ash.'

So for the first ten days he drilled us only with the spear. He taught us to hold the weapon high in our right hands, the shaft projecting behind the shoulder, so that we could thrust downwards and use our body weight behind the thrust. It was tiring work, but nothing as exhausting as when we were issued with round limewood shields. 'Close up! Close up! Close up tighter!' he ranted as we shuffled sideways on the parade ground, shoulder to shoulder, holding our shields before us and trying to fill every gap in the line to make a wall. 'Closer together, you louts!' he would scream, and then come charging at us and deliver a massive flat-footed kick at the weakest man in the line. When his victim staggered back, leaving a gap, the instructor charged in, wielding a heavy baton and lashing out at the two men on each side who were now exposed. As they rubbed their bruises, he would bellow at the unfortunate man who had wilted, 'You fall and the comrades on each side of you die! Shoulder to shoulder, shield to shield, that's your only hope.'

Gradually we became better at withstanding his frenzied assaults. The line buckled, but did not break, and we learned when it was safe to stand with our shields rim to rim or – in the face of a massed charge – to form up in even closer order, our shields overlapping so that the rim touched the shield boss of the man to our left. Then our shield wall, the burg as our instructor called it, seemed to be nearly impregnable.

We became so confident in our defensive skills that the big Dane felt bold enough to question our instructor when he told us that we had to repeat all our training, but this time dressed in byrnies, the hot and heavy chain-mail shirts.

Our instructor smiled grimly. He ordered us to set up a shield on a wooden frame and place behind it a pig's carcass. He then went to the armoury and fetched a throwing spear. Marking off twenty paces, he took aim and threw the first javelin. The missile struck the shield, the metal head passed clean through and pierced the dead pig a hand's breadth deep. 'Now,' barked our instructor, 'you can see why in future you will drill wearing Odinn's web, your byrnies.'

So it was back to the armoury to try to find byrnies that would fit us, and then we spent an entire day scouring and oiling their metal rings so they slid more smoothly and restricted our movements to a minimum. I still felt like a crab in its shell after I had tugged the mail shirt over my head and put on the cone-shaped metal helmet that the armourer issued to me. The helmet's central noseguard made me squint and I tried easing the chin strap and shifting the helmet so that I could see straight. A moment later a blow from behind me sent the helmet spinning to the ground and my instructor was snarling in my face.

'See this scar here?' he yelled, pointing at a groove that ran across his scalp. 'Got that from Courlander's sword when I left my helmet strap too loose.'

Recalling those sweaty, dusty days of training on the parade ground, I now understand that our instructor knew we were too raw to be any use on the battlefield unless we could be trained to work in unison. So he made us rehearse again and again the basic battlefield manoeuvres — staying in a tightly packed group as we wheeled to left or right, retreating in good order one step at a time, or forming a disciplined front when the first rank dropped on one knee so the spears of the second rank projected over their shoulders in a bristling hedge. Then, on his command, we all sprang to our feet and went charging forward, spears at the ready. Even in close combat, our instructor did not trust us to fight singly, one on one. He made us fight as pairs, one man knocking aside his opponent's shield, while his comrade stabbed a spear through the gap.

Only after we were reasonably proficient with the spear did he allow us to handle axes and swords. Then he showed us how to aim our blows rather than chop, hack and thrust indiscriminately. For our graduation class we learned the 'swine array', an arrowhead formation, a single man at the point, two men behind him in the second rank, three men in the third rank, four men behind them and so forth. On his command we all lumbered forward and to our amazement, for we were rehearsing against a shield burg of the older men, the weight of our charge broke their line, and our point man, the beefy Dane again, was thrust right through the opposition.

Each day, after drill and training, the recruits joined the senior members of the felag for the evening meal. I never imagined that so many words could be expended on discussing, for instance, the relative merits of the spear with a broad flange against the narrow-bladed spear, or whether it is better to sling a sword scabbard from the right or the left shoulder, and whether it should hang vertically or horizontally. Usually these discussions were accompanied by practical demonstrations. Some burly warrior would get up from his bench and strike a pose, grasping his spear shaft or sword hilt to show what he considered the proper grip, then making a series of mock passes with the weapon. After much drink had been consumed and arguments arose, it was remarkable that these differences of opinion did not lead to open fights between armed men who were both boastful and belligerent. But the rules of the Jomsviking fellowship held: each man considered the others to be his brothers.

Thrand, like myself, found many of these discussions tedious, and the two of us would leave the barracks and spend the evening strolling about the town of Jomi. Our initial impression of its prosperity had been correct. The place was thriving. Traders came from as far afield as the Greek lands to purchase the amber carvings for which the place was famous, though the majority of the merchants were from the other major Baltic ports – Hedeby, Bjorko, Sigtuna and Truso. Besides their pottery, furs, leather goods and other wares, they brought news of what was going on in the outside world. Knut, it seemed, had grown so powerful and rich that there was talk he might proclaim himself emperor of the north. Already he held both England and Denmark, and he was claiming sovereignty over Norway as well. The merchants, whose trade depended on continued peace, were divided as to the merits of Knut's ambition. Some thought it would be beneficial if all the northern lands were united under a single ruler; others feared that Knut's pretensions would lead to war. The traders who arrived from Sweden were the most sceptical. They were followers of the Old Ways and pointed out that Knut was increasingly under the influence of the followers of the White Christ, and that where Knut ruled the Christians followed. Among the townsfolk of Jomi, the Swedes had a sympathetic hearing, for although Christians were allowed to practise their religion in Jomi, the city council had ruled that their observances must be done discreetly. No church bells were allowed.

The traders had a finely tuned instinct for politics. One evening Thrand and I had gone to visit the temple of Svantevit, the local four-faced Wendish God. His sacred animal is a white stallion used for divination, and we had seen the priests lead out the horse and coax him between three rows of wooden stakes as they watched anxiously, believing that if the horse steps first with its right foot then their presaging is true. As Thrand and I re-entered the Jomsviking citadel, we found a delegation from Knut himself. To my delight the embassy was led by a man I recognised – one-legged Kjartan who had stood beside me when Edgar died in the boar hunt and had assisted my escape from London.

'Thorgils!' he exclaimed, thumping me on the shoulder with his fist. 'Who would have thought to find you here! It's good to see you.'

'How's Gisli the One Hand?' I asked.

'Fine, fine,' Kjartan replied, looking around at the parade ground. 'You can't imagine how good it is to be here, away from those canting Christians. I've still got those wax coins you gave me. I suppose you know that Archbishop Wulfstan, that wily schemer, died.'

'No, I hadn't heard.'

'Last year he finally went to meet his maker, as he would have

put it, and good riddance. But sadly his departure to join his
precious angels has had little effect on the king's court. There seem
to be just as many Christians in positions of power, and they are
making life difficult for the Old Believers. Queen Emma encourages
them, of course. She goes nowhere unless she is accompanied by a
pack of priests.'

'What about Aelfgifu?' It was a question I could not hold
back.

Kjartan gave me a shrewd glance and I wondered just how
much he knew.

'She's well, though we don't see much of her now. Either
she's at her father's place in Northampton or she travels overseas
as Knut's representative.'

At that point a trumpet sounded. The felag was called to
attend to a meeting in the great hall and Kjartan turned to go. 'I
hope we'll have the chance to remember our days in Northampton
and London,' he said.

The meeting was packed. Every Jomsviking, whether veteran
or recent recruit, had assembled to hear what Kjartan had to say.
He was escorted into the hall by two leading members of the
felag's ruling council, who introduced him to his audience. He
spoke clearly and firmly, and his soldierly bearing and battle
injury made his audience listen respectfully. His message was clear
enough: King Knut, ruler of England and Denmark and rightful
heir to the throne of Norway, invited the Jomsvikings to join his
cause. War was looming. The enemies of the king – Kjartan
described them as a league of resentful earls forgetful of their
oaths of loyalty, warlords from Norway and Sweden, and a false
claimant to the Norwegian throne – were assembling an army to
challenge Knut's authority. King Knut, of course, would crush
them, and in victory he would remember and reward those who
had helped him. There would be much booty to distribute – here
an appreciative murmur rose from the listening warriors – and
there was fame to be won.

Kjartan reminded his listeners of the renown of the Jomsvikings, their illustrious history and their prowess as fighting men. Finally, he proffered the bait that, all along, he knew would most tempt his audience. 'King Knut holds you in such high regard,' he announced, 'that he has authorised me to offer each one of you fifteen marks of silver if you agree to fight on his behalf, half to be paid now, and half to be paid on the conclusion of the campaign.'

It was a munificent offer and characteristic of Knut's statecraft: silver coins rather than iron weapons were his tools of preference.

When Kjartan had finished speaking, a senior member of the Jomsviking council rose to reply. It was a generous proposal, worthy of a generous ruler, he began. He himself would recommend acceptance, but it was the custom of the Jomsviking assembly that any member of the felag could state his views, whether for or against, and he called upon anyone who wished to express an opinion to speak up. One after another, Jomsvikings came forward to address the assembly. All were in favour of accepting Knut's offer, which was not surprising. The advance payment of fifteen marks for every man was an enticing prospect and it seemed that further discussion was a mere formality. Until Thrand spoke.

He had been sitting with the other members of the council, and when he rose to give his opinion a hush fell on the gathering. Everyone in the hall also knew that he was a survivor of the original felag.

'Brothers of the felag,' he began, 'before you make your decision whether or not to accept the King of England's offer, I want his emissary to answer one question.' Turning to Kjartan, he asked, 'Is it true that in agreeing to join King Knut's army, we could find ourselves fighting alongside, or even under the command of, Knut's deputy in military affairs: the leader of the royal huscarls, his earl known as Thorkel the Tall?'

The man standing beside me abruptly sucked in his breath, as though a raw nerve had been exposed. Behind Thrand several older members of the council looked uncomfortable.

'And am I right in thinking,' Thrand continued, 'that this same Thorkel, more than thirty years ago, broke his Jomsviking vow when he, with his crew, turned tail and abandoned his brothers who were left, unaided, to fight the Norwegian Haakon and his fleet?'

A terrible hush had fallen over the assembly. A few paces from me someone was whispering to his neighbour the story of the disgrace, when the honour of the Jomsvikings was shattered.

Kjartan rose to give his answer. All could see that he had been shaken. He had not anticipated this. Thrand's question implied that no Jomsviking should go to the assistance of a man who had betrayed the fellowship. We waited expectantly. The pause lengthened slowly and became an embarrassment. I felt sorry for Kjartan. He was a soldier, not a diplomat, and he could not come up with the fine words to wriggle out of the dilemma.

When he finally spoke he was hesitant. 'Yes, Knut's most trusted earl is the same Thorkel who was a member of your fellowship. Thorkel has become a great war leader, won riches, earned the confidence of the king. I believe that you should be proud of what he has become, rather than remember what happened thirty years ago.'

His words made little impression. I could feel the scepticism of the crowd grow around me, their mood suddenly changed. Kjartan felt it too. He knew that his mission was on the verge of collapse. He scanned the faces of the crowd. I was standing close to the front, looking up at him and, like all the others, waiting for him to continue. Our eyes met, and suddenly Kjartan announced.

'You don't have to take my word for it. One of your own brotherhood has met Thorkel the Tall at King Knut's court, and he can tell you about him now.' He beckoned to me and, after a moment's surprised hesitation, I stepped forward to stand beside him. He gripped my elbow and whispered in my ear, 'Thorgils, for the memory of Edgar the huntsman, try to say something to make them accept my proposal.'

Turning to face my audience, my breath seemed to leave my

lungs. A couple of hundred warriors were looking at me curiously and I could scarcely breathe. For the first time in my life I had been called upon to address a large gathering and my mind was in turmoil. I realised that I held the balance between two men to whom I owed great debts: Thrand, who had been my mentor over the years, and Kjartan, who had stood by me when I was in desperate need in England. I had to find a middle way without dishonouring either man.

Odinn came to my rescue.

I cleared my throat and, stammering over the first few syllables, said, 'I am Thorgils, a follower of Odinn, and I have always let the High One be my guide — Kjartan is my friend and I know him to be an honest man, so I believe he is carrying an honest message. Thrand is also my friend and has told me of the cowardice of Thorkel and the others in the fight against Earl Haakon. Yet I have seen how high Thorkel the Tall then rose in the court of King Knut, and I know that he would never have achieved such fame and wealth if he had stayed to fight and die. So I say — let Odinn's wisdom guide you, and accept this as his sign. Seventy survivors of our felag came before Earl Haakon for judgement, and this is the seventieth of the High One's sayings.'

Here I paused to draw breath before reciting:

'It is better to live than to lie a corpse,
I saw flames rise before a rich man's pyre
and before his door he lay dead.'

Kjartan saw his chance. He quoted the next verse for me.

'The lame rides a horse, the handless is herdsman
The deaf in battle is bold
No good can come of a corpse.'

A low mutter of approval came from the crowd, and a voice from the back shouted, 'Forget about Thorkel. Odinn had other plans for him. I'm all for the accepting Knut's silver.'

One by one, the members of the council spoke up and all

were in favour of Kjartan's proposition. Only Thrand failed to speak. He sat there silent, and on his face was the same distant expression that I had seen while he gazed into the ship's wake and thought of the defeat at Hjorunga Bay.

As the assembly began to dissolve, Kjartan took me aside to thank me. 'Your speech made all the difference,' he said. 'Without it, the men would not have committed themselves to fight for Knut.' Then he smiled. 'With my wooden leg, I liked the bit about the lame being able to ride a horse. But I'm not sure that when I get back to London I should tell Gisli One Hand that, according to you and Odinn, he should become a cowherd.'

'It was All-Father Odinn who spoke through me and swayed the minds of the audience,' I replied. What I did not tell Kjartan was that, after a month in Jomsburg, I knew that the new order of Jomsviking could never resemble the felag Thrand had known. The new Jomsvikings were driven by their thirst for silver, not glory, and in the end they would have accepted Knut's bribe whatever Thrand had said. By citing the High One, I had given Thrand a reason to accept their decision with no loss to his own sense of honour or duty to his fallen comrades.

ELEVEN

WE WERE SUMMONED to earn our fifteen marks of silver early in September. Knut moved against the forces massing to oppose him, and sent a messenger to tell the Jomsvikings to join his fleet, now on its way from England. His messenger slipped into our citadel disguised as a Saxon trader because Knut's enemies already lay between us and the man whose pay we had taken. To the west of Jomsburg a great Norwegian force was raiding Knut's Danish territories, while their allies, the Swedes, were harrying the king's lands in Skane across the Baltic Sea. This left the felag dangerously isolated and our council met to discuss how best we should respond. After much debate it was decided to send two shiploads of volunteers, the most experienced warriors, to run the gauntlet and join the king. The rest of the Jomsvikings, fewer than a hundred men, would remain to garrison the citadel against any enemy attack.

'Stay and complete your training,' Thrand advised me. He was packing his war gear into the greased leather bag which also served as his sleeping sack while on campaign. As one of the most experienced fighters in the felag, he had been appointed second in command of one of the two ships in our little expeditionary force. My speech in defence of Thorkel the Tall at the assembly seemed to have done no damage to our friendship, though Thrand was so taciturn that it was difficult to tell what he was thinking.

'I've already volunteered to join the expedition,' I told him. 'If I'm to take Knut's silver, then I feel I ought to earn it. Besides, our battle drills are becoming very repetitive.'

'As you wish,' said Thrand. He slid his sword halfway out of its scabbard to check the blade for rust, and then carefully eased it back into the sheath. The scabbard was lined with unwashed sheep wool, the natural oils in the fleece protecting the metal from decay. As an added precaution he began to wind a linen strip around the hilt to seal the gap where the blade entered the scabbard. He paused from the work and looked up.

'Be warned: Knut wants the Jomsviking as warriors in his line of battle. That is what you have trained for. But if it comes to a sea action, all that training is next to useless. There's no chance for the swine array or shield walls. Ship fights are close up and brutal. Most of the engagement is pitiless and chaotic, with a good deal of luck as to who emerges the victor.'

That afternoon I went to the armoury to withdraw my weaponry for the expedition. When I had been a new recruit, the crippled armourer had been casual, issuing me with a mail shirt in need of repair and the weapons that were closest to hand. This time, knowing that I was going into action, he took greater care, and I emerged from the armoury with a helmet that fitted me properly and a byrnie of a new design. Attached to the helmet was a small curtain of mail that hung across my lower face, protecting my throat. He also produced for me a good sword with an inlaid metal handle, two daggers, half a dozen javelins, an ash spear and a round limewood shield, as well as a short-handled battleaxe. When I stacked this assortment of weaponry on the ground beside Thrand, he commented, 'if I were you, I would change the grip on that sword. Wrap that showy metalwork with tarred cord so that your hand does not slip when your palm gets sweaty. And you'll need a second shield.'

'A second shield?'

'Every man brings a second shield. Nothing fancy, just a light wooden disc. They'll be arranged along the side of the vessel —

there's a special slot along the upper strake to hold them – and they'll make a fine display. In my experience much of warfare is decided by appearances. Strike fear into your enemy by how you look or act before the first blow and you've won half the battle.'

A spoked wheel with alternating fields of red, black and white was the pattern that the council chose for our insignia, and I had to admit it looked imposing when the shields were set in place. They gave our two ships a professional air, though a trained eye would have noted that the vessels, like the Jomsviking harbour, were antiquated and in a poor repair. The two drakkar, longships of medium size, were all that now remained of a Jomsviking fleet of thirty vessels, the great majority of which had been sunk or captured in Earl Haakon's time. These two survivors were leaky and their timbers were suspect. The felag's shipwrights had struggled to make them seaworthy, caulking seams and applying a thick layer of black pitch to the outside of the hulls. But the deck planks were warped and cracked, and there were splits and shakes in the masts. Fortunately the Jomsburg lowlands grew flax so we were able to obtain new sails and rigging at short notice. But nothing could hide the fact, as we set out on a bright and crisp September day, that our two vessels were unhandy and slow, and their sixty-man crews were badly out of practice as sailors.

A fully manned drakkar offers little comfort to her crew. By the time we had loaded aboard all our weapons and equipment, the spaces between the sea chests which served as our oar benches were so crammed with gear that there was very little room to move about. Our only gangway was a walkway of planks, laid along the middle of the vessel to connect the small platform in the bows of the drakkar with the stern deck, where our captain stood. He was a squat thug of a man, a Jute who had lost one eye in a minor skirmish and the wound made him look like a bandit. Indeed, as I glanced round at my companions with their diversity of homelands and racial features, I thought they looked more like a pirate crew than a trained fighting unit. The truth was that we were hired mercenaries, setting out for money and the chance of loot – I wondered how long our discipline and our loyalty to the felag would last.

Our inexperience showed in the chaos of our embarkation. We found our places about the drakkars, unlashed the oars from their stowage and fitted them to the thole straps. Men took practice pulls with their oars to test their length and find their own best position. Unless they were careful, they knocked into their neighbours or struck the man sitting directly in front, hitting him in the back with the loom of the oar. There were oaths and angry grumbling in several languages and it was some time before our captain was able to order the lines to be cast off. Our drakkars pulled slowly out of the harbour, their oars moving to an uneven beat as though we were two crippled insects.

The current was in our favour once we emerged through the disused harbour gates, and as we rowed towards the river mouth it became obvious which of our oarsmen had learned to row on rivers and lakes and which were proper seamen. Those from calmer waters pulled their oars in a long flat sweep, while the experienced mariners used a shorter, chopping action, and of course the two styles did not match. So there were more oaths and arguments among the rowers, until our drakkars began to pitch and roll on the first waves from the sea, and one of the river rowers sprained his wrist. Luckily there was a brisk east wind to speed us on our way, so we hoisted our brand-new sail, hauled the oars inboard and relaxed, leaving the Jutish captain and his helmsman to steer.

'Thank Svantevit for this wind,' said the Wend beside me, reaching inside his shirt and producing a little wooden image of his God. He found a niche for the talisman beside his seat and put it there, then nodded towards the flat shoreline on our left. 'Anyone know this coast?'

A man three places from us must have been a Sjaellander, for he answered, 'Used to sail past it with my uncle when we were bringing his farm produce to Rugen. Not much to see, but easy enough once you know the channels. Have to watch out for sand

and mudbanks, but there are plenty of creeks and bays handy for shelter if the wind blows up.'

'Rich country?' asked another voice hopefully.

'No, just farmlands; nothing of note until you get to Ringsted and that's Knut's domain, so I guess we'll be on our best behaviour if we stop there.'

'We won't be making any stops,' said a heavily bearded Skanian, one of our Danish volunteers. 'Rumour has it that Knut's fleet has left Limfiord and is heading for the sound and we're to rendezvous with him there.'

He spat over the side, and watched the spittle float away in our wake, judging the speed of our vessel. 'She's no racer,' he commented. 'In a wind like this she ought to be half as fast again.'

'Ballast's all wrong,' said a voice from somewhere amidships. 'She's too heavy in the bow.'

'Reckon the mast isn't stepped quite right either,' came a third opinion. 'Should be shifted aft a hand's breadth and the main halyard set up tighter.' As the discussion gathered pace I realised that sailors could spend as much time discussing the rig of their vessels as warriors in barracks spent comparing the merits of weapons.

That evening we landed on a stretch of deserted shore to make a meal and rest. There is no cooking hearth aboard a drakkar, so the crew eat cold food if they do not land. We brought the vessels close inshore, turned stern on, and after setting anchors to haul them off next morning, we backed water with the oars until the sterns touched the sand. That way, if there was an emergency or we needed to depart in a hurry, we could scramble aboard and leave in double-quick time. Not that we expected trouble. Few villages could muster enough men or courage to dispute the landing of two shiploads of armed men. The only glimpse we had of the local inhabitants was the distant figure of a shepherd running away down sand dunes to take a warning to his people. He left his flock behind, so we butchered ten of his sheep and feasted.

Next morning the wind was fluky, changing in strength and direction as we resumed our coastal passage. But the sun shone in a sky flecked with high, fast-moving white clouds. It felt like a holiday as we headed onward under sail, keeping well offshore.

'Wish all campaigning was like this,' commented the Sjaelander, who was proving to be the ship's chatterer.

By now most of the crew had learned how to make best use of the cramped space, stretching out on the lids of the storage chests that held their war gear. Folded sails and padded jerkins were their cushions. Thrand, I noticed, never joined us. As we sailed onward, he took up his position on the little foredeck, standing there watching the forward horizon or, more often, scanning the shoreline as we moved steadily northward.

Shortly before noon I became aware that Thrand's gaze had not shifted for some time. He was looking towards the land, his attention fixed. Something about his posture alerted me to turn around and look back at our captain. He was glancing in the same direction too, and then looking astern at the waves and sky, as if to check the wind speed and direction, and watching the bronze weathervane on our stern post. Everything seemed to be in good order. Our two ships were moving steadily forward, nothing had changed.

The Sjaelander, who had been stretched out on his back enjoying the warmth of the sun on his face, lazily rolled over on his side and raised his head to peer over the side of the drakkar. 'Soon be passing the entrance to the Stege Bight,' he said, and then, 'ah yes, there it is, I can see sails on the far side of that little island. They must be coming out from West Sjaelland.' He rolled back on his side and settled himself comfortably. 'Probably merchantmen on their way out to the sound.'

'If so, they've come to trade with swords not purses. Those are warships,' said the big Dane. He was standing on the oar bench, an arm shielding his eyes from the sun's reflection on the water, as he looked towards the distant sails. There was a sudden

stir among our crew. Men sat up and looked around, several got
to their feet and squinted in the same direction.

'How do you know they're warships?' asked one of the
Wends. He had been one of the river rowers and this was clearly
the first time he had been to sea.

'Some of those sails have stripes. Sign of a fighting ship,'
answered the Dane.

I looked at our own new sail. It was unmarked. 'Maybe they'll
mistake us for merchant ships as well.'

'I doubt it,' said the Dane. 'Merchant ships don't carry low,
broad sails like ours. Their sails are taller and not so wide. As
soon as they clear the island and get a good view of us, they'll
recognise the outline of a drakkar hull and know we're not a pair
of harmless trading ships. However, this may be a piece of luck.
West Sjaelland is ruled by Earl Ulf, one of Knut's liegemen, and
those ships could be on the way to reinforce Knut's war fleet.
We'll be able to sail in company with them and if we run into the
king's enemies they'll think twice about attacking such a large
force.'

When the strange ships emerged from behind the dunes and
into plain view, we saw that the big Dane had been correct, at
least in part. Five ships came out from the sound. Three were
drakkars like our own and two were trading knorrs, apparently
under escort. Their position put them slightly upwind of us, and
we watched them set their course to match our track, gradually
closing the gap between us, as if to join us.

It is a commonplace to say that everything happens slowly at
sea until the last moment, then all is haste and flurry, but it is
true. For a while very little happened as all seven vessels carried
steadily on their way – the five Danish ships sailing in company
while our own helmsmen kept the two Jomsviking vessels close
together, no more than fifty paces apart. As the gap between us
and the approaching squadron dwindled, we gazed across at the
strangers trying to learn more about them, until eventually our

own Dane was able to confirm that they were indeed Earl Ulf's men. He knew the earl's livery and even thought he recognised some of the warriors aboard. Their two knorrs were clearly troopships carrying Danish levies, and their slower speed meant that the junction between our squadrons was leisurely.

Finally, in early afternoon, the leading Danish drakkar had pulled slightly ahead of her consorts, and was close enough for our Jutish captain to call out a greeting. 'Well met,' he bellowed, cupping his hands around his mouth so the sound carried over the waves washing along his vessel's side. 'Any news of Knut's fleet? We go to join the king.'

There was a long delay and I saw the Danish captain turn to consult his colleagues on the aft deck. Then he looked back at us and shook his head to indicate that he had not understood. He gestured for us to slow down so the ships drew closer, and held his hand to his ear.

'We go to join the king!' our skipper called out yet again. The Danish captain stepped up on the bulwarks of his ship, and one of his men reached and gripped him by the belt to hold him steady as if a slightly smaller gap would make the sound carry more clearly. 'Have you news of the royal fleet?' yelled our captain, adjusting the helm so that the wind spilled from our sail and our drakkar lost speed through the water.

'Watch out!' — a sudden roar from our fore deck. Most of our crew swung round to see Thrand standing there, waving an arm in warning. Those who did not look at Thrand saw one of the Danes on the aft deck stoop down and produce a javelin, hidden behind the bulwark, and hand it up to their skipper. He drew back his arm and threw the missile across the narrowing gap. Either it was a very lucky throw or the Dane was a champion spearsman, for the weapon flew across between the ships and struck our Jutish captain in his side. Even above the sound of the waves I heard the soft thump as the metal point of the weapon sank into his unprotected ribs. The Jute staggered and fell, knocking down the helmsman. There was a rush of feet, and

Thrand raced past us along the central walkway, his feet pounding the boards. He reached the aft deck, leaped to the helm and flung his weight on the bar, heaving it across so that our vessel sheered away downwind, and presented her stern to the attacking Danish ship.

'Ease the starboard sheet, square away,' he shouted.

The rest of us had been taken completely off guard. We were sitting or standing, numb with shock.

'Jump to it!' bellowed Thrand. He glanced back over his shoulder, judging the distance between our vessel and the hostile Danish longship. Our drakkar's sudden swerve had taken the Danes by surprise and for a moment they had overshot their quarry. There was confusion on their deck as they too adjusted sail to follow in our wake.

'I thought Ulf's people were king's men,' shouted the Wend beside me.

'Not all of them, it seems,' muttered the Sjaellander, as shocked as any of us by the sudden attack. 'There's treachery somewhere.'

Our entire crew was in turmoil. Some were searching for shields and weapons, others frantically donning their padded jackets, and opening the store chests to pull out their byrnies. Only a handful who were sensible enough to attend to the ship were checking that sheets and halyards were set up taut, and our venerable drakkar was sailing to best advantage.

Our consort, the second Jomsviking drakkar, had seen the ambush and was also adjusting sail. Our sudden swerve had taken them by surprise too, and we nearly collided with them as we changed course, passing within ten paces of the startled crew. That close encounter was nearly their undoing, for we were to windward and, as we passed, we took the wind from their sail and their drakkar lost speed. The pursuing Danes promptly switched their pursuit from us to our floundering consort. They swooped in close enough to launch a barrage of spears and stones, which rained down on the hapless Jomsvikings and we saw several men fall.

Now the Danes were roaring in triumph. One of them held up a red-painted shield, the sign of war. A warrior seated ahead of me cursed and left his oar bench to run aft to the stern deck, javelin in hand. He made ready to throw, but Thrand, without even looking round, reached out and held his arm.

'Don't waste the weapon,' he said. 'They are out of range. Keep your strength for rowing if it comes to that.'

By now our consort had managed to adjust her sail to the course and was beginning to pick up speed. The captain of the leading Danish longship was unwilling to close and board her in case we turned back to help and he found himself tackling two drakkars at the same time. We watched his crew delicately spill the wind from her huge sail with its red, green and white stripes, so she slowed in the water and allowed the two other Danish longships to catch up. The troop-carrying knorrs were left behind now that the trap was sprung. The Danes were intent on finishing off their prey, but they would do so in their own time.

The outcome of the chase was clear from the start. Our drakkars were built to an outmoded design. Old and worn-out, they could not match the speed of the Danish ships and the inexperience of our crews increased our handicap. The landsmen among us fumbled vital ropes and got in the way of those who knew what they were doing as they went about the delicate task of extracting the best possible speed from our drakkar. These novices were harshly commanded to sit still and shift position only when ordered to, and then to move smartly to the place indicated and stay there until instructed otherwise. They were movable ballast. The only time they were actively involved was when Thrand, who had assumed command, ordered every loose item on board, except our weapons and oars, to be thrown overboard to lighten the ship. Then the landsmen were set to prising up from the bilges the heavy stones which acted as our ballast and tossing them in our wake. But it made little difference to the pursuit. We watched the splashes as the pursuing Danes lightened their vessels too and slowly gained on us.

With the wind directly aft, our hope was that we could keep ahead of the chasing Danes long enough to evade them in the darkness or, better, meet friendly vessels from Knut's war fleet who would scare them off. Until then every member of our crew watched intently, trying to gage whether the gap between ourselves and the pursing longships was increasing or diminishing. Occasionally we glanced across at our consort, who copied our every manouevre and stratagem because it was vital that the two of us kept together. For when − not if − the Danes caught up with us, at least the odds would be no worse than three to two against us.

The Gods, whether Wendish or the Aesir, seemed to smile on us. The wind, which had continued to be erratic, picked up strength. This helped the older vessels because, in a strong wind, there was less difference in their speed against the newer Danish ships, and the more ground we covered the better were our chances of meeting Knut's fleet. So we kept up full sail, even though we could all hear the mast foot grinding in its wooden socket. The wind raised a succession of fast-moving swells which swept beneath us, heaving up the ancient hulls and making them twist and groan. The swell turned into long breaking waves, the spray flew back from the bows and as our craft began to swoop and sway the stress on the elderly hulls became more and more obvious.

That was when disaster struck. Perhaps it was the absence of ballast, or it might have been the clumsiness of her inexperienced crew which brought our companion, the second Jomsviking drakkar, to make a fatal error. The accident happened so suddenly that we did not know whether a main sheet snapped or the mast step slipped on the keelson, or whether it was just plain bad fortune that a larger swell lifted up our accompanying drakkar's stern at the very moment she dipped her bow to leeward and skidded sideways on the forward rush of water. The drakkar abruptly buried her nose in the back of a wave, tripped and slewed, and water began to pour into her open hull. Without her ballast to hold her steady, her sail was driving her forward at full tilt, and the inrush of water plunged her even further downwards. She ran herself underwater. One moment she was sailing at full speed on the surface, the next moment she was on her side, bow down and half submerged. The halt was so abrupt that most of her crew were flung headlong into the water, while the remainder were left clinging onto the stern deck, which was all that was left above the surface of the sea.

From the Danes came a roar of triumph and there were frantic signals from the leading longship, clearly the commander of their squadron. In answer the vessel nearest to the stricken drakkar swiftly dropped sail, put out oars and began to row, bearing down on her disabled victim. As our own boat fled on, we looked back, unnerved, and saw the Danes reach our comrades. They began spearing them like salmon trapped in a net, stabbing repeatedly downward on the swimmers. Those who were not massacred, had already drowned, pulled down by the weight of their mail. There would be no survivors.

Only Thrand seemed unmoved by the calamity. He stood on the aft deck, gaunt and intense, the helm still in his hand, his face showing no emotion as he kept his attention fixed on the set of our sail, the strength and direction of the wind and the balance of our vessel. Just twice he glanced back over his shoulder at the slaughter in our wake and then – without warning – he suddenly pushed across the helm so that our drakkar heeled over and came hard on the wind, heading for the distant shore. He gave no explanation for the sudden change of course, and once again the abruptness of the manoeuvre caught the Danes by surprise. We gained a few precious boat lengths on them. Along the oar benches we looked at one another, wondering what Thrand had in mind. Not one of us challenged his decision. From the moment he had seized the helm, he became our unquestioned leader. I swivelled in my seat and looked forward over the bows. Ahead the Sjaelland coast stretched away on either hand, low and flat without any sign of a harbour or a channel into which we might escape. Yet Thrand was aiming our vessel straight towards the distant shore as if he had a plan to save us.

The captains of the two Danish ships must have been equally perplexed because the furious pace of their pursuit slackened while they conferred, shouting across the gap between their vessels. Then they decided that, whatever we intended, they could still overhaul us before we reached the land. I saw their white bow waves surge up again and the slant of their masts increase as the two ships hardened up against the wind and resumed the chase. Aboard our drakkar the entire crew except for five sail handlers had scrambled to the windward side to improve the vessel's trim. Even the greenest of our recruits now knew that our lives depended on how well we coaxed our venerable vessel to her best performance.

Slowly and inexorably the Danish ships gained on us, while in the far distance the third of their vessels, having finished off our comrades, hoisted sail and set out to join in the hunt. We could only sit and watch the advancing enemy, and note how the best of their warriors had assembled in the bows, ready to hurl javelins at our helmsman the moment they were in range, hoping to strike him down and cripple our flight.

One of the Wends reached under his oar bench, pulled out his chain-mail shirt and began to tug it over his head.

'That'll drown you if we capsize,' warned his neighbour. 'Didn't you see what happened with our other drakkar?'

'Makes no difference,' the Wend replied. 'I don't know how to swim.'

The tension mounted as we watched the shoreline rush closer. It still appeared featureless, a low, sandy, yellow beach backed by dunes and sea grass. The place was uninhabited. There were no fishing skiffs drawn up on the beach, no houses, nothing – only gulls circling hungrily, squabbling amongst themselves over a shoal of sprats.

'No one lives here. It's too barren,' said the Sjaellander who had previously sailed this coast. 'There are only shallows, mudbanks and the occasional sand spit.'

The Danes very nearly caught us. Their leading ship was close enough for the first javelins to be thrown, and an arrow or two whizzed overhead, but without any harm. Judging his moment, Thrand again pushed over the rudder bar and altered course abruptly. Our drakkar swerved, and like two greyhounds which overshoot the hare as it jinks, the Danish vessels overreached and had to check their onward rush before they picked up the hunt again. Thrand had managed his manoeuvre well. The leading Danish ship cut across the bows of its companion and for a few moments there was confusion as they adjusted sails to avoid a collision.

By then Thrand had turned our drakkar back onto her original course and once again we were heading straight for the shore at full pace. He was staring forward intently, ignoring the chasing ships behind him as we sped towards the strand. We were already in the outer surf before I understood what he intended. Ahead of us a long outer bank of sand ran parallel to the beach itself. Waves were breaking across the ridge of the sandbank, washing into the shallow lagoon which lay on the far side.

'We're going to smash to pieces when she hits,' muttered the man seated next to me. 'At this speed she'll burst her planks like a barrel loses staves when the hoops let go.'

'We've no choice,' I answered. 'It's either that or be run down by the longships.'

Our course did seem suicidal. In the last fifty paces approaching the sandbar our drakkar was picked up by each wave and flung forward bodily. We heard the surf hissing all around us. Our bellying sail continued to drive the vessel onward, the pace never slackening, until our progress had a wild, lurching motion. When the water shallowed and the waves became steeper, I saw Thrand suddenly snatch out the bar from the rudder. A moment later the rudder blade, projecting below our keel, struck the sand beneath us and the rudder head swung forward. Now we were completely out of control, without any steering. A sudden scraping shock ran through the hull as the keel hit the ridge of the sandbar. Then came a deeper hissing sound as the keel ploughed on through the sand, and we felt the hull scrape on the sandbank beneath our feet. The impact snapped the mast. It toppled forward, taking the sail with it and knocking the foredeck man into the water. Luckily he grabbed the side of the ship as he fell and managed to hang on, dangling there until he could heave himself back aboard. For a moment the drakkar floundered on the flat crest of the sandbank, her mast lying over the side, sail dragging in the water. But the sheer weight of her headlong rush had carried her to the crest of the submerged barrier, and a moment later a fortunate wave broke at just the right instant and washed her over the sandbar. With a grinding, slithering wrench our vessel scraped into the lagoon, more of a wreck than a ship.

The pursuing Danes promptly put up their helms and swerved away. Their captains had seen how close we had come to complete destruction. 'Reckon their keels draw maybe a span more water than we do,' commented one of our sailors. 'Reckless to try the bar and risk such fine new ships as theirs, not like our ramshackle old hull.'

'She did us well, didn't she?' enquired one of our landsmen.

'Yes' answered the sailor. 'For now.'

'What do you mean?' the man asked, but after a moment's thought he added, 'we're trapped, aren't we?'

Before anyone could reply, Thrand called for our attention. He stood on the stern deck looking down at us as our crippled vessel floated gently on the lagoon. After the hustle and panic of the chase everything had gone so quiet that he barely had to raise his voice. 'Brothers of the felag,' he began, 'now is the time we honour our oath to our fellowship. Even now our enemies are patrolling the sandbank, searching for a channel where they can safely enter the lagoon. When they find it, they will advance on us and we must prepare to fight and, if the Gods so decide, die as Jomsvikings.'

We had a respite before the Danes came at us again. We spent the interval cutting away the wreckage of the mast and disposing of the sail, and the tallest of our men waded ashore to collect large stones where a small stream washed into the lagoon and had exposed the bedrock. Then we put our drakkar in fighting trim, the decks cleared fore and aft, our sea chests arranged to make a fighting platform, and every man armed and wearing his byrnie and knowing his battle station. Thrand himself took up position once again on the bow platform, where the extra height of the upswept bow would give him best advantage. I went to join him, but he gently pushed me back. 'No,' he said, 'I need men here who are battle-tried,' and he beckoned to a Gothlander to join him. I was puzzled because the man seemed slightly mad. While we had been readying the ship for battle, he had stayed off to one side by himself, muttering and laughing into his beard, then suddenly scowling as if he saw an imaginary demon.

'Thorgils, there is something more important you must do,' Thrand said quietly. He was unwinding a cloth which had been tied around his waist like a sash. 'Go aft to the weathervane,' he continued. 'Remove the vane from its staff and in its place put this.' He handed me the cloth. The fabric was a dirty white, old and frayed. 'Go on,' Thrand said sharply, 'Hurry. It is Odinn's banner. It flew when we met Earl Haakon.'

Then I knew. Thrand had told me about the banner when I was his pupil in Iceland, but he had not mentioned that he was speaking from personal experience. Odinn's flag bears no emblem. But in battle all those who truly believe in the All-Father can read their fate upon it, for they see the figure of Odinn's bird, the raven, upon the cloth. If the raven struts and spreads its wings, then victory is assured. When it lowers its head and mopes, defeat is due. As I fastened the cloth to its staff, I tried my hardest to see the raven sign. But I could detect nothing, only a few creases and ancient stains on the fabric.

The banner hung limp from the staff, for the wind had died completely. I glanced up at the sky. It was the calm before a storm. Far to the north black clouds were gathering and the sky had an ominous, heavy overcast. In the distance I saw the flicker of a lightning strike and much later heard the faint and distant echo of thunder. Thor, not Odinn, seemed to be the God of that day.

I had barely lashed the banner in place when the Danes appeared, rowing along the length of the lagoon. They must have found a safe entry channel through the sandbar. Seeing that we made no move to escape and were helpless, they paused deliberately to lower their masts for fighting action. Then they set course to approach us, one from each side, forcing us to divide our defence. But to carry out the manoeuvre they had to row, and this cancelled out their advantage in numbers because a third of their men stayed seated as oarsmen. Also they failed to anticipate how well we had prepared. Their first over-confident approach was met with a hail of the stones and rocks we had gathered, which caught them completely off guard. The Danes could respond only with a few arrows and thrown spears which did little harm, while our barrage of well-directed missiles sent three of their men sprawling on top of their comrades at the oars. Our second barrage was even better aimed and the oarsmen on both Danish ships hurriedly backed water as their captains ordered a temporary withdrawal while they reassessed the situation. It was then that I heard a strange, wild howling burst out. Looking round to where Thrand stood on the foredeck, I saw that the Gothlander had thrown off his helmet and removed his byrnie. He was now standing on the foredeck, naked from the waist and baying like a wild animal as he faced the enemy. He was a hulking, hairy-chested man and his pelt of body hair made him look a gross animal or a troll. He was raving and grimacing, now leaping up on the top rail and dancing in derision as he hurled insults at the enemy, then jumping down to the deck and capering back and forth and waving his war axe so wildly that I thought he would accidentally strike Thrand, who stood beside him. Eventually the berserker quietened down, but then picked up his shield and began biting its top edge furiously.

The savage sight made our foes even more cautious and for their second attack they took their time. They circled our ancient drakkar like a pair of wolves despatching a lame stag. In unison they darted in, one from each side, and then quickly pulled back after the warriors on their bow platforms had thrown a javelin or two and drawn our response of stones and rocks. Three or four times they launched these brief attacks until they saw that our supply of missiles was exhausted, then they came again, this time to close and board us.

I was standing in the waist of our drakkar, facing the starboard side so all I saw was the onslaught from that direction. It was terrifying. Four heavily armed Danes stood in the bows, ready to leap down on us as their vessel struck us amidships. They were big men, and made even bigger by the fact that they had the advantage of height and towered over us. Remembering our war instruction, I stood upon a sea chest and overlapped my shield with the Wend beside me on my left, while the man on my right did the same for me, though it was difficult to find secure footing on the uneven platform. We tried to slant our spears upward, hoping to impale our enemies as they leaped down upon our deck, but our awkward stance made the shield wall ragged and unstable, and the spear points wavered. As it turned out, our preparations were ineffectual. We were braced for the shock of the oncoming bows when, behind us, the second Danish ship rammed our vessel amidships, and our drakkar gave a sudden lurch so that we stumbled and slipped, and our shields separated, leaving wide gaps between them. If our enemies had been alert they could have burst through the gaps, but instead they misjudged. The first of the Danes jumped for our vessel too soon, and only his right foot landed on the edge of our drakkar. He stood there momentarily off balance, and I had the presence of mind to step forward and thrust the metal rim of my shield in his face, so that he overbalanced backwards and fell into the sea. Out of the corner of my eye I saw a spear point come from behind me and pass over my left shoulder to thrust neatly into the unprotected groin of the second Danish boarder. The Dane doubled up in pain and grasped the spear shaft. 'Like sticking boar in a forest,' said my companion the Wend with a satisfied grin, as he wrenched the weapon free. He had little time to gloat any further. The Danish longship was well handled. Their oarsmen were already swinging the vessel so she lay alongside us and the rest of their fighting men could board. A moment later there was a thud as the two ships came together and there was a yelling, stampeding rush as our enemies leaped into our ship.

If the Danes had expected an easy victory, they were quickly disillusioned. The Jomsvikings may have been inept sailors, but they were dogged fighters. We held our own, against odds of two to one, and the first Danish onslaught was met with skill and discipline. We remembered our training and we fought as brothers. Shoulder to shoulder with the unknown Wend, I deliberately jabbed my spear point into the shield of the next Dane to charge us, and his onward rush drove the weapon deep into the wood. Then I twisted on the spear shaft so the shield was forced aside. At that instant the Wend stepped forward nimbly with his axe and struck the unprotected Dane at the base of the neck, felling him as neatly as an ox in a slaughterhouse. I heard the Wend give a grunt of satisfaction. I tugged my spear to retrieve it, but the weapon was stuck fast. I abandoned it, as I had been trained to do, and stepped back into line, reaching for the battleaxe that hung by my left shoulder. On all sides men were shouting and roaring, and there was the constant thud of blows and the ring of metal striking metal. Over the clamour I heard the shout of the Danish captain calling on his men to fall back and regroup. Suddenly the enemy were at arm's length, backing away from us and then scrambling aboard their longship, which was then pushed clear and drifted free.

In the breathing space which followed I turned to see what had happened behind us. Here, too, the initial Danish attack had been beaten off. Several bodies lay on the deck of the other vessel, which had also pushed away from us. Our own losses had been minimal. Half a dozen wounded and one man dead. The wounded were slumped on the deck and their sea chests, moaning in pain.

'Close up! Stand fast! There'll be another attack,' came Thrand's shout. He was still on the foredeck, the shield on his left arm splintered and battered, and a bloodied battleaxe held loosely in his right hand. Instantly recognisable, he alone of all the Jomsvikings had chosen to wear the old-fashioned battle helmet with its owl-like eye guards, while the rest of us wore the armoury's conical helmets. Thrand's antiquated war gear reminded me of our time-honoured battle standard and I squinted aft at Odinn's banner. The flag was now flapping and snapping in the wind. In the heat of battle I had failed to notice that the leading edge of the storm was now upon us. The sky was black from horizon to horizon. Gusts of wind tore the surface of the sea. I felt the old drakkar swing as the wind buffeted her ancient hull. We were drifting, all three ships, across the surface of the lagoon and towards the shallows. I also caught a glimpse of the third Danish longship. She was arriving with fresh men aboard and soon the odds would be three to one. I knew then that we had no hope. I glanced again at Odinn's banner, but still saw only the plain white cloth slatting in the gathering gale.

The Danes were shrewd. The crew of the newly arrived longship lashed their vessel to another one and the two ships together formed a single fighting platform. Then they rowed upwind of us, shipped their oars and began to drift down on our drakkar. Now they had no need of oarsmen. Every one of their men was free to fight. Their third vessel positioned herself to attack, once again, on our opposite side.

The crunching impact of the rafted longships stove in our

drakkar's topmost plank. I heard the ancient wood crack as the vessels collided. Our boat heeled with the weight of the sudden rush of the main Danish fighting force as their warriors jumped aboard. Some tripped and stumbled, and these men were despatched with an axe blow to the back of the head. But the sheer weight of comrades piling aboard behind them pushed their vanguard forward and broke our line. We were forced to give way and in a pace or two found ourselves back to back with our comrades who were trying to defend themselves against the attack from the opposite side. We fought viciously, either in desperation or because we believed in our oath to felag. Certainly not a single Jomsviking broke ranks. Spears were useless at such close quarters so we hacked with axes and stabbed with daggers. It was impossible to draw or to swing a sword. Shields were thrown aside as they split or splintered, and soon we were relying on our helmets and byrnies to turn aside the weapons of our enemies.

Gradually we retreated, step by step, towards the stern of our drakkar, our dwindling band packed so tightly that when the Wend beside me took an axe blow in the neck, his body stayed upright for several moments before it eventually slipping down at my feet. My shield arm shook to the impact of blows from the Danish axes and clubs, and the leather-bound shield began to disintegrate. I gasped for breath through the chain-mail curtain which hung across my face. My whole body ran with sweat within the padded jacket under the byrnie. Rivers of sweat ran down from my helmet and stung my eyes. I felt desperately tired, scarcely able to swing a counter-blow with my own axe. From sheer exhaustion I longed to drop my shield arm and rest. My vision blurred with glimpses of open-mouthed, yelling Danes hacking and thrusting and slashing, sometimes the blows directed at me, sometimes at my comrades on each side. I began to stagger and sway with a strange lassitude. I felt as if I was wading through a swamp of mud that sucked at my feet and legs.

I was slipping away into oblivion and a great blackness began to gather around me when an icy stinging sensation flicked at my eyes. Peering past the noseguard, I realised that our battle was shrouded in a sudden summer hailstorm. A clatter of large hail-stones struck my metal helmet and suddenly my feet were slipping and skidding on the crunching white surface that covered the deck. It became very cold. The hail was so intense that gusts of the squall blew ice grains under the rims of our helmets and into our faces. It was difficult to see the full length of the drakkar, yet in the distance I glimpsed Odinn's banner waving at the stern post. I blinked to clear my eyes, and it might have been my utter exhaustion or the roaring of the blood in my ears that affected my sight, but I saw the raven, black and bloodthirsty, and it turned to look towards me and slowly lowered its knowing, wise head. At that moment a great agony erupted in my throat. My breath stopped.

I woke to a terrible pain in my gullet every time I breathed. I was lying face downwards, wedged between two oar benches. My left arm was trapped underneath something heavy which proved to be the corpse of the Abdorite who had been our instructor at Jomsburg. In his death throes he had toppled across me, pinning me down. Cautiously and painfully, each breath drawn as gently as possible through my tormented windpipe, I wriggled clear and raised my head to look along the length of the vessel. I could hear nothing except the faint slap of waves against the hull. There was no movement, no one standing on the deck. Everything seemed very still, and dark. It was night-time and our drakkar was silent. Pain sliced through me as I shifted my weight and carefully eased myself along the thwart. I heard a groan, but could not tell where it came from. All around me the oar benches were littered with bodies, Danes and Jomsvikings together. Dizzy from the effort, I began to crawl towards the foredeck where I had last seen Thrand.

I found him slumped down on the deck, his back against the bulwark. Even in the dim light I could see the rent in his byrnie over his chest. He was still wearing his antiquated helmet and I thought he was dead until I saw the faint movement of his eyes behind eye guards.

He must have seen my crab-like approach for his voice said softly, 'Odinn must love you, Thorgils.'

'What happened? Where are we?' I croaked.

'Where we met our fate,' he replied.

'Where are the Danes?'

'Not far away,' he said. 'They withdrew to their ships when it became too dark. Nightfall came early in the storm and they dread killing anyone in the dark in case the victim returns to haunt them as undead. At dawn they will return to finish off the wounded and strip the corpses.'

'Is there no one left?' I asked.

We fought well,' he answered. 'None better. The Jomsvikings are finished.'

'Not all of them. I can help you get away from here.'

Thrand made a faint gesture and I looked down. His legs were stretched out flat on the deck before him and I saw that his right foot was missing.

'Always the weak point in a ship battle,' he said. 'You defend yourself with your shield and someone crouches beneath a thwart until you are close enough for him to hack at your leg.'

'But I can't abandon you,' I said.

'Leave me, Thorgils. I'm not afraid to die.' And he quoted the High One:

> 'The sluggard believes he shall live for ever
> If the fight he faces not
> But age shall not grant him the gift of peace,
> though spears may spare his life.'

Reaching forward, he grasped my forearm.

'Odinn sent that storm for a purpose. He brought the early darkness to preserve you from the final slaughter of the wounded. You must go now and find King Knut. Tell him that the Jomsvikings kept their word. He must not think we failed to honour our hire. Tell him also that Earl Ulf is a traitor, and inform Thorkel the Tall that the dishonour of Hjorunga Bay has been expunged, and that it was Thrand who led the felag to their duty.'

He sank back, exhausted. There was a long silence. I was so tired that, even had I wanted to, I felt I had no strength to leave the drakkar. I only wanted to lie down on the deck and rest. But Thrand would not let me. 'Go on, Thorgils, go,' he said softly, and then as if there was no doubt, he added, 'you saw the raven. Defeat was Odinn's will.'

Every movement was agony as I took off the heavy byrnie. Its chain-mail throat guard had stopped the sword slash from taking off my head but had left me choking. I dragged off the padded undercoat and pulled myself across to the gap in the bulwark where the Danes had smashed into us. I was too bruised and exhausted to do anything more than lower myself though the gap and into the lagoon. The shock of the cold water revived me for a moment and I tried to swim. But I was too tired. My legs sank downward and I resolved to let go of the boat and allow myself to drown. To my surprise my feet touched the ground. Our drakkar must have drifted far enough into the shallows for me to stand. Slowly, half swimming, half walking, I headed for the shore, until I was able to lurch up the beach. My feet sank into the drier sand, and I stumbled over the first clump of dune grass and fell. I picked myself up, knowing that I had to put as great a distance as possible between myself and the Danes.

As I crossed the first of the dunes I looked back towards the drakkar and saw a point of light. It was a tiny burst of flame. It died down and then flared up and grew brighter. I remembered the pitch which the shipwrights had used to revive our ancient vessel inside and out, and knew that she would burn well. But whether it was Thrand who set the fire, or some other survivor of the fight, it was impossible to tell. I only knew that by daylight the last warship of the Jomsvikings would have burned down to the waterline.

TWELVE

It took me nearly two weeks to walk or, rather, stumble to Knut's headquarters at the town of Roskilde. I was crossing the lands of Earl Ulf, whom I knew to be a traitor, so I avoided human contact, skirting around villages and sleeping under hedges or in the lee of earth banks. I have no clear memory of how each day of that grim journey was spent, only that my nights were filled with terrible visions of violence and death. When it rained, I awoke shivering with cold and fear, the rain drops on my face reviving images of grotesquely swirling storm clouds, the vanquished raven and an image which at the time had seemed so malevolent that I had buried it deep in my thoughts – a black hag riding on the wind. Once or twice I could have sworn that Thrand sat somewhere close to me in the shadows, a pool of black blood leaking from his leg. I lay numb with despair, wondering if my second sight had summoned his ghost from the dead, only to realise that I was alone and close to madness. When hunger drove me to knock on the doors of cottages along my path to beg for charity, my throat was so badly bruised that the inhabitants thought I was a mute. I had to gesture with my hands to make myself understood. They gave me scraps of food occasionally. More often they drove me away with kicks and curses, or set their dogs on me.

In the end it was Odinn who relieved my plight. I crept into Roskilde like a vagrant, filthy and wild-eyed, and was promptly arrested by a sentry. Odinn had arranged that Kjartan, the one-handed huscarl, was commander of the guard that day, and when I was brought before him, he looked at me with astonishment.

'Thorgils, you look as though you have been chewed over by Nidhoggr, the corpse-tearer!' he said. 'What in Thor's name has happened to you?'

I glanced towards my captor, and Kjartan took the hint. He sent the sentry back to his post, then made me sit down and eat a meal before he heard my story. My battered throat allowed me only to swallow a bowl of lukewarm gruel before I told him of the ambush and destruction of the Jomsviking expedition sent to join Knut.

When I finished, Kjartan sat silent for a moment. 'This is the first I've heard of it,' he said. 'Your battle with the Danes was fought at a place so remote that no one knows about it. I presume the victors put to sea after binding up their wounds and, if they were Earl Ulf's men acting treacherously, then they would have kept quiet because events overtook them.'

'What do you mean?' I asked hoarsely.

'While you and the Jomsvikings were waylaid off Sjaeland, the king and his fleet caught up with his enemies off the coast of Skane. There was a great battle in the estuary of Holy River. Both sides are claiming the victory, and frankly I think we were lucky that we did not suffer a major defeat. But at least the Swedes and Norwegians have been thwarted for the time being.' Then he paused and asked, 'I need to be sure about this – when did you say the Jomsvikings were ambushed?'

'I lost track of time during my journey here,' I said, 'but it was about two weeks ago.'

'You had better tell your story to the king in person. I can arrange that. But don't say a word to anyone else until you've had your audience with him.'

'I would like to tell Thorkel the Tall,' I said. 'Thrand's last words to me were that I was to inform Thorkel that the dishonour of Hjorunga Bay had been wiped away.'

Kjartan looked at me. 'So you don't know about the changes at Knut's court.'

'What's happened?' I asked.

'You can't speak to Thorkel, that's for sure. He's dead. Died in his bed, amazingly enough. Never expected it from such an inveterate warrior. So he'll never get Thrand's message unless the two of them exchange news in Valholl, if that's where they have both gone. Thorkel's death was a setback for Knut. The king had appointed him regent here in Denmark, and when he died Earl Ulf took his place.'

'But it was Earl Ulf's men who attacked us,' I blurted.

'Precisely. That is why it would be wise if you did not tell anyone else about the Jomsvikings' ambush.'

Kjartan must have had considerable influence with the royal secretariat because my interview with the king took place that same evening. It was held in secret, away from the king's official residence. Only the three of us were present – Kjartan, myself and the husband of the woman I still loved.

For the first time I was able to see Knut close to, and of course I judged him jealously. The king was on his way to an official banquet, for he was wearing a brilliant blue cloak held at the right shoulder by a gold buckle, a tunic of fine linen with a thread of gold running through it, gold-embroidered bands at the hem and cuffs, scarlet leggings and cross gaiters. Even his soft leather shoes had lines of gold stitched in square patterns. He radiated authority, privilege and virility. What impressed me most was that he was almost my own age, perhaps three or four years older. I did a quick mental calculation. He would have been leading an army while he was in his teens and I was still a youngster in Vinland. I felt inadequate by comparison. I doubted that Aelfgifu had found me a satisfactory substitute. Knut had a magnificent physique, well proportioned and robust. Only his nose marred his good looks. It was prominent, thin and slightly hooked.

But that deficit was more than made up for by his eyes, which were large and wide-set and gave him a level, confident gaze as he stared at me while I stumbled huskily through my account.

When I had finished, Knut looked at Kjartan and asked bluntly, 'Is this true?'

'Yes, my lord, I've known the young man for some time and I can vouch for his honesty as well as his bravery.'

'He's not to tell his story to anyone else?'

'I've told him not to, my lord.'

'Well, he's certainly earned his pay. How much did we promise the Jomsvikings?'

'Fifteen marks of silver each man, my lord. Half in advance. Final payment to be made after they had fought for you.'

'Well, that's a bargain! They fought, it seems, and now there's only one of them to collect his pay. I'll double it. See to it that the paymaster gives him thirty marks. And make sure, also, that he's kept out of sight. Better yet, arrange to have him sent away, somewhere far off.'

The king turned on his heel, and was gone. Knut's brusque dismissal left me wondering whether he knew about my affair with Aelfgifu.

As Kjartan escorted me back to his own lodgings, I dared to ask, 'Is the queen, Aelfgifu, I mean, is she here with the king?'

Kjartan stopped. He turned to me in the darkness, and I could not see his expression but his voice sounded more serious than I had ever heard him. 'Thorgils,' he said, 'let me give you some advice, though I know it is not what you want to hear. You must forget Aelfgifu. Forget her completely, for your own safety. You do not understand about life at court. People act differently when they are close to the seat of power. They have particular reasons and motives and they pursue them ruthlessly. Aelfgifu's son, Svein, is now ten years old. He takes after his father in looks and manner, and she is ambitious for him to be Knut's heir rather than the children of Queen Emma. She will do anything to further his chances.'

I tried to interrupt. 'I never knew she had a son; she never told me.'

Kjartan's voice ground on remorselessly, overriding my half-hearted objection. 'She has two sons, in fact. If she failed to mention them to you, that makes my point. They were fostered out at an early age. They grew up in Denmark while Aelfgifu was in England. Right now she's playing for very high stakes – no less than the throne of England. If she thinks that you are a threat because of anything that happened at Northampton . . . I'm not accusing you of anything, Thorgils. I just want you to realise that Aelfgifu could be a danger to you. She has a ruthless streak, believe me.'

I was stunned. First I had lost Thrand and now my cherished vision of Aelfgifu was smashed. Mother of two, ambitious royal consort, deceitful, conniving – this was not the sweet, high-spirited woman whose memory I had cherished these two years past.

Kjartan's voice softened. 'Thorgils, give thanks to Odinn that you are still alive. You could be a corpse along with your ship-mates on the drakkars. You are young, you are free of restraints and from tomorrow you'll have money to spare. Tomorrow I'll take you to see the king's paymaster and you'll have your royal bounty. Look upon Knut's wish to be rid of you as another sign that Odinn protects you. The court is a snake pit of intrigue and you are best away from it. You may think that the king was generous in his payment to you, but if the Danish vessels which attacked you had reached Holy River in time for the battle, King Knut might have lost his crown. And monarchs do not like to know that they are in another's debt.'

His last observation made no sense. 'I don't understand how the defeat of the Jomsvikings could have saved the king. We never reached the rendezvous. We were no use to him,' I said.

'Think of it this way,' Kjartan replied. 'Recently Knut has been increasingly mistrustful of Ulf. He fears that the earl is plotting against him and your story of the ambush of the Joms-vikings confirms Ulf's double dealing. His ships attacked the

Jomsvikings, knowing them to be reinforcements for the king. They did not expect any survivors to live to tell the tale. But as it turned out, the ambush delayed Ulf's ships so they missed the vital engagement at Holy River. Had they been there, Ulf might have felt strong enough to switch sides and join the Swedes. And that would have been the end for King Knut.'

I thought that Kjartan was being overly cynical, but he was proved right. Soon afterwards matters came to a head between the king and Earl Ulf. They were playing a game of chess when Knut, a chess fanatic, made a wrong move on the board. Ulf promptly took one of his knights. Knut insisted in replaying the move, and this so angered Ulf that he got up from his seat, tipped over the chessboard and stalked out of the room. Knut called after him that he was running away. Ulf flung back the jibe that it was Knut who would have run away from Holy River if Ulf's force had not fought on his side.

That night the earl fled for sanctuary in Roskilde's White Christ church. It did him little good. At dawn Knut sent a huscarl to the church with orders to kill Ulf. There was uproar among the Christians that murder had been committed in one of their churches. But when I heard the story, I felt a more immediate chill. Ulf was married to Knut's sister. If a brother-in-law could be assassinated in the struggle for the throne, how much more likely a victim would be the queen's illicit lover.

'I NEED THE DETAILS!' said Herfid excitedly. 'It's perfect material for a saga — "The Last Fight of the Jomsvikings!" Can you describe to me the leader of the Danes? Was there any exchange of insults between him and Thrand? Hand-to-hand combat between the two of them? That would be a nice touch, to catch an audience's imagination.'

'No, Herfid, it was just as I described it. Chaotic and savage. I didn't see who chopped off Thrand's foot and I don't even know who led the Danes. At first we thought they were on our side, on their way to join the king. But then they attacked us.' My throat hurt. Sometimes, when I was tired, my voice suddenly changed pitch like a boy in his puberty.

By a happy coincidence Herfid was travelling on the ship that Kjartan had found to take me clear of court intrigue. Herfid had finally given up his attempts to find a permanent job as a royal skald, and was heading back to Orkney where the new earl might have work for him. 'Knut's got too many skalds as it is,' Herfid lamented. 'Sighvatr Thordarsson, Hallvardr Hareksblesi and Thorarin Loftunga, not to mention Ottar the Black, who is his favourite. They didn't welcome more competition.' He looked woebegone. 'But if I could compose a really good saga about the Jomsvikings, that might get me some attention.'

'I think not, Herfid,' I said. 'Knut may not want to be reminded of the episode.'

'Oh well ... if you ever change your mind. Meanwhile perhaps you could tell me some of the Irish sagas you heard when you were in that country, maybe I could work parts of them into my own compositions. In exchange I'll give you a few more lessons on style and structure. They could prove useful should you ever decide to make a living by story telling. Besides, it will help pass the hours at sea.'

The captain taking us towards Orkney was in a hurry. It was late in the season to be attempting the trip, but he was a man with weather luck and his crew trusted his judgement and sea skill. Herfid, by contrast, probably knew at least a hundred poetic phrases for the sea and its ships, but had no practical knowledge. He made a singular impression on our hard-bitten crew as he walked about the deck referring to the little vessel as a 'surge horse' and a 'twisted rope bear', even 'a fore-sheets snake'. When we cleared the Roskilde anchorage the waves became 'the whale's housetops', and the jagged rocks were 'the water's teeth'. I noticed several crew members raise their eyebrows in astonishment when he referred to our hard-driving skipper as a 'brig elf', and I feared the captain had overheard.

Fortunately, just when I was thinking that Herfid was going to get himself tossed overboard for his presumption, we ran into the sea race off the tip of Caithness. It was an intimidating experience, as unnerving as anything I had yet experienced at sea, except perhaps for being wrecked on the Greenland skerries, but I was too young to remember that. The west-going tide ripped past the headland, creating overfalls and strange, swirling patches of water, until it seemed we were riding a huge river in full spate rather than the ocean. I could see why his men trusted our captain so implicitly. He timed his vessel's entry into the race with perfection. He thrust boldly into the torrent just as the tide was gathering, and we were swept along like a wood chip on the spring flood. Our vessel began to make a strange swooping motion, lifting up, then sliding forward and down as if we would be sucked to the bottom of the sea, only to rise again, check, and begin the next plunge. It required prime seamanship to keep the vessel straight. The captain himself manipulated the side rudder, which Herfid had called 'the broad-blade ocean sword', and by some smart handling of the sheets the crew made sure that we did not broach and roll. We hurtled through the race, our ears filled with the grumbling roar of the tide.

Poor Herfid fell silent as the motion of the ship increased. Soon he had found his way to the rail and was hanging on to a mast stay, then in a sudden lurch he was doubled over the rail, throwing up the contents of his stomach. He was bent in that position for some time, retching and heaving miserably. When we were clear of the waves, and the motion had subsided enough for the skipper to be able to relinquish the helm, he sauntered over to Herfid and asked innocently, 'And what do you call the sea — "breakfast swallower" or "vomit taker?"' Herfid raised his green-white face and gave him a look of pure loathing.

BIRSAY, THE HOME of the Earl of Orkney, was just as I remembered it — a modest settlement of a few houses huddling behind tussock-covered sand dunes. As a port of call, Birsay only existed because it was on the crossroads of the shipping lanes between the seas of England, Ireland and Iceland. The anchorage was so exposed to the fierce winter gales raging in from the west that the local boats had been hauled ashore and secured in half-sunk sheds or bedded behind barriers of rock and sand. Our captain had no intention of staying a moment longer than necessary in such a dangerous place, and he paused only long enough for us to visit the long hall to pay our respects to the earl, and for Herfid to ask permission to stay.

Like Knut, the new Earl of Orkney was of the coming generation – energetic, ambitious and completely without qualms. His name was Thorfinn, and Herfid was in luck. The young earl was looking for a skald to enhance his reputation and Herfid was given the job, initially on approval. Afterwards – as I learned – his post was made permanent when Thorfinn heard that he was becoming known as 'the Mighty', a phrase that Herfid had used to describe him.

To my astonishment, the earl's grandmother Eithne was still alive. I had not seen her for almost eight years, yet she seemed to have changed hardly at all. Perhaps she was a little more stooped, and even more of her hair had fallen out, so that she kept her headscarf knotted securely under her chin. But her mind was as alert as ever.

'So another battle nearly killed you,' she wheezed at me by way of greeting. I was not surprised. Eithne was acknowledged to be a volva, a seeress, and there was little that she did not know or divine. She was the one who had told me that I was a spirit mirror, my second sight occurring most frequently when I was with someone else who had the gift.

'There's something I want to ask you about,' I said. 'There was a vision which I do not understand, and I have not mentioned to anyone as yet.'

'Tell me about it.'

'It was during a sea fight. In the midst of the battle a hailstorm

suddenly lashed us, chilling us to the bone. The wind which
brought the hailstones always seemed to be in our faces, never to
hamper our enemies. It blew so powerfully that it turned our
arrows, nor could we hurl our spears against it. It was unearthly.
Everyone thought so. Some of our men from Wendland and
Witland cried out that magic was being used against us.'

'What did you think?' the old woman asked.

'I think our enemies had a supernatural ally. I saw her — it
was a woman — she appeared in the hailstorm. At first I thought
she was a Valkyrie come to carry away our dead, for she seemed
unearthly and she rode the wind. But this woman was different.
She had a cruel face, a cold eye and was in a frenzy, shrieking
and raging at us, and pointing at us with a clawlike hand.
Whenever she appeared, the hail flew thicker and the wind came
in stronger gusts.'

Eithne gave a snort of derision at my ignorance. 'A Valkyrie
indeed. Have you never heard of Thorgerd Holgabrud? That's
who you saw.'

'Who's she?' I asked.

'Thrand could have told you,' she replied. 'She appeared at
Hrojunga Bay, the first time the Jomsvikings were defeated. She
is the patron Goddess of the northern Norwegians. Earl Haakon,
who led the battle against the Jomsvikings, sacrificed his own
seven-year-old son to her to obtain the victory. That sacrifice was
so powerful that, even now, Thorgerd Holgabrud returns to
ensure the extinction of the Jomsvikings. She is a blood drinker, a
war witch.'

I must have looked sceptical because Eithne reached out and
gripped me by the arm. 'Listen to me: signs appeared in Caithness
and Farroes soon after the great slaughter at Clontarf. There the
Valkyries did appear to Old Believers — twelve Valkyries, riding
horses. They set up a loom in each place, using the entrails of
dead men as weft and warp, fresh skulls as the loom weights and
a sword as the beater. An arrow was their shuttle. As they wove,
they sang of the men who had fallen. You may never have heard

of Thorgerd Holgabrud, or her sister Irpa, but those Wends and Witlanders were right. A volva was working against you that day, someone invoking the hailstorm and the gale and inciting Thorgerd to fight against you. Learn from this event. Be on your guard against those who use the occult to defeat you.'

I forgot her words over the next few months and paid the price.

I ARRIVED BACK IN Iceland to find that Grettir was now a legend. Against all odds he was still at large and evading every attempt to hunt him down. What made his survival all the more remarkable was that no outlaw had ever had such a high bounty put on his head. Thorir of Gard had redoubled the reward he and his family would pay to anyone who killed or captured Grettir, and several bounty hunters had tried and failed to collect the prize money. I heard a great deal of chuckling about the fate of one of them. Grettir had overpowered him and forced him to undress and return home in only his underclothes. Other stories were more far-fetched and reminded me of when Grettir and I had robbed the barrow grave together. It was claimed that Grettir had thrown an evil troll-woman to her death over a cliff, that he had swum under a waterfall and found a giant living in a cave carpeted with men's bones, that he had shared a remote cave with a half-giant. On one point, everyone was agreed: Grettir was now living on an island in the north-west fiords.

'Why doesn't someone get together a group of like-minded fellows to go and capture him?' I asked.

My informant, a farmer from Reykholt with whom I was staying overnight, shook his head. 'You should see the island he's chosen for his retreat,' he said. 'Sheer cliffs that are near impossible to climb. The only way to the summit is by ladders and Grettir hauls them up whenever he sees a strange boat approaching. And he is not alone. His younger brother Illugi is living there with him and there's said to be a servant as well. A man called

Glaum or some name like that. There may be others, too. It's difficult to be sure. Grettir has allowed no one on the island since he took it over, though I've heard that the local farmers are furious. Previously they grazed a few sheep on the flat top of the island. Someone would go ashore, lower down a rope and the sheep would be hauled up one by one. After you got the sheep on the summit, you could go away and leave them there without a shepherd. There was no way the animals could get off.'

He said the island was called Drang, meaning 'sea cliff', and it was in the mouth of Skagafiord.

'Is there any way of getting out there?' I asked.

'There's a story that Grettir occasionally swims ashore, but that's impossible,' the farmer said. 'The island is too far out in the entrance to the fiord, and there are powerful currents that would sweep away a man and drown him. I think that tale is pure fantasy.'

It was odd, I thought to myself, how a farmer would believe in trolls and giants living under waterfalls, but not in a man's ability to swim long distances. Yet I had seen Grettir do just that in Norway.

When I stood on the shore of Skagafiord a few days later, I understood why the farmer had been so sceptical. Drang Island was far in the distance. Its shape reminded me of the massive blocks of ice which occasionally drifted into harbour at Eiriksfiord in Greenland when I was a boy. These ice mountains had stayed in the channel for weeks at a time, slowly melting. But the ice blocks had been a cheerful, sparkling white tinged with blue, and Drang Island was a dark, square, brooding oblong. It gave me the shivers. The thought of swimming across the intervening expanse of sea – I could see the tide swirl – was daunting. Someone on the mainland must be acting as a go-between, occasionally rowing out to the island to bring supplies and news.

I made a circuit of the fiord's shoreline, staying at one farmhouse after another, claiming to be looking for land to buy. Already I was travelling under an assumed name as I had no wish for Gunnhildr and her father to learn that I was back in Iceland. The only man to know of my return was Snorri Godi, that wily old chieftain, on whom I had called in order to discuss the redemption of my fire ruby. He still held the gem in safe keeping, and I had left with him the bulk of my silver hoard, asking that he wait before handing on the cash to Gunnhildr's family so that I had time to meet Grettir. I kept only enough silver with me to show the farmers of Skagafiord that I could afford their land prices.

I quickly identified the farmer most likely to be Grettir's contact. He owned the farm closest to Drang and there was a landing beach and boatshed on his property. More important, he was not a member of the group taking its lead from Thorbjorn Ongul, the chief landholder in the region. Thorbjorn Ongul I judged to be a hard man. Everything about him was off-putting. He had a scarred eye socket. He had lost the eyeball in his youth when his stepmother had struck him in the face for being disobedient and had half-blinded him. Now he was surly and belligerent, and obviously a bully. 'We'll get that bastard off our island, if it's the last thing I do,' he assured me when I raised the subject of Grettir on the island. 'Half the men around here are too faint-hearted to take any action. But I've been buying out their shares of the island – we used to own it jointly – so that whoever takes the decision about its future, it'll be me.' He paused, and looked at me suspiciously. 'Anyway, what's your interest in the place?'

'I just wondered: if I get a farm around here would I be able to purchase a share in the island and put some sheep on it?'

'Not without my permission, you couldn't,' he said rudely. 'By the time you finalise any land deal, I'll have seen to it that I hold the majority share in the island. Grettir is dead meat. He's due for a surprise, the murderous son of a bitch.'

I returned to the farmer whom I had guessed was supplying Grettir on Drang. Sure enough, when I offered him enough silver, he agreed to row me over to the island after dark. He

warned me, however, that Grettir was dangerous and unpredictable. 'You want to be careful,' he said. 'When the mood is on
him, the outlaw turns violent. He swam over from the island last
autumn and broke into my farm building. He was looking for
supplies, but I wasn't at home at the time. So he stripped off his
wet clothes, lay down by the fire and went to sleep. Two of the
women servants walked in on him and found him stark naked.
One woman made some sort of giggling remark about his penis
being rather small for such a powerfully built man. Grettir had
been half-asleep and heard the remark. He jumped up in a rage
and grabbed for her. The other woman fled and Grettir proceeded
to rape the woman he got his hands on. I know that he's been
out on that island for a long time, but it was a brutal thing to
do.'

The farmer's story depressed me. I had known that Grettir
was moody and unpredictable. I had seen enough examples of his
loutish behaviour for myself. But he had never before been violent
towards women. According to rumour, he had even been saved
from capture several times by women who had taken pity on him
and hidden him in their houses. I was appalled that he should use
rape to punish what was nothing more than impudence. I began
to fear that prolonged outlawry had unhinged Grettir, and he had
become half-savage. It made me wonder what reception my sworn
brother would give me.

I paid the farmer handsomely to deliver me out to Drang
under cover of darkness on the next windless night, and to keep
my presence secret. He landed me on the small shelf of beach
below the sheer cliff face, and I heard the splash of his oars
receding in the distance as I felt my way to the foot of the wooden
ladder he had told me I would find. All around me in the darkness
I could hear the rustlings and scratchings of roosting seabirds, and
my nostrils were filled with the acrid smell of their droppings.
Cautiously I felt my way up the rickety wooden rungs, pulling
myself up step by step. The first ladder brought me to a ledge on
the cliff face. Groping around I found the foot of a second ladder

leading even further upward. I wondered at Grettir's confidence that he should leave the ladders in position at night, not fearing the approach of an enemy.

It was when I had reached the flat crest of the island and was stumbling my way forward through tussock grass that I tripped over the body of his lookout. The man was sound asleep, wrapped in a heavy cloak and half buried in a shallow trench. He gave a startled grunt as I trod accidentally on his legs, and I sensed, rather than saw, him sit up and peer in my direction.

'Is that you, Illugi?' he asked.

'No, it's a friend,' I replied. 'Where's Grettir?'

The half-seen figure merely grunted and said, 'Well, that's all right then,' and sank back into his hole to return to sleep.

Fearful of stumbling over the cliff edge in the darkness, I sat down on the ground and waited for the dawn.

Daylight showed me that the summit of the island was covered with pasture, closely cropped by sheep. I could see at least a score of animals. In every direction the surface of the island stopped abruptly, ending in thin air where the cliff edge began. Only behind me, where the wooden ladder reached the summit, was there any access. And between me and the ladder I could see the little hump of cloth which marked the location of Grettir's watchman. He was still asleep.

I rose to my feet and went in search of Grettir. I could see nothing except for the sheep grazing quietly. There was no hut, no cabin, no sign of habitation. I walked across to the west side of the island. It took just a couple of hundred paces and I was at the cliff edge, looking straight down several hundred feet to the sea. I could see the white shapes of gulls circling and wheeling far beneath me in the updraughts. Puzzled by Grettir's absence, I turned back, retraced my steps, and searched towards the south end of the island. I had almost reached the lip of the furthest cliff when, coming round a large boulder jutting up from the soil, I came upon my sworn brother's home. It was a dug-out shelter, more like a bear's den than a human dwng. He had scraped out the soil to make an underground chamber roofed with three or four tree trunks he must have salvaged from the beach, for there were no trees on the island, not even a bush. Over the tree trunks was laid a layer of turf sods. A smoke hole at the back of the dugout provided a vent for the smoke from his cooking fire. It was a bleak, miserable place.

Grettir must have sensed my presence. I was still taking in the depressing scene when he emerged from the shelter. I was shocked by his appearance. He looked haggard and worn, his hair grey and streaked, and his skin was grimed with soil and smoke. His eyes were red-rimmed from the foul air in the dugout and his clothes were tattered and squalid. I realised that I had not seen a freshwater spring on the island, and wondered how he and his companions found their drinking water. Washing clothes did not seem possible. Despite his grotesque and shabby appearance, I felt a surge of pride. There was no mistaking the self-assurance in the look my sworn brother directed at me as, for a moment, he failed to recognise who I was.

'Thorgils! By the Gods, it's Thorgils!' he exclaimed and, stepping forward, gave me a great hug of affection. He stank, but it did not matter.

A moment later, he pulled back. 'How did you get here?' he asked in astonishment, which for a moment turned to suspicion. 'Who brought you? And how did you get past Glaum?' Glaum must have been the lazy sentinel I had stumbled on.

'All of Iceland knows that you are living on this island,' I replied, 'and it wasn't difficult to work out who your ferryman is. He dropped me off last night. As for Glaum, he doesn't take his duties very seriously.'

At that point, a second figure emerged from the dugout behind Grettir. It had to be his younger brother Illugi. He was at least ten years younger than Grettir, thin and undernourished looking, with black hair and a pale skin. He too was dressed in little better than rags. He said nothing, even when Grettir introduced me as his sworn brother, and I wondered if he was mistrustful of my intentions.

'Well, what do you think of my kingdom?' said Grettir, waving his arm expansively towards the southern horizon. The entrance to the dugout looked down the length of Skagafiord to the distant uplands on the mainland. To left and right extended the shores of the fiord, and rising behind them were the snow-streaked flanks of the mountains. 'Wonderful view, don't you agree, Thorgils? And practical too. From this spot I can see anyone approaching by boat down the length of the fiord, long before they reach the landing beach. It's impossible for anyone to sneak up on me.'

'At least in daylight,' I murmured.

'Yes,' said Grettir. 'No one has been bold enough to try a night landing previously, and in future I'll not trust that lazy servant Glaum to keep a look out. He's idle, but he amuses me with his chatter, and the Gods know, one needs a bit of humour and light-heartedness out here, especially in winter.'

'What do you live on?' I asked. 'Food must be very scarce.'

Grettir showed yellow teeth through his dirty tangle of beard. 'My neighbours kindly donate a sheep every couple of weeks,' he said. 'We ration ourselves, of course. There were about eighty animals on the island when we took over, and now we are down to about half that number.'

I did a quick mental calculation. Grettir had been living on Drang for at least a year, probably longer.

'There's one old ram who'll be the last one to be eaten. He's quite tame now. Visits the dugout every day and rubs his horns on the doorway, waiting to be petted.'

'What about water?' I asked.

'We gather rain, of which there is plenty, and when we get really short, there's a freshwater seep over on the east, in an over-hang. It oozes a few cupfuls of water every day, enough to keep us alive.'

'Enough to keep four people alive?' I asked.

Grettir took my meaning at once. 'You mean you want to stay?' he asked.

'Yes,' I said. 'If you and Illugi have no objection.'

So it was that I became the fourth member of the outlaw community and for almost a year Drang Island was my home.

THIRTEEN

GRETTIR WAS RIGHT: there was no shortage of food on the island, even with an extra mouth to feed. We were able to fish from the beach whenever the winter storms abated, and Grettir and Illugi had already saved an ample store of dried fish and the smoked carcasses of seabirds. For vegetables we ate a dark green weed which grew luxuriantly on the slopes too steep for the sheep to graze. The succulent leaves of this weed – I do not know its name – had a pleasant salty taste, and gave welcome variety to our diet. We had neither bread nor whey, the staple of the farmers on the mainland, but we never went hungry.

Our real struggle was how to keep warm and dry. The roof of the dugout kept out the rain, but the interior was constantly damp from the wetness rising up through the soil and we found it impossible to keep our garments dry. The fireplace was at the back of the dugout against the great boulder so that the stone reflected every bit of precious heat. But the ever-present problem was the scarcity of firewood. We depended on the chance discovery of driftwood. Each day one or other of us would descend the ladders and make a circuit of the island's narrow beach, hoping that the sea had brought us its bounty. Salvaging a good-sized log suitable for firewood was a greater cause for satisfaction than bringing back a string of freshly caught fish. When we found a log or dead branch, however small, we used ropes to hoist it back up the cliff and put it to dry in a sheltered spot. Then we would use an axe to chop the driftwood into kindling or shape a log to keep the fire at a gentle glow all night.

Grettir and I spent many hours in conversation, sometimes seated in the dugout, but more usually out in the open air where our discussions could not be overheard. He confessed to me that he was feeling more and more worn down by his long period of outlawry. 'I've lived over two-thirds of my life as an outlaw,' he said. 'I've scarcely known any other condition. I've never married, never been able to drop my guard in case there is someone ready to kill me.'

'But you've also become the most famous man in Iceland,' I said, trying to cheer him up. 'Everyone knows of Grettir the Strong. Long ago you told me that your reputation was all that mattered to you and that you wanted to be remembered. You've certainly achieved that. The Icelanders will never forget you.'

'Yes, but at what cost?' he replied. 'I've become a victim of my own pride. You'll remember how I swore no one would ever drive me away from Iceland by sending me into exile. Looking back, I see that was a mistake. I trapped myself here with those words. I often regret that I have travelled no further than Norway. How I would have loved to see the foreign lands you have known – Vinland, Greenland, Ireland, London, the shores of the Baltic Sea. I envy you. If I were to travel abroad now, people would say that I am running away. I have to stay here for ever, and that means until someone catches up with me when I am weak or old and kills me.'

Grettir looked out across the fiord. 'I have a premonition that this view is the one I will live and die with. That I will finish out my time on this small island.' Disconsolately he threw a pebble over the cliff edge. 'I feel cursed,' he went on. 'Everything I do seems to have the reverse effect of what I intend. If I start something for the best of reasons, it usually turns out quite differently. People are hurt or harmed by my actions. I never intended to kill that young man who insulted me in the church in Norway, and when I burned those unfortunates in that shore house it was largely their fault. If they had not been so drunk, they would have escaped the fire, which they themselves started.'

'What about that woman over at the farm? I'm told you raped her.'

Grettir looked down at the ground and mumbled his answer. 'I don't know what came over me. It was a black rage, not something I'm proud of. Sometimes I think that living like a hunted animal makes you into an animal. If you live too long away from normal company, you lose the habits of normal behaviour.'

'What about your brother Illugi? Why don't you send him away from here? He doesn't have to be bound to your fate.'

'I've tried a dozen times to persuade Illugi to go back home,' Grettir replied, 'but he is too much like me. He's stubborn. He sees my outlawry as a matter of personal pride. No one is going to dictate to him or his family what they should do and he has a strong sense of family. That's how we were brought up. Not even my mother wants me to surrender. When Illugi and I said goodbye to her before coming here, she said that she never expected to see either of us alive again, but she was pleased we were protecting the family's good name.'

'Then what about Glaum?' I said. 'What part does he play in all this? To me he seems nothing more than a lazy lout, a jester.'

'We met Glaum on our way to the island,' Grettir said. 'It was pure chance. Glaum is a nobody. He has no home, no land, nothing. But he's amusing, and his company can be entertaining. He volunteered to come to the island with us and until he decides to leave I'm willing to let him stay. He tries to make himself useful, collecting firewood, helping haul up the ladders, doing some fishing, generally being about the place.'

'You're not concerned that Glaum might try to attack you, like Redbeard, hoping to gain the bounty money?

'No. Glaum's not like that. He's too lazy, too weak. He's not a bounty hunter.'

'But there's something foreboding about Glaum,' I said. 'I can't define what it is, but I have a feeling that he represents misfortune. I would be happier if you sent him away.'

'Maybe I will,' said Grettir, 'but not yet.'

'Perhaps matters will improve,' I suggested. 'I've heard it said that if a man survives outlawry for a span of twenty years then the sentence is complete. In a couple of years that will be the case for you.'

'I think not,' Grettir answered gloomily. 'Something is bound to go wrong before then. My luck is dire and my enemies will never give up. My reputation and the reward for my death or capture means that any young hothead will have a try at killing me or taking me prisoner.'

His forebodings came true in the early spring. This was the season when the farmers would normally bring out their sheep to Drang and leave them there for the summer grazing. Doubtless this prompted them, under Thorbjorn Ongul's leadership, to launch a plan to retake the island. A young man from Norway, Haering by name, had arrived in the area. Like everyone else, he soon heard about Grettir living on Drang Island and of the huge reward being offered for his death. He contacted Thorbjorn Ongul and told him that he was an expert climber of cliffs. Haering boasted that there was no cliff which he could not scale single-handed and without ropes. He suggested that if he could be landed on Drang without Grettir knowing, he would surprise the outlaw and either kill or wound him so severely that the others would be able to storm the island. Thorbjorn Ongul was shrewd. He decided that the best way to approach Drang without alerting Grettir's suspicions would be in a large, ten-oared boat with a cargo of live sheep. From his boat he would call up to Grettir, asking for permission to land the animals. Ongul calculated that Grettir would agree because he had already depleted the flock on the island. Meanwhile Haering would climb the cliffs on the opposite side of Drang and creep up on Grettir from behind.

Grettir and I worked out Ongul's stratagem only after it had failed and it was a narrow escape. We saw the ten-oared boat approaching from a great distance down the fiord, and watched as it slowly drew closer. Soon we could see the four or five men aboard and the dozen or so sheep. Haering himself was not visible. He must have crouched down and hidden among the animals. Ongul was at the helm and steered for the landing place at the foot of the ladder leading up to the summit. But he took a slightly unusual course and, at the time, we failed to understand why. There was a short interval when the boat was so close under the cliffs and passing round the end of the island that it was lost to sight from anyone standing at the cliff top. This was the moment when Haering must have slipped overboard and swum ashore. Moments later Ongul and his boat reappeared in view, the oars-men rested on their oars, and Ongul shouted up to Grettir, asking him to agree to let more sheep graze on the island. Grettir called back down, and the negotiations began. Grettir, usually so alert, was hoodwinked. He warned Ongul that the moment anyone tried to climb the ladders, the upper ladder would be withdrawn. Mean-while, with a great deal of deliberate fumbling, the men in the boat began to get the sheep ready to be hoisted.

Unknown to us up on the summit, Haering had begun to climb. The young man was inching his way up the cliff face by a route which no one had attempted or even imagined possible. It was, by any standards, an extraordinary feat of agility. Unaided, the young man managed to find one handhold after another. He hauled himself upward past the ledges of nesting seabirds. Some-times the rock face leaned out so far that Haering was obliged to cling on, hanging by his fingers as he searched for a grip, then clambered upwards like a spider. His feet, to prevent them slipping, were clad only in thick woollen socks, which he had wetted to give them a better grip.

I know about the wet socks because it was I who first saw Haering after he had hauled himself over the topmost rim of the cliff. It was the old grey ram which alerted me. Grettir, Illugi and Glaum were clustered at the top of the ladder, looking down at

Ongul and his farmer colleagues as they discussed the landing of the sheep. Their attention was completely distracted. By contrast, I had deliberately stayed back from the cliff edge so I could not be seen from below. No one apart from the farmer who had brought me to Drang knew that I was on the island, and it seemed a good idea to keep my presence a secret. So I noticed the sudden movement among the sheep grazing near the cliff edge opposite where Grettir was standing. The animals raised their heads from grazing, and stood stock still, staring out into space. They were alarmed and I saw them tense as if to flee. The old grey ram, however, trotted confidently forward as though he expected to be petted. A moment later I saw a hand rise over the cliff edge, as if from the void, and feel around until it found a grip. Then Haering's head appeared. Slowly, very slowly, he eased himself over the rim of the cliff until he was lying face down flat on the grass. That was when I saw the wet socks and noted that, to lighten himself for the climb, his only weapon was a small axe tied with a leather thong to his back.

I gave a low whistle to warn the others. Grettir and Illugi both looked round and immediately saw the danger. As Haering got to his feet, Grettir said something to Illugi, and it was the younger man who turned and advanced on a now-exhausted Haering. His older brother stayed behind in case his great strength was needed, with Glaum's help, to haul up the wooden ladder.

Poor Haering, I felt sorry for him. He was utterly spent by the spectacular climb, and instead of finding Grettir and Illugi alone on the island, he now found himself confronted by four men, and without any advantage of surprise. He unslung the axe. He may have been a superb mountaineer, but he was an inexpert warrior. He held the axe loosely in from of him, and when Illugi struck at him with a sword the axe was knocked spinning out of his grasp.

Haering offered no further resistance. There was something manic about Illugi's headlong rush at the unarmed young man. Illugi may have felt that his refuge had been violated, or maybe he had never killed a man before and was desperate to finish the job. He ran at Haering wildly, swinging his sword. Unnerved, the Norwegian turned and fled, running in his socks over the turf. But there was nowhere to go. Illugi chased his prey grimly, still cutting and slashing with his sword as Haering dodged and turned. He ran towards the boulder which masked the entrance to the dugout. Perhaps he was seeking to shelter behind it, but he did not know the lie of the land. Beyond the rock the ground suddenly fell in a steep slope at the far end of which was the edge of the cliff. From there to the sea was a sheer drop of four hundred feet. Haering ran headlong down the slope towards the precipice. Perhaps he thought his speed would carry him far enough out. Perhaps he panicked. Maybe he wanted to die by his own hand and not on Illugi's sword. Whatever his intention was, he ran straight to the edge of the cliff and without hesitating flung himself outward ... and continued running, as though still on solid ground. His legs and arms flailed as he dropped from view.

I joined Illugi at the cliff edge, crouching cautiously on the ground and then crawling forward on my belly, so that my head looked out over the vast drop. Far below, the cliff climber's body lay broken and twisted on the beach. To my right Ongul's people had seen the tragedy and were already rowing to the spot to retrieve the corpse.

No other attempt was made to dislodge us from Drang during the next three months. Probably Haering's death had shocked the farmers who supported Ongul and anyhow they had their summer chores to do. Grettir, Illugi, Glaum and I stayed on the island. The friendly farmer visited us only twice, bringing us news from the mainland. The main event was the death of Snorri Godi that winter, full of years and honour, and his son Thorodd – the man whom Grettir had spared – had succeeded to the chieftainship. I wondered if Thorodd had also inherited charge of my fire ruby which I had left in his father's safe keeping and if Snorri had told him of its history.

My sworn brother reacted glumly to the news of Snorri Godi's death. 'So vanishes my last hope of obtaining justice,' he said to me as we sat in our favourite spot near the cliff edge. 'I know that Snorri refused to take up my case at the Althing when we first arrived back in Iceland and you went to see him on my behalf. But as long as Snorri was alive, I nursed a secret hope that he would change his mind. After all, I spared his son Thorodd when he tried to kill me and win his father's approval. But now it is too late. Snorri was the only man in Iceland who had the prestige and law skill to have my sentence of skogarmadur annulled.'

After a short pause Grettir turned to face me and said earnestly, 'Thorgils, I want you to promise me something: I want you to give me your word that you will make something exceptional of your own life. If my life is cut short at the hands of my enemies, I don't want you to mourn me uselessly. I want you to go out and do the things that my ill luck has never allowed me to do. Imagine that my fylgja, my other spirit, has attached itself to you, my sworn brother, and is at your shoulder, always present, seeing what you see, experiencing what you experience. A man should live his life seeking out his opportunities and fulfilling them. Not like me, cornered here on this island and becoming famous for surviving in the face of adversity.'

As Grettir spoke, a memory came back. It was of the day when Grettir and I were leaving Norway, and Grettir's half-brother, Thorstein Galleon, had said goodbye. He had promised to avenge Grettir's death if he was killed unjustly. Now, sitting on a cliff top on Drang, Grettir had taken me one step further. He was asking me to continue his life for him, in remembrance of our sworn brotherhood. And behind the request was an unspoken understanding between us: neither Grettir nor I expected that he would live out the full twenty years of outlawry and reach the end of the sentence imposed upon him.

The conversation had a remarkable effect on me. It changed my perception of life on Drang. Previously I had been despondent about the future, fearing the outcome of Grettir's seemingly

endless difficulties. Now I saw that it was better to enjoy whatever
time there was left for us together. The change of season helped
my pessimism to lift. The arrival of the brief Icelandic summer
wiped away the memory of a dank and melancholy winter. I
watched the tiny island change from a remote, desolate outpost
to a place full of life and movement. It was the birds that did it.
They arrived in their thousands, perhaps from those distant lands
which Grettir dreamed of. Flock after flock came in until the sky
was filled with their wings and their constant mewing and screaming mingled with the sounds of the sea and the wind. They came
to breed, and they settled on the ledges, crevices and tiny outcrops
of the cliffs until it seemed that there was not a single hand's
breadth that was not occupied by some seabird busily building a
new nest or refurbishing an old one. Even in Greenland I had not
seen so many seabirds clustered together. Their droppings ran
down the cliff faces like streaks of wax when a candle gutters in
the draught, and there was a constant movement of fluttering and
flight. Of course, we took their eggs, or rather we took a minus-
cule portion of them. This was when Grettir was at his best. With
his huge strength he lowered Illugi on a rope over the cliff edge
so that his young brother could gather the eggs from the ledges
while the angry gulls beat their wings around his head, or if they
stayed on their nests, shot green slime from their throats into the
face of the thief. Perhaps the proudest moment of all my relationship with Grettir was when he turned to me and asked if I would
go down the precipice on the rope and I agreed. As I dangled
there, high above the sea, swinging in space, with only my sworn
brother's strength to prevent me falling to my death like Haering,
I felt the satisfaction of utter trust in another.

So the summer weeks passed by: sudden rain showers were
interspersed with spells of brilliant sunshine when we stood on the
cliff tops and watched the whales feeding in the waters around
the island; or we traced the evening spread of white mist over the
high moors on the mainland. Occasionally I would go by myself
to a little niche on the very lip of the precipice and lie on the turf,

deliberately gazing across the void and imagining I was no longer in contact with the solid ground. I hoped to achieve something my seidr mentors had long ago described to me: spirit flying. Like a small bird beginning to take wing, I wanted to send my spirit out over the sea and distant mountains and away from my physical body. For brief moments I succeeded. The earth fell away beneath me, and I felt a rush of wind on my face and saw the ground far beneath. But I never travelled far or stayed out of my body for long. I had brief glimpses of dense forest, a white landscape and felt a piercing cold. Then, like the fledgling which flutters uncertainly back to the branch, my spirit would return to where I lay, and the rush of air on my cheeks often proved to be no more than the rising wind.

The intrusion of awful dread into this pleasant life was shocking. The day was bright and fresh, and the waters of Skagafiord had that intense dark blue into which one could look for ever. Grettir and I were at a spot where the small black and white seabirds which nested in their millions regularly flew towards their nests, a row of tiny fish neatly arranged in their rainbow beaks. As they skimmed low over the cliff, riding up-draughts, we would rise from ambush and with woven nets on sticks pull them down from the sky and break their necks. Smoked over our fire, their dark brown flesh was delicious, a cross between lamb's liver and the finest venison. We had netted perhaps a dozen of the birds when we heard Illugi call out that a small boat was coming down the fiord. We gathered at the cliff edge and saw a little skiff rowed by just one man heading our way. Soon we could make out Thorbjorn Ongul at the oars.

'I wonder what he wants this time,' said Grettir.

'He can't be coming to negotiate,' Illugi commented. 'By now he must know that we can't be shifted, whatever he offers us, whether threats or payment.'

I, too, had been watching the boat, and as it drew nearer, I began to feel uncomfortable. A chill came over me, a cold queasiness. At first I thought it was an expression of my mistrust of

Thorbjorn Ongul. I knew that he was the man from whom Grettir had the most to fear. But as the little boat came closer, I knew that there was something else, something more powerful and sinister. I broke out in a cold sweat and felt the hairs on the back of my neck rise. It seemed ridiculous. In front of me was a small boat, rowed by an aggressive farmer who could not climb the cliffs, floating on a pleasant summer sea. There could be no menace there.

I glanced at Grettir. He was pale and trembling slightly. Not since our shared vision of fire emerging from the tomb of old Kar on the headland had we both been touched by the second sight simultaneously. But this time the vision was blurred and indistinct.

'What is it?' I asked Grettir. I did not have to explain my question.

'I don't know,' he answered throatily. 'Something's not right.'

The fool Glaum broke our concentration. Suddenly he began capering on the cliff edge, where he could be seen by Ongul in the boat. He shouted obscenities and taunts, and went so far as to turn his back, drop his breeches to his ankles and expose his buttocks at the Ongul.

'Stop that!' ordered Grettir brusquely. He went across to Glaum and cuffed him so hard that the vagrant was knocked backwards. Glaum scrambled to his feet, pulling up his breeches, and shambled off, muttering crossly. Grettir turned back to face Ongul. He had stopped rowing and was keeping the little skiff a safe distance away from the beach.

'Clear off!' Grettir bellowed. 'There's nothing you can say that I want to hear.'

'I'll leave when I feel like it,' Ongul yelled back. 'I want to tell you what I think of you. You're a coward and a trespasser. You're touched in the head, a murderer, and the sooner you're dealt with the better it will be for all decent men.'

'Clear off!' repeated Grettir, shouting at the top of his lungs. 'Go back to minding your farm, you miserable one-eye. You're the one who is responsible for bringing death. That young man would never have tried to climb up here if you hadn't encouraged him. Now he's dead, and with your scheme unstuck so badly you've been made to look a fool.'

As the exchange of insults continued, I felt shooting pains in my head. Grettir did not seem affected. Perhaps he was distracted by his anger at Ongul. But I began to feel feverish. The day which had begun with such promise was turning heavy with menace. The sky was clouding over. I felt unsteady and sat down on the ground to stop myself retching. The shouting match between the two men echoed off the cliffs, but then I heard something else: a growing clatter of wings and a swelling volume of bird calls, rising in pitch. I looked back towards the north. Huge numbers of seabirds were taking to the sky. They were launching themselves in droves from the cliff ledges, gliding down towards the sea and then flapping briskly to gain height as they began to group together. They reminded me of bees about to swarm. The main flock spiralled upward as more and more birds joined in, flying up to meet their companions. Soon the flock was so immense it had to divide into ranks and squadrons. There were thousands upon thousands of them, too many to count or even guess their numbers. Many birds still stayed on the ledges, but most were on the move. Section by section, breed by breed, the great mass of flying creatures circled higher and higher like a storm cloud, until smaller groups began to break away and head out towards the sea. At first it seemed that their departure was random, in all directions. But then I realised there was one direction which all the birds avoided: none of them was returning to Drang. The birds were abandoning the island.

I dragged myself upright and walked unsteadily to where Grettir stood. My head and muscles ached. I felt terrible. 'The birds,' I said, 'they're leaving.'

'Of course they are,' he answered crossly over his shoulder, 'they leave every year about this time. It is the end of their breeding season. They go now, and come back in the spring.'

He searched around in the grass until he found a rounded

stone, about the size of a loaf. Plucking it from the grass, he heaved it above his head with both hands and let fly, aiming at Ongul in the boat far below. Ongul had imagined he was safely out of range. But he had not reckoned with Grettir the Strong who, since boyhood, had amazed everyone with just how far he could pitch a rock. The stone flew far out, its arc greater than I had imagined possible. Grettir's aim was true. The stone plummeted down, straight at the little skiff. It missed Ongul by inches. He was standing amidships, working the oars. The stone landed with a thump on a bundle of black rags on the stern thwart. As the stone struck, I saw the bundle shiver and flinch, and over the crying of the myriad departing birds, I heard distinctly a hideous cry of pain. At that moment I remembered where I had felt that same chill, the same sense of evil, and heard the same vile cry. It was when Thrand and I had fought the Danes in the sea ambush and I had had a vision of Thorgerd Holgabrud, the blood drinker and witch.

As Ongul rowed away, I was swaying on my feet.

'You've got a bad attack of some sort of fever,' said Grettir and put his arm around me to stop me falling. 'Here, Illugi, give me a hand to carry Thorgils inside.' The two of them lifted me down into the dugout and made me comfortable on some sheepskins on the earth floor.

I had just enough strength to ask, 'Who was in the boat with Ongul? Why didn't they show themselves?'

Grettir frowned. 'I don't know,' he said, 'but whoever it was is nursing a very bad bruise or a broken bone and won't forget this day in a hurry.'

Perhaps the birds began their migration because they knew that the weather was about to change, or perhaps – and this was my own private explanation – they were disturbed from their roosts by the evil that visited us that day. At any rate that was the last day of summer we enjoyed. By evening the rain had set in and the temperature began to fall. We did not see the sun again for a fortnight, and by then the first of the autumn gales had mauled the island unseasonably early. The ledges on the cliffs were empty of all but a handful of seabirds, and Drang had settled back prematurely into its gloomy routine though the autumn equinox had barely passed.

I continued very ill and weak with fever and from my sick bed I could see that Grettir was more subdued than usual. There was despondency in his face, perhaps at the thought of another winter spent in the raw, cramped isolation of Drang. He took to leaving the dugout at first light and often did not reappear until dusk. Illugi told me that his brother was spending much of his time alone, sitting staring out towards the mainland, saying nothing, refusing to be drawn into conversation. At other times Grettir would descend the ladders and, when the low tide permitted, walk around the island, furiously splashing through the shallows, always by himself. It was from one of these excursions that he returned with that look I had never seen before: a look of dismay.

'What's worrying you?' I asked.

'Down on the beach, I had that same feeling we both sensed the day that Ongul came to visit us and I threw the stone. I felt it mildly at first, but as I walked around the island it came on me more strongly. Oddly, I also had a stroke of luck. On the far side of the island I came across a fine piece of driftwood. The current must have brought it there from the east side of the fiord. It was a good, thick log, an entire tree trunk, roots and all, ideal for firewood. I was bending down to drag it further up the beach when I felt ill – I thought I was going down with your fever. But then it occurred to me that my feeling might have something to do with that particular spot on the beach – it faces across to that ruffian Ongul's farm – or perhaps it was to do with the log. I don't know. Anyhow, I took the wave of nausea to be a warning. So instead of salvaging the log, I shoved it out to sea again. I didn't want to have anything further to do with it.'

The very next day Glaum appeared with a smug expression at the door of the dugout. 'I've done well,' he said. 'Better than the lot of you, though you treat me as if I'm useless.'

'What is it, Glaum?' asked Grettir sourly.

We had all become weary of Glaum's endless vulgarities – his favourite amusement was to let out controlled farts, which did not help the fug of the dugout, and he snored so much that, unless the night was wild, we made him sleep outside. He had made a noxious lair for himself in the hollow by the ladders where I had first stumbled across him. There he pretended to play sentry, though there was little likelihood of any surprise attack now that the weather was so bad.

'I've salvaged a fine log,' said Glaum. 'Took me enough trouble too. Found it on the beach by the foot of the ladders and I've managed to hoist it up with ropes. There's enough timber to burn for three or four nights at least.'

It was one of those days when there was a brief break in the dreary weather and Grettir had half-carried me out of the fetid dugout so I could sit in the open air and enjoy the watery sunshine.

Glaum went on, 'Better cut up the log now. Before it rains again.'

Grettir picked up our axe. It was a fine, heavy tool, the only axe we had, too important for our well-being to let Glaum handle in case he lost it or damaged the blade. Grettir walked to where Glaum had dragged the log. I was lying on the ground so I could not see the log itself because it was concealed in the grass. But I heard Grettir say, 'That's strange, it's the same log I threw back into the water the other day. The current must have carried it right around the island and brought it back in the opposite beach.'

'Well, it's a good log wherever it came from. Well seasoned and tough,' said Glaum, 'and it took me enough trouble to get it up here. So this time it's not going to waste.'

I saw Grettir raise the axe with both hands and take a hefty swing. A moment later I heard the sound of a blow that has been mis-aimed – the false echo – as Grettir fell.

Illugi had been idling nearby. He rushed over to his brother, and was kneeling on the ground. I saw him rip off a piece of his own shirt and guessed that he was applying a bandage. Then Grettir's arm came up and took a hold around his brother's neck, and as Illugi strained back, the two men rose, Grettir with one leg bent up. Blood drenched the bandage. Slowly and painfully, Grettir hobbled past me into the dugout. Too fever-racked to move, I lay there worrying about how badly Grettir had hurt himself. Eventually, when Illugi and Glaum helped me inside, I found Grettir sitting on the ground with his back against the earth wall of the dugout. Instantly I was reminded of the last time I had seen Thrand, sitting in the same position when he had lost his foot to a Danish axe. But at least Grettir had both legs, though the injured one was leaking what seemed a huge amount of blood through the makeshift bandage.

'A fine lot we are,' said Grettir, his face twisted with pain, 'We've got two invalids now. I don't know what came over me. The axe bounced off that tough old log and twisted in my hand.'

'It's cut very deep,' said Illugi. 'Any deeper and you would have chopped off your leg. You'll be out of action for months.'

'That's all I need,' said Grettir, 'plain bad luck again.'

Illugi busied himself in rearranging the interior of the dugout to give Grettir more space. 'I'll light the fire,' he said to his brother. 'It'll be cold tonight, and you need to keep warm.' He called to Glaum to bring in some firewood, and there were sounds of grunting and mumbling as Glaum slowly backed into the dugout, dragging the unlucky log which had been the cause of Grettir's accident.

'That's too big to fit into the hearth. Get something smaller,' said Illugi.

'No, it isn't,' replied Glaum argumentatively. 'I can make it fit. You've seen for yourself that it's too tough to chop up into pieces.'

Illugi, I realised, lacked Grettir's authority over Glaum and I knew that the balance within our tight little community had gone. Glaum was wrestling the log into position in the hearth and turning it over so that it rested against the stone. As he did so, I

saw something on the underside of the wood and called, 'Stop!'
I crawled over to take a closer look. Part of the underside of the
log had been cut smooth. Somebody had deliberately shaved down
the surface, leaving a flat area as long as my forearm. On the
surface were a series of marks cut deep into the wood. I knew
what the marks were even before I saw the faint red stain in their
grooves. Thrand, my mentor in the Old Ways, had warned me
against them. They were curse runes, cut to invoke harm against
a victim, then smeared with the blood of the volva or seidrmann
to make the evil in the runes more effective. I knew then that
Grettir was the victim of black seidr.

For the next three days Grettir's injury appeared to be on the
mend. The gash began to close and the edges of the wound were
pink and healthy. Then, on the third night, he started to suffer
from a deep-seated throbbing pain and by dawn he was in agony.
Illugi unwrapped the bandage and we saw the reason. The flesh
around the wound was puffed and swollen. Fluid was seeping
from the gash. The next morning the flesh was beginning to
discolour, and as the days passed the area around the wound
turned dark blue, then a greenish-black, and we could smell the
putrefication. Grettir could not sleep – the pain was too bad. Nor
could he get to his feet. He lost weight and looked drained. By
the end of the week he knew that he was dying from the poison
in his leg.

That was when they unleashed their assault. How they knew
that Grettir was in a coma, I have no way of knowing.

The end was swift and bloody. More than a dozen farmers
came up the ladders, which had been left in place now that we no
longer had Grettir's strength to pull them clear. They came at
dusk, armed with axes and heavy spears, and overpowered Glaum
as he lay half asleep. They prodded him in front of them as he
led them to our dugout, though they would have found the place
soon enough for themselves. I heard them coming first, for they
were working themselves up into a battle rage. Illugi, in an
exhausted sleep, was slow to wake and scarcely had time to jam

shut the makeshift door. But the door was not designed to withstand a siege — it was nothing more than a few sticks of wood covered with sheepskins — and it burst open after the first few blows. By then Illugi was in position, sword in one hand, axe in the other. The first farmer who ventured in lost his right arm to a terrific blow from the same weapon that had been Grettir's bane.

For an hour or more the attack continued. I could hear Ongul's voice urging on his men. But they found it was deadly work. Two more farmers were badly wounded and another killed, all trying to rush the door. Our attackers were like men who corner a badger in its sett and try to take the prey alive. When Ilugi held them off with sword and axe, they began to dig down through the earth roof of our refuge. From inside we heard the sounds of digging and soon the roof began to shake. I was as weak as water and unable to intervene, only to observe. From where I lay on the floor I saw the earth rain down from the ceiling and then the point of a spear poked through. I knew the end could not be long in coming.

Another rush at the door and the frame split. Our defence was collapsing around us. A spear thrust through the doorway caught Illugi in the shoulder. Grettir struggled to his knees to face the attack. In his hand was the short sword that he and I had robbed from old Kar's burial mound. At that moment a section of the roof fell in close to the hearth. Amid the shower of earth, a farmer jumped down. Grettir turned to meet the new threat, stabbed with the sword and impaled the intruder, killing him. But the man fell forward so that Grettir's sword arm was trapped. As he struggled to withdraw the blade a second man dropped through the hole and stabbed Grettir in the back. I heard Grettir call out and Illugi turned to help, throwing up his shield to protect his brother. This left the door unguarded and suddenly the dugout was filled with armed men. In moments they had knocked Illugi to the ground and were hacking and stabbing him to death. One man, seeing me, stepped forward and planted the point of his spear against my blankets. He had only to press down his weight and I too was dead. But he made no move, and I watched as Ongul darted behind Grettir to avoid the outlaw's sword and knifed him several times in quick succession. Grettir did not even turn to look at his killer. He was already so weak that he slumped to the ground without a sound. I lay there, unable to move, as Ongul leaned down and roughly tried to prise Grettir's fingers from Kar's sword. But the death grip was too strong and Ongul pulled aside my sworn brother's hand until it lay across the fatal fire log. Then, like a skilful butcher, he severed the fingers so that the sword fell free.

Picking up the sword, Ongul cut Grettir's head from his shoulders. It took four blows. I counted every one as Ongul hacked down on the corpse. By then the blood-splattered remains of the ruined dugout were crammed with sweating, jubilant farmers, all shouting and talking and congratulating themselves on their victory.

FOURTEEN

I BOUGHT MY life for five and a half marks. That was the sum the
farmers found on me, and I gave them a promise of ten marks
more if they delivered me, alive, to Snorri Godi's son Thorodd
for judgement. They accepted the bargain because, after the
slaughter of Grettir and Illugi, some of them had had enough of
bloodshed. They buried the corpses of Illugi and Grettir in the
ruins of our dugout, then lowered my sick and aching body down
the cliff face on a rope and placed me in the stern of the ten-oar
boat they had come in. Destitute Glaum was not so lucky. On the
way back to the mainland, they told him he had betrayed his
master, cut his throat and threw his body overboard. Grettir's
head they kept, wrapped in a bag, so Ongul could present the
gruesome evidence to Thorir of Gard and claim his reward.
Eavesdropping, I learned how we had been defeated: Ongul had
gone to his aged foster-mother Thurid for help in evicting Grettir
from Drang. Thurid was a volva, rumoured to use black arts. It
was she who had lain concealed beneath the pile of rags when
Ongul rowed out to quarrel with Grettir. She needed to hear and
judge the quality of her victim before she chose her curse runes.
She then cut the marks, stained them with her own blood and
selected the hour on which Ongul should launch the cursed tree
on the tide. My only consolation, as I listened to the boastful

farmers, was to learn that the old crone was hobbling and in dreadful pain. The rock that Grettir threw had smashed her thigh bone and crippled her for life.

Ongul, as it turned out, never received his head money. Thorir of Gard refused to pay up. He said that, as a Christian, he would not reward the use of witchcraft. Ongul took this as a weasel excuse and sued Thorir before the next assembly of the Althing. To his rage the assembled godars supported Thorir's view – he may have bribed them – and went so far as to banish Ongul. They ruled that there had been enough bloodshed and, to forestall revenge by Grettir's friends, it was better that Ongul left Iceland for a while. I was to meet Ongul later, as I will relate, but in the meantime the Gods provided me with a way to honour the memory of my sworn brother.

Thorodd was lenient in his judgement, as I had anticipated. When I was brought before him, he remembered that Grettir had spared his own life when he had challenged the outlaw on the road, and now repaid his debt by declaring that I should be set free after I had paid my captors the ten marks I had promised. This done, Thorodd returned to me my fire ruby, saying that this was what his father had instructed him to do, and undertook to settle my affairs with Gunnhildr's family. He also surprised me by handing over Thrand's old hoard chest. Apparently Thrand had left instructions that if he failed to come back from Jomsburg, I was to be his heir. I donated the entire contents of the chest to Thor. Half the silver paid for a temple mound to be erected in the God's honour on the spot where Thrand's old cabin had stood, and the remainder I buried deep in its earth.

At the feast which followed the temple dedication, I found myself seated next to one of Snorri Godi's sons-in-law, an intelligent and well-to-do farmer by the name of Bolli Bollason. It turned out that Bolli was suffering from that itch for travel which is so characteristic of the northern peoples. 'I can hardly wait for the day when my oldest son can take over my farm, Thorgils,' he confessed. 'I'm going to put it in his care, pack and head off.

I want to see other countries, meet foreign peoples and see how they live while I am still fit and active. Iceland is too small and remote. I feel cooped up here.'

Naturally his words recalled Grettir's words, begging me to travel.

'If you had your choice, Bolli,' I asked, 'which of all the places in the world would you most want to see?'

'Miklagard, the great city,' he responded without a moment's hesitation. 'It's said that there is nowhere else on earth like it – immense palaces, public baths, statues which move of their own accord. Streets paved with marble and you can stroll along them after dark because the emperor who rules there decrees that blazing torches be set up at every corner and kept lit throughout the night.'

'And how does one get to Miklagard?' I asked.

'Across the land of the Rus,' he answered. 'Each year Rus traders bring furs to sell at the imperial court. They have special permits to enter the emperor's territories. If you took a load of furs yourself, you would make a profit from the venture.'

Bolli fingered the collar of his cloak. It was an expensive garment, worn specially for the feast, and the collar was trimmed with some glossy fur.

'The trader who sold me this cloak told me that the Rus get their furs from the northern peoples who trap the animals. I haven't seen it for myself, but it is said the Rus go to certain known places on the edge of the wilderness and lay out their trade goods on the ground. Then they go away and wait. In the night, or at dawn, the natives come out secretly from the woods, pick up the trade goods and replace them with the amount of furs that they think is a fair bargain. They are a strange lot, those fur hunters. They don't like intruders on their territory. If you trespass, they're likely to put a spell on you. No one else is more skilled in seidr, men and women both.'

This last remark decided me. Thor may have put the words

in Bolli's mouth as a reward for my offerings to him, but it was Odinn who determined the outcome. A journey to Miklagard would not only carry out Grettir's wish, it would also bring me closer to my God's mysteries.

So it was that, less than a month later, I had a trader's pack on my back and was plodding through the vast forests of Permia, wondering if Odinn had been in his role as the Deceiver when he lured me there. After a week in the wilderness I had yet to glimpse a single native. I was not even sure what they were called. Bolli Bollason had called them the Skridfinni, and said that the name meant 'the Finni who run on wooden boards'. Others referred to them as Lopar or Lapu and told me, variously, that the name meant 'the runners', 'witches' or 'the banished'. All my informants agreed that the territory they occupied was barren beyond belief. 'Nothing except trees grows up in their land. It's all rock and no soil,' Bolli had warned. 'No crops at all, not even hay. So you won't find cows. Therefore neither milk nor cheese. It's impossible to grow grain . . . so no beer. And as for vines to grow grapes, forget it. Not even sheep can survive. So the Gods alone know what the natives do for clothing to keep out the cold when they haven't any wool to weave. They must do something. There's snow and ice for eight months in the year, and the winter night lasts for two months.'

No one at the trading post where I had bought my trade stock had thrown more light on these mysteries. All they could say was that I should fill my pack with coloured ribbons, brass rings, copper figurines, fish hooks and knife blades. They thought I was mad. Winter was coming on, they pointed out, and this was not the time to trade. Better wait until the spring when the natives emerged from the forest with the winter pelts of their prey. Stubbornly I ignored their advice. I had no intention of spending several months in a remote settlement on the fringes of a wasteland. So I had slung my pack on my back and walked away. Now, with the chill wind beginning to numb my fingers and face,

I was wondering – and that not for the first time – if I had been incredibly foolish. The footpath I had been following through the forest was more and more difficult to trace. Soon I would be lost.

I blundered on. Everything around me was featureless. Each tree looked like the last one I had passed and identical to the trees that I had seen an hour earlier. Very occasionally I heard the sound of a wild animal fleeing from me, the sounds of its alarmed progress fading into the distance. I never saw the animals themselves. They were too wary. The straps of my pack were cutting into my shoulders, and I decided that I would set up camp early and start afresh in the morning. Casting around for a sheltered spot where I could light a fire and eat a meal of dried fish from my pack, I left the faint trace of the path and searched to my left. After fifty paces or so I came across such a dense thicket that I was forced to turn back. I tried in the opposite direction. Again I was thwarted by the thick undergrowth. I returned to the path and walked forward a little further, then tried again. This time I got only twenty paces – I counted them because I did not want to lose my track – before I was again forced to a halt. Once more I returned to the path and moved forward. The bushes were crowding closer. I limped on. There was a raw blister on my right heel where the shoe was rubbing and my foot hurt. I was concentrating on this pain when I noticed that the path led to an obvious gap between the dense thickets. Gratefully I quickened my pace and walked forward, then tripped. Looking down, I saw my foot was entangled in a net laid out on the ground. I was bending down to untangle the restraint when I heard a sharp, angry intake of breath. Straightening up, I saw a man step from behind a tree. He was carrying a hunting bow, its arrow set to the string and he drew it back deliberately and quietly, aiming at my chest. I stood absolutely still, trying to look innocent and harmless.

The stranger stood no higher than my chest. He was wearing the skin of an animal, some sort of deer, which he wore like a loose blouse. His head poked through a slit cut in the skin and the garment was gathered in at his waist by a broad belt made from the skin of the same animal. This blouse reached down to his knees and his lower legs were clad in leather leggings, which extended down to strange-looking leather slippers with turned-up toes. On his head was a conical cap, also of deerskin. For a moment he reminded me of a land wight. He had appeared just as silently and magically.

He made no further move towards me, but clicked his tongue softly. From behind other trees and out of the thickets emerged half a dozen of his companions. They ranged from one youngster who could only have been about twelve years old, to a much older man, whose scraggly beard was turning grey. Their precise ages were difficult to tell because their faces were unusually wrinkled and lined, and they were all dressed in identical deerskin garments. Not one of them was tall enough to come up to my shoulder, and they all had similar features – broad foreheads and pronounced cheekbones over wide mouths and narrow chins, which gave their faces a strangely triangular shape. Several of the men, I noted, had watery eyes as if they had been staring too long into the sun. Then I remembered what Olaf had told me about the long months of snow and ice, and recognised what I had seen in my childhood in Greenland – the lingering effects of snow blindness.

They were not aggressive. All of them were carrying long hunting bows, but only the first man kept an arrow aimed at me, and after a few moments he lowered his bow and let the tension relax. Then followed a brief discussion in a language that I could not understand. There seemed to be no leader – everyone including the youngster had an opinion to express. Suddenly they turned to leave and one of them jerked his head at me, indicating that I was to follow. Mystified, I set out, walking behind them along the trail. They did not even look over their shoulders to see if I was there and I found that, despite their small size, the Lopar – as I knew they must be – travelled remarkably quickly through the forest.

A brisk march brought us to where they lived. A cluster of
tents stood on the bank of a small river. At first I thought this
was a hunters' camp, but then I saw women, children and dogs
and even a baby's cradle hanging from a tree, and realised that
this was a nomad home. Tethered at a little distance were five
unusual-looking animals. That they were deer was evident because
they had antlers which would have done justice to the forest stags
I had hunted with Edgar in England. Yet their bodies were less
than half the size. Somehow their smallness seemed appropriate
among a people who – by Norse standards – were diminutive.

The man who had first revealed himself to me in the forest led
me to his tent, indicated that I should wait and ducked inside. I
eased the pack from my shoulders, lowered it to the ground and
sat down beside it. The man reappeared and silently handed me a
wooden bowl. It contained pieces of a cake. I tasted it and recognised fish and wild berries mashed together.

As I ate the fish cake, everyone in the camp continued about
their normal business, fetching water from the river in small
wooden buckets, bringing in sticks of firewood, moving between
the tents, all the while politely ignoring me. I wondered what
would happen next. After an interval, during which I finished
my meal and drank from a wooden cup of water brought to me
by one of the Lopar women, my guardian – which was how I
thought of him – again emerged from his tent. In his hand was
what I thought was a large sieve with a wooden rim. Then I saw
it was a drum, broad, flat and no deeper than the span of my
hand, an irregular oval in shape. He placed the drum carefully
upon the ground and squatted down beside it. Several of the other
men strolled over. They sat in a circle and another quiet discussion
followed. Again I could not understand what they were saying,
though several times I heard the word vuobman. Eventually my
guardian reached inside his deerskin tunic and produced a small
wedge of horn, no bigger than a gaming counter, which he placed
gently on the surface of his drum. From the folds of his blouse he
next pulled out a short hammer-shaped drumstick and began to

tap gently on the drum skin. All the onlookers leaned forward, watching intently.

I guessed what was happening and rose to my feet. Walking over to the group, I joined the circle, my neighbour politely shifting aside to give me space. I was reminded of the Saxon wands. The surface of the drum was painted with dozens of figures and symbols. Some I recognised: fish, deer, a dancing, stick-like man, a bow and arrow, half a dozen of the Elder runes. Many symbols were new to me and I could only guess their meaning — lozenges, zigzag lines, irregular star patterns, curves and ripples. I supposed that one of them must represent the sun, another the moon and perhaps a third depicted a forest of trees. I said nothing as the little horn counter hopped and skipped on the drum skin as it vibrated to the regular tapping of the drummer. The counter moved here and there, then seemed to find its own position, remaining on one spot — over the drawing of a man who seemed to have antlers on his head. Abruptly my guardian stopped his drumming. The counter stayed where it was. He picked it up, placed it on the centre of the drum and began again, tapping a slow, repeated rhythm. Again the counter advanced across the drum and came to the same position. A third time my guardian cast the lot, this time starting the counter at the edge of the drum skin before he began to urge it into life. Once more the wedge of horn moved to the figure of the antlered man, but then moved on until it came to rest on the symbol of a triangle. I guessed it was a tent.

My guardian slipped the drumstick back inside his blouse, and there was complete silence in the assembled group. Something had changed. Where the Lopar had previously been courteous, almost aloof, now they seemed a little nervous. Whatever the drum had told them, its message had been clear.

My guardian returned the drum to his tent and beckoned to me to follow him. He led me to a tent set slightly apart from the others. Like them it was an array of long thin poles propped together and neatly covered with sheets of birch bark. Pausing

outside the tent flap, he called, 'Rassa!' The man who came out
from the tent was the ugliest Lopar I had yet seen. He was of the
same height and build as all the others in the camp, but every
feature of his face was out of true. His nose was askew and
bulbous. Eyes, bulging under bushy eyebrows, gave him a perpet-
ually startled expression. His lips failed to close over slightly
protruding teeth, and his mouth was definitely lopsided. Compared
to the neat foxy-faced Lopars around him, he looked grotesque.

'You are welcome among us. I am glad you have arrived.'
said this odd-looking native. I was startled. Not just by what he
said, but that he had spoken in Norse, heavily accented and
carefully phrased but clearly understandable.

'Your name is Rassa?' I asked hesitantly.

'Yes.' he replied. 'I told the hunters that the vuodman would
provide an unusual catch today and they should not harm it, but
bring it back to camp.'

'The vuodman?' I asked. 'I don't know what you mean.'

'The vuodman is where they lie in wait for the boazo.' He
saw that I was looking even more mystified. 'You must excuse
me. I don't know how to say boazo in your tongue. Those animals
over there are boazo.' He nodded towards the five small tethered
deer. 'Those are tame ones. We place them in the forest to attract
their wild kind into the trap. Now is the season when the wild
boazo leave the open ground and come into the forest to seek
food and find shelter from the coming blizzards.'

'And the voudman?'

'That was the thicket that kept turning you back when you
were walking. Our hunters were watching you. I hear you tried
to leave the trail several times. You made much noise. In fact they
nearly lost our prize boazo who was frightened by your approach
and ran off. Luckily they recaptured it before it had gone too far.'

I recalled the hunting technique Edgar had showed me in the
forest of Northamptonshire, how he had placed me where the deer
would be directed towards the arrows of the waiting hunters. It

seemed that the Lopar did the same, building thickets of brush to funnel the wild deer in the place where the hunters lay in ambush.

'I apologise for spoiling the hunt,' I said. 'I had no idea that I was in Lopar hunting grounds.'

'Our name is not Lopar,' said Rassa gently. 'That word I heard when I visited the settled peoples — at the time when I learned to speak some words of your language — we are Sabme. To call us Lopar would be the same as if we called you cavemen.'

'Cavemen? We don't live in caves.'

Rassa smiled his crooked smile.

'Sabme children learn how Ibmal the Creator made the first men. They were two brothers. Ibmal set the brothers on the earth and they flourished, hunting and fishing. Then Ibmal sent a great howling blizzard with gales and driving snow and ice. One of the brothers ran off and found a cave, and hid himself in it. He survived. But the other brother chose to stay outside and fight the blizzard. He went on hunting and fishing and learning how to keep alive. After the blizzard had passed over, one brother emerged from the cave and from him are descended all the settled peoples. From the other brother came the Sabme.'

I was beginning to take a liking to this forthright, homely little man. 'Come,' he said, 'as you are to be my guest, we should find out a little more about you and the days that lie ahead.'

With no more ceremony than Thrand consulting the rune tablets, Rassa produced his own prophecy drum. It was much bigger and more intricately decorated than the one I had seen before. Rassa's drum had many, many more symbols. They were drawn, he told me, with the red juice from the alder tree, and he had hung coloured ribbons, small amulets and charms of copper, horn and a few in silver round the drum's edge. I carried copies of the same charms in my trade pack.

Rassa dropped a small marker on the drum skin. This time the marker was a brass ring. Before he began to tap on the drum, I intervened.

'What do the symbols mean?' I asked.

He gave me a shrewd glance. 'I think you already know some of them,' he replied.

'I can see some runes,' I said.

'Yes, I learned those signs among the settled peoples.'

'What about that one? What does that signify?' I pointed to a wavy triple line. There were several similar symbols painted at different places on the drum skin.

'They are the mountains, the places where our ancestors dwell.'

'And that one?' I indicated the drawing of a man wearing antlers on his head.

'That is the noiade's own sign. You call him a seidrmann.'

'And if the marker goes there what does it mean?'

'It tells of the presence of a noiade, or that the noaide must be consulted. Every Sabme tent has a drum of prophecy, and someone to use it. But only a noiade can read the deeper message of the arpa, the moving marker.'

Abruptly he closed his eyes and began to sing. It was a thin, quavering chant, the same short phrase repeated over and over and over again, rising in pitch until the words suddenly stopped, cut off mid-phrase as if the refrain had fallen into a pool of silence. After a short pause, Rassa began the chant again, once more raising the pitch of his voice until coming to the same abrupt halt. As he chanted, he tapped on his drum. Watching the ugly little man, his eyes closed, his body swaying back and forth very slightly, I knew that I was in the presence of a highly accomplished seidrmann. Rassa was able to enter the spirit world as easily as I could strike sparks from a flint.

After the fourth repetition of his chant, Rassa opened his eyes and looked down at the drum. I was not surprised to see that the arpa was resting once again on the antlered man. Rassa grunted, as if it merely confirmed what he had expected. Then he closed his eyes and resumed tapping, more urgently this time. I watched the track of the brass ring as it skittered across the face of the drum. It visited symbol after symbol without pausing, hesitated and then retraced a slightly different track. Rassa's drumming ended and this time he did not look down at the drum but straight at me. 'Tell me,' he said.

Strangely, I had anticipated the question. It was as if a bond, an understanding, existed between the noiade and myself. We both took it for granted that I possessed seidr skill and had come to Rassa for enlightenment.

'Movement,' I said. 'There will be movement. Towards the mountains, though which mountains I do not know. Then the drum spoke of something I do not understand, something mysterious, obscure, a little dangerous. Also of a union, a meeting.'

Rassa now looked down at the drum himself. The brass ring had come to rest on a drawing of a man seated on horseback. 'Is that what you meant by movement?' he asked.

The answer seemed obvious, but I answered, 'No, not that sign. I can't be sure how to interpret it, but whatever it is, it concerns me closely. When the ring approached the symbol and then came to rest, my spirit felt strengthened.'

'Look again and tell me what you see,' the noiade replied.

I examined the figure more closely. It was almost the smallest symbol on the drum, squeezed into a narrow space between older, more faded figures. It was unique. Nowhere else could I see this mark repeated. The horse rider was carrying a round shield. That was odd, I thought. Nowhere among the Sabme had I seen a shield. Besides, a horse would never survive in this bleak cold land. I looked again, and noticed that the horse, drawn in simple outline, had eight legs.

I looked up at Rassa. He was gazing at me questioningly with his bulging eyes. 'That is Odinn,' I said. 'Odinn riding Sleipnir.'

'Is it? I copied that sign from something I saw among the settled folk. I saw it carved on a rock and knew that it had power.'

'Odinn is my God,' I said. 'I am his devotee. It was Odinn who brought me to your land.'

'Later you can tell me who is this Odinn,' Rassa answered, 'but among my people that symbol has another meaning. For us it is the symbol of approaching death.'

WITH THIS ENIGMATIC forecast I began my time among the forest Sabme. My days with them were to be some of the most remarkable, and satisfactory, of my life, thanks almost entirely to Rassa and his family. Rassa was no ordinary noaide. He was acknowledged as maybe the greatest noaide of his time. His unusual appearance had marked him out from his earliest childhood. Ungainly and clumsy, he had differed from other boys. Trying to play their games, he would sometimes fall down on the ground and choke or lose his senses entirely. Norse children would have mocked and teased him, but the Sabme treated him with special gentleness. No one had been surprised when, at the age of eight, he began to have strange and disturbing dreams. It was the proof to the Sabme that the sacred ancestors had sent Rassa as their intermediary, and Rassa's parents unhesitatingly handed over their son to the local shaman for instruction. Thirty years later his reputation extended from the forest margins where his own people lived as far as the distant coast, to those Sabme who fished for seal and small whale. Among all the Sabme bands, the siida, it was known that Rassa was a great noaide, and from time to time he would come to visit them in his spirit travels. So high was his reputation when I arrived among them that no one questioned why he decided to take a lumbering stranger into his tent and instruct him in the sacred ways. His own siida believed that their great noaide had summoned me. Their drums told them so. For my part, I believed sometimes that Rassa was Odinn's agent. At other times I thought he might be the All-Father himself, in human guise.

Our siida (as I soon came to think of it) shifted camp the morning after my arrival. They did not trouble to dismantle their birch-bark tents. They merely gathered up their few belongings, wrapped them in bundles, which they slung on rawhide cords over their shoulders or tied to their backs, and set off along the trail that followed the river bank. The fishing had been disappointing, Rassa explained. The local water spirit and the Fish Gods were displeased. The reason for their anger he did not know. There was a hole in the bottom of the river, leading to a subterranean spirit river, and the fish had all fled there. It would be wise for the siida to move to another spot, where the spirits were more friendly. There was no time to waste. Soon the river would be frozen over and fishing – on which the siida depended at least as much as hunting – would become impossible. Our straggle of twenty families, together with their dogs and the six haltered boazo, walked for half a day before we came to our destination, further downstream. Clearly the siida had occupied the site previously. There were tent frames already standing, which the Sabme quickly covered with deerskins.

'Birch bark is not strong enough to withstand the snows and gales, nor warm enough,' Rassa explained. 'For the next few weeks we will use a single layer of deerskin. Later, when it gets really cold, we'll add extra layers to keep in the warmth.'

His own family consisted of his wife, a married daughter with her husband and their small baby, and a second daughter who seemed vaguely familiar. Then I realised that she had been with the hunting party at the vuodman. With all the Sabme dressed in their deerskin blouses, leggings and caps, it was difficult to tell men from women, and I had not expected a girl to be among the hunters. Nor, during the previous night spent in Rassa's tent, had I noticed that he had a second daughter because the Sabme removed only their shoes before they lay down and they slept almost fully clothed. I had crawled into Rassa's tent to find the place half filled with smoke. There was a fireplace in the centre, and the chimney hole in the apex of the tent had been partly covered over because several fish were hanging to cure from a pole projecting over the fire. Staying close to the ground was the only place where it was possible to breathe freely. Arranged around the outer edge of the tent were the family possessions and these became our pillows when we all lay down to sleep on deerskins over a carpet of fresh birch twigs. There was no furniture of any kind.

Rassa asked me to walk with him to the river bank. I noticed that all the other Sabme stayed well back, watching us. The water was shallow, fast flowing over gravel and rocks. Rassa had a fish spear in one hand and a birch-bark fish basket in the other. Without pausing, he waded out to a large, slick boulder which projected above the water. Rassa scanned the surface of the river for a few moments, then stabbed with his fish spear, successfully spiking a small fish about the length of my hand. He carefully removed the fish from the barbs, knocked its head against the rock and laid the dead fish on the rock. Next he placed the fish basket on his head, and spoke some words in the Sabme tongue, apparently addressing the rock itself. Scooping up water in the palm of his hand, he poured it onto the rock, and bowed three times. With the curved knife which every Sabme wore dangling from his belt, he scraped some scales from the fish. Cradling the scales in the palm of his hand he returned to the camp, where he distributed them to the man of each family. Only then did the siida begin to prepare their nets and fishing lines and approach the water. 'The rock is a sieidde,' Rassa explained to me, 'the spirit of the river. I asked fishing luck for every family. I promised that each family that catches fish will make an offering to the sieidde. They will do this at the end of every day that we stay here, and will do so whenever we return to this place in the future.'

'Why did you give fish scales only to the men?' I asked.

'It is bad luck for a woman to approach the sieidde of the river. Ill luck for the siida and dangerous for the woman herself. It can harm her future children.'

'But didn't I see your daughter with the hunters at the vuodman. If the women can hunt, why can't they fish?'

'That is the way it has always been. My daughter Allba hunts because she's as good as many of the men when it comes to the chase, if not better. They can hardly keep up with her. She's quick and nimble even in dense forest. She was always like that, from when she was a little child. Her only fault is that she likes to talk all the time, a constant chatter. That's why my wife and I named her after the little bird that hops around in summer in the bushes and never stops saying "tik-a-tik".'

With every sentence, Rassa was strengthening my desire to stay among the Sabme if they would allow it. I wanted to learn more of Rassa's seidr and to honour my promise to Grettir by sharing in their way of life. Remembering the store of fish hooks in my trade pack, I went to fetch them and handed my entire stock to Rassa. He accepted the gift almost casually, as if it was the most natural thing in the world. 'We make our own fish hooks of wood or bone. But metal ones are far better,' he said as he began to distribute them among the different families.

'Do you share out everything?' I asked.

He shook his head. 'Not everything. Each person and each family knows what is theirs – clothes, dogs, knives, cooking gear. But they will lend or give that item to someone else if it meets a need. Not to do so would be selfish. We have learned that only by helping one another can we survive as a siida.'

'Then what about the other siida? What happens if you both want to fish on the same river or hunt boazo in the same area of forest?'

'Each siida knows its own territory,' he answered. 'Its members have hunted or fished in certain places down through the generations. We respect that custom.'

'But if you do have a dispute over, say, a good fishing place when there is a famine, do you fight for your rights?'

Rassa looked mildly shocked. 'We never fight. We use all our energy in finding food and shelter, making sure that our children grow up healthy, honouring our ancestors. If another siida is starving and needs a particular fishing spot or hunting ground, then they ask us and if possible we agree to lend it to them until their lives have improved. Besides, our land is so broad that there is room enough for all.'

'I find that strange,' I told him. 'Where I come from, a man will fight to defend what he owns. If a neighbour tries to take his land, or a stranger comes to seize his property, we fight and try to drive him away.'

'For the Sabme that's not necessary,' said the noaide. 'If someone invades our territory, we hide or we run away. We wait until the winter comes and the foreigners have to leave. We know that they are not fit to stay.'

He gestured towards the clothes I was wearing – woollen shirt and loose trousers, a thick travelling cloak and the same ill-fitting leather shoes which had given me blisters earlier. 'The foreigners dress like you. They don't know any better. That is why I've asked my wife and Allba to prepare clothes more suitable for the winter. They've never made clothes so big before, but they will have them ready for you in a few days.'

The unexpected benefit of Rassa's request for clothes that would fit me was that it silenced, temporarily, the constant chatter of his daughter Allba. She talked without pause, mostly to her mother, who went about her work quietly, scarcely bothering to reply. I had no idea what Allba was saying, but did not doubt that I was often the topic of her conversation. Now, as she sat with her mother stitching my winter wardrobe, Allba's mouth was too full of deer sinew for her to keep up her constant chatter. Every thread in the garment had to be ripped with teeth from dried sinew taken from a deer's back or legs, then chewed to soften the fibre and rolled into thread. While the women chewed and stitched, I helped Rassa prepare the family meals. One of the novel features of life among the Sabme was that the men did the cooking.

It must have been in about my fourth week with the siide that two events occurred which changed my situation. The first event was anticipated, but the second was a complete surprise. I woke up one morning at the usual time, just after first light, and as I lay on my deerskin rug I noticed that the interior of the tent was much lighter than usual. I rolled over and peered at the small gap between the edge of the tent and the ground. The daylight was shining through the gap so brightly that it made me squint. Quietly I got up, pushed aside the door flap, and stepped out. The entire camp was shrouded in a covering of heavy snow. The first great snowfall had come upon us in the night. Everything we had left outside the tents — firewood, fish baskets, the nets, the sleeping dogs — were humps in the snow. Even the six boazo had snowy coats. Winter had arrived.

That was the day that Rassa's wife and daughter finished my deerskin garments. There was much mirth among the Sabme as they came to our tent to see me being shown how to put them on. First came a deerskin shirt, worn with the fur against my skin, then close-fitting deerskin trousers, which were awkward to pull on though they had slits at the ankles, and a pair of hand-sewn shoes. These had the characteristic turned-up toes but no heels. 'For when you wear skis,' Rassa explained. He was teasing out some dried sedge grass by separating the strands, then arranging them into two soft padded squares. 'Here put these in your shoes,' he said, 'You'll find them better than any woollen socks. They'll keep your feet warmer, and when they get wet they'll dry out in moments if you hold them near the fire.' Finally he helped me into the long Sabme deerskin blouse. It reached down to my knees. A broad belt held the garment tight around my waist. When I took a few experimental steps, the sensation was quite different from any other clothes I had ever worn before — my body warm and protected, my legs free.

The second event took place on the night after the snowfall. When I entered the family tent, I found a second deerskin had been left on my usual sleeping place. As the weather had turned much colder, I pulled the deerskin over me as a blanket when I lay down. I was on the verge of falling asleep, when I felt the edge of the deerskin lift and someone crawl in beside me. There was enough light from the fire's embers to see that my visitor was Rassa's daughter, Allba. I could see the gleam of the firelight in her eyes and her face had a mischievous look. She placed her mouth against my ear and said softly, 'Tik-a-tik,' then giggled and snuggled down beside me. I did not know what to do. Close by slept her father and mother, her sister and brother-in-law. I feared Rassa's reaction should he wake up. For several moments I lay there, pretending to be asleep. Then Allba's hand began to explore. Very quietly she loosened my Sabme belt and removed my leggings. Then she slid inside my Sabme blouse and nestled against me. She was naked.

I woke up to find that I had overslept. Allba lay curled up within my outstretched arm and the tent was empty. Rassa and the other members of his family had already begun their day. I could hear them moving about outside. Hurriedly I began to pull on my clothes, and this woke Allba. Her eyes were pale blue-grey, a colour sometimes found among the Sabme, and she gazed up at me without the slightest trace of embarrassment. She looked utterly content. She wriggled across to where her clothes lay and, a moment later, she was dressed and ducking out of the tent flap to join her parents. Slowly I followed, wondering what reception I would receive.

Rassa looked up at me as I emerged, and seemed utterly unconcerned. 'You know how to use these, I hope,' was all he said. He was wiping the snow off two long flat lathes of wood.

'I rode on a ski when I was a child, but only a few times, and mostly as a game,' I answered.

'You'll need to know more than that. Allba can show you.'

It dawned on me that Rassa was taking my relationship with his second daughter as normal. Later I was to discover that he actively approved of it. The Sabme thought it natural for a man and woman to sleep together if both were willing. They considered it a sensible arrangement if it is satisfactory for both partners. For a while I worried that Allba was anticipating that our relationship would become a permanent bond. But later, after she had instructed me in a few words of the Sabme language and I had taught her to speak some Norse, she laughed at me when I expressed my concern.

'How can one expect something like that to go on for ever? That's how the settled people think. It would be like staying in one spot permanently. The Sabme believe that in life, the seasons change and it is better to travel than to stay.' I began to say something more, but she laid a finger on my lips and added, 'I could have come to your bed as an act of kindness, as you are the guest in my tent. But that is not why I joined you. I did so because I wanted you and you have not disappointed me.'

Allba was the remedy for an ailment that I scarcely knew I suffered. My shabby treatment at the hands of Gunnhildr, my disenchantment with Aelfgifu, and my youthful heartbreaks had left me disillusioned with the opposite sex. I viewed women with caution, fearing either disappointment or some unforeseen calamity. Allba cured all that. She was so full of life, so active, so natural and uncomplicated. In love-making she was skilled as well as lustful, and I would have been a dullard not to have revelled in my good fortune. Beneath those layers of deerskin clothes, she was very seductive. She had small, fine bones which made her seem as fragile and lightweight as the little snow bird after which she had been named. Constant exercise while hunting and skiing meant that her body was in perfect condition, with slim shoulders and hips. Tiny, high, arched feet gave her a quick, graceful step, and I was roused to discover that the skin of her body and limbs was a smooth dark ivory in contrast to the dark tanned elfin face, its lines etched by snow glare and the wind. Although neither of us became hostage to the other, I think Allba relished our relationship. She was proud of my role as a foreign noaide. For my part I was entranced by her. In short, I fell in love with Allba and my love was unfettered and free.

She taught me how to travel on skis. Not as well as any Sabme, of course. The Sabme learn the skill of travelling across the country on wooden boards as soon as they learn to walk, and no one can really acquire their expertise. Just as the Norse are the finest ship handlers and shipbuilders, so the Sabme excel at snow travel. Nature seems to have designed them for it. Their light weight ensures that they glide across snow that would crack beneath a heavier burden, and their agility means they can thread their way across broken terrain that would thwart a clumsier man. They do not use the ski as the Norse do, riding a single board, with a stick to steer and propel themselves downhill or across a frozen surface. The Sabme attach a board to each foot and can stride at the speed of a running man. They keep up the pace for as long as daylight will allow them. Where Norse craftsmen know how to shape a hull or cut and stitch a sail to best advantage, the Sabme know how to select and shape the skis that bear them, birch wood when the snow is soft, pine when the surface hardens; every ski – they are unequal in length – is hand-crafted to suit the style and size of the user. In the end I learned to travel on the wooden lathes well enough to keep up with siida when we moved, or to travel slowly alongside when Rassa wanted to show me some remote sacred place. But I could never match Allba and the other hunters. They moved so confidently across the snow that they could run down a wolf and get its pelt. For hour after hour they would pursue their prey across the snow, the animal tiring as it leaped through the drifts over which the hunters glided effortlessly. Finally, when the exhausted wolf turned snarling on its pursuers, the leading Sabme would ski close enough to spear or knife the beast to death.

FIFTEEN

ALLBA WORE AROUND her neck an amulet in the shape of a bird. She never took it off, even when we were making love. The bird was her companion, she said, and she asked why I did not wear my own. As a man I should carry it on a cord looped round from my neck and under my arm, so that the talisman hung within my armpit. 'Are you so brave that you risk travelling alone?' she asked. 'Even my father does not do that.' I thought she was talking of a good-luck charm and I made a joke of it, telling her that I had a dozen talismans in my trade pack and was well guarded. It was one of the few times I saw Allba angry. She told me not to play the fool.

When I asked Rassa why his daughter had reacted with such intensity, he asked if I remembered where I had first joined the siida. 'The fishing had been very bad in that place,' he reminded me. 'The fish had gone away. They were still there, but they were not there. We had to move to where another sieidde would accept our sacrifices.'

'How could the fish be there and not there?'

'They had gone away to their own saivo river. I could have followed them, or sent my companion to plead with the water spirit who sent them there. But if the water spirit was still angry, the fish might not have returned.'

The saivo, according to Rassa, is a world which lies alongside
our own. It is a mirror of our world, yet more substantial and in
it live the spirits of the departed and the companions of the living.
These companions come into our world to join us as wraiths and
sometimes we can visit the saivo ourselves, but we need our
guardian wraiths to guide and protect us.

'Our companions are animals, not people,' Rassa said, putting
aside the wooden bowl he had been carving. 'Every Sabme has
one – whether it is a fox, a lynx, a bird or some other animal.
When we are very young the drum tells our parents which creature is to be our saivo companion through life. Occasionally the
wrong choice is made and then the child gets sick or has an
accident. So we ask the drum again and it indicates a new companion, one that will be more suitable. Since Allba was a baby her
saivo wraith is the bird whose image she wears.'

'Among my people,' I said, 'there are fylga, the fetches. I have
seen them myself at times of death. They are our other-persons
from another world. When they appear, they resemble us directly.
Do you mean that I have an animal companion as well?'

Rassa reached across to where his drum lay on the ground. It
was always close to his hand. He placed the arpa on the taut drum
skin, and without even closing his eyes or singing his chant, he
gave a single hard rap on the drum with his forefinger. The arpa
leaped, struck the wooden rim and bounced back. It landed on the
outline figure of a bear.

I chose to doubt him. 'How do I know that my companion is
a bear?'

'It was decided for you at the time of your birth.'

'But I was born on an island in the ocean where there are no
bears.'

'Perhaps a bear entered the lives of your parents.'

I thought for a moment. 'I was told that when my father first
met my mother, he was on his way back from a voyage to
Norway to deliver a captive polar bear. But he had handed over

the bear many weeks before he met my mother, and anyhow the bear died soon afterwards.'

'You will find that the bear died about the time you were born,' said Rassa firmly. 'The bear's spirit has protected you since then. That is your good fortune. The bear is the most powerful of all creatures. It has the intelligence of one man and the strength of nine.'

Before the sun vanished below the horizon for winter, Rassa suggested that if I wanted to know more about the saivo I should enter it myself. I hesitated. I told him that my experience of the other world had been in brief glimpses, through second sight, usually in the company of others who also possessed the ability, and that sometimes the experience had been disturbing and unpleasant. I said I was doubtful that I had the courage to enter the spirit world deliberately and alone. He assured me that my spirit companion would protect me, and that he himself could assist me to pass through the barrier that separated us from the saivo. 'Your second sight shows that you already live close enough to the saivo to see through the veil that divides it from us. I am only proposing that you pass through the veil entirely and discover what lies on the other side.'

'How do I know that I will be able to return?' I asked.

'That, too, I can arrange with Allba's help,' he answered.

He woke Allba and me long before dawn the next day. He had already lit a small fire in the central hearth and cleared a space at the back of the tent. There was enough room for me to sit cross-legged on a square of deerskin. The hide was placed fur side down, and its surface had been painted with the four white lines in the pattern that I had known from throwing the rune counters and the Saxon wands. Rassa indicated that I should sit within the central square and that Allba would squat facing me. 'As my daughter, she has inherited some of my powers,' he said. 'If she is near at hand, you may meet her in the saivo.'

Allba's presence gave me more confidence, for I was feeling

very nervous. She untied the small leather pouch she wore on her belt when she went on her hunting trips and shook out the contents onto the deerskin in front of me. The red caps with their white spots were faded to a dull, mottled pink, but I could still recognise the dried and shrivelled mushrooms. Allba picked them over carefully, running her small fingers over them delicately, feeling their rough surface. Then she selected three of the smallest. Carefully putting the others back into the pouch, she left two of the mushrooms on the deerskin, placed the third in her mouth and began to chew deliberately. She kept her eyes on me, her gaze never wavering. After a little time, she put her hand to her mouth and spat out the contents. She held out her palm to me. 'Eat,' she said. I took the warm moist pellet from her, placed it on my tongue and swallowed. Twice more she softened the mushrooms and twice more I swallowed.

Then I sat quietly facing her, observing the firelight play across her features. Her eyes were in shadow.

Time passed. I had no way of judging how long I sat there. Rassa stayed in the background and added several dry sticks to the fire to keep it alight.

Slowly, very slowly, I began to lose touch with my body. As I separated from its physical presence, I felt my body trembling. Once or twice I knew I twitched. But there was nothing I could do about it and I felt unconcerned. A hazy contentment was settling over me. My body seemed to grow lighter as my thoughts relaxed. Everything except for Allba's face became indistinct. She did not move, yet her face came closer and closer. I saw every tiny detail with extraordinary clarity. The lobe of her right ear filled my vision. I detected the gentle blush of blood beneath the skin, the soft fuzz of hair. I wanted to reach out and nibble it in my teeth.

Suddenly there was no ground beneath me. I was suspended in a comfortable space. I knew that my body was there with me, but it had no importance. Without any sensation of movement I was in an endless landscape of trees, snow and rock, but I felt no cold. I glided over the surface without contact. It was as if I was riding on a gentle air current. The trees were a vivid green and I could examine every leaf and wrinkle of the bark in minute detail. The snow reflected the colours of the rainbow, the crystals shifted, merged and rippled. A small bird flew up from a bush and I knew that it was Allba's companion. Between two trees I glimpsed the upright form of a white bear, close, yet not close. It was standing upright, its two eyes gazing at me with a human expression and motionless. I heard someone speaking to me. I recognised my own voice and replied. The conversation was reassuring. I felt peaceful. A bear, dark brown this time, appeared to one side of my path, head down, lumbering and swaying as it walked along and our tracks were converging. When the animal was in touching distance, we both halted. I felt the brush of a bird's wing against my cheek. The bear slowly turned to face me and its muzzle beneath the eyes seemed to smile.

The eyes were grey-blue, and I realised that I was looking into Allba's face. I was back on the deerskin, still seated.

'You have come back from the saivo,' said Rassa. 'You were there only a short time, but long enough to know how to return there if you wish.'

'It seemed very like our own world,' I said, 'only much larger and always just beyond reach, as though it withheld itself.'

'That is appearance only,' said the noaide. 'The saivo is full of spirits, the spirts of the dead as well as the spirits who rule our lives. By comparison our world is temporary and fragile. Our world is in the present, while the saivo is eternal. Those who travel into the saivo glimpse the forces that determine our existence, but only when those spirits wish to be seen. Those who visit the saivo regularly become accepted there and then the spirits reveal themselves.'

'Why should a bear smile?' I asked.

Opposite me Allba suddenly got to her feet and left the tent. Rassa did not answer. Without warning I felt dizzy and my stomach heaved. More than anything else, I wanted to lie down and close my eyes again. I could barely drag myself back to my sleeping place and the last thing I remembered was Rassa throwing a deerskin over me.

Snow fell almost daily now, heavy flakes drifting down through the trees and settling on the ground. Our hunters made repeated sweeps of the forest to lay out their wooden traps because the fur-bearing animals had grown their winter coats and were in their prime. The siida made one final move. It was laborious because our tents were now double- or triple-layered to keep out the cold and difficult to dismantle and we were hampered by our heavy winter clothing. We went to ground, quite literally. The siida had its midwinter camp in the lee of a low ridge, which gave shelter from the blizzards. Over the generations each family had dug itself a refuge, excavating the soft earthen side of the ridge, then covering the crater with a thick roof of logs and earth. The entrance to Rassa's cabin was little more than a tunnel, through which I crawled on hands and knees, but the place was surprisingly spacious once inside. I could stand upright and though the place was smoky from the small fire in the central hearth it was cosy. I admitted to myself that the thought of spending the next few months here with Allba was appealing. Rassa's wife had spread the floor with the usual carpet of fresh spruce twigs covered with deerskins, and had divided the interior into small cubicles by hanging up sheets of light cotton obtained from the springtime traders. The contrast with the squalid dugout where Grettir had died could not have been greater. I said so to Rassa and described how my sworn brother had met his end through a volva's malign intervention, with curse runes cut on a log.

'Had your sworn brother met with such an accident among the Sabme, injuring himself with that axe,' commented Rassa, 'we would have known that it was surely a staallu's doing. The staallu can disguise himself as an animal, a deer perhaps, and allows himself to be hunted down and killed. But when the hunter begins to cut up the animal to take its flesh and hide, the staallu turns the knife blade on the bone, so that the hunter cuts himself badly. If the hunter is far from his siida, he bleeds to death beside the carcass of his kill. Then the staallu returns to his normal shape, drinks the blood and feasts on the corpse of his victim.'

Allba, who was listening, gave a little scornful hiss. 'If I ever meet the staallu, he will regret the day. That's just a story to frighten children.'

'Don't be so sure, Allba. Just hope you never meet him,' her father murmured, then turning to me said, 'The staallu roams the forest. He's big and a bit simple and clumsy. We say he's like those coarse traders who come to acquire our furs in the spring-time, though the staallu's appetite is even more gross. He eats human flesh when times are hard, and has been known to carry off Sabme girls.'

That same week I gave away the rest of the contents of my trader's pack. I had lost any ambition to barter with the members of the siida for furs and I was ashamed to hold back items which could be useful to the band. The Sabme were so generous and hospitable to me that it seemed wrong not to contribute my share to their well-being. Apart from mending nets and doing some primitive metalwork, I was useless to them, so I handed the pack over to Rassa and asked that he distribute the contents to who-ever needed it most. The only item I kept back was the fire ruby – and that I gave to Allba as a love token. The jewel delighted her. She spent hours in the cabin, sitting by the fire with the ruby in her fingers and turning the gem this way and that so that the red light flickered within the gem. 'There is a spirit dancing inside the stone,' she would say. 'It is the spirit which brought you to me.'

The effect of giving away all my trade goods was the reverse of what I had expected – instead of ending my chances of obtain-ing furs to take to Miklagard, I was deluged with them. Nearly every day a hunter left outside Rassa's cabin the frost-stiffened carcass of an ermine, a sable, a squirrel or a white fox, whose luxurious pelt Allba would skin and prepare for me. There was no way of knowing which hunter was responsible for the gift. They

came and went silently on their skis. Only the blizzards stopped
them. When the blizzard spirit raged the entire siida would disappear inside their underground shelters and wait for the terrible
wind and driving snow to end. Then, cautiously, the Sabme dug
themselves out of the snow-covered lairs and, like the animals
they hunted, sniffed the wind and set out to forage.

Of course we ate the flesh of the animals we skinned. Some
were rank and disagreeable – marten and otter were particularly
unpleasant. But squirrel was tasty and so too was beaver. Whatever meat was left over we placed in the little larders each Sabme
family had built close to their cabin, a small hutch on a pole or
set on top of a rock, so as it was out of reach of animals. The
food never spoiled in the bitter cold. If a hunter was lucky enough
to kill a wild boaz, he stored wooden bowls of the fresh deer's
blood in the same place. Within hours it had frozen hard and
could be chopped in pieces with an axe and brought within the
cabin as required.

Rassa was called away by the spirits from time to time, though
not always when he wanted. Without warning he would begin to
twitch and writhe, then lose his balance and fall to the ground. If
the spirit call was urgent, he foamed at the mouth. He had told us
to press a rag into his mouth if his tongue lolled out, but not to
restrain him if he was in spasms because, as his body writhed, his
spirit was entering the saivo, and soon all would be calm. Rassa's
family were accustomed to these sudden departures. They would
lay the unconscious noiade comfortably on his face, place his
drum beneath his outstretched right hand in case he had need of
it in the saivo, and then await his return to our world. When
Rassa did rejoin us, his mood depended on what he had experienced in his absence. Sometimes, if he had been fighting evil
spirits, he would come back exhausted. At other times he was
elated, telling us of the great spirits that he had encountered.
Ibmal the Sky God was untouchable and unknowable, but Rassa
sometimes met Biegg-Olbmai, the God of Wind, and wrestled

with him to prevent a three-day blizzard. On another occasion he had asked the God responsible for hunting, a spirit he called 'Blood Man', that the siida's hunters should be rewarded. Two days later they tracked and killed an elk. The Gods and spirits whom Rassa revered were new to me, but his words aroused a faint recollection of a spirit world far older than the Elder Faith. I sensed that my own Gods, Odinn, Frey, Thor and the others, had all emerged from Rassa's saivo to take the shapes in which I knew them.

It was when Bolive, the Sabme Sun God, had begun to appear regularly over the southern horizon that one of our neighbours came to the entrance of Rassa's cabin and called excitedly down the tunnel. He gabbled his words so fast that I could not understand what he was saying, though Allba had spent many hours teaching me a working knowledge of her language. Whatever the hunter's message, Rassa immediately put aside the drum he was repainting and rose to his feet. Reaching for his heavy wolfskin cloak, he gestured for me to follow, and the two of us emerged from the cabin to find a group of eight Sabme hunters, looking towards him, impatient for instructions. One of the Sabme said something about 'honey paws', and when Rassa replied, the hunters began to disperse towards their cabins, calling out to their families excitedly.

'What's happening?' I asked Rassa.

'The time has come to leave our cabins and live in our tents again, though this is much earlier in the season than is usual,' he said, 'but the Old One wants it to be that way.'

'The Old One? Who's he?'

Rassa would not answer directly. He asked his wife and Allba to get ready to leave the cabin. So uncomplicated was the Sabme life that our entire siida was on the move within the time it took for the men, women and children to load our belongings onto light sledges, strap infants to their mothers' backs in tiny boat-shaped cradles lined with moss, and fasten on skis. I had no sledge to pull as I was so clumsy on skis, nor was I given a pack because I was already heavier than the Sabme and would have broken through the crust of snow.

We returned to the camp that we had left before we went into the cabins, and once again triple-covered the standing tent frames with deer hides. Everyone seemed in great good humour, leaving me confused as to what was going on.

'What is it?' I asked Allba, 'Why did we leave the cabins so quickly?'

'It's time for the most important hunt of the entire year,' she replied. 'The hunt that will ensure our siida's future.'

'Are you going on the hunt?'

'That is forbidden.'

'But you're almost our best hunter,' I objected. 'You will be needed.'

'Brothers are needed, not women,' she replied enigmatically as she tugged the final layer of the tent's deerskin into position.

I was still bemused the next morning when I woke up to find myself covered with a layer of snow a hand's breadth deep. The smoke hole in the top of the tent had been left open, and a late heavy fall of snow had half-buried the camp. No one seemed perturbed.

'Here, wear these,' said Allba, handing me a pair of shoes she had been working on all winter.

I turned them over in my hand. 'Can't I wear my usual shoes?'

'No,' she said. 'I stitched those with the seams inside so that the snow does not gather on them and I made them from the skin from a boaz head. The thickest and strongest hide, it is fitting that you should wear them today.' She also insisted that I put on my best winter garment – a heavy wolfskin cape – though it looked strange on me because the cape had previously belonged to Rassa, and Allba had lengthened it with a skirt of reindeer hide to make it fit my extra height. Rassa himself was donning his noaide's belt hung with the jawbones of the various fur-bearing animals we hunted, a cap sewn with sacred amulets and a heavy bearskin cloak. I had never seen him wear all these items at the same time, nor the short staff wound with red and blue ribbons and its cluster of small hawk's bells. When I offered to carry his sacred drum for him, Rassa shook his head and gestured for me to leave the tent ahead of him. Outside I found every hunter in our siida already waiting and dressed as if for a festival. Some had put on dark blue surcoats made of cloth acquired from the traders, and their wives had sewn the hems with strips of red and yellow ribbon. Others wore the familiar deerskin hunting garments, but had added colourful hats and belts and tied sprigs of spruce to their sleeves. They all looked excited and eager, and it took me several moments to realise that they were not equipped with their usual hunting bows and arrows, throwing sticks and wooden traps. Each man was armed with a stout spear, its shaft of rough wood, the tip a broad metal head.

I had no time to ask the hunters why they had changed their equipment because Rassa now made his formal appearance. He emerged from the tent and tramped through the snow to the flat boulder at the centre of our camp. With each step he softly jingled the bells on his noaide's wand and chanted a song I had never heard before. The words were very strange. They came from a language which bore no relation to that I had learned over the winter. When Rassa reached the rock he placed his magic drum on it, then faced towards the south. He raised the wand three times and called out what I took to be an invocation. Then he reached inside his cloak with his right hand and pulled something out from under his left armpit. He held it up for all to see. It was an arpa ring, but not of brass. From where I stood, I guessed that it was of gold and was sure of it when Rassa tossed the ring onto the drum skin. It fell with a dull and heavier thud than a token made of baser metal.

Rassa struck the drum's wooden rim with the end of his noaide's wand. The golden arpa skidded across the taut deerskin and came to a halt. Everyone craned forward to see the symbol

where it rested. It lay on the serpent sign of the mountains. A
shiver of delight ran through the crowd. The small, nimble men
glanced at one another and nodded happily. The ancestors were
observing and approving. Again the noiade rapped the drum with
his staff and this time the golden ring came to rest on the figure
of a bear. Now I detected that the onlookers were puzzled, almost
doubtful. Rassa sensed their hesitation. Instead of striking the
drum a third time with his wand, he snatched up the golden arpa
and with a cry like a heron's angry croak he tossed it in the air so
that it landed on the drum skin. By chance the ring landed on its
edge, and began to roll, first to the edge of the drum, then
rebounding it began to trace its path erratically. It wobbled along
as if uncertain until it finally slowed, remained for a heartbeat on
its edge, then toppled gently to one side and settled with the
gentle reverberation that a coin makes as it falls upon a gaming
table. Again all the spectators leaned forward to see where it had
come to rest. This time the arpa lay upon the sign of my saivo
companion – the bear.

Rassa did not hesitate. He picked up the ring, walked across
to the nearest hunter and took away his heavy spear. Next he
placed the golden ring over the spear tip. Finally he turned to
where I stood and, with a formal gesture, placed the spear in my
hand.

The drum had decided. The hunters dispersed to their tents to
collect their skis and Rassa led me to where his wife and Allba
were standing by our tent, watching. Allba knelt down in the
snow to tie on my skis and, as she rose to her feet, I made a
movement as if to embrace her. To my chagrin, she leaped back
as if I had struck her and moved away from me, making it plain
that she wanted nothing to do with me. Puzzled and a little hurt,
I accompanied her father to where a little procession was forming
up. It was led by the man who had first called Rassa from our
cabin. I recognised his voice. He was the only one without a
heavy spear in his hand. Instead he carried a long hunting bow of
willow bound with birch bark. The bow was unstrung and a

spruce twig was fastened to the tip. Behind him came Rassa in his
bearskin cape, then myself, and finally the remainder of the
brightly dressed hunters in single file. In complete silence we left
the camp and began to ski through the forest, following the man
with the bow. How he picked his way I could not tell, for the
snowfall had obliterated all tracks. But he did not falter and I was
hard put to it to keep up with the pace. From time to time he
slowed so that I could catch my breath, and I marvelled at the
patience of the Sabme hunters behind me who must have thought
me half-crippled on my skis.

At mid-morning our leader abruptly came to a stop. I looked
around, trying to see what had made him halt. There was nothing
different. The forest trees stretched away on all sides. The snow
lay thick on the ground and clung in little piles to the branches.
I could hear no sound. There was utter stillness apart from the
sound of my own breathing.

Our leader bent down and unfastened his skis. Still holding his
bow, he stepped to one side and began to walk in a wide circle,
sinking deep into the snow with each step. The rest of us waited,
watching him, not saying a word. I looked across at Rassa, hoping
for some guidance, but he was standing with his eyes closed, his
lips moving as if in prayer. Slowly the bowman walked on, leaving
his footmarks in the snow and finally coming back to his starting
point. Again I tried to understand the significance of his actions.
Everything was done so quietly and deliberately that I knew it
had to be a ritual. I scanned the circle of footprints he had made.
I still saw nothing. The circle enclosed a small rise in the ground,
not even large enough to be called a knoll. For want of any other
explanation, I presumed that it was a sieidde place. We had come
to pay homage to the nature spirit.

I waited for Rassa to begin his incantation to the spirit. But
the noiade was now removing his own skis and so too were the
other Sabme. I did the same. My hands were stiff with cold and it
took me several attempts to undo the knots in the thongs holding
the skis to the new shoes Allba had made for me. I was pleased

to see that, as she had promised, the snow had not stuck to them.
I laid down the heavy spear to use both hands to undo the knots,
and fearing that the gold ring would slip off and be lost in the
snow, I pushed it more firmly in place. I put my skis to one side
and straightened up. Glancing round, I saw that the other hunters
had spread out to either side of me. Rassa was standing slightly
aside. The only person directly ahead of me was the bowman and
he was walking to the middle of the circle he had made with his
footprints. He still had his bow in his right hand, but it was not
yet strung. Coming almost to the centre of the circle, the hunter
took three or four steps to one side, then another five or six steps
forward, and turned to face me. Some instinct warned me, and
made me grasp the heavy spear more firmly. I wondered if he
would string the bow and attack me. Instead he raised the bow
with both hands, and plunged it into the snow at his feet. Nothing
happened. Two or three times more he repeated the same action.
Then, shockingly, the snow directly in front of him cracked open,
and a massive shape came bursting out. In the next instant I
recognised the snow-covered form of an angry bear charging
straight towards me.

To this day I do not know whether I was saved by my natural
sense of self-preservation or by following Edgar's hunting instructions given long ago in an English forest. I had no time to turn
and flee. The snow would have hampered my flight and the bear
would have caught and ripped me in an instant. So I stood my
ground, rammed the butt of the crude spear into the snow behind
me and felt it strike solid, frozen earth. Scattering snow in all
directions, the bear came careering towards me. When it saw
the obstacle in its path, its angry warning growl rose to a full
threatening roar and it rose on its back legs, its paws ready to
strike. If the bear had stayed on all fours, I would not have known
where to aim the spear. Now I was confronted with the hairy
belly, the small eyes glaring down at me in rage, the open mouth
and pink gullet, and I guided the spear point into the open and
inviting chest. The bear impaled itself and I did nothing more

than hold the shaft firm. It gave a deep coughing grunt as the broad metal spear head entered its chest, and then it began to sink down onto all fours, shaking its head as if in surprise. The end was swift. For a moment the bear looked incredulous. Even as it tried to turn and lumber away and my spear was wrenched from my grasp, the Sabme were closing in from either side. I looked on, shaking with shock, as they ran up and with cool precision speared the bear in its heart.

Rassa approached the carcass where it lay on the blood-smeared snow. The hunters reverentially stepped back several paces to give him space. The noiade leaned down and felt the bear's body. I saw him reach behind the bear's left front leg, against the chest. A moment later the noiade stood up and gave a thin wailing shout of jubilation. Holding up his right hand, he showed what he had retrieved. It was the golden ring arpa.

Pandemonium broke out among the hunters. I thought they had lost their senses. Those with sprigs of spruce on their garments snatched them free and ran up to the bear and began to flog the carcass. Others picked up their skis and laid them across the dead animal. All of them were yelling and shouting with joy, and I heard cries of thanks, praise and congratulation. Some of the men kept chanting phrases from the arcane song that Rassa had sung in camp before we began the hunt, but still I could not understand a word. When the hunters had capered and danced themselves to exhaustion, Rassa knelt in the snow, facing the bear and called out solemnly to the dead animal, 'We thank you for the gift. May your spirit now roam happily in the saivo, and be born again in the spring, refreshed and in full health.'

Very soon it would be dark. Leaving the dead animal where it lay, we began to make our way back towards the camp. This time instead of skiing through the forest in solemn silence, the Sabme called out to one another, laughed and joked, and while still some distance from home they sent out long whooping calls that echoed far ahead of us among the trees to announce our return.

I shall never forget the sight which greeted us when we

entered the camp. The women had lit a blazing fire on the flat-topped rock, and were standing where the light from the flames flickered across their faces. Every one of their faces was stained a bloody red. For a moment I thought there had been a terrible atrocity. Then I saw the movements of a dance, the gestures of welcome and recognised a song of praise for our hunting skill. I was exhausted. All I wanted to do was lie down and rest, preferably with Allba beside me. But when I headed towards our tent, Rassa took me by the arm and led me away from the entrance flap and around to the back. There he made me drop on all fours, and crawl under the hem of the tent. As I entered I found Allba standing facing me across the hearth. Her face too was stained red, and she was looking at me through a brass ring held up to one eye. As I crawled into view, she backed away from me and disappeared. Too tired to care, I crawled fully dressed to our sleeping place and fell into a deep sleep.

Rassa prodded me awake at first light. Neither Allba nor his wife were anywhere to be seen. 'We go to fetch the Old One now,' he said. 'I thank you for what you have done for the siida. Now it is the time to celebrate.'

'Why do you keep on calling him the Old One?' I asked, feeling peevish. 'You might have warned me we were hunting for bear.'

'We can call him a bear now that he has given his life for us,' he replied cheerfully, 'but if we had spoken directly of him before the hunt, he would have been insulted. It removes respect if we call him by his earth name before the hunt.'

'But my saivo companion is a bear? Surely it is not right that I killed his kind?'

'Your saivo companion protected you from the Old One's charge when he emerged from his long winter sleep. You see, the Old One you killed was killed many times before. Yet he always comes again, for he wishes to give himself to the siida, to strengthen us because he is our own ancestor. That is why we returned the gold ring under his arm, for that is where our great-

great-grandfathers first found the golden arpa, and knew that he was the original father of our siida.'

We skiied back to the dead bear, taking a light sledge with us, and hauled its carcass to the encampment. Under Rassa's watchful gaze the hunters removed the large pelt – the bear was a full-grown male – and then with their curved knives separated the flesh from the bones, taking exquisite care. Not a bone was broken or even nicked with a knife blade, and each part of the skeleton was carefully put on one side. 'Later,' said Rassa, 'we will bury the skeleton intact, every bone of it, so that when the Old One comes again to life he will be as well and strong as he was this year.'

'Like Thor's goats,' I said.

Rassa looked at me questioningly. 'Thor is a God of my people,' I said. 'Each evening he feasts on the two goats which draw his chariot through the sky – the thunder is the sound of his passing – and after the meal he sets aside their bones and skins. In the morning, when he awakes, the goats are whole again. Unfortunately one of Thor's dinner guests broke open a hind leg to get at the marrowbone, and ever since that goat has walked with a limp.'

The siida made a great fuss of me for the three days of feasting it took to consume every last morsel of the animal I had killed. 'Scut of boaz, paw of bear,' was Rassa's recommendation as he helped me to the delicacy, explaining that to set aside or keep any portion of the dead animal would be an insult to the generosity of its death. 'The Old One made sure that the blizzard did not destroy us, and that the spring will come and the snow will melt. Already he is roaming the hills ahead of us, calling upon the grass and the tree shoots to appear and for the birds that left to return.'

My only regret was that Allba still kept her distance from me. 'If she comes to your bed within three days of the hunt,' her father enlightened me, 'she will turn barren. Such is the power of our father-ancestor whose presence came so close to you. Even as

you set off to hunt the Old One, his power was already reaching
out towards you.' This seemed to explain why Allba had been
behaving so strangely, and only when Rassa wore on his face the
muzzle we had flayed from the Old One and every hunter –
myself included – had danced around the central rock in imitation
of Old Honey Paws on the final night of feasting, did she once
again snuggle against my shoulder.

She also made me a fine cloak from the pelt, long enough for
my height. 'You are wearing the presence of the Old One, a sign
that he himself gave you,' Rassa said. 'Even a Sabme from another
band would know that and treat you with respect.' He was anxious
to press ahead with my instruction, and as the days grew longer
he took me on trips into the forest to show me strange-shaped
rocks, trees split by lightning or bent by the wind into human
shapes, and ancient wooden statues hidden deep in the forest.
They were all places where the spirits resided, he explained, and
on one special occasion he brought me to a long, low rock face
shielded from the snow by an overhanging cliff. The grey rock
was painted with many pictures and I recognised the images that
appeared on the siida's magic drums, as well as some I had not
seen before – outlines of whales, boats and sledges. Others were
too old and faded to decipher.

'Who painted these?' I asked Rassa.

'I do not know,' he said. 'They have always been here for as
long as our siida has existed. I believe they were left for our
instruction, to remind us who has gone before and to guide us
when we are in need of help.'

'And where are they now, the painters?' I asked.

'In the saivo, of course,' he replied. 'And they are happy. In
the winter nights when the curtains of light hang and twist and
mingle in the sky, the spirits of the dead are dancing with joy.'

With each day came more signs of spring. Our footprints in
the snow, once clear and distinct, now had softer edges, and I
heard the sound of running water from small rivulets hidden
beneath the icy crust and the patter of drips falling from the forest

branches. A few early flowers emerged through the snow and flocks of birds began to pass overhead in increasing numbers. Their calls heralded their arrival, then faded into the distance as they flew onward to their nesting grounds. Rassa took the chance to teach me how to interpret the meanings hidden in their numbers, the directions which they appeared from or vanished to, even the messages in the manner of their calls. 'Birds in flight or smoke rising from the fire. It is the same,' he said. 'For those who can read them, they are signs and portents.' Then he added 'though in your case it requires no such skill.' He had noted how my gaze lingered towards the south even after the birds had gone. 'Soon the siida will be heading north for our spring hunting grounds and you will be going in the opposite direction and leaving us,' he said. I was about to deny it, when his crooked smile stopped me. 'I have known this since the very first day you arrived among us, and so has every member of our siida, including my wife and Allba. You are a wanderer just as we are, but we retrace the paths laid down by our ancestors, while you are restless in a deeper way. You told me that the spirit God you serve was a seeker after knowledge. I have seen how he sent you among us, just as I know that he now wishes you to continue onward. It is my duty to assist and there is little time left. You must leave before the melting snow makes it impossible to travel easily on skis. Soon the staallu men will be arriving to trade for furs. For fear of them, we will retreat deeper into our forests. But before that happens, three of our best hunters will take our winter furs to the special place for the trading. You must go with them.'

As usual, the Sabme, once they came to a decision, carried it out quickly. The next morning there was every sign that they were breaking camp. Deerskin coverings were being stripped from the tent poles and the three designated hunters were stacking two sledges with tight-packed bundles of furs. Everything was done with such bewildering speed that I had no time to think what I should say to Allba, how best to say goodbye. I need not have worried. She left her mother to attend to the dismantling of our tent and led me a little way from the camp. Stepping behind the shelter of a spruce tree, she took my hand, and pressed something small and hard into my palm. I knew that she was returning to me the fire ruby. It was still warm from where it had lain against her flesh.

'You must keep it,' I objected. 'It is yours, a token of my love for you.'

'You don't understand,' she said. 'For me it is much more important that the spirit that flickers within the stone continues to guard and guide you. Then I know you will be safe wherever you are. Besides, you have left with me something just as precious. It stirs inside me.'

I took her meaning. 'How can you be sure?'

'Now is the season that all creatures can feel the stirrings of their young. The Sabme are no different. Madder Acce, who lives beneath the hearth, has placed within me a daughter. I knew she would, from that day that we both visited the saivo.'

'How can you be sure that our child will be a girl?'

'Do you remember the bear you met on your saivo journey?' she answered. 'I was there with you as my companion bird, though you did not see me.'

'I felt your wings brush my cheek.'

'And the bear? Don't you remember the bear you met at that time?'

'Of course, I do. It smiled at me.'

'If it had growled, that would have meant my child would be a boy. But when the bear smiles then a girl child is promised. All Sabme know that.'

'Don't you want me to stay, to help you with our child?'

'Everyone in the siida will know that she is the child of a foreign noaide and the grandchild of a great noaide. So everyone will help me because they will expect the girl will become a great noaide too, and help our siida to survive. If you stayed among us for my sake, it would make me sad. I told you when you first arrived among us that the Sabme believe it is far, far better to travel onward than to remain in one place. By staying you imprison your spirit, just as the fire is held within that magic stone you lent me. Please listen to me, travel onward and know that you have left me happy.'

She turned her face up towards me for one last kiss, and I took the opportunity to close her fingers once more around the fire ruby. 'Give it to our daughter when she is grown, in memory of her father.' There was a tiny moment of hesitation and then Allba acquiesced. She turned and walked back towards her family. Rassa was beckoning to me. The men with the fur sledges were anxious to leave. They had already strapped on their skis and were adjusting the leather hauling straps of the sledges more comfortably across their shoulders. I went across to thank Rassa for all he had done for me. But, strangely for him, he looked worried.

'Don't trust the staallu men,' he warned me. 'Last night I visited the saivo to consult your saivo companion about what will happen. My journey was shadowy and disturbed, and I sensed death and deceit. But I could not see from where it came, though a voice told me that already you knew the danger.'

I had no idea what he was talking about, but I respected him too much to doubt his sincerity. 'Rassa, I will remember what you have said. I can look after myself, and it is you who have the greater task — to look after the siida. I hope that the spirits guard and protect your people, for they are in my memory always.'

'Go now' said the stunted little man. 'your companions are good men and they will bring you to the staallu place safely. After that you must guard yourself. Goodbye.'

It took four days of steady skiing, always southward, to reach the place where my siida traded with the outsiders. At night the four of us wrapped ourselves in furs and slept beside our sledges. We ate dried food or, on the second evening, a ptarmigan which one of the hunters knocked down with his throwing stick. As we drew closer to the meeting place, I sensed my comrades' growing nervousness. They feared the foreign traders and the last day we travelled in complete silence, as if we were on our way to hunt a dangerous wild beast. We detected the staallu men from a great distance. In that pristine, quiet forest we heard them and smelled the smoke from their cooking fire. My companions halted at once, and one of them slipped out of the hauling harness and glided off quietly to scout. The others pulled the sledges out of sight and we waited. Our scout returned to say that two staallu men were camped in the place where they usually waited for the silent trade. With them were four more men, boaz men. For a moment I was puzzled. Then I understood that he was talking about the slaves who would act as porters for the traders.

The foreign traders had already displayed their trade goods in a deserted clearing, the bundles hung like fruit from the trees. That night our little group furtively approached, and in the first light of dawn my companions examined what was on offer – cloth, salt, metal items. Apparently they were satisfied, for we hurriedly unloaded the sledges of the furs, replaced them with the trade goods, and soon the Sabme were ready to depart. They embraced me and skiied away as silently as they had arrived, leaving me among their furs.

This is how the traders found me, to their amazement: seated on a bundle of prime furs in a deserted forest glade, as if I had appeared by magic, and wearing my noiade's heavy bearskin cloak.

SIXTEEN

THEY SPOKE CRUDE Norse.

'Frey's prick! What have we got here?' the first one called out to his companion. The two men were clumsily pushing themselves forward across the snow with stout poles, each on a single ski in the Norse fashion. I thought how ungainly they looked compared with the agile Sabme. Both men were bundled up in heavy coats, felt hats and thick loose trousers gathered into stout boots.

'Nice cape he's got on,' said the other. 'A bearskin that size would fetch a good price.'

'So would he,' replied his companion. 'Go up to him slowly. I'll see if I can get behind him. They say that once those Skridfinni get going, there's no hope of catching up with them. Act friendly.'

They sidled closer, the leader wearing a false smile which only emphasised that his bulbous nose was dripping a slimy trail down his heavy moustache and beard.

I waited until they were within a few paces and then said clearly, 'Greetings. The bearskin is not for sale.'

The pair of them stopped in their tracks. They were too astonished to speak.

'Nor are the furs in the pack I am sitting on,' I continued. 'Your furs are lying over there. They are fair exchange for the goods you left.'

The two men recovered from their shock that I had spoken in their language.

'Where did you drop from?' the leader asked belligerently, mistaking me for a rival. 'This is our patch. No one trespasses.'

'I came with the furs,' I said.

For a moment they did not believe me. Then they read the ski tracks of my Sabme companions. They clearly came from the rim of the silent forest and then returned again. Then the traders noted my Sabme fur hat, and the deerskin shoes that Allba had sewn for me.

'I want to get to the coast,' I said. 'I would pay you well.'

The two men looked at one another. 'How much?' asked the snot-nosed individual bluntly.

'A pair of marten skins, perfectly matched,' I suggested.

It must have been a generous offer because both men nodded at once. Then the leader turned to his companion and said, 'Here, let's see what they've left for us,' and began to grub among the furs that the Sabme hunters had left behind. Apparently satisfied, he turned back towards his camp and let out a huge bellow. Out of the thickets appeared a sad little procession. Four men bundled up against the cold in ragged and dirty clothes trudged along on small square boards attached to their feet, dragging crude sledges. They were what my Sabme companions had called the boaz people, porters and hauliers for the fur traders. As they loaded the sledges, I saw they had the beaten air of thralls and did not understand more than a few words of their masters' language. Every command was accompanied by kicks and blows as well as simple gestures to show what needed to be done.

The two fur traders, Vermundr and Angantyr, told me they were collecting the furs on behalf of their felag. It was the same word the Jomsvikings had used to describe their military fellowship, but in the mouths of the fur traders the meaning was much debased. Their felag was a group of merchants who swore to help one another and share profits and expenses. But it was soon apparent to me that Vermundr and Angantyr were both prepared to cheat their colleagues. They demanded my marten skins in advance, hid them in their personal belongings, and when we reached the rendezvous with the felag at the trading town of Aldeigjuborg they failed to mention the extra pelts.

I had never seen so much mud in my life as I found at Aldeigjuborg. Everywhere you walked you sank almost ankle deep, and within a day I had lost both of Allba's shoes and had to buy a pair of heavy boots. Built on a swampy riverside, Aldeigjuborg lies in that region the Norse call Gardariki, the land of forts, and is the gateway to an area stretching for an unimaginable distance to the east. The place is surrounded by endless forest, so all the houses are made of wood. The logs are cut, squared and laid to make walls, the roofs are wooden shingles, and a tall fence of wooden stakes encloses each house's yard. The houses have been erected at random so there is no single main street, and barely any attempt is made to keep the roadways passable. Occasionally a layer of tree trunks is laid down on the earth to provide a surface, but in the spring these trees sink into the soft soil and are soon slippery with rain. Everywhere the puddles are fed by the filth seeping out from the house yards. There is no drainage and, when I was there, each householder used his yard as a latrine and rubbish dump, never clearing away the squalor. As a result the place stank and rotted at the same time.

Yet Aldeigjuborg was thriving. Flotillas of small boats were constantly coming and going at the landing staithes along the river. They were laden with the commercial products of the northern woodlands – furs, honey, beeswax, either obtained cheaply by silent barter such as I had witnessed or, more usually, by straightforward extortion. Gangs of heavily armed traders travelled into the remoter regions and demanded tribute from the forest-dwelling peoples. Often they obliged the natives to provide them with porters and oarsmen as well, so the muddy lanes of Aldeigjuborg were thronged with Polians, Krivichi, Berendeis, Severyane,

Pechenegs and Chuds, as well as people from tribes so obscure that they had no known name. A few were traders in their own right, but the majority were kholops – slaves.

With such a rapacious and mixed population, Aldeigjuborg was a turbulent place. The town was nominally subject to the overlord of Kiev, a great city several days' journey to the south, and he appointed a member of his family as regent. But real power lay in the hands of the merchants, particularly the better armed ones. They were commonly known as Varangians, a name by which I was proud to call myself in later days, but when I first met them I was appalled by their behaviour. They were out-and-out ruffians. Mostly of Swedish descent, they came to Gardariki to make their fortunes. They took the var – the oath which formed them into felags – and became a law unto themselves. Some hired themselves out as mercenaries to whoever would pay the highest price; others joined felags which masqueraded as trading groups, though they were little more than pirate bands. The most notorious of all the felags when I arrived was the one to which Vermundr and Angantyr belonged, and no Varangian was more feared than its leader, Ivarr known as the Pitiless. Vermundr and Angantyr were so terrified of him that the moment we arrived in Aldeigjuborg they took me straight to see their leader to report on their mission and seek his approval of what they had done.

Ivarr held court – that is the only phrase – in a large warehouse close to the landing place. Like all the other buildings of Aldeigjuborg, it was single-storey though far bigger than most. Two scruffy guards lounged at the entrance gate and checked everyone who entered, removing any weapons they found and demanding a bribe to let visitors past. Led across the filthy yard, I was taken into Ivarr's living quarters – a scene of barbaric squalor. The single main room was decorated in what I learned was a style favoured by tribal rulers in the east. Rich brocades and carpets, mostly patterned in red, black and blue, hung from the walls. Cushions and couches provided the only furniture and the room was lit by heavy brass lamps on chains. Even though it was midday, these were burning and the place smelled of candle wax and stale food. Half-eaten meals lay on trays on the floor, and the rugs were stained with spilled wine and kvas, the local beer. Half a dozen Varangs, dressed in their characteristic baggy trousers and loose, belted shirts, stood or squatted around the edge of the room. Some were playing dice, others were talking idly among themselves, but all took care to show that they were there in attendance upon their leader.

Ivarr was one of those remarkable men whose physical presence arouses immediate fear. I have met much bigger men in my life of travel, and I have observed men who make it their style to inspire dread with threatening gestures or a cruel manner of speech. Ivarr imposed his will by exuding sheer brute menace, and he did so naturally without conscious effort. Between forty and fifty years old, he was short and so thick-set that he could have been a wrestler, albeit a dandified one, for he was wearing a rust-coloured velvet tunic, and silk pantaloons, and his feet were encased in soft yellow leather boots trimmed with fur. His short, powerful arms had small hands, and his stubby fingers were decorated with expensive rings. The most striking feature about him was his head. Like his body, it was round and compact. The skin was the colour of antique walrus ivory and hinted of mixed ancestry, maybe part-Norse and part-Asiatic. His eyes were dark brown, and he had greased and perfumed his ample beard so that it lay on the front of his tunic like a glossy black animal. By contrast his scalp was shaved clean except for a single lock of hair, which hung from the side of his head in a long curl and touched his left shoulder. This, it seemed, was regarded as a sign of royalty, which Ivarr claimed to be. But for the moment my attention was caught by his right ear. It was decorated with three studs – two pearls and between them a large single diamond.

'So you are the poacher,' he said, thrusting his head forward pugnaciously, as if he was about to spring up from his couch and knock me to the ground. I tore my gaze away from the ear studs.

'I don't know what you're talking about,' I said calmly. There was a tremor of surprise from the Varangs in the room behind me. They were not accustomed to hearing their master addressed in this way.

'My men tell me that you were collecting furs from the Skrid-finni in an area where my felag alone deals with them.'

'I did not collect the furs,' I answered. 'They were given to me.'

The truculent brown eyes regarded me. I noted that they held a look of quick intelligence.

'Given to you? For nothing?'

'That's correct.'

'How did that happen?'

'I lived the winter among them.'

'Impossible. Their magicians make their people vanish if any strangers approach.'

'A magician invited me to stay.'

'Prove it.'

I glanced around the room. The other Varangs were like a pack of hungry dogs awaiting a treat. They expected their leader to quash me. Two stopped the game of dice that they had been playing and another filled the pause before I gave my answer, by spitting noisily onto the carpet.

'Give me some dice and a tray,' I said, trying to sound disdainful.

The remnants of a meal were swept from a heavy brass tray, and I indicated that it should be placed on the carpet in front of me. I held out my hand to the dice players and they gave me the dice they had been using. Seated on his couch Ivarr adopted a bored look as if already unimpressed. I was sure he expected me to claim magical assistance in throwing the dice. Instead I asked for five more pairs of dice. This brought a stir of interest. Each of the Varangs carried his own set and I laid the twelve dice down on the tray, arranging them in the pattern of nine squares, three by three. In the first square I placed a single dice so that the number four showed. In the next square I put two dice whose combined total was nine. In the third square I again laid a single dice showing two. In the second row, the numbers were three, five and seven. The last row was eight, one and six.

The pattern looked thus:

$$4 \quad 9 \quad 2$$
$$3 \quad 5 \quad 7$$
$$8 \quad 1 \quad 6$$

I stepped back and said nothing. There was a long, long silence. My audience was puzzled. Perhaps they expected that the dice would move on their own, or that they would burst into flames. They looked long and hard at the dice, then at me, and nothing whatsoever happened. I gazed straight at Ivarr, challenging him. It was for him to see the magic. He looked down at the dice and frowned. Then he looked a second time and I could see the sudden light of understanding. He glanced up at me and we shared the knowledge. My gamble had paid off. I had flattered his raw intelligence.

His lackeys still looked puzzled. None of them dared question their master. They were too frightened of him.

'You learned well,' said Ivarr. He had seen the magic of the pattern: whichever way you read the lines, across, sideways, downwards, or on both diagonals, the total that they gave was always fifteen.

'I am told that you will soon be going to Miklagard,' I said. 'I would like to accompany your boats.'

'If you are as good at trading as you are at numbers, you would be a useful addition,' Ivarr replied, 'but you still have to convince my men.'

The Varangians, still puzzled, were collecting up their dice from the tray. I stopped one of them as he was picking up his two gaming pieces. 'I'll gamble on it. Highest wins.' I said. The Varang smirked, then threw his dice. I was not surprised that they fell showing double six. The dice were almost certainly loaded and I wondered how many games he had won by cheating. His score was unbeatable. I picked up his two dice, made as if to throw them on the tray, then checked myself. I set one of the dice aside and picked up a replacement from the pile. It was a dice that had seen much use. Made of bone, it was old and cracked. Now it was not Rassa's magic that I used, but something that I had learned among the Jomsvikings. As I held the two dice in my hand, I pressed them together hard and felt the older dice begin to split. With a silent prayer to Odinn, I flung the two dice down upon the tray with all my strength. Odinn, who invented dice for man's amusement, heard my plea. As the two dice struck the metal tray, one of them broke apart. My opponent's dice still read its false six, while the other gave a six and a two. 'I win, I think,' I said and the other Varangs broke into guffaws of laughter.

The Varang I had beaten scowled and would have struck me if Ivarr had not said sharply, 'Froygeir! That's enough!' Froygeir snatched up his dice and stalked away, furious and humiliated, and I knew that I had made a dangerous enemy.

The felag had been waiting for the return of Vermundr and Angantyr, and was now ready to depart for Miklagard. I counted nine Varangians of the felag, including Ivarr, and about thirty kholops, whose task was to row the flotilla of light river boats they loaded with our bales of furs. Several of the Varangians also brought along their women as cooks and servants, and it was clear these unfortunates were part slave, part concubine. Ivarr, as befitted his rank, was accompanied by three of his women and also two of his sons, lads no more than seven or eight years old of whom he seemed extremely fond. So our expedition totalled rather more than fifty.

The way to Miklagard lay upriver through Kiev, so I was surprised when our flotilla pushed off from the river landing place and headed downstream in the opposite direction. I thought it best not to ask the reason. I was well aware that I was still unwelcome in Ivarr's felag. It was not just Froygeir who disliked me. His colleagues resented the ease with which I seemed to have won

Ivarr's favour and they envied the rich stock of furs that I had brought with me. I had not taken the var, the oath of fellowship, so I was a private trader taking advantage of their journey and this meant that my profit would not be shared. The Varangians grumbled among themselves and pointedly left me to fend for myself when it came to preparing meals or finding a place to sleep. So, by default, I spent most of my time on Ivarr's boat as we travelled the waterways across Gardariki, and I slept in his tent when we stopped at night and pitched camp on the river bank. This only made matters worse because the other Varangs soon saw me as Ivarr's favourite, and sometimes I wondered if it was our leader's deliberate policy to provide his followers with a focus for their malcontent. My travelling companions were a ferocious lot and, like the pack of wild dogs they resembled, they were only partly tamed. They held together only as long as they submitted to Ivarr's savage rule, and the moment that was lifted they would fight amongst themselves to divide the spoils and decide upon their next leader.

Ivarr himself was an unpredictable mixture of viciousness, pride and shrewdness. Twice I saw him stamp his authority on the group by brute violence. He liked to carry a short thick-handled whip, whose strands were weighted with thin strips of lead and the butt decorated with silver. I thought it was a badge of office or perhaps an instrument for striking lazy kholops. But the first time I saw him use it was when a Varangian hesitated in carrying out one of his orders. The man paused for the briefest moment, but it was enough for Ivarr to lash out – the blow was all the more shocking because Ivarr did not give the slightest warning – and the weighted thongs caught the man full across the face. He fell to his knees, clutching his face for fear that he had been blinded. He got back to his feet and stumbled away to carry out his orders, and for a week afterwards a crust of dried blood marked the welts across his cheeks.

On the second occasion the challenge to Ivarr's authority was more serious. One of the Varangians, drunk on too much kvas,

openly contested Ivarr's right to lead the group. It happened as
we sat around a cooking fire on the river bank eating our evening meal. The Varangian was a head taller than Ivarr and he drew
his sword as he rose to his feet and shouted across the fire, calling on Ivarr to fight. The man stood there, swaying slightly,
as Ivarr calmly wiped his hands on a towel held out to him by
his favourite concubine, then turned as if to reach for his own
weapon. In the next instant he had uncoiled from the ground and
in a blur of movement ran across the burning fire, scattering
the blazing sticks in all directions. Head down, he charged his
challenger, who was too drunk and too surprised to save himself.
Ivarr butted the man in the chest and the shock threw him flat on
his back. Scorning even to remove the contender's sword, Ivarr
grabbed his opponent's arm and hauled him across the ground
back to the fire. There, in front of the watching Varangians, he
thrust the man's arm into the embers and held it there as his
enemy howled with pain and we smelled the burning flesh. Only
then did Ivarr release his grip and his victim crawled away, his
hand a blackened mess. Ivarr calmly returned to his place and
beckoned to his slave girl to bring him another plate of food.

The following day I made the mistake of calling Ivarr a
Varangian, and he bridled at the name. 'I am a Rus,' he said. 'My
father was a Varangian. He came across the western sea with the
rops-karlar, the river rowers, to trade or raid, it did not matter
which. He liked the country so much that he decided to stay and
took a job as captain of the guard at Kiev. He married my mother,
who was from Karelia, of royal blood, though she had the
misfortune of being taken captive by the Kievans. My father
bought her for eighty grivna, a colossal sum which goes to show
how beautiful she was. I was their only child.'

'And where's your father now?' I enquired.

'My father abandoned me when my mother died. I was eight
years old. So I grew up in the company of whoever would have
me, peasants mostly, who saw me as a useful pair of hands to help
them gather crops or cut firewood. You know what the Kievans

call their peasants? Smerdi. It means "stinkers". They deserve the name. I ran away often.'

'Do you know what happened to your father?'

'Most likely he's dead,' Ivarr answered casually. He was seated on a carpet inside his tent – he liked to travel in style – and was playing some complicated child's game with his younger son. 'He left Kiev with a company of his soldiers who thought they would get better pay from the great emperor in Miklagard. Rumour came back that the entire group was wiped out on their journey by Pechenegs.'

'Are we likely to meet Pechenegs too?'

'I doubt it,' he replied. 'We go a different way.' But he would not say where.

By the fifth day after leaving Aldeigjuborg, we had rowed and sailed our boats around the shores of two lakes, along the river connecting them and turned into yet another river mouth. Now we were heading upstream and progress became more difficult. As the river narrowed we were obliged to get out of the boats and push them across the shallows. Finally we reached a point when we could go no further. There was not enough water to float our craft. We unloaded the boats and set our kholops to cutting down small trees to make rollers. The larger boats and those which leaked badly we deliberately set on fire to destroy them and then searched the ashes to retrieve any rivets or other metal fastenings. To me it seemed a prodigious waste because I had grown up in Iceland and Greenland, countries where no large trees grow. But Ivarr and the felag thought nothing of it. Timber in abundance was all they had known. Their main concern was that we had enough kholops to manhandle our remaining boats across the portage.

There was a track, overgrown with grass and bushes but still discernible, leading eastward through dense forest. Our axemen went ahead to clear the path. The kholops were harnessed like oxen, ten in a team, to ropes attached to the keels of our three remaining boats. The rest of us steadied the boats to keep them level on the rollers, or worked in pairs, picking up the rollers as they passed beneath the hulls and throwing them down ahead of the advancing keels. It took us four days of sweating labour, plagued by flying insects, to drag our boats to the headwaters of a stream that flowed to the east. There we rested for another week while our shipwright – a Varangian originally from Norway – directed the building of four replacement craft. He found what he needed less than an arrow-shot from our camp – four massive trees, which were promptly felled. Then he directed the kholops in hollowing out the trunks with axe and fire to make the keels and lower hulls of our boats. Other kholops split the planks which were attached to the sides of these dugouts, building up the hulls until I recognised the familiar curves of our Norse vessels. I complimented the shipwright on his skill.

He grimaced. 'Call these boats?' he said. 'More like cattle troughs. You need time and care to build proper boats, and skilled carpenters, not these clumsy oafs. Most of them would be better off chopping firewood.'

I pointed out that two of the kholops from the far north had proved useful when the supply of metal rivets for fastening the planks had run out. The men had used lengths of pine-tree root to lash the planks in place, a practice in their own country.

The Norse shipwright was still unimpressed. 'Where I come from, you get only knife and needle.'

'What do you mean?' I asked.

'When you think you are good enough to call yourself a boatbuilder, the master shipwright who taught you gives you a knife and a needle and tells you to make and rig a boat, using no other tools. Until you can do that, you're considered a wood butcher, like this lot here.'

The Norwegian seemed the least vicious of our company. He spoke the best Norse, while all the others mixed so many local words into their sentences that it was often hard to understand them. I asked him how it was that, as a skilled shipwright, he found himself a Varangian. 'I killed a couple of men back home,' he said, 'and the local earl took offence. It turned out that they were his followers, so I had to make myself scarce. Maybe I'll go back home one day, but I doubt it. This life suits me – no need to break your back hauling logs or lose a finger carving planks when there are slaves to do the work, and you can have as many women as you want without marrying them.'

As we recommenced our journey, we saw only the occasional trace of human habitation, a footpath leading from the water's edge into the forest, a tree stump that had been cut with an axe, the faint smell of a fire from somewhere deep in the forest, which stretched without a break along both banks. But we did not meet the natives themselves, though once or twice I thought I saw far in the distance the outline of a small boat disappearing into the reeds as we approached. By the time we reached the spot there was nothing to show, the reeds had sprung back into position and I wondered if I had been imagining it. 'Where are all the people who live here?' I asked Vermundr. He gave a coarse laugh and looked at me as if I was weak in the head.

We did eventually come to a couple of trading posts and a sizeable town. The latter, situated on a river junction, was very like Aldeigjuborg, a cluster of log-built houses sheltering behind a wooden palisade, and protected on at least two sides by the river and a marsh. We did not stop. The inhabitants shut their gates and regarded us warily as we drifted past. I guessed that the reputation of Ivarr's felag had preceded us.

The river was much wider now, and we steered our course in midstream so I saw little of the countryside except the monotonous vista of green forest moving slowly past on either hand. I thought, naively, that we stayed in midstream to take best advantage of the current. Then I began to see plumes of smoke rising from the forest cover. The smoke arose ahead of us or from some vantage point, usually a high bluff overlooking the river. It did not require much intelligence to guess that unseen inhabitants were signalling our progress to one another, keeping track of our flotilla. Now whenever we came ashore for the night we set guards around our camp and, on one occasion when the smoke signals were very frequent, Ivarr refused to let us go ashore at all. We spent the night anchored in the shallows and ate a cold supper.

Finally we left behind the area of watchful natives and the land around us became more level. Here we turned aside into a small river that flowed into the main stream from the north, and began to steer much closer to the left-hand bank. I noticed that Ivarr scanned the shore intently, as if he was searching for a particular sign. He must have seen what he was looking for because at the next suitable landing place he beached our boat. All the other vessels followed.

'Empty the two lightest boats and set up camp here,' Ivarr ordered.

I saw the Varangians glance at one another in anticipation as the kholops unloaded the goods and carried them up to a patch of level ground. Ivarr spoke to the Varangian whose burned hand was still wrapped in rags soaked in bear's grease. 'You stay here till we get back. See to it that no one lights a cooking fire or uses an axe.' The man had learned his lesson well. He dropped his gaze submissively as he accepted his assignment.

'You, you and you.' Ivarr walked amongst the kholops and touched about a dozen of them on the shoulder with the silver butt of his whip. They were the tallest and strongest of our slaves. He pointed to where Vermundr and Angantyr were unwrapping one of the cargo bales. I saw that it contained weapons – cheap swords and a heap of light chain. For a moment I thought it was anchor chain, but then I saw that the links were longer and thinner than any ship's chain, and that it came in sections about an arm's span long. There was a large metal loop at the end of each length and I recognised what they were: fetters.

Ivarr handed each kholop a sword. This was taking a risk, I thought to myself. What if the kholops decided to rebel? Yet Ivarr seemed unconcerned as several of the kholops began to swing their swords through the air to test their weight. He was confident enough to turn his back on them.

'Here, Thorgils,' he said, 'you'd better come with us. You can make yourself useful, if necessary, by making us all disappear.' The rest of the Varangians laughed sycophantically.

With five Varangians and half a dozen kholops aboard each boat, we set off to row upstream. Again, Ivarr was watching the river bank closely. The oarsmen took care to make as little noise as possible, dipping their blades gently into the water as we glided forward. Both Vermundr and Angantyr were with me in Ivarr's vessel and seemed tense. 'We should have waited until dawn,' said Vermundr under his breath to his companion. Ivarr must have overheard his comment because he turned round from where he stood in the bow and looked at Vermundr. His glance was enough to make Vermundr cringe.

Late in the afternoon Ivarr held up his hand to attract our attention, then silently gestured towards the bank. The slope was marked with footprints leading down to the water's edge. A large, half-submerged log was worn and smooth. Its upper surface had been used as a surface for washing clothes. A broken wooden scoop lay discarded close by. Ivarr made a circular gesture and waved on the second boat, indicating that it was to row further upstream. He pointed to the sun, then brought his arm down towards the horizon and made a chopping motion. The Varangians in the second boat waved in acknowledgement and they and the kholops rowed onwards silently. Very soon they were out of sight round a bend in the river.

Aboard our own vessel, the current carried us gently back back downstream until we were out of sight of the washing place. A few oar strokes and the boat slid under the shelter of some overhanging branches, where we hung on and waited. We sat in silence and listened to the pluck and gurgle of the water on the hull. Occasionally there was the splash of a fish jumping. A heron glided down to settle in the shallows a few paces away from us. It began its fishing, stalking cautiously through the water, step by step until suddenly it noticed our vessel and its human cargo. It gave a sudden twitch of panic, leaped up into the air and flew off, releasing a loud and angry croak once it was safely clear. Beside me Angantyr muttered angrily at the heron's alarm call. Another glance from Ivarr quietened him instantly. Ivarr himself sat motionless. With his glistening shaven head and his squat body, he reminded me of a waterside toad waiting in ambush.

Finally Ivarr rose to his feet and nodded. The sun was about to dip below the treeline. The oarsmen eased their blades into the water and our boat emerged from its hiding place. Within moments we were back at the washing place and this time we landed. The boat was drawn up on the mud and the men formed up into a column, Ivarr at its head, Angantyr right behind him. Vermundr and I brought up the rear, behind the kholops. All of us were armed with swords or axes, and each Varangian carried a set of manacles, wrapped around his waist like an iron sash.

We walked briskly along the track, which led inland. The path was sufficiently well worn for us to make quick progress and we made scarcely any noise. Very soon I heard the shouts of children at play and a sudden burst of barking, indicating that dogs had detected us. Within moments there came the urgent clamour of a horn sounding the alarm. Ivarr broke into a run. We burst out of the forest and found ourselves in open ground where the trees had been cleared to provide space for small plots of farmland and vegetable gardens. A hundred paces away was a native village of forty or fifty log huts. The place was defenceless – it did not even have a palisade. The inhabitants must have thought they were too isolated and well hidden to take any precautions.

In the next few moments they learned their error. Ivarr and the Varangians swept into the settlement, waving their weapons and yelling at the top of their voices to terrorise the villagers. To my surprise the kholops joined in the charge with just as much relish. They ran forward, howling and bellowing and swinging their swords. A man who had been working in his vegetable patch tried to delay our onslaught. He swung his spade at Angantyr, who cut him down with a back-handed swing, barely pausing in his stride. Women and children appeared in the doorways. They took one look at our attack and ran screaming. An old woman hobbled out of a house to see what was the matter. One of our kholops smashed her in the face with the hilt of his sword and she dropped to the ground. A child, no more than three years old, wandered into our path. Dirty and dishevelled, probably woken from sleep, the child gazed at us wonderingly as we raced past. An arrow whizzed past me and struck one of the kholops in the back. He sprawled on the ground. The arrow had come from behind. Vermundr and I turned to see a man armed with a hunting bow setting a second arrow to his bowstring. Vermundr may have been an uncouth brute, but he had his full share of courage. Though he had no shield to protect himself, he gave a blood-curdling roar as he charged straight at the archer. The sight of the raging Varangian running towards him unnerved the bowman. He missed his second shot and a few strides later Vermundr was on him. The Varangian had chosen an axe for his weapon and now he swung the blade so hard that I heard the thud as he chopped his opponent in the waist. His victim was lifted off his feet and fell sideways in a heap.

'Come on, Thorgils, you arse-licker,' Vermundr yelled in my face as he rushed back past me to continue the sweep through the village. I ran after him, trying to make out what was happening. One or two corpses were lying on the ground. They looked like bundles of abandoned rags until you saw a battered head, a bloody outflung arm, or dirty, shoeless feet. Somewhere in front of me were more shouts and yells and out from a side alley burst the figure of an older man, running for his life. I recognised the short bearskin cape. It must have been the village shaman. He was unarmed and must have doubled back through our cordon. At that moment Ivarr stepped into view. He had a throwing axe in his hand. As smoothly as a boy throws flat pebbles to skip across a pond, he skimmed the axe towards the fugitive. The weapon went whirling across the gap as if the target was standing still.

The axe struck the shaman in the back of his skull and he
sprawled forward and lay still. Ivarr saw me standing there,
looking appalled. 'Friend of yours, I suppose,' he said.

There was no further resistance from the villagers. The
shocking swiftness of our attack had taken them by surprise and
they lacked the weapons or skill to defend themselves. We
herded those still alive into the central square of their little settlement, where they stood in a huddled and dejected group. They
were an unremarkable people, typical of those who scratch a living from the forest. In appearance they were of medium height,
with pale skin but dark hair, almost black. They were poorly
dressed in homespun clothes of wool and none of them wore any
form of jewellery apart from simple amulets on leather thongs
around their necks. We knew this because the Varangians
promptly searched everyone, looking for valuables, and found
nothing.

'Miserable lot of shitheads. Hardly worth the trouble,' complained Vermundr.

I looked at our prisoners. They gazed at the ground dully,
knowing what was coming next.

Angmantyr and my particular enemy, Froygeir, whom I had
humiliated at dice, strode over to the prisoners and began to
divide them into two groups. To one side they shoved the older
men and women, the smaller children and anyone who was
deformed or blemished in some way. These formed the larger
group since many of the villagers had badly pock-marked faces.
This left the younger, fitter men and children over the age of
eight or nine standing where they were. Except for one mother
weeping bitterly at being separated from her small child, who had
been sent to join the others, this second group contained almost
no women. I was puzzling about the reason for this, when the
crew of our second raiding boat strode into the square. In front
of them they were herding, like a flock of geese, the women of
the village. I realised that Vermundr, Froygeir and the rest of us
in the first boat had been the beaters. The second boat's crew had

been given enough time to circle around behind the village and wait for us to flush out the game. The real prey in our manhunt had fled straight into the trap, as Ivarr had intended.

There were about twenty women in the group. Their faces and arms were scratched and torn from branches, several of them had raw bruises on their faces and all of them had their wrists bound together with leather thongs. With their straggly hair and grimy faces they looked a sorry lot. However, Vermundr, standing next to me, disagreed. 'Not a bad catch,' he said. 'Give them a good scrub and they'll be worth a tidy sum.' He went forward to inspect them more closely. The women huddled together, several looking piteously across towards their children, who had been set aside. Others kept their heads down so that their tangled hair concealed their features. Vermundr was clearly a veteran slave catcher for he now went from one woman to the next, seizing each by the chin, and forcing back her head so that he could look into the woman's face and judge her worth. Suddenly he let out a whoop of delight. 'Ivarr's Luck!' he called, 'Look at this.' He seized two women by their wrists, dragged them out from the group, and made them stand side by side in front of us. Judging by their bodies the girls were aged about sixteen, though with their shapeless gowns it was difficult to tell precisely, and they kept their heads bowed forward so it was impossible to see their faces. Vermundr changed that. He went behind the girls, gathered up their hair in his hands, and like a trader in a market who flaunts his best produce with a flourish, pulled back their heads so we could see straight into their faces. They were identical twins, and even with their tear-streaked faces it was clear that they were astonishingly beautiful. I remembered how I had bribed Vermundr and Angantyr with a pair of marten skins, perfectly matched. Now I saw in front of me the human equivalent: two slave girls of perfect quality, a matching pair. Ivarr's felag had found riches.

We did not linger. The light was fading. 'Back to the boats!' Ivarr ordered. 'These people may have friends, and I want us well

clear by the time they get together to launch an attack.' The last
rivets were hammered tight on the fetters of the male slaves, and
the felag began to withdraw to the sounds of wailing and sobbing
from the despairing villagers. Several of the women captives fell
to the ground, either because they fainted or because their limbs
simply would not carry them away from their children. They
were picked up and carried by the kholops. One male captive who
refused to budge received a savage blow from the flat of a sword,
which sent him stumbling forward. The majority of our captives
meekly began to shuffle out of the village.

Ivarr beckoned to me. 'Come with me, Thorgils,' he said.
'Here's where you might be useful.'

He led me back through the empty village to where the corpse
of the shaman lay. I thought he had only gone to retrieve his
throwing axe.

'That's the same sort of cloak that you wear, isn't it?' he
asked.

'Yes,' I said. 'It's a noiade's cloak. What you call a magician.
Though I don't know anything about this tribe. They are completely different from the Skridfinni among whom I lived.'

'But if these people had a magician, then that means they had
a God. Isn't that so?'

'Very likely,' I said.

'And if they had a god and a magician, that means they probably had a shrine to worship at,' Ivarr looked about us, then
asked, 'And as you know so much about these noiades or whatever you call them, where would you guess that shrine is to be
found?'

I was at a loss. I genuinely wanted to answer Ivarr's question
because, like everyone else, I was frightened of him. But the
village we had raided bore no resemblance to a Skridfinni camp.
These people were settled forest dwellers, while the Sabme had
been nomads. The village shrine could be anywhere nearby,
hidden in the forest. 'I really have no idea,' I said, 'but if I were

to guess, I would say that the noiade was running towards it, either to seek sanctuary there or to plead to his God for help.'

'That's just what I was thinking,' said Ivarr and set off at a brisk walk towards the edge of the dark forest in the direction that the shaman had been fleeing.

The shrine was less than an arrow flight away once we had left the open, cultivated ground and entered the forest. A tall fence of wooden planks, grey with age, concealed the sacred mystery. We walked around the fence — it was no more than thirty paces in circumference — looking for a gateway, but did not find one. I expected Ivarr simply to batter open a gap, but he was cautious. 'Don't want to make too much noise,' he said. 'We've not much time, and the villagers will soon be gathering their forces. Here, I'll help you over.' I found myself hoisted up to the top of the fence and I dropped down on the other side. As I had expected, the shrine was a simple place, suitable for such a modest settlement. The circular area inside the fence was plain beaten earth. In the centre stood what I first took to be a heavy wooden post set in the ground. Then I saw that the villagers had worshipped what Rassa would have called a sieidde. It was the stump of a tree struck by lightning and left with the vague resemblance to a seated man. The villagers had enhanced the similarity, carving out the shape of knees, and folded arms, and whittling back the neck to emphasise the head. The image was very, very old.

I spotted the latch that allowed a section of the surrounding fence to swing open, and went to let Ivarr in. He approached to within touching distance of the effigy and halted. 'Not as poor a village as it seemed, Thorgils,' he said. He was looking into the plain wooden bowl which the effigy held on its knees. It was where the villagers placed their offerings to their God. I stepped up beside Ivarr and glanced down into the bowl to see what they had given. Abruptly the breath had left my lungs. I felt giddy, not because I saw some gruesome offering, but because a poignant memory came surging into my mind and left me reeling. The bowl was half full of silver coins. Many of them were old and worn and indecipherable. They must have lain there for generations. But several coins on the surface were not yet tarnished and their patterns were instantly readable. All of them bore that strange rippling writing that I had seen during my days in London – a time I would never forget. It was when I had first made love with Aelfgifu and she had worn a necklace of those coins around her graceful neck.

Ivarr ripped the sleeve from his shirt, and knotted the end to create a makeshift sack. 'Here, Thorgils, hold this open,' he said as he lifted the wooden bowl from its place and poured in the cascade of coins. Then he tossed the bowl aside. He looked up at the roughly carved head of the wooden statue. Around its neck was a torc. The neck ring was so weatherbeaten that it was impossible to tell whether it was plain iron or blackened silver. Clearly Ivarr thought it was precious metal because he reached up to tug it free. But the torc remained fast. Ivarr was reaching for his throwing axe when I intervened.

'Don't do it, Ivarr,' I said, trying to sound calm and reasonable. I feared his violent reaction to anyone who thwarted him.

He turned to face me, and scowled. 'Why not?'

'It is a sacred thing,' I said. 'It belongs to the sieidde. To steal it will call down his anger. It will bring bad luck.'

'Don't waste my time. What's a sieidde?' he growled, beginning to look angry.

'A God, the local God who controls this place.'

'Their God, not mine,' Ivarr retorted and swung his axe. I was glad the blow was directed at the statue not me, for it decapitated the wooden effigy with a single blow. Ivarr lifted off the torc and slid it up his naked arm. 'You're too timid, Thorgils,' he said. 'Look, it even fits.' Then he ran for the gate.

It was dark by the time we arrived back at the river bank. The crews were already on board the two boats and waiting. They had made the captives lie in the bilges and the moment

Ivarr and I took our places the oarsmen began to row. We fled from that place as fast as we could travel and the darkness hid our withdrawal. No natives intercepted us and as soon as we reached our camp Ivarr stormed up the beach, insisting that everyone make ready to depart at once. By dawn we were already well on our way back to the great river highway.

SEVENTEEN

THE SUCCESS OF the slave raid greatly improved the temper of the felag. The underlying feeling of ferocity was still there, but the Varangians showed Ivarr a respect which bordered on admiration. Apparently it was very rare to find girl twins among the tribes, let alone a pair as exquisite as the ones we had captured. There was much talk of 'Ivarr's Luck', and a mood of self-congratulation spread among the Varangians as they preened themselves on their decision to join his felag. Only I was morose, troubled by the desecration of the shrine. Rassa had taught me to respect such places and I had a sense of foreboding.

'Still worrying about that piddling little village idol, Thorgils?' said Ivarr that evening, sitting down beside me on the thwart.

'Don't you respect any God?' I asked.

'How could I?' he answered. 'Look at that lot there.' He nodded towards the Varangians in the nearest accompanying boat. 'Those who don't worship Perun venerate their ancestors. I don't even know who my mother's ancestors were, and certainly not my father's.'

'Why not Perun? From what I've heard he's the same God we call Thor in the Norse country. He is the God of warriors. Couldn't you venerate him?'

'I've no need of Perun's help,' Ivarr said confidently. 'He

didn't assist me when I was a youngster. I made my own way. Let others believe in forest hags with iron teeth and claws, or that Crnobog the black God of death seizes us when we die. When I meet my end, if my body is available for burial and not hacked to pieces, it will be enough for my companions to treat my corpse as they wish. I will no longer be there to be concerned with their superstitions.'

For a brief moment I thought to tell him about my devotion to Odinn the All-Father, but the intensity of his fatalism held me back and I changed the subject.

'How was it,' I asked, 'that our kholops took part in the raid for slaves with such enthusiasm when they themselves are slaves?'

Ivarr shrugged. 'Kholops are prepared to inflict on others what they themselves suffer. It makes them accept their own condition more easily. Of course I took back their weapons once they had completed the task and now they are kholops once again.'

'Aren't you afraid that they, or our new captives, will attempt to escape?'

Ivarr gave a grim laugh. 'Where would they find themselves if they did? They are far from home, they don't know which way to turn, and if they did run away, the first people to find them would merely turn them back into slaves again. So they accept their lot.'

In that opinion, Ivarr was wrong. Two days later he gave our male captives a little more space. The prisoners' wrist and ankle fetters had been fastened to the boats' timbers, so they were forced to crouch in the bilges. Ivarr ordered that the shackles be eased so they could stand and move about. As a precaution he kept them chained in pairs. This did not prevent two of our male captives from taking their chance to leap overboard. They flung themselves into the water and made no attempt to save their lives. They deliberately raised their arms and sank beneath the water, dragged down by the weight of their manacles, so there was no chance that our cursing oarsmen could turn and retrieve them.

The great river was now so wide that it was as if we were

floating on an inland sea, and we were able to raise sail and greatly increase the distance we travelled each day. A full cargo of slaves and furs meant we had no reason to halt except to revictual the flotilla at the riverside towns which began to appear with increasing frequency. The townsfolk recognised us from a distance because only the Varangian craft had those curved profiles from the northern lands and the local traders were waiting with what we required.

We bought food for our slaves, mostly salted and dried fish, and cheap jewellery to prettify them. 'A well-turned-out slave girl gets ten times the price than one looking like a slut,' Ivarr told me, 'and if she has a pretty voice and can sing and play an instrument, then there's almost no limit to the money a rich man will pay.' He had taken me to the market in the largest of the river cities where he had a commercial arrangement with a local merchant. This man, a Jewish Khazar, specialised in the slave trade. In exchange for our least favoured slave, a male, he provided us with lengths of brightly coloured fabric for women's clothes, necklaces of green glass, beads and bangles, and an interpreter who knew the languages spoken along the lower river.

'What about the men and children we've captured?' I asked Ivarr as we waited in the Khazar's shop for the goods to be delivered.

'The children, that depends. If they are sprightly and show promise, they are easy to sell. Girls are usually more saleable than boys, though if you have a really intelligent male you can sometimes be lucky in Miklagard, the great city, particularly if the lad has fair skin and blue eyes.'

'You mean for men who like that sort or for their wives?'

'Neither. Their masters arrange to have their stones removed, then educate them. They become trusted servants, secretaries and bookkeepers and such like. Some have been bought for the imperial staff and have risen to power and responsibility. At the highest levels of the emperor's government are men who have been gelded.'

I wondered what was in store for the twins we had captured. The Khazar Jew had offered to buy them, but Ivarr would not hear of it. 'The Jews rival us for mastery of the slave trade,' he said, 'but they are middle men. They don't take the risks of raiding among the tribes. If I can sell the twins direct to a client, the felag will make a far greater profit.'

He had given the two girls into the care of his favourite concubine. She was gentle with them, showing them how best to wash and braid their hair, how to apply unguents to their faces and wear the clothes and jewellery we supplied. When the sun shone brightly, she insisted that the girls wear heavy veils to protect their fair complexions. There was no possibility that the girls would be molested by any of our men. Everyone knew that untarnished twins were far too valuable.

The weather was very much warmer now. We set aside our heavy clothes and took to wearing loose shirts and baggy trousers made of many folds of cotton. The loose trousers meant that we could scramble unhampered about the boat, yet remain cool in the increasing heat of summer. At dusk we landed on sandbanks and slept in the light tents we had purchased so we could take advantage of the night breeze. The river had left behind the dense forests, and now flowed through flat, open country grazed by the cattle of the local tribes whose language, according our interpreter, was spoken by the horse-riding peoples further east. Whenever we encountered the boats of other river travellers, they sheered off like frightened minnows. It did not matter whether people thought of us as Varangian or Rus, it was clear that we had an unsavoury reputation.

'Ivarr! On the river bank! Serklanders!' Vermundr called out one hot afternoon. The excitement in his voice made me look round to see what had made him so eager. In the distance was a small riverside village and beside it a cluster of long, low tents made of dark material. In front of the tents half a dozen river boats were drawn up on the shore.

Ivarr squinted across the glare of the river's surface. 'Thorgils, you bring good fortune with you yet again,' he said. 'I've never known Serklanders so far north.' He ordered the helmsman to steer for land. With our slave raid fresh in my mind, I wondered if Ivarr planned to swoop down on the strangers and rob them like a common pirate.

I said as much to Vermundr, and he sneered back at me. 'Perun knows why Ivarr thinks so much of you. Serklanders travel well protected, by Black Hoods usually.'

As we came closer to the landing place, I saw what he meant. A squad of men, wearing long dark hooded gowns, emerged from the tents and took up positions on the river bank, facing us. They deployed with the discipline of trained fighting men and were armed with powerful-looking double-curved bows, which they trained on us. Ivarr stood up in the bow of our boat, his brawny arms held well away from his body to show that he was unarmed.

'Tell them we come to talk of trade,' he told our interpreter, who shouted the message across the gap. The leader of the Black Hoods brusquely gestured that we were not to land close to the tents, but a little further downriver. To my surprise, Ivarr meekly obeyed. It was the first time I had seen him accept an order.

He then sent our interpreter to talk with the strangers while we set up our camp. On Ivarr's instructions, we took more care than usual. 'Expect to be here for a few days,' he said. 'We need to make a good impression.' By the time the interpreter returned, we had pitched our tents in a neat row and Ivarr's favourite concubine had shepherded our batch of slave girls to their own accommodation, a separate tent set beside our leader's pavilion with its array of rugs and cushions.

'The Serklander says he will visit you tomorrow after his prayers,' our interpreter reported. 'He asks that you prepare your wares for his inspection.'

'The land of silk, that's Serkland.' Ivarr said to me, wiping the beads of sweat from his scalp. He was sweating more than usual. 'I've never been there. It's beyond the mountains, far to the south. Their rulers like to buy slave girls, particularly if they are beautiful and accomplished. And they pay in honest silver.'

Thinking back to my time with Brithmaer the royal moneyer and his clever forgeries, I hoped that Ivarr was right. 'If it's called the land of silk why do they pay in silver?'

Ivarr shrugged. 'We'll be paid in silk when we sell our furs in the great city but the Serklanders prefer to use silver. Sometimes they exchange for gems which they bring from their country, like these.' He tugged at his pearl ear studs and the diamond.

I wondered if, yet again, my life was turning back upon itself. It was Brithmaer who had told me the rumour that fire rubies came from lands beyond the mountains.

So I awaited the arrival of the mysterious Serklander with great interest to see what he was like.

I do not know what I had been expecting, perhaps a giant clad in glistening silks or a gaunt bearded sage. Instead the Serklander proved to be a small, jovial, tubby man with a pale brown skin and dark eyes. He was dressed in a simple white cotton gown, with a cloth of the same material wrapped around his head, and plain leather sandals. To my disappointment he wore no jewellery of any kind. His affable manner was emphasised by the dourness of his escort of Black Hoods, who looked every bit as suspicious as when they had warned us off. By contrast the Serklander smiled at everyone. He trotted round our camp on his short legs, beaming at everyone, kholops and Rus alike. He patted Ivarr's two children on the head in a fatherly way, and even laughed at himself when he tripped over a tent rope and almost went headlong. But I noticed that his alert gaze missed nothing.

Finally Ivarr brought him to where the slave girls were waiting. Their tent was like a market booth and Ivarr had ordered that the front flap should be hanging down as we approached. Our little procession consisted of Ivarr, the Serklander and his guards, the Serklander's interpreter and our own, and myself as Ivarr's lucky mascot. Everyone else was kept well back by the

Black Hoods. We came to a halt, facing the curtain. There was a pause and I saw two of the Black Hoods exchange a quick glance. They suspected an ambush and made a move as if to step forward and check. But the little Serklander was too quick for them. He was enjoying Ivarr's showmanship. He made a small restraining gesture and waited expectantly, a cheery smile on his face. Ivarr stepped forward, took hold of the edge of the tent curtain and threw it open, revealing the tableau inside. The slave girls had been arranged so that they stood in a line, hands demurely clasped in front of them. They were dressed in all the finery that Ivarr's concubine had been able to muster — flowing gowns, bright belts, coloured necklaces. Their hair had been washed and combed and arranged to best advantage. Some had flowers braided in their hair.

I watched the Serklander's face. His glance swept along the line of the dozen women on offer and the cheerful smile remained on his lips as if he was highly amused. Then I saw his gaze halt and — just for an instant — his eyes widened a fraction. He was looking at the far end of the line of slave girls where Ivarr's woman had positioned the twins, so that the sunshine filtering through the tent cloth bathed them in a luminous light. Daringly she had decided not to decorate the two girls at all. They wore only plain, cotton gowns, belted with a simple pale blue cord. Their feet were bare. The twins looked virginal and pure.

I knew instantly that Ivarr had made the sale.

Nevertheless, it took a week to settle a price for the girls. Neither the Serklander nor Ivarr were involved directly. The trading custom was that the two interpreters proposed bid and counter-bid, though of course their masters were the ones who dictated the value of their offers. Ivarr mistrusted the man whom the Khazar Jew had provided, so instructed me to accompany our interpreter whenever he visited the Serklander camp to negotiate, to keep an eye on him. I found this difficult because the two men carried on their negotiation entirely by touch, not word. After the usual formalities and a glass of some sweet drink, they would sit down on the ground facing one another and clasp their right hands. A cloth was then placed over the hands to shield them from the gaze of onlookers and the bargaining began. It must have been done by the varying pressures and positions of fingers and palms in a code to signal the offers and responses. All I could do was sit and watch, and try to read their faces.

'It's impossible,' I said to Ivarr after returning back to his camp after one session. 'I can't tell you if the trading is fair and honest, or if the two of them are making a private deal and you are being cheated.'

'Never mind, Thorgils,' he said. 'I still want you to be there. You are my good luck.'

So I continued with my visits to the Serklander's camp, and thus I came to his attention. His name was Salim ibn Hauk, and he was both merchant and diplomat. He was returning from an embassy to the Bolgars of the river on behalf of his master, whom he referred to as Caliph al-Qadir. Meeting with our felag had been as much a stroke of good fortune for him as it had been for us. He had been charged with collecting information about the foreign lands, and wished to know more about the Rus.

A Black Hood was sent to fetch me to ibn Hauk's tent.

'Greetings,' said the cheerful little man, speaking through his interpreter. Ibn Hauk was seated cross-legged on a carpet in his tent, a light airy canopy spread over slender supports which allowed the maximum of breeze. In front of him was a low wooden desk and he held a metal stylus in his hand. 'I would be very grateful if you could tell me something about your people.'

'Your excellency, I'm not sure that I can tell you very much,' I answered.

He looked at me quizzically. 'Don't be alarmed,' he said, 'I only want to learn about your customs. Nothing that would be considered as spying.'

'It's not that, your excellency. I have only lived among the Rus for a few months. I am not one of them.'

He looked disappointed. 'You are a freed slave?'

'No, I joined them of my own wish. I wanted to travel.'

'For profit?'

'To fulfil a vow I made to a friend before his death. They are on their way to the great city, to Miklagard.'

'How remarkable.' He made a note with his stylus on the page in front of him and I saw that he wrote from right to left. Also he used a version of the curving script which had haunted me since I had seen it on Aelfgifu's necklace coins.

'Excuse me, your excellency,' I asked. 'What is it that you write?'

'Just a few notes,' he said. 'Never worry. There's nothing magical in making marks on paper. It does not steal away the knowledge.'

He thought me illiterate like most members of the felag.

'No, your excellency. I was wondering just how your script conveys the spoken word. You write in the opposite direction from us, yet you begin at the top of the page just as we do. If there is more than one page of writing, which page is the first? I mean, do you turn the pages from left to right, or in the other direction? Or is there perhaps another system?'

He looked astonished. 'You mean to say that you can read and write!'

'Yes, your excellency, I have been taught the Roman script and the Greek. I know also the rune letters.'

He laid down his stylus with an expression of delight. 'And I thought that I had found only two gems for my master. Now I discover that I have a treasure of my own.' He paused, 'And just for your information, yes, I do write letters from right to left, but numbers in the opposite direction.'

The Serklander summoned me several times to his tent to question me, and he detained me for many hours so I could supply the information he required. That might have been one reason why he did not hurry the negotiations over the sale of the twins, and this meant, in turn, that our felag stayed camped on the river bank for longer than was wise. The Varangians had not troubled to dig latrines, and our original neat encampment grew dirty and foul. As I have noticed in my travels, pestilence soon appears in such conditions, and this time the first victim was Ivarr himself.

His guts turned to water. One day he was healthy, the next he was staggering in his walk and vomiting incessantly. There were small white flecks in his bile and in the liquid that began to pour from his bowels. He retreated to his tent and, despite his bull-like strength, collapsed. His concubines hurried to minister to him, but there was little they could do. Ivarr shrivelled. His cheeks fell in, his skin took on a dull grey pallor and his eyes sank back in their sockets. It was like watching the contents of a full wine skin drain away. Occasionally he groaned and writhed with cramp and his skin was cold to the touch. His breath came in short, shallow gasps and by the third day ceased altogether. I knew that it was the vengeance of the village sieidde he had defiled, but the felag thought otherwise. They blamed the Serkander or his servants for poisoning Ivarr and they may have had a point. When I reported the signs of Ivarr's illness to ibn Hauk, he immediately asked me to leave his presence and the Black Hoods struck camp that same evening. Before sunset the Serklander and his people were embarking on their boats and heading downstream, taking the twins with them. The felag took their hasty departure as evidence of their guilt.

Sudden death was commonplace for the felag. Their first response to Ivarr's death was to calculate how much extra profit would accrue to each member of the felag now that he was gone. Then, from respect to his memory or perhaps because it gave an excuse for much drinking, they resolved to celebrate his funeral rites. What followed is scarred into my memory.

They found themselves a gand volva – a black witch – in the nearby village. Who she was or from whom she had learned her seidr I do not know. But her knowledge was partly of things that I had learned from Thrand and Rassa, and partly of other elements more evil and malign. She was a woman perhaps in her sixtieth

year, emaciated but still active and possessed of a sinewy strength.
When she arrived at our camp I looked for her noaide emblems –
such as a sacred staff, a girdle of dried fungi, gloves of fur worn
inside out or a string of amulets. But I saw nothing that might
signify her calling, except a single large pendant, a polished green
and white stone dangling from her belt. But there was no doubting
who she was. I felt the presence radiate from her as powerfully as
I could smell a rotting carcass and the sensation made me queasy.

She ordered the materials for a scaffold. It was to be built on
the shore, and as she drew the outline of the structure in the sand
with the point of a stick my fears were calmed. It was to be a
wooden platform similar to one Rassa had shown me when he
took me through the northern forests. The height of a man, the
scaffold was where a noaide often chose to keep vigil when
seeking to enter the saivo world, sitting above the earth in the
cold air until the spirit chose to leave the body. When the kholops
had brought timber for the structure, the volva called for Ivarr's
favourite knife. She used it to cut runes on the main cross timber
and as I watched her I shivered. I had seen those runes only once
before: on the log which had been the cause of Grettir's death,
the log that turned the axe to wound him. They were curse runes.
Of course the volva sensed my dismay. She turned to look straight
at me and the venom in her glance was like a blow to the head.
She knew that I possessed the second sight and she dared me to
intervene. I was helpless and afraid. Her power, I knew, was far
greater than mine.

Ivarr's funeral began an hour before dusk. By then the
members of the felag were already well and truly drunk. They
had supervised the kholops as they dragged the leakiest of our
boats from the river bank up to the scaffold and placed firewood
under and around the hull. The crone had then taken charge. She
ordered Ivarr's tent to be taken down, then reassembled amidships
on the boat. In it the kholops placed his carpets, rugs and cushions.
Finally Ivarr's corpse, dressed in a gown of brocade, was carried
aboard and laid upon the cushions. When all had been arranged

to her satisfaction, the volva went to fetch Ivarr's favourite concubine. She was a plump, obedient girl with long, black braids which she wore coiled round her head. I guessed that she was the mother of at least one of Ivarr's boys, for she wore a heavy neck ring of gold, a sign of her master's favour. I liked her because she had shown kindness when she supervised the preparation of the twins for sale. Now I feared that she would fall into the hands of owners as vicious as Vermundr or Froygeir. When the volva arrived to collect her, she was standing on the patch of bare earth where Ivarr's tent had stood and looking bereft. I saw the volva whisper something in her ear and take her by the wrist.

Walking as if in a dream, the girl was led towards the scaffold. From her wavering steps it seemed to me that she had been drugged or was intoxicated. Certainly every member of the felag was tipsy and I confess I was far from sober myself. Overwhelmed with dread, I had taken several cups of mead to repel the sense of doom.

'You should go with her. You were just as much his favourite,' Vermundr jeered, his drunken breath in my face as we watched the concubine approach the scaffold. Two hefty Varangians took her by the waist and lifted her to the platform. Three times they raised and lowered the girl in some sort of ceremony, and I saw her lips move as she mumbled an incantation or maybe a plea for help. On the third occasion the volva handed her a living cockerel. For a moment, the girl hesitated and I heard the volva scream urgently at her. What language was used I do not know, but the girl put the head of the cockerel in her mouth and bit it off, then flung its corpse, still fluttering, so that it landed upon the funeral ship. I saw the spray of chicken blood scatter through the air.

The girl was lifted from the scaffold one more time and, weaving and stumbling, brought to her master's ship. She slipped and fell as she tried to climb the stacked firewood and the volva had to help her. Four members of the felag, including Vermundr, followed her and so did the volva. The light was fading, which made it difficult to see the details, but the girl lost her balance and toppled into the open door of the tent. Perhaps the volva had deliberately tripped her. She slumped on the cushions and one of the four Varangians began to fumble drunkenly at his trousers. Then he advanced on the girl and raped her. The volva stood to one side, looking on dispassionately. Each of the Varangians took the girl, then stood up and, turning towards us where we were clustered around the campfire, shouted, 'That I have done in honour of Ivarr.' Afterwards he descended from the boat and allowed the next man to take his turn.

When all four men were back on the ground, the volva reached down, seized the girl by the hair and dragged her further into the tent. By that stage the concubine was completely limp. The flickering light of the campfire illuminated the final death rite. I saw the volva make a noose with the cord to which the blue and green stone was attached, and slip it over her victim's head. Next she placed one foot on the girl's face, and leaning back, pulled tight the noose with a powerful jerk. Lastly she took Ivarr's knife from her belt, and repeatedly stabbed down on the human sacrifice.

Only then did the volva descend and, selecting a brand from the camp fire, thrust it into the kindling heaped around the boat. The wood was dry from the summer heat and immediately caught fire. The breeze fanned the flames and within moments the funeral pyre was burning fiercely. As the blaze sucked in more air, I threw up my arm to protect my face from the heat. Flames roared and crackled, sending columns of blazing sparks into the air. In the heart of the conflagration, great holes suddenly appeared in the fabric of the tent sheltering Ivarr's corpse. The holes spread their burning edges, eating away the cloth so rapidly that for an instant the frame of the tent stood alone as if to defy the inferno. Then the tent poles collapsed inwards across the bodies of Ivarr and his murdered concubine.

That night I drank myself into oblivion. The heat radiating from the blaze had brought on a powerful thirst, but I drank to forget what I had just seen. All around me the Varangians caroused and celebrated. They drank until they threw up, wiped their beards and then went back to drink. Two of them came to blows over an imagined insult. They groped for their swords and daggers and made futile stabs and slashes at one another until too weak to continue the dispute. Others guzzled mead and ale until they fell senseless on the ground. Those who could still stand, staggered off to the tent where our slave girls slept, and molested them drunkenly. The volva was nowhere to be seen. She had vanished, gone back to her village, no doubt. Nauseous with too much drink, I crept away to a quiet corner behind some cargo bales and fell asleep.

I awoke with a racking headache, a queasy stomach and a foul taste in my mouth. It was well past daybreak and the sun was already high above the horizon. It promised to be another scorching day. Holding onto the cargo bale for support, I pulled myself to my feet and looked across to where Ivarr's funeral pyre had stood. There was nothing but a heap of charred wood and ash. Only the volva's scaffold remained. Beside it a chicken feather stirred in the breeze on the scorched ground.

A few kholops were moving about the camp in an aimless way, lacking orders. Their masters, those I could see, lay snoring on the ground, motionless after their debauch.

Gingerly I made my way slowly across the camp, then down the river bank to the water's edge. I felt defiled and in desperate need of a wash even if the river water looked far from clean. It was a dark brown, almost black. I pulled off my soiled shirt and wrapped it around my waist as a loincloth, and removed my loose Varangian trousers. Slowly and carefully I waded out into the river until the tepid water reached the middle of my thighs. I stopped there for a moment, letting the sun warm my back, feeling the mud ooze up between my toes. I was in a back eddy. The water was barely moving. Cautiously I leaned forward, fearing that a sudden movement would bring on an attack of nausea. Gradually I brought my face closer to the dark water, and got ready to splash water in my face. Just before I plunged my cupped

hands into the river, I paused and looked at my reflection. The
sun was at such an angle that I saw my head and shoulders as a
vague outline. Suddenly I was assailed by a violent swaying
sickness. My head spun. A chill washed over me, and I was about
to faint. I thought it was the result of my debauchery, but then
realised that I had seen the very same reflection before. It was the
image I had seen when I peered into the well of prophecy that
Edgar the royal huntsman had shown me in the forest at
Northampton. Even as I came to that understanding, I saw the
flash of something bright in the mirror of the river. For a heartbeat
I mistook it for the silver flicker of a fish, then I recognised the
reflection of a knife blade and the upraised arm that held it as I
fell to one side and the assassin struck.

There was an agonising pain high up in my left shoulder. The
blow aimed at my back had missed. A swirl of water, a growl of
rage and I felt a hand grab for me, slip on wet skin and then
another slash of pain as a second knife stroke sliced my left side.
I flung myself forward, desperate to avoid the dagger. Again a
hand tried to hold me and this time seized the shirt wrapped
around my waist. I ducked underwater, twisted and pushed down
with my feet. The ooze gave no grip and I panicked. My flailing
feet touched the legs of my attacker. Even without seeing his face,
I knew who it was. It had to be Froygeir. He had hated me since
the day I humiliated him at dice in front of the other Varangians.
Now, with Ivarr dead, the time for his revenge had come.

I wriggled like a salmon trying to avoid the barbs of a fishing
spear. Froygeir was a big, agile man, well used to fighting at close
quarters with a knife. Normally he would have finished me off
with ease. Perhaps he was feeling the effects of his night's debauch
or maybe he wanted to haul me out of the water, turn me so I
could see my killer and then cut my throat. So, instead of stabbing
again, he made the mistake of trying to pull me close by heaving
on my loincloth. Its knot came undone and I squirmed free.

As Froygeir stumbled backwards, I seized my chance to swim

clear. The pain in my wounded left shoulder was so excruciating that I forgot the cut to my ribs. Terror drove me as I found the strength to move my arms and legs and swim a dozen frenzied strokes. I had no idea in which direction I was going. All I knew was that I had to get away from Froygeir. I thrashed forward blindly, expecting at any moment to feel his hand grasp my ankle and pull me back.

My nakedness saved me. I can think of no other explanation. Froygeir was a river man. He knew how to swim and should have overhauled his wounded prey with no difficulty, but he was wearing Varangian trousers with their many folds of material and, waterlogged, they hampered him. I heard him surge after me, wading at first, then forced to swim in my wake. As my initial panic receded, I took a quick look to see where I was heading – directly away from shore, out into the broad river. I forced myself to breathe deeply and move through the muddy water in some sort of rhythm. Only when I had swum at least two hundred strokes did I risk glancing back. Froygeir had abandoned the chase. I could see the back of his head as he returned towards the shore. There, I knew, he would be waiting for me if I was so foolish as to return to the camp.

Utterly exhausted, I stopped swimming and trod water. A red stain was spreading from my shoulder all around me. I had heard of giant fish in the river – it was said they were longer than a man – and wondered if they fed on flesh and would be attracted by blood. I prayed to Odinn for help.

Slimy and ancient, the log was floating so low in the water that I did not see my salvation until it nuzzled against me and I flinched, thinking of those meat-eating fish. Then I wrapped my arms gratefully around the slippery wood and let the timber take my weight. Another circle of my life was closing, I thought to myself. Driftwood had caused the death of my sworn brother and now another floating log would prolong my life if only I could hang on. Bleeding to death would be better than drowning. I clenched my teeth against the pain from my shoulder, squeezed my eyes tight shut, and deliberately sought the relief of darkness.

I KNEW NOTHING MORE until a sour smell roused me. Fumes stung my nose and brought tears in my eyes. A trickle of liquid, sharp and astringent, ran into my throat and made me cough. Someone was bathing my face with a sponge. I opened my eyes. I must have fainted while clinging to the log – I had no idea how I came to be lying on my back on a carpet and looking up into the chubby face of ibn Hauk. For once, his expression was sombre. He said something in his own language and I heard the voice of his interpreter.

'Why were you floating in the river?'

I licked my lips and tasted vinegar.

'They tried to kill me.'

The Serklander did not even bother to ask who had made the attempt. He knew.

'Then it was lucky that one of my Black Hoods spotted you.'

'You must get away,' I said urgently. 'The man who sold you the slaves, Ivarr, is dead. His comrades think you poisoned him. Now the Varangians are leaderless they are very dangerous and will try to catch up with you to get back the twin girls.'

'No more than I would expect of those savages,' he answered. 'We are already on our way downriver.'

I tried to sit up.

'My master asks you to lie still,' said the interpreter. 'You will disturb the dressing.'

I turned my head and saw that my left shoulder was bandaged. Again I smelled vinegar and wondered why.

Ibn Hauk answered before I had time to enquire.

'The vinegar is against the pestilence,' he said. 'It is to cleanse you from the sickness that killed Ivarr. Rest now. We will not be stopping, but will travel through the darkness. I do not think that your Rus will catch up with us. And if they do the Black Hoods will deal with them.'

I relaxed and thought about this turn of events. Everything I owned – my precious furs, my clothes, even the knife that Thrand had given me and which I treasured – was lost irretrievably. They were in the hands of the Varangians, who would already have divided the spoils amongst themselves. I was glad that I had given away the fire ruby to Allba. I was destitute and now I did not even have clothes to wear. Under the loose cotton sheet which covered me I was naked.

Ibn Hauk personally attended to me as we sailed downriver. He carried a stock of healing drugs from his own country and prepared the poultices of herbs and spices which were applied to my knife wounds. Certainly he was very skilled in their use, for eventually the wounds closed up so cleanly that they left barely the faintest scars. Each time he came to change the dressings he took the chance to question me about the customs of the Varangians and the countries where I had travelled. He had never heard of Iceland or Greenland, and of course he knew nothing of Vinland. But he had heard of King Knut of England and had some vague information about the northern lands.

When I told him how Ivarr's corpse had been burned, he was shocked. 'That is utter barbarism,' he said. 'No wonder the pestilence spreads among those river pirates. My religion demands that we wash before our prayers, but I observed that your former travelling companions are more filthy in their habits than donkeys.'

'Not all are so uncouth,' I said. 'There are men who know the use of herbs and simples just as you do, and the true Varangians, the men who come from the northern lands, are strict about their personal cleanliness. They bathe regularly, keep their hair and fingernails clean and take a pride in their appearance. I know because I have had to wield the heavy stones they use to press their clothes.'

'But burning a corpse to ashes,' ibn Hauk observed, 'that is abominable.'

'In your country what do they do?' I asked.

'We bury our dead,' he answered. 'Often the grave must be

shallow because the soil is rocky, but we put the dead into the ground as quickly as possible before putrefaction sets in. Our climate is very hot.'

'That is what the Christians also do – bury the dead,' I said, and found myself repeating what Thrand had said long ago. 'You see, for those who follow the Old Ways that is an insult to the deceased. We – for I am an Old Believer – find it repugnant to let a man's corpse decompose or be eaten by worms. We prefer that it is destroyed neatly and cleanly, so that the soul rises to Valholl.'

Then, of course I had to explain what I meant by Valholl, while ibn Hauk busily made notes. 'Your Valholl sounds very much like the valley that some of our believers, a strange sect, think they will achieve if they die in battle sacrificing their lives for their leader.'

He was so amiable and outgoing that I took the chance to ask him if he had ever seen precious stones that were the colour of pigeon's blood and had a burning fire within them.

He recognised the description instantly.

'Of course. We call them laal. My master owns several – they are among the pride of his royal jewels. The best ones he received as gifts from other great potentates.'

'Do you know where they come from?'

'That's not an easy question to answer. The gem dealers refer to these jewels as badakshi, and this may have something to do with the name of the country where they are found,' he said. 'It is said that the mines lie in high mountains, close to the borders of the country we call al-Hind. Their precise location is kept a secret, but there are rumours. It is reported that the rubies are found encased in lumps of white rock, which are broken open with great care by the miners, using chisels, to reveal the jewel within. If they find a small jewel of poor quality, they call it a foot soldier. A better jewel is known as a horse soldier, and so on up through an amir jewel, a vizier jewel, until the very best – the emperor jewel – which is reserved for royalty.'

In such intelligent and informative company the journey south passed rapidly, and it was with genuine regret that I heard ibn Hauk announce one afternoon that our paths were about to separate.

'Tomorrow we reach the outer frontiers of Rumiyah,' he said. 'I expect we will meet with a border patrol. The great river curves away to the east and the way to Rumiyah, where you want to go, is south and west. You have to cross from this river to another, which takes you to a port from where you take ship and finally, after a passage of two or three weeks, you will arrive at its capital, Constantinople, or Miklagard as you call it.'

I must have looked dejected because he added, 'Don't worry. One traveller should always help another and my religion tells me that acts of charity will be rewarded. I promise that I will see to it that you reach your Miklagard.'

Only when the commander of the frontier guard came to interview ibn Hauk did I fully appreciate how influential was my modest travelling companion. The commander was a Pecheneg mercenary, hired with his troop of tribal cavalry to patrol the buffer zone between the empire and the wilder region to the north. The Pecheneg was either arrogant or looking for a bribe. He spoke to ibn Hauk rudely, demanding proof of his claim that he was an ambassador. Quietly ibn Hauk produced a small metal tablet. It was about the length of my hand and three fingers broad. There were lines of Greek script engraved on it, though I doubted that the Pecheneg could read them. However, the soldier had no need of literacy. The tablet was solid gold. He blenched when he saw it and became very obsequious. Was there anything the ambassador wanted? He asked. He would be happy to oblige.

'Allow myself and my retinue to continue downriver,' answered the Arab gently, 'and provide an escort, if you would be so kind, for this young man. He is carrying a message to his majesty the emperor.'

I had the presence of mind not to gape with astonishment.

The moment the Pecheneg had left the tent, I asked, 'Your excellency, what was meant about a message for Constantinople?'

'Oh, that.' Ibn Hauk waved his hand dismissively. 'It will do no harm if I send the compliments of the caliph to the emperor of Rumiyah. Indeed it would be much appreciated. The imperial court positively relishes the niceties of diplomacy, and the protocol department might take it as an insult if they heard that I had visited a corner of imperial territory without sending a few flattering words to the great emperor of the Romans, for that is how he styles himself. You can carry the note for me. In fact you can help write it out in Greek letters.'

'But I don't understand why the Pecheneg should go to the trouble of arranging my journey.'

'He has little choice,' said ibn Hauk. 'The imperial office only issues gold passport tablets to the representatives of the most important fellow rulers. Each tablet carries the authority of the emperor himself. If the Pecheneg failed in his duty, he would be lucky to hold onto his job, if not thrown into gaol. The bureaucrats of Constantinople are corrupt and conceited, but they hate disobedience. To smooth your passage, I will give you enough silver to sweeten them on arrival. Here, let us compose the message you will carry.'

So it was that I had my first and only lesson in transcribing from Serkland script to Greek. I found the task not that difficult because many of the letters had their close equivalents, and with the help of the interpreter I made what I think was a reasonable translation of ibn Hauk's flowery congratulations and compliments to the basileus, as the Byzantines call their emperor.

'I doubt he will ever see the letter, anyhow,' commented ibn Hauk. 'It will probably get filed away somewhere in the palace archives, and be forgotten. A pity as I'm rather proud of my calligraphy.'

He had taken great care with his penmanship, delicately inking in the lines of script on a fresh, smooth parchment. He reminded me of the monks whom I had seen at work in the scriptorium of the monastery where I had served a brief novitiate. His hand-writing was a work of art. I said as much and he looked even more cheerful than usual.

'You will have noted,' he said, 'that I used a different script from the one I wrote when I was making my notes about your travels. That was my everyday working hand. This letter I have penned in our formal lettering, which is reserved for important documents and inscriptions, copies of our holy book and anything which bears my master's name. Which reminds me: you will need money to cover your travelling expenses on the way to Constantinople.'

Which is how I came to travel the final stage of my journey to Miklagard dressed in a cotton Arab gown and carrying coins which I had first seen around the neck of the queen of England, and which I now knew were struck in the name of the great caliph of Baghdad.

EIGHTEEN

MUCH HAS BEEN written of the splendours of Constantinople, the city we northerners know as Miklagard and others call Metropolis, the queen or – simply – the great city. Yet nowhere have I read of the phenomenon which intrigued me as I arrived at the mouth of the narrow strait on which Constantinople stands. The phenomenon is this: the sea water runs only one way through the strait. This is against nature. As every sailor knows, if a sea is tidal, there is a regular ebb and flow in such a constricted place. If there is no tide or very little, as at Constantinople, there should be no movement of the water at all. Yet the captain of the cargo vessel which had brought me to the strait, assured me that a sea always flows through in the same direction.

'You can count on it running from north to south,' he said, watching my expression of disbelief, 'and sometimes the current is as swift as a powerful river.' We were passing between the two rocky headlands which mark the northern entrance to the channel. 'In ancient times,' he continued, 'it was said that those rocks could clash together, smashing to splinters any vessel that tried to slip through. That is mere fable, but it is certain that the current always goes one way.'

I watched our speed increase as we came into the current. On the beach a gang of men were man-hauling a vessel upstream, so

to speak, with tow ropes tied to their bodies. They reminded me
of our kholops dragging our light boats in the land of the Rus.

'Now I will show you something still more remarkable,' said
the captain, pleased to teach an ignorant foreigner the wonders of
his home port. 'That vessel over there, the one that looks as if it
is anchored in midstream.' He pointed to a tubby little trading
ship, which appeared to have dropped anchor far from shore,
though quite why its crew were rowing when the ship was at
anchor, was a mystery. 'That ship is not anchored at all. You
couldn't reach the bottom with the longest line. The skipper is
dangling a big basket of stones overboard. He's done it to catch a
current deep down. It flows the other way, from south to north,
and is helping to drag his vessel in the way he wants.'

I was too astonished to comment, for the strait ahead of us
was widening. Its banks, with their villas and country houses,
were opening out to frame a spectacle which was nothing like
anything I had imagined could be possible. Constantinople had
come full into view.

The city was immense. I had seen Dublin from the Black Pool
and I had sailed up the Thames to arrive in London's port, but
Constantinople far exceeded anything I had ever witnessed. There
was no comparison. Constantinople's population was said to
number more than half a million citizens, ten times the size of the
next largest city in the known world. Judging by the immense
number of palaces, public buildings and houses covering the entire
width of the peninsula ahead of me, this was no exaggeration. To
my right a capacious harbour opened out, an entire gulf crowded
with merchant shipping of every shape and description. Looming
over the wharves were buildings which I identified as warehouses
and arsenals and I could see the outlines of shipyards and dry
docks. Beyond the waterfront rose an imposing city wall, whose
ramparts encircled the city as far as the eye could see. Yet even
this tall city wall was dwarfed by the structures behind it. There
was a skyline of lofty towers, columns, high roofs and domes, all
built of marble and stone, brick and tile, not of wood, plaster and

thatch like the cities with which I was familiar. But it was not the magnitude of the place that silenced me, nor its air of solid permanence, for I had carried a wondrous vision of the city in my head ever since Bolli Bollason had sung the praises of Miklagard, and I had promised Grettir to travel in his memory. The reason for my stunned amazement came from something else: the panorama of the city was dominated by a vast assembly of churches and oratories and monasteries, most of them built to a design that I had never seen before – clusters of domes surmounted by the cross-shaped symbol of the White Christ. Many of the domes were covered with gold leaf and glittered in the sunshine. I had totally failed to realise that my destination was the greatest stronghold of the White Christ faith on earth.

Despite all this magificence I had little time to gaze. The current rapidly brought our ship into the anchorage, which my captain proudly informed me was known throughout the civilised – and he emphasised the word civilised – world as the Golden Horn for its prosperity and wealth. 'There'll be a customs man waiting on the dock to check my cargo and charge me taxes. Ten per cent for those grasping rogues in the state treasury. I'll ask him to arrange for a clerk to escort you to the imperial chancery, where you can hand over that letter you are carrying.' Then he added meaningfully, 'If you have to deal with the officials there, I wish you luck.'

My monastery-learned Greek, I rapidly discovered, either made people smile or wince. The latter was the reaction of the palace functionary who accepted ibn Hauk's letter on behalf of the court protocol department. He made me wait for an hour in a bleak antechamber before I was ushered into his presence. As ibn Hauk had anticipated, I was greeted with supreme bureaucratic indifference.

'This will be placed before the memoriales in due course,' the functionary said, using only his fingertips to touch ibn Hauk's exquisitely written letter, as if it was tainted.

'Will the memoriales want to send a reply?' I asked politely.

The civil servant curled his lip. 'The memoriales,' he said, 'are the secretaries of the imperial records department. They will study the document and decide if the letter should be placed on file or if it merits onward transmission to the charturalius –' he saw my puzzlement – 'the chief clerk. He in turn will decide whether it should be forwarded to the office of the dromos, the foreign minister, or to the basilikoi, who heads the office of special emissaries. In either case it will require the secretariat's approval and, of course, the consent of the minister himself, before the matter of a response is brought forward for consideration. ' His reply convinced me that my duty towards ibn Hauk had been amply discharged. His letter would be mired in the imperial bureaucracy for months.

'Perhaps you could tell me where I might find the Varangians,' I ventured.

The secretary raised a disdainful eyebrow at my antiquated Greek.

'The Varangians,' I repeated. 'The imperial guardsmen.'

There was a pause as he deliberated over my question, it was as if he was smelling a bad odour. 'Oh, you mean the emperor's wineskins,' he answered. 'That drunken lot of barbarians. I haven't the least idea. You'd better ask someone else.' It was quite plain that he knew the answer to my question, but was not prepared to help.

I had better luck with a passer-by in the street. 'Follow this main avenue,' he said, 'past the porticos and arcades of shops until you come to the Milion – that's a pillar with a heavy iron chain round the base. There's a dome over it, held up on four columns, rather like an upside-down soup bowl. You can't miss it. It's where all the official measurements for distances in the empire start from. Go past the Milion and take the first right. In front of you you'll see a large building, looks like a prison, which is not surprising because that is what it used to be. That's now the barracks for the imperial guard. Ask for the Numera if you get lost.'

I followed his directions. It seemed natural to seek out the
Varangians. I knew no one in this immense city. In my purse I
had a few silver coins left over from ibn Hauk's generosity, but
they would soon be spent. The only northerners whom I knew
for certain lived in Miklagard were the soldiers of the emperor's
bodyguard. They came from Denmark, Norway, Sweden and
some from England. Many, like Ivarr's father, had once served in
Kiev before deciding to come on to Constantinople and apply to
join the imperial bodyguard. It occurred to me that I might even
ask if I could join. After all, I had served with the Jomsvikings.

My scheme, had I known it, was as clumsy and whimsical as
my knowledge of spoken Greek, but even in the city of churches
Odinn still watched over me.

As I reached the Numera, a man emerged from the doorway
to the barracks and started to walk across the large square away
from me. He was obviously a guardsman. His height and breadth
of shoulder made that much clear. He was a head taller than the
majority of the citizens around him. They were small and neat,
dark haired and olive skinned, and dressed in the typical Greek
costume, loose shirt and trousers for the men, long flowing gowns
and veils for the women. By contrast, the guardsman was wearing
a tunic of red, and I could see the hilt of a heavy sword hanging
from his right shoulder. I noticed too that his long blond hair
hung in three plaits down his neck. I was staring at the back of
his head as he moved through the crowd, when I recognised
something about him. It was the way he walked. He moved like a
ship rolling and cresting over the swell of the sea. The faster-
moving civilians had to step aside to get past him. They were like
a river flowing around a rock. Then I remembered where I had
seen that gait before. There was only one man that tall, who
walked in that measured way – Grettir's half-brother, Thorstein
Galleon.

I broke into a run and chased after him. The coincidence
seemed so far-fetched that I did not yet dare say a prayer of
thanks to Odinn in case I was deluded. I was still wearing an

Arab gown that ibn Hauk had given me and to the pedestrians I must have looked a strange sight indeed, a fair-haired barbarian in a flapping cotton robe pushing rudely through the crowd in pursuit of one of the imperial guard.

'Thorstein!' I shouted.

He stopped, and turned. I saw his face and knew I would make a sacrifice to Odinn in gratitude.

'Thorstein!' I repeated, coming closer. 'It's me Thorgils, Thorgils Leifsson. I haven't seen you since Grettir and I were at your farmhouse in Tonsberg, on our way to Iceland.'

For a moment Thorstein looked puzzled. My Arab dress must have confused him, and my face was tanned by the sun. 'By Thor and his goats,' he rumbled, 'it is indeed Thorgils. What on earth are you doing here and how did you find your way to Miklagard?' He clapped me on the shoulder and I flinched. His hand had touched the wound left by Froygeir's knife.

'I only arrived today,' I answered. 'It's a long story but I came here through Gardariki and along the rivers with the fur traders.'

'But how is it that you are alone and inside the city itself?' Thorstein asked. 'River traders are not allowed inside the city walls unless they are accompanied by an official.'

'I came as an ambassadorial courier,' I said. 'It's so good to see you.'

'You too,' answered Thorstein heartily. 'I heard that you became Grettir's sworn brother after you got back to Iceland. Which makes a bond between us.' Abruptly he checked himself, as though his initial enthusiasm was misplaced. 'I was on my way to report for duty at the palace guardroom, but there's time for us to go and share a glass of wine in a tavern,' and, strangely, he took me by the arm, and almost pushed me away from the open square and into the shelter of one of the arcades. We turned into the first tavern we came to and he led me to the back of the room. Here he sat us down where we could not be observed from the street.

'I'm sorry to seem so brusque, Thorgils,' he said, 'but no one else knows that Grettir was my half-brother and I want it to stay that way.'

For a moment I was scandalised. I had never imagined that Thorstein would conceal his relationship to Grettir, even though his half-brother had earned such an unsavoury reputation as a brigand and outlaw. But I was misjudging Thorstein badly.

'Thorgils, you remember the promise I made to Grettir at my farm in Norway. On the day that you and he were about to set sail for Iceland?'

'You promised to avenge him if ever he was killed unjustly.'

'That's why I'm here in Constantinople, because of Grettir,' Thorstein went on. His voice had a new intensity. 'I've come here in pursuit of the man who killed him. It's taken a long time to track him down and now I'm very close. In fact I don't want him to know just how close. It's not that I think he will make a run for it, he's come too far for that. What I want is to pick the right moment. When I'm to take my revenge, it won't be a hole-in-the-corner deed. It will be out in the open, something to make men remember.'

'That's exactly what Grettir would have said,' I replied. 'But tell me, how does Thorbjorn Ongul come to be here in Miklagard?'

'So you know it was that one-eyed bastard who caused the deaths of Grettir and Illugi,' said Thorstein. 'That's common knowledge in Iceland but nowhere else. He was condemned to exile by the Althing for employing the help of a black witch to cause Grettir's death. Since then he's taken care to keep out of sight. He went to Norway, then came here to Miklagard, where there's little chance of running into any other Icelanders or being recognised. In fact the other members of the guard know nothing about his background. He applied to the service about a year ago, met the entry requirements, greased a few palms and has established himself as a reliable soldier. That's another reason why I have to strike at the right moment. The regiment won't like it.'

He paused for a moment and then said quietly, 'Thorgils, your arrival has complicated matters for me. I cannot allow anything which might interfere with my promise or risk its outcome. I would prefer if you stayed out of Constantinople, at least until I have settled matters with Thorbjorn Ongul.'

'There's another way, Thorstein,' I said. 'Both of us are honour bound to Grettir's memory, whether as half-brother or sworn brother. As witness to your oath to Grettir I have a duty to support you, should you ever need my help. I am utterly certain that it was Odinn who brought about this meeting between us and that he did it for a purpose. Until that purpose becomes clear, I ask you to reconsider. Try to think how I might remain in Constantinople and be close at hand. For instance, why don't I join the guard as a recruit? Anonymously of course.'

Thorstein shook his head. 'Out of the question. Right now there are many more volunteers than vacancies and a long waiting list. I paid a hefty bribe to get in. Four pounds of gold is the going rate for the greedy officials who maintain the army list. Of course the pay scales are so good that you earn the money back in three or four years. The emperor knows enough to keep his guardsmen happy. They're the only troops he can trust in this city of intrigues and plots.' He thought for a moment, then added, 'Maybe there is a way of arranging for you to be close at hand, but you will have to be very discreet. Each guardsman has the right to have one valet on regimental strength. It's a menial job, but it provides you with a billet in the main barracks. I have not yet exercised my nomination.'

'Won't there be a risk that Ongul will see and recognise me?' I asked.

'Not if you keep in the background,' Thorstein answered. 'The Varangian guard has grown in size. There are nearly five hundred of us nowadays and we no longer all fit into the Numera Barracks. Two or three platoons are quartered in the former barracks of the excubitors – they are the palace regiment of Greek guardsmen. Their regimental strength is in decline, while ours is

growing. That's where Thorbjorn Ongul has his room – another
reason why it's been difficult for me to find the right moment to
challenge him over Grettir's death.'

So it was that I became Thorstein Galleon's valet, not a very
demanding task as it turned out. At least not for someone who,
as a youngster, had been on the palace staff of that great dandy,
King Sigtryggr of Dublin. I had learned a long time ago how to
comb and plait hair, wash and press clothes, and polish armour
and weapons till they gleamed. And it turned out to be the
Varangians' pride in their weapons which provided Thorstein with
the opportunity to take revenge, far earlier than he or I had
expected.

The Byzantines love pomp. More than any other nation I have
seen, they adore pageantry and outward show. I can scarcely
recall a single day when they did not have some sort of parade or
ceremony in which the basileus took a prominent part. It might
be a procession from the palace to attend a service in one of the
many churches, a formal parade to commemorate a victory of the
army, or a trip to the harbour to inspect the fleet and the arsenal.
Even a local excursion to the horse races at the Hippodrome –
less than a bow shot from the palace outer wall – was organised
by the master of ceremonies and his multitude of officious staff.
They kept an immensely long list of precedence, detailing who
held what rank in the palace hierarchy, what their precise title
was, who was senior to whom, how they must be addressed, and
so forth. When an imperial procession formed up to leave the
palace grounds, these busybodies could be seen rushing around,
making sure that everyone was in their correct place in the column
and carried the proper emblem of rank – a jewelled whip, a gold
chain, inscribed ivory tablets, a rolled-up diploma, a sword with a
golden hilt, a jewelled gold collar, and so forth. For onlookers it
was easy to identify the imperial family: only they were allowed
to wear the colour purple, and immediately in front and behind of
them marched the guards, just in case of trouble.

The Varangians carried the symbols of their trade: battleaxe and sword. The axe had a single blade, often inlaid with expensive silver scrollwork. The haft was waxed as far as the two-handed grip with its fancy, hand-stitched leatherwork. Both blade and shaft were polished until they gleamed. The heavy sword was worn, as I have mentioned, dangling from the right shoulder, but there was a problem when it came to its embellishment because a sword with a gold hilt was the emblem of a spartharios, a court official of middle rank whose rights and privileges were jealously preserved. So the guardsmen found other ways to ornament their weapons. In my time in Constantinople silver sword handles were popular, and some soldiers had their swords fitted with grips made of exotic wood. Nearly all the men had paid the scabbard makers to have their sword sheaths covered in scarlet silk to match their tunics.

Less than a week after I had taken up my duties as Thorstein's valet, a message arrived at the Numera barracks from the logo- thete, a high official of the chancery. The basileus and his entourage were to process to a service of thanksgiving in the church of Hagia Sophia, and the guard was to provide the usual imperial escort. However, the logothete – he was far too grand to speak for himself but sent a deputy – stressed that the occasion was sufficiently important for the entire guard to be on parade in full regalia. The procession was scheduled to take place in three days' time.

Typically, the first response of the senior officers was to order a dress rehearsal, which took place in the great square before the Numera barracks. I watched from an upper window and had to admit that I was impressed. The Varangian guard looked awe- inspiring, rank upon rank of burly, heavily bearded axemen, fierce enough in appearance to terrify any opposition. Even Thorstein, with his great height, was overtopped by several colleagues, and I spotted Thorbjorn Ongul with his villainous one-eyed look.

The moment the dress rehearsal ended, I and the other orderlies hurried out into the square to collect up the tunics, sword belts and other accoutrements which we would have to keep clean and neat until the procession itself. Naturally a number of the soldiers gathered in groups to gossip and at that point I saw Thorstein walk across and join the group which included Thorbjorn Ongul.

Rashly, I followed.

Taking up my position on the edge of the circle, I took care to keep out of Thorbjorn Ongul's sight, but moved close enough to see what was going on. As I had noted with the Jomsvikings, soldiers love nothing better than to compare their weaponry and this is precisely what the guardsmen were doing. They were showing off their swords, axes and daggers to one another and making claims, mostly exaggerated, about the merits of each item – its excellent balance, its sharpness, how it kept an edge when hacking at a wooden shield, the number of enemies the weapon had despatched, and so on. When it came to Ongul's turn, he unhitched his scabbard, withdrew his sword and flourished it proudly.

My mouth went dry. The sword which Ongul held up for all to see was the very same sword which Grettir had looted from the barrow mound in my company. I recognised it at once. It was a unique weapon, beautifully made with that wavy pattern in the metal of the blade that denotes the finest workmanship of the Frankish swordsmiths. It was the sword Ongul had wrenched from Grettir's hand, chopping off his fingers to release his grip as my sworn brother lay dying on the squalid floor of his hideout on Drang. I made a mental note to tell Thorstein how the sword came to be in Ongul's possession, but Grettir's killer did it for me. The guardsman standing next to Ongul asked if he might look more closely at the weapon and Ongul proudly handed over the sword. The guardsman sighted along the blade and pointed out to Ongul that there were two nicks on the cutting edge.

'You should get those attended to. It's a shame that such a fine blade has such marks,' he said.

'Oh no,' announced Ongul boastfully as he took back the sword. 'I made those nicks myself. They come from the day that

I used this sword to put an end to the perverted outlaw, Grettir the Strong. This was his sword. I took it from him and those two nicks were made when I hacked off his head. Grettir the Strong was like no other man. Even his neck bones were like iron. It took four good blows to cut through his neck and that was when the sword edge was chipped. I wouldn't grind out those marks even if the commander-in-chief himself asked me to.'

'Can I see the weapon?' asked a voice. I recognised the deep tones of Thorstein Galleon, and saw Ongul hand over the weapon. Thorstein swung the sword from side to side experimentally to find what a true swordsman calls the sweet spot, the balance point where the edge carries the most impact and a blade should meet its target. The sweep of Thorstein's swing made the crowd move back to give him more space and, to my horror, the man standing in front of me stepped aside and left me exposed to Ongul's view. He glanced round the circle and the gaze of his single eye settled on my face. I knew that he recognised me immediately as the man who had been carried off Drang after Grettir's death. I saw him frown as he tried to understand why I was there. But it was too late.

'This is to avenge Grettir Asmundarson, the man you foully murdered,' Thorstein called out as he stepped across the watching circle of men, raised the nicked sword and from his great height brought it slicing down directly on Ongul's unprotected skull. Thorstein had found the sweet spot. The sword bit through Ongul's skull and split his head like a melon. The man who had killed my closest friend died instantly.

For a moment there was stunned silence. The onlookers gazed down at Ongul's corpse, sprawled on the flagstones of the parade ground. Thorstein made no move to escape. He stood with bloody sword in his grasp, an expression of profound satisfaction on his face. Then he calmly wiped the blood from the sword, walked across to where I stood and handed it to me with the words, 'In Grettir's memory.'

As soon as word of the killing reached the excubitors, who

were responsible for police duties, a Greek officer arrived to place Thorstein under arrest. He offered no resistance but allowed himself to be led quietly away. He was at peace with himself. He had done what he had set out to do.

'He hasn't got a hope,' said Thorstein's platoon commander, looking on. He was a tough veteran from Jutland with ten years' service in the guard. 'To kill within the palace precincts is a capital offence. The pen pushers in the imperial secretariat dislike us so much that they will lose no opportunity to damage the regiment. They will say that Ongul's death was just another squalid brawl amongst bloodthirsty barbarians. Thorstein's as good as dead.'

'Isn't there anything that can be done to help him?' I asked from the edge of the little group of onlookers. The Jutlander turned to look at me, standing there with Grettir's sword in my hand.

'Not unless you can oil the wheels of justice,' he said.

Grettir's sword felt like a living thing in my grasp.

'What happens when a guardsman dies on active service?' I asked.'

'His possessions are divided among his comrades. That's our custom. If he leaves a widow or children, we auction off his personal effects and the money goes to them, along with any back pay that is outstanding.'

'You say that Thorstein is as good as dead. Could you organise an auction of his possessions in the barracks, including the sale of this sword? Ongul told you how he looted it from Grettir the Strong, even used it for his death blow, and you've seen how Thorstein took it back.'

The Jutlander looked at me in surprise. 'That sword's worth two years' salary,' he said.

'I know, but Thorstein presented me with the weapon and I would gladly put it up for auction.'

The platoon commander looked intrigued. He knew me only as Thorstein's valet and was probably curious to know what role

I had played in this affair. Perhaps he was wondering if he could acquire the sword for himself. 'It's irregular, but I will see what I can do,' he said. It'll be better if the auction is held without the Greeks knowing. They would only claim that we were so avaricious that we sold off Thorstein's effects before he was even dead. Not that they can accuse others of avarice. They're the past masters.'

'There's one more thing I would ask,' I continued. 'A lot of people heard Thorstein shout out the name of Grettir the Strong just before he cut down Thorbjorn Ongul. No one really knows why he did so, though there's a lot of speculation. If the auction could be held tonight, just when interest is at its height, it would attract the largest number. More than just his platoon.'

In fact nearly half the regiment crowded into the courtyard of the Numera barracks to attend the auction that evening, cramming themselves into the porticos that surrounded the yard. It was precisely what I had wanted.

Thorstein's platoon commander, Ragnvald, called them to silence. 'All of you know what happened this afternoon. Thorstein, nicknamed the Galleon, took the life of his fellow countryman, Thorbjorn Ongul, and none of us know why. Thorbjorn can't tell us because he's dead and Thorstein is in solitary confinement awaiting trial. But this man, Thorgils Leifsson, claims he can answer your questions, and he wants to auction the sword that Thorstein gave him.' He turned to me. 'Now it's your turn.'

I climbed up on a block of stone and faced my audience. Then I held up the sword so all could see it and waited until I had their complete attention. 'Let me tell you where this sword comes from, how it was found among the dead, where it travelled, and the story of the remarkable man who owned it.' And then I proceeded to tell the tale of Grettir the Strong and his remarkable career, from the night we had robbed the barrow grave, through all our times together, both good and bad: how he had twice saved my life, first in a tavern brawl and then aboard a foundering ship. I told them about the man: how perverse and stubborn he could be, how often his best intentions had led to tragedy, how he could be violent and brutal, how he did not know his own strength and yet had struggled to remain honest to himself in the face of adversity. I went on to describe his life as an outlaw in the wilderness, his victories in hand-to-hand combat over those who had been sent to kill him and how, finally, he had been defeated by black seidr invoked by Thorbjorn Ongul's volva foster-mother, and had died on Drang.

It was Grettir's saga and, as I told it, I knew that the men who heard it would remember and repeat the tale so that Grettir's name would live on in honoured memory. I was fulfilling my final promise to my sworn brother.

When I had finished my tale, the Jutlander stood up. 'Time to auction the sword of Grettir the Strong,' he called out. 'From what we have just heard, Ongul's death was not murder, but an act of honourable revenge, justified under our own laws and customs. I suggest that the money raised from the sale of this sword is put towards the expense of defending Thorstein Galleon in the law courts of Constantinople. I call upon you to be generous.'

Then something remarkable happened. The bidding for the sword began, but it was not in the manner I had anticipated. Each of the Guardsmen shouted out a price far less than I had expected. One after another they called out a number and the Jutlander carved marks on a tally stick. Finally the bidding stopped. The Jutlander looked down at the marks. 'Seven pounds in gold, and five numisma. That's the total,' he announced. 'That should be enough to see that Thorstein avoids the hangman's rope, and receives instead a prison sentence.'

He looked round the circle of watching faces. 'My platoon has a vacancy,' he called. 'I propose that it is filled, not by purchase, but by acclamation of our general gathering. I propose to you that the place of Thorstein Galleon is taken by the sworn brother to Grettir Asmundarsson. Do you agree?'

A general mutter of agreement came back. One or two

guardsmen banged their sword hilts on the stones. The Jutlander turned to me. 'Thorgils, you may keep the sword. Use it as a member of the guard.'

And that is how I, Thorgils Leifsson, was recruited into the imperial guard of the basileus in Metropolis, and was on hand to pledge my allegiance to the man called the 'thunderbolt of the north' or, to some, the last of the Vikings. In his service I would travel to the very hub of the world, win spoils of war sufficient to rig a ship with sails of silk, and – as his spy and diplomat – come within an arrow's length of placing him on the throne of England.

AFTERWORD

THORSTEIN GALLEON DID take his revenge on the murderer of Grettir his half-brother, according to Grettir's Saga written c. AD 1325. That saga traces the celebrated events in Grettir's life, from his rebellious childhood, through the plundering of a barrow grave and his many escapades as a notorious outlaw, to his eventual death on Drang Island at the hands of Thorbjorn Ongul and a posse of local farmers. Thorstein Galleon is said to have tracked down Thorbjorn Ongul to Constantinople and confronted him at a weapons inspection of the Varangian guard. Ongul was boasting how he had killed the outlaw with Grettir's own sword, taken from him as he lay dying. The weapon was passed from hand to hand among the guardsmen and when it came to Thorstein, in the words of the saga, 'Thorstein took the short sword, and at once raised it up and struck at Ongul. The blow landed on his head, and it was so powerful that the sword went right down to his jaws. Thorbjorn Ongul fell dead to the ground. Everyone was speechless . . .'

from *Grettir's Saga*, translated by Denton Fox and Hermann Palsson, University of Toronto Press, 1998

VIKING: King's Man

Read on for an exclusive extract from the third volume
of this brilliant epic Viking adventure . . .

Published by Macmillan in 2005

ONE

THE EMPEROR WAS pretending to be a whale. He put his head under water and filled his mouth, then came back up to the surface and squirted little spouts across the palace plunge pool. I watched him out of the corner of my eye, not knowing whether to feel disdainful or sympathetic. He was, after all, an old man. Past seventy years of age, he would be relishing the touch of warm water on his blotchy skin as well as the feeling of weightlessness. He was afflicted with a bloating disease which had puffed up his body and limbs so grossly that he found walking very painful. Only the week before I had seen him return to the palace so exhausted after one of the endless ceremonials that he had collapsed into the arms of an attendant the moment the great bronze doors closed behind him. Today was the festival the Christians call Good Friday, so in the afternoon there was to be yet another imperial ceremony and it would last for hours. I decided that the emperor deserved his moment of relaxation, though his whalelike antics in the pool might have surprised his subjects, as the majority of them considered him to be their God's representative on earth.

I shifted the heavy axe on my shoulder. There was a damp patch where the haft had rested on my scarlet tunic. Beads of sweat were trickling down under the rim of my iron helmet with its elaborate gold inlay, and the heat in the pool room was making me drowsy. I struggled to stay alert. As a member of the Hetaira, the imperial household troops, my duty was to protect the life of the Basileus Romanus III, ruler of Byzantium, and Equal of the Apostles. With five hundred fellow members of his personal Life Guard, the palace Varangians, I had sworn to keep the emperor safe from his enemies, and he paid us handsomely to do so. He trusted us more than his fellow countrymen, and with good reason.

At the far end of the baths were clustered a group of the emperor's staff, five or six of them. Sensibly they were maintaining their distance from their master, not just to give him privacy, but also because his advancing illness made him very tetchy. The Basileus had become notoriously short-tempered. The slightest wrong word or gesture could make him fly into a rage. During the three years I had served at the palace, I had seen him change from being even-handed and generous to waspish and mean. Men accustomed to receiving rich gifts in appreciation from the imperial bounty were now ignored or sharply criticized. Fortunately the Basileus did not yet treat his Life Guard in a similar fashion, and we still gave him our complete loyalty. We played no part in the courtiers' constant plotting and scheming as various factions sought to gain advantage. The ordinary members of the guard did not even speak their language. Our senior officers were patrician Greeks, but the rank and file were recruited from the northern lands and we continued to speak Norse among ourselves. A court official with the title of the Grand Interpreter for the Hetaira was supposed to translate for the guardsmen, but the post was in name only, another high-sounding title in a court mesmerized by precedence and ceremonial.

'Guardsman!' The shout broke into my thoughts. One man in the group was beckoning to me. I recognised the Keeper of the Imperial Inkwell. The post, despite its pompous name, was one of real importance. Officially the keeper proffered the bottle of purple ink whenever the Basileus was ready to sign an official document. In reality he acted as secretary of the emperor's private office. The post gave him open access to the imperial presence, a privilege denied even to the highest ministers, who had to make a formal appointment before being brought before the Basileus.

The keeper repeated his gesture. I glanced across at the Basileus. Romanus was still wallowing and spouting in the pool, eyes closed, happy in his warm and watery world. The pool had recently been deepened in its centre, yet was still shallow enough for a man to stand upright and keep his head above the surface. There seemed no danger there. I strode over towards the keeper, who held out a parchment. I caught a glimpse of the imperial signature in purple ink even as the keeper indicated that I was to take the document to the adjacent room, a small office where the notaries waited.

It was not unusual for a guardsman to act as a footman. The palace officials were so preoccupied with their own dignity that they found it demeaning to carry out the simplest tasks like opening a door or carrying a scroll. So I took the parchment, cast another quick look over my shoulder and walked to the door. The Basileus was still blissfully enjoying his swim.

In the next room I found the Orphanotrophus waiting. He was in charge of the city orphanage, an institution financed from the royal purse. Once again the title was no reflection of his real importance. John the Orphanotrophus was the most powerful man in the empire, excluding only the Basileus. Thanks to a combination of raw intellect and shrewd application, John had worked his way up through the various grades of the imperial hierarchy and was prime minister of the empire in all but name. Feared by all, he was a thin man who had a gaunt face with deep-sunk eyes under startlingly black eyebrows. He was also a beardless one, a eunuch.

I came to attention in front of him, but did not salute. Only the Basileus and the immediate members of the imperial family warranted a guardsman's salute, and John the Orphanotrophus was certainly not born to the purple. His family came from

Paphalagonia on the Black Sea coast, and it was rumoured that the family's first profession when they came to Constantinople was to run a money exchange. Some said that they had been forgers.

When I handed over the parchment, the Orphanotrophus glanced through it, and then said to me slowly, pronouncing each word with exaggerated care, 'Take this to the logothete of finance.'

I stood my ground and replied in Greek, 'My apologies, your excellency. I am on duty. I cannot leave the imperial presence.'

The Orphanotrophus raised an eyebrow. 'Well, well, a guardsman who speaks Greek,' he murmured. 'The palace is finally becoming civilised.'

'Perhaps someone could call a dekanos, ' I suggested. 'That is their duty, to carry messages.' I saw I had made a mistake.

'Yes, and you should do yours,' the Orphanotrophus retorted acidly.

Smarting at the rebuff, I turned on my heel and marched back to the baths. As I entered the long chamber with its high, domed ceiling and walls patterned with mosaics of dolphins and waves, I knew immediately that something was terribly wrong. The Basileus was still in the water, but now he was lying on his back, waving feebly with his arms. Only his corpulence was keeping him from sinking. The attendants who had previously been in the room were nowhere to be seen. I dropped my axe to the marble floor, wrenched off my helmet and sprinted for the pool. 'Alarm! Alarm!' I bellowed as I ran. 'Guardsmen to me!' In a few strides I was at the edge of the pool and, fully clothed, dived in and swam as fast as I could manage towards the Basileus. Silently I thanked my own God, Odinn, that we Norse learn how to swim when we are still young.

The Basileus seemed unaware of my presence as I reached him. He was barely moving and occasionally his head slipped underwater. I put one hand under his chin, lowered my legs until I could touch the bottom of the pool, and began to tow him towards the edge, taking care to keep his head on my shoulder, clear of the water. He was limp in my arms, and his scalp against my chin was bald except for a few straggly hairs.

'Guardsmen to me!' I shouted again. Then in Greek I called out, 'Fetch a doctor!'

This time my calls were answered. Several staff members — scribes, attendants, courtiers — came running into the room and clustered at the edge of the pool. Someone knelt down to grab the Basileus under the armpits and haul him dripping out of the water. But the rescue was clumsy and slow. The Basileus lay on the marble edge of the pool, looking more than ever like a whale, a beached and dying one this time. I clambered out and pushed aside the courtiers.

'Help me lift him,' I said.

'In Thor's name what's going on?' said a voice.

A decurion, the petty officer of my watch, had finally arrived. He glowered so fiercely at the gawking courtiers that they fell back. The two of us picked up the emperor's limp body and carried him towards a marble bench. One of the bath attendants had the wit to spread a layer of towels over it before we laid down the old man, who was moving feebly. The decurion looked round and ripped a brocaded silk gown off the shoulders of a courtier and laid it over the emperor's nakedness.

'Let me through, please.'

This was one of the palace physicians. A short, paunchy man, he lifted up the emperor's eyelids with his stubby fingers. I could see that he was nervous. He pulled his hands back as if he had been scalded. He was probably frightened that the Basileus would expire under his touch. But the emperor's eyes stayed open and he shifted his head slightly to look around him.

At that moment there was a stir among the watching courtiers, and their circle parted to allow a woman through. It was Zoë, the empress. She must have been summoned from the gynaeceum, the women's quarters of the palace. It was the first time I had seen her close to, and I was struck by her poise. Despite her age, she held herself with great dignity. She must have been at least fifty years old and had probably never been a beauty, but her face retained that fine-boned structure which hinted at aristocratic descent. She was the daughter and granddaughter of emperors, and had the haughty manners to prove it.

Zoë swept through the crowd, and stepped up to within an arm's length of her husband where he lay on the marble slab. Her face showed no emotion as she gazed down at the emperor, who was ashen pale and breathing with difficulty. For a brief moment she just stared. Then, without a word, she turned and walked out of the room.

The courtiers avoided looking at one another. Everyone, including myself, knew that there was no love between the emperor and his wife. The previous Basileus, Constantine, had insisted that they marry. Zoë was Constantine's favoured daughter, and in the last days of his reign he had searched for a suitable husband for her from among the ranks of Constantinople's aristocracy. Father and daughter had both wanted to ensure the family succession, though Zoë was past childbearing age. That had not prevented her and Romanus when they ascended the throne together from attempting to found their own dynasty. Romanus had dosed himself with huge amounts of aphrodisiacs – the reason for his hair loss, it was claimed – while his elderly consort hung herself with fertility charms and consulted quacks and charlatans who proposed more and more grotesque ways of ensuring pregnancy. When all their efforts failed, the couple slid into a mutual dislike. Romanus had taken a mistress and Zoë had been bundled off to the gynaeceum, frustrated and resentful.

But that was not the whole story. Zoë had also acquired a lover, not two years since. Several members of the guard had come across the two of them coupling together and turned a blind eye. Their tact had not been out of respect for the empress – she conducted her affair openly – but because her consort was the younger brother of John the Orphanotrophus. Here was an area where high politics mingled with ambition and lust, and it was better left alone.

'Stand back!' ordered the decurion.

He took up his position a spear's length from the Basileus's bald head, and as a reflex I stationed myself by the emperor's feet and also came to attention. My axe was still lying somewhere on the marble floor, but I was wearing a dagger at my belt and I dropped my hand to its hilt. The doctor paced nervously up and down, wringing his hands with worry. Suddenly Romanus gave a deep moan. He raised his head a fraction from the towel that was his pillow and made a slight gesture with his right hand. It was as if he was beckoning someone closer. Not knowing whom he gestured to, no one dared move. The awe and majesty of the imperial presence still had a grip on the spectators. The emperor's gaze shifted slowly, passing across the faces of his watching courtiers. He seemed to be trying to say something, to be pleading. His throat moved but no sounds emerged. Then his eyes closed and his head fell back and rolled to one side. He began to pant, his breath coming in short shallow gasps. Suddenly, the breathing paused, and his mouth fell open. Out flowed a thick, dark brown substance, and after two more choking breaths, he expired.

I stood rigidly to attention. There were the sounds of running feet, of tumult, and in the distance a wailing and crying as news of the emperor's death spread among the palace staff. I took no notice. Until a new Basileus was crowned, the duty of the guard was to protect the body of the dead emperor.

'Thorgils, you look like the village idiot standing there in your soaking uniform. Get back to the guardroom and report to the duty officer.'

The instructions were delivered in Norse and I recognised the voice of Halfdan, my company commander. A beefy veteran, Halfdan had served in the Life Guard for close on ten years. He should have retired by now, after amassing a small fortune from his salary, but he liked the life of a guardsman and had cut his ties with his Danish homeland, so he had nowhere else to go.

'Tell him that everything is under control in the imperial presence. You might suggest that he places a curfew on the palace.'

I squelched away, pausing to collect my helmet and the spiked axe which someone had obligingly picked up off the floor and leaned against the wall. My route to the guardroom lay through a labyrinth of passages, reception rooms and courtyards. Romanus III could have died in any one of his palaces – they all had swimming pools – but he had chosen to expire in the largest and most sprawling of them, the Great Palace. Standing close to the tip of the peninsula of Constantinople, the Great Palace had been extended and remodelled so many times by its imperial occupants that it had turned into a bewildering maze of chambers and anterooms. Erecting ever grander buildings was a fascination bordering on mania for each occupant of the purple throne. Every Basileus wanted to immortalise his rule by leaving at least one extravagant structure, whether a new church, a monastery, a huge palace, or some ostentatious public building. Romanus had been busily squandering millions of gold pieces on an immense new church to the mother of his God, though it seemed to me that she already had more than enough churches and monasteries to her name. Romanus's new church was to be dedicated to her as Mary the Celebrated, and what with its surrounding gardens and walkways and fountains – and the constant changes of design, which meant pulling down half-finished buildings – the project had run so far over budget that Romanus had been obliged to raise a special tax to pay for the construction. The church was not yet finished and I suspected it never would be. I surprised myself by realising how easily I was already thinking of Romanus in the past tense.

'Change into a dry uniform and join the detail on the main gate,' the duty officer ordered when I reported to him. No more than twenty years old, he was almost as edgy as the physician who had attended the dying emperor. A Greek from one of Constantinople's leading families, his family would have paid handsomely to buy his commission in the Life Guard. Merely by placing him inside the walls of the palace, they hoped he might attract the attention of the Basileus and gain preferment. Now their investment would be wasted if a new Basileus decided, out of concern for his own safety, to replace all the Greek officers. It was another deception so characteristic of palace life. Byzantine society still pretended that the Hetaira was Greek. Their sons prided themselves on being officers of the guard, and they dressed up in uniforms which denoted the old palace regiments – the Excubia, the Numeri, the Scholae and others – but when it came to real work our Basileus had trusted only us, the foreigners, his palace Varangians.

I joined twenty of my comrades at the main gate. They had already slammed the doors shut without asking permission of the keeper of the gate, whose duty it was to supervise the opening of the main gate at dawn, close it again at noon, and then reopen it for a few hours in the early evening. But today the death of the emperor had removed his authority and the keeper was at a loss to know what to do. The decurion decided the matter for him. He was refusing to let anyone in or out.

Even as I arrived, there was a great hubbub outside the gate, and I could hear thunderous knocking and loud, impatient shouts.

'Glad you've got here, Thorgils,' said the guard commander. 'Maybe you can tell me what those wild men out there want.'

I listened carefully. 'I think you had better let them in,' I said. 'It sounds as though you've got the Great Patriarch outside, and he's demanding admittance.'

'The Great Patriarch? That black-clad old goat,' grumbled the guard commander, who was a staunch Old Believer. 'Lads, open the side door and allow the monks through. But hold your breath. They don't wash very often.'

A moment later a very angry group of monks, all with chest-length beards and black gowns, stormed through the gap between the doors, glared at us, and hurried off down the corridor with a righteous-sounding slap of sandals and the clatter of their wooden staffs on the marble floor slabs. In their midst I saw the white-bearded figure of Alexis of the Studium, the supreme religious authority of the empire.

'Wonder what's brought them down from their monastery in such a hurry,' muttered a Varangian as he pushed shut the door and dropped the bar back in place.

His question was answered later, when we came off duty and returned to the guardroom. Half a dozen of my colleagues were lounging there, smirking.

'The old bitch has already got herself a new husband. The moment she was sure that old Romanus was definitely on his way out, she sent someone to fetch the high priest.'

'I know, we let him and his crows in.'

'Well, she certainly didn't summon them to give her beloved husband the last rites. Even while the priests were on their way, the old lady called an emergency meeting of her advisors, including that foxy creep, the Orphanotrophus. She told them that she wanted her fancy-boy to be the new Basileus.'

'Not the handsome rattle-brain!'

'She had it all worked out. She said that, by right of imperial descent, she represented the continuity of the state, and that it was in the best interests of the empire if "my darling Michael", as she called him, took the throne with her.'

'You must be joking! How do you know all this?'

The guardsman gave a snort of derision. 'The Orphanotrophus had ordered four of us to act as close escort for the empress in case there was an attempt on her life. It was a ruse, of course. When the other courtiers showed up to dispute the idea of Michael's succession, they saw the guard standing there, and came to the conclusion that the matter had already been settled.'

'So what happened when the high priest arrived?'

'He plunged straight into the wedding ceremony for the old woman and her lover-boy. She paid him a fat bribe, of course, and within the hour they were man and wife.'

This bizarre story was interrupted by the arrival of another of our Greek officers, who scuttled into the room, anxiously demanding a full sovereign's escort. We were to don our formal uniforms and accompany him to the Triklinium, the grand audience chamber. He insisted that there was not a moment to be lost.

Thirty of us formed up and marched through the passageways to the enormous hall, floored with mosaics, hung with silk banners and decorated with rich icons, where the Basileus formally received his ministers, foreign ambassadors and other dignitaries. Two ornate thrones stood on a dais at the far end of the hall and our officer led us straight to our positions – to stand in a semicircle at the back of the dais, looking out across the audience chamber. A dozen equerries and the marshal of the Triklinium were busily making sure that everything was in order for the arrival of their majesties. Within moments the Empress Zoë and Michael, her new husband, entered the room and hurried up to the thrones. Close behind came the Orphanotrophus, some high-ranking priests, and a gaggle of courtiers associated with the empress's faction at court. Zoë and Michael stepped up on the dais, our Greek officer hissed a command, and we, the members of the Life Guard, obediently raised our axes vertically in front of us in a formal salute. The empress and emperor turned to face down the hall. Just as they were about to sit down there came a tense moment. By custom the guard acknowledges the presence of the Basileus as he takes his seat upon the throne. As the emperor lowers himself on to his seat, the guards transfer their axes from the salute to their right shoulders. It is a signal that all is well and that the business of the empire is continuing as normal. Now, as Zoë and Michael were about to settle on their throne cushions, my comrades and I glanced at one another questioningly. For the space of a heartbeat nothing happened. I sensed our Greek officer stiffen with anxiety, and then, raggedly, the guard placed their axes on their shoulders. I could almost hear the sigh of relief from Zoë's retinue.

That crisis safely past, the proceedings quickly took on an air of farce. Zoë's people must have sent word throughout the palace, summoning the senior ministers and their staff, who came in one by one. Many, I suspected, arrived thinking that they would be paying their respects to the body of their dead emperor. Instead they were confronted with the astonishing spectacle of his widow already remarried and seated beside a new husband nearly young enough to be her grandson. No wonder several of the new arrivals faltered on the threshold, dumbfounded. The matronly empress and her youthful consort were clutching the emblems of state in their jewelled hands, their glittering robes had been carefully arranged by their pages, and on Zoë's face was an expression which showed that she expected full homage. From the back of the dais I watched the courtiers' eyes take in the scene – the aloof empress, her boyish husband, the waiting cluster of high officials, and the sinister, brooding figure of John the Orphanotrophus, Michael's brother, noting how each new arrival responded. After a brief moment of hesitation and calculation, the high ministers and courtiers came forward to the twin thrones, bowed deeply to the empress, then knelt and kissed the ring of her bright-eyed husband, who, less than six hours earlier, had been known as nothing more than her illicit lover.

The next day we buried Romanus. Overnight someone – it must have been the supremely efficient Orphanotrophus – arranged for his swollen corpse to be dressed in official robes of purple silk and laid out on a bier. Within an hour of sunrise the funeral procession had already assembled, with everyone in their correct place according to rank, and the palace's main gates were thrown open. I was one of the one hundred guards who marched, according to tradition, immediately before and after the dead Basileus as we emerged on to the Mese, the broad main avenue which bisects the city. I was surprised to see how many of the citizens of Constantinople had left their beds this early.

Word of the Basileus's sudden death must have spread very fast. Those who stood at the front of the dense crowd lining the route could see for themselves the waxen skin and swollen face of the dead emperor, for his head and hands had been left uncovered. Once or twice I heard someone shout out, 'Poisoned!', but for the most part the crowd remained eerily silent. I did not hear a single expression of sorrow or regret for his passing. Romanus III, I realised, had not been popular in Constantinople.

At the great Forum of Amastration we wheeled left, and half a mile further on the cortège entered the Via Triumphalis. Normally an emperor processed along this broad avenue to the cheers of the crowd, at the head of his victorious troops, as he displayed captured booty and files of defeated enemy in chains. Now Romanus was carried in the opposite direction in a gloomy silence broken only by the creaking wheels of the carriage which carried his bier, the sound of the horses' hooves and the muted footfalls of hundreds upon hundreds of the ordinary citizens of Constantinople, who, simply out of morbid curiosity, joined in behind our procession. They went with us all the way to the enormous unfinished church of Mary the Celebrated that was Romanus's great project, and where he was now the first person to benefit from his own extravagance. Here the priests hurriedly placed him into the green and white sarcophagus which Romanus had selected for himself, following another curious imperial custom that the Basileus should choose his own tomb on the day of his accession.

Then, as the crowd was dispersing in a mood of sombre apathy, our cortège briskly retraced its steps to the palace, for there was not a moment to be lost.

'Two parades in one day, but it will be worth it,' said Halfdan cheerfully as he shrugged off the dark sash he had worn during the funeral and replaced it with one that glittered with gold thread. 'Thank Christ it's only a short march this afternoon, and we would have to be doing it anyway as it's Palm Sunday.'

Halfdan, like several members of the guard, was part-Christian and part-pagan. Superficially he subscribed to the religion of the White Christ – and swore by him – and he attended services at the new church to St Olaf, recently built near our regimental headquarters down by the Golden Horn, Constantinople's main harbour. But he also wore Thor's hammer as an amulet on a leather strap around his neck, and when he was in his cups he often announced that when he died he would much prefer to feast and fight in Odinn's Valholl than finish up as a bloodless being with wings like a fluffy dove in the Christians' heaven.

'Thorgils, how come you speak Greek so well?' The question came from one of the Varangians who had been at the palace gate the previous day. He was a recent recruit into the guard.

'He licked up a drop of Fafnir's blood, that's how,' Halfdan interjected. 'Give Thorgils a couple of weeks and he could learn any language, even if it's bird talk.'

I ignored his ponderous attempt at humour. 'I was made to study Greek when I was a youngster,' I said, 'in a monastery in Ireland.'

'You were once a monk?' the man asked, surprised. 'I thought you were a devotee of Odinn. At least that is what I've heard.'

'I am,' I told him. 'Odinn watched over me when I was among the monks and got me away from them.'

'Then you understand this stuff with the holy pictures they carry about whenever we're on parade, the relics and bits of saints and all the rest of it.'

'Some of it. But the Christianity I was made to study is different from the one here in Constantinople. It's the same God, of course, but a different way of worshipping him. I must admit that until I came here I had never even heard of half of the saints they honour.'

'Not surprising,' grumbled the Varangian. 'Down in the market last week a huckster tried to sell me a human bone. Said it came from the right arm of St Demetrios, and I should buy it because I was a soldier and St Demetrios was a fighting man. He claimed the relic would bring me victory in any fight.'

'I hope you didn't buy it.'

'Not a chance. Someone in the crowd warned me that the huckster had sold so many arm and leg bones from St Demetrios that the holy martyr must have had more limbs than a centipede.' He gave a wry laugh.

Later that afternoon I sympathised with the soldier as we marched off for the acclamation of our young new Basileus, who was to be pronounced as Michael IV before a congregation of city dignitaries in the church of Hagia Sophia. We shuffled rather than marched towards the church because there were so many slow-moving priests in the column, all holding up pictures of their saints painted on wooden boards, tottering under heavy banners and pennants embroidered with holy symbols, or carrying precious relics of their faith sealed in gold and silver caskets. Just in front of me was their most venerated memento, a fragment from the wooden cross on which their Christ had hung at the time of his death, and I wondered if perhaps Odinn, the master of disguise, had impersonated their Jesus. The Father of the Gods had also hung on a wooden tree, his side pierced with a spear as he sought to gain world knowledge. It was a pity, I thought to myself, that the Christians were so certain that theirs was the only true faith. If they were a little more tolerant, they would have admitted that other religions had their merits, too. Old Believers were perfectly willing to let people follow their own gods, and we did not seek to impose our ideas on others. But at least the Christians of Constantinople were not as bigoted as their brethren further north, who were busy stamping out what they considered pagan practices. In Constantinople life was tolerant enough for there to be a mosque in the sixth district where the Saracens could worship and several synagogues for the Jews.

A hundred paces from the doors of Hagia Sophia, we, the members of the guard, came to a halt while the rest of the procession solemnly walked on and entered the church. The priests had no love for the Varangians, and it was customary for us to wait outside until the service was concluded. Presumably it was thought that no one would make an attempt on the life of the Basileus inside such a sacred building, but I had my doubts.

Halfdan let my company stand at ease, and we stood and chatted idly among ourselves, waiting for the service to end and to escort the acclaimed Basileus back to the palace. It was then that I noticed a young man dressed in the characteristic hooded gown of a middle-class citizen, a junior clerk by the look of him. He was approaching various members of the guard to try to speak to them. He must have been asking his questions in Greek, for they either shook their heads uncomprehendingly or ignored him. Eventually someone pointed in my direction and he came over towards me. He introduced himself as Constantine Psellus, and said he was a student in the city, studying to enter the imperial service. I judged him to be no more than sixteen or seventeen years old, about half my age.

'I am planning to write a history of the empire,' he told me, 'a chapter for each emperor, and I would very much appreciate any details of the last days of Basileus Romanus.'

I liked his formal politeness and was impressed by his air of quick intelligence, so decided to help him out.

'I was present when he drowned,' I said, and briefly sketched what I had witnessed.

'You say he drowned?' commented the young man gently.

'Yes, that's seems to have been the case. Though he actually expired when he was laid out on the bench. Maybe he had a heart attack. He was old enough, after all.'

'I saw his corpse yesterday when it was being carried in the funeral procession, and I thought it looked very strange, so puffed up and grey.'

'Oh, he had had that appearance for quite some time.'

'You don't think he died from some other cause, the effects of a slow-acting poison maybe?' the young man suggested as calmly as if he had been discussing a change in the weather. 'Or perhaps you were deliberately called away from the baths so someone could hold the emperor underwater for a few moments to bring on a heart attack.'

The theory of poisoning had been discussed in the guardroom ever since the emperor's death, and some of us had gone as far as debating whether it was hellebore or some other poison which was being fed to Romanus. But it was not our job to enquire further: our responsibility was to defend him from violent physical attack, the sort you block with a shield or deflect with a shrewd axe blow, not the insidious assault of a lethal drug in his food or drink. The Basileus employed food-tasters for that work, though they could be bribed to act a sham, and any astute assassin would make sure that the poison was slow-acting enough for its effect not to be detected until too late.

But the young man's other suggestion, that I had been lured away to leave Romanus unguarded, alarmed me. If that was the case, then the Keeper of the Inkwell was certainly implicated in the Basileus's death, and perhaps the Orphanotrophus as well. I remembered how he had tried to send me on to the logothete of finance with the parchment. That would have delayed me even more. The thought that I might have been a dupe in the assassination of the Basileus brought a chill to my spine. If true, I was in real danger. Any guardsman found to be negligent in his duty to protect the Basileus was executed by his company commander, usually by public beheading. More than that, if Romanus had indeed been murdered, I was still a potential witness, and that meant I was a likely target for elimination by the culprits. Someone as powerful as the Orphanotrophus could easily have me killed, in a tavern brawl, for example.

Suddenly I was very frightened.

'I think I hear the chanting of the priests,' said Psellus, interrupting my thoughts and fidgeting slightly. Maybe he realised he had gone too far in his theorising, and was close to treason. 'They must have opened the doors of Hagia Sophia, getting ready for the emergence of our new Basileus. It's time for me to let you

go. Thank you for your information. You have been most helpful.'
And he slipped away into the crowd.

We took up our positions around Michael IV, who was mounted on a superb sorrel horse, one of the best in the royal stables. I remembered how Romanus had been a great judge of horseflesh and had built up a magnificent stud farm, though he had been too sick to enjoy riding. Now I had to admit that the youthful Michael, though he came from a very plebeian background, looked truly imperial in the saddle. Perhaps that was what Zoë had seen in him from the beginning. Halfdan had told me how he had been on duty when Zoë had first gazed on her future lover. 'You would have been an utter dolt not to have noticed her reaction. She couldn't take her eyes off him. It was the Orphanotrophus who introduced him to her. He brought Michael into the audience chamber when Zoë and Romanus were holding an imperial reception, and led him right up to the twin thrones. Old Romanus was gracious enough, but Zoë looked at the young man as if she wanted to eat him on the spot. He was good looking, all right, fresh-faced and ruddy-cheeked, likely to blush like a girl. I reckon the Orphanotrophus knew what he was doing. Set it all up.'

'Didn't Romanus notice, if it was that obvious?' I asked.

'No. The old boy barely used to look at the empress by then. Kept looking anywhere except in her direction, as though her presence gave him a pain.'

I mulled over the conversation as we marched back to the Grand Palace, entered the great courtyard and the gates were closed behind us. Our new Basileus dismounted, paused for a moment while his courtiers and officials formed up in two lines, and then walked down between them to the applause and smiles of his retinue before entering the palace. I noted that the Basileus was unescorted, which seemed very unusual. Even stranger was the fact that the courtiers broke ranks and began to hurry into the palace behind the Basileus, almost like a mob. Halfdan astonished me by rushing off in their wake, all discipline gone. So did the guardsmen around me, and I joined them in pushing and jostling as if we were a crowd of spectators leaving the hippodrome at the end of the games.

It was unimaginable. All the stiffness and formality of court life had evaporated. The crowd of us, ministers, courtiers, advisers, even priests, all flooded into the great Trikilinium. There, seated up on the dais, was our young new emperor, smiling down at us. On each side were two slaves holding small strongboxes. As I watched, one of the slaves tilted the coffer he held and a stream of gold coins poured out, falling into the emperor's lap. Michael reached down, seized a fistful of the coins, and flung them high into the air above the crowd. I gaped in surprise. The shower of gold coins, each one of them worth six months' wages for a skilled man, glittered and flashed before plummeting towards the upstretched hands. A few coins were caught as they fell, but most tumbled on to the marble floor, landing with a distinct ringing sound. Men dropped to their hands and knees to pick up the coins, even as the emperor dipped his hand into his lap and flung another golden cascade over our heads. Now I understood why Halfdan had been so quick off the mark. My company commander had shrewdly elbowed his way to a spot where the arc of bullion was thickest, and was clawing up the golden bounty.

I, too, crouched down and began to gather up the coins. But at the very moment that my fingers closed around the first gold coin, I was thinking to myself that I would be wise to find some way of resigning from the Life Guard without attracting attention before it was too late.